JOURNEY TO A PLUGGED IN STATE OF MIND

First published in Great Britain in 2010 by Cherry Red
Books (a division of Cherry Red Records Ltd), Power Road
Studios, 114 Power Road, Chiswick, London W4 5PY

Copyright © Dave Henderson 2010

ISBN: 978 1 901447 42 2

Design by: Black Creative Limited
www.blackcreative.co.uk
Cover Design: David Black
Edited by Richard Anderson

Printed in the UK by Ashford Colour Press

Dedicated to all the robots of this world.

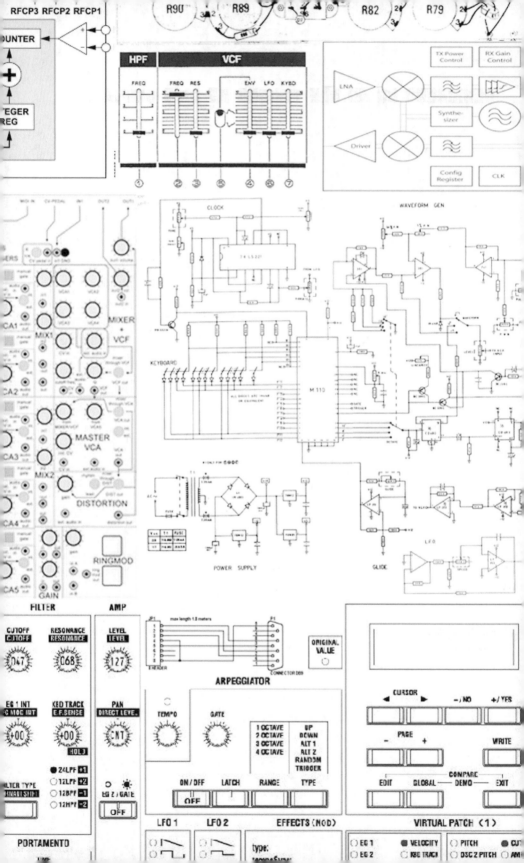

CONTENTS

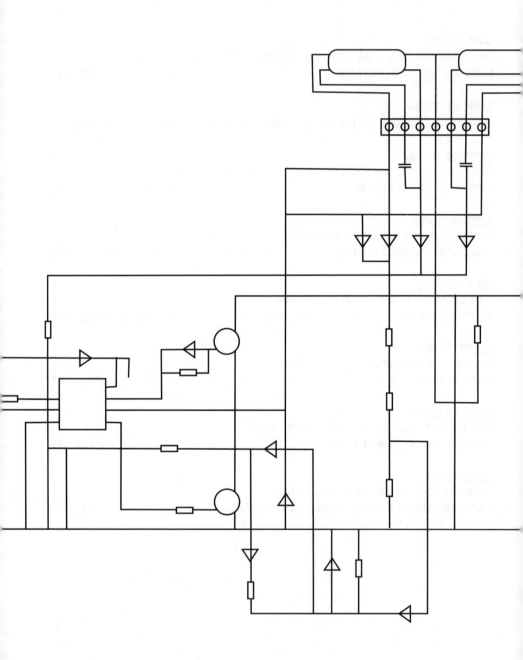

ONE

THE EARLY YEARS – ARTISTS, INVENTORS AND ECCENTRICS GO ELECTRONIC

Why is it that when we think of music, we don't often think of how it was made, what circumstances brought about that noise, or that sound, and how the layers of this and that make something that we've never heard before? By its very nature the possibilities of music should be finite, but there are people – and we will name names in due course – apparently born to study and test every item under the sun to see if it *could* be music. Most people just aren't conditioned and ready for that.

Music is now ubiquitous. CDs, the radio, TV, advertisements, the internet, file sharing, ringtones, blue-toothed tune-swapping, game soundtracks, film scores, DJs at sports events, music in restaurants, in the gym, in lifts, clothes shops et al – they've all become part of our everyday life. It's everywhere. Music isn't hard work any more - it doesn't have to be. It doesn't take effort for us to consume, so why should we consider what lengths people went to to make it?

These days, our ears act as a multi-tasking jukebox jury, vetoing things we don't like and moving on rapidly, flicking the channel, locating the next tune, even if that sounds vaguely like something we've filtered away that may have been a version of a song that was sampled from the soundtrack of *Pulp Fiction* that sounds like something else when played at speaker-splitting volume from your daughter's bedroom upstairs. It may then sound like a synthetic replica of a remote fragment of that when cranked out from her phone in all its tinny tackiness. But perhaps that experience is no different to the swirls of interference that underpinned Pink Floyd when they were played on pirate radio through your pillow decades ago, the sound re-arranged, mixed up with every day stuff, taking on a life of its own in your own personal mix.

Music hasn't been simple for a long time. In the 1940s and '50s, people's established ideas of music became old fashioned. Technology marched on - the generation gap marched back from war and genius classical composers writing their symphonies and scores knew that nothing would be the same again. The confines of creativity had been lifted and technological breakthroughs from the war effort meant that electronic music could become a reality. People were sick of strings and woodwind, they just didn't know that yet. But nobody really knew what electronic music was. People were confused. At the time music really stood for something. It was ordered. It was sensible. The idea of music, though, suddenly became an old fashioned concept. The world order had been revamped and everyday routine was about to be called into question.

After the Second World War, people had time on their hands and technology to conjure with. Long before the war, similarly off the wall approaches to music had been attempted, but by either artists, who were allowed to be eccentric, or inventors who were allowed to experiment as long as they wore white coats and wrote a paper about it at the end. People built things that looked like the inside of Dr Who's TARDIS, which was fine, as long as they could carry a tune. Centuries of traditional classical composition was carefully filed away and newness for the sake of being different was given extended attention. Structure and order in music were brought into question. Many of these developments produced sounds that were similar to putting your head inside a washing machine. Some people liked that.

As the 1900s dawned, it seemed that any new device that could make a sound like no other would be accepted. In some cases these were used at face value to augment existing sounds, in others they were utilised to play the right music, "real music", but with a sound that was just plain wrong. In 1912, Thaddeus Cahill launched the Telharmonium or Dynamophone after 15 years in the laboratory. Brow sweating, a slow organised perspiration, his monster machine arrived without Rolf Harris and a TV ad campaign, and fell on deaf ears. Its immense size and complex construction somewhat limited its potential as a post-dinner musical accompaniment. The Dynamophone was at the XX end of XXL.

Half a century later, in the swinging '60s, a working computer would still fill a whole room with whirling tapes, flickering lights and clunking gears as neighbouring villages' electricity stuttered as it had at the awakening of Frankenstein's monster. But, somehow, amid this cod-futuristic set up, the arrival of the pocket-sized Stylophone changed everything. Again. It was a revolution.

Cahill must have whirred in his grave when Rolf first whizzed his pen across the synthetic keyboard that came to prominence in 1967. Sounding like a cross between Joe Meek's 'Telstar' and a burst from the *Dr Who* theme on helium, the Stylophone was affordable science in your hand, promoted by a man famous for using a wobble board for percussion. But the roots of Rolf go further back than Thaddeus Cahill, and way beyond a time we can really comprehend, when cave paintings were the new Banksy and nature made music.

According to Dr Kristine H Burns, whose essay 'History Of Electronic And Computer Music Including Automatic Instruments And Composition Machines' lurks in cyberspace, it was as early as the second century BC that this all began:

"The Hydraulis was invented by Ktesibios sometime in the second century BC. Ktesibios, the son of a Greek barber, was fascinated by pneumatics and wrote an early treatise on the use of hydraulic systems for powering mechanical devices."

Sadly, Ktesibios was centuries ahead of his time and no recordings of his piece exist, and it wouldn't be until 1877, when Edison invented the phonograph, and 1898, when Poulson's Telegraphone magnetic recording tape was perfected, that the hit 45rpm single began to loom closer and the concept of Jimmy Saville became a reality. Even five years before Cahill's solder-heavy creation, people were locked into existing classical music and oblivious to the musical revolution that was beginning to unfold.

In 1907 when the Italian composer Ferruccio Bosoni published a series of 'thoughts' about the future of music, he questioned the status quo. What did it mean? What did music stand for?

Surely it was sweet relief, not something to be pondered over by chin-stroking theorists. Bosoni's 'The Sketch Of A New Aesthetic Of Music' bemoaned the fact that conventional keyboards were limiting music's progress. He was distraught that the noises he heard in his head couldn't be made available for mass consumption. He had a vision, something that, much later, his pupil Edgard Varese would recall:

"He was very much interested in the electrical instruments we began to hear about, and I remember particularly one he had read of called the Dynamophone. All through his writings one finds over and over again predictions about the music of the future, which have since come true. In fact, there is hardly a development that he did not foresee, as for instance in this extraordinary prophecy: 'I almost think that in the new great music, machines will also be necessary and will be assigned a share in it. Perhaps industry, too, will bring forth her share in the artistic ascent'".

If Bosoni was desperate for progress and Cahill was ham-fistedly providing an alternative, the Futurist art movement of the early 1900s acted as the catalyst for change by simply being bloody minded about everything. With a manifesto that desired to "present the musical soul of the masses, of the great factories, of the railways, of the transatlantic liners, of the battleships, of the automobiles and airplanes. To add to the great central themes of the musical poem the domain of the machines and the victorious kingdom of Electricity," the Futurists threw down the gauntlet, and by 1913 they'd rewritten the rulebook on music.

LUIGI RUSSOLO
The Art Of Noises
Originally published: 1913
Examples available on 'Musica Futurista: The Art of Noises'
LTM Records

Luigi Russolo was an Italian painter who became a composer and theorist on music. Through his desire to augment what already existed, he prepared a reasoned evaluation of sound and a theoretical manifesto on how it could be changed. In his 'Art Of Noises' transcript, Russolo wrote: "In this inventory we have encapsulated the most characteristic of the fundamental noises; the others are merely the associations and combinations of these. The rhythmic movements of a noise are infinite: just as with tone there is always a predominant rhythm, but around this numerous other secondary rhythms can be felt."

It wasn't just words. Russolo and his Futurist contemporaries were looking for a reaction. They had a vision and had heard the rumblings, they thought everyone else should too. To prepare for their live actions, they created a list of "interesting" sounds and, much in the same way that latter day composers like John Cage, Stockhausen and their many imitators would, they then edited from the list of sounds to create something new, different and, in many cases, vaguely annoying.

Their live performances would mix poetry and prose, sound collages and material from their armoury of listed noises, whilst the listener would simply marvel at how murmurs and mumbles could replace the romantic classical stylings of Mahler and Sibelius which, at the time, ruled the day. Was it a musical joke? A set of extremes set out to flush out a reaction? The 'Anarchy In The UK' of its day? Of course it was.

Prior to 1910, the Impressionist music of Debussy and Ravel was rubbing shoulders with the free dissonance of Charles Ives and Edgard Varese, who would both directly influence Frank

Zappa, but it was the Italian Futurist movement, founded in 1909 by Fillipo Marinetti and quickly embraced by the Russian avant garde, that led to Russolo's manifesto which called for the incorporation of noises of every kind into music. Italian Futurists Silvio Mix, Nuccio Fiorda, Franco Casavola, and Pannigi (whose 1922 'Ballo Meccanico' piece included two motorcycles - how cool does that sound?), took the idea to heart and in turn inspired Prokofiev, Ravel, Stravinsky, Varese and George Antheil.

In the early days of this new diversion they used many treated or affected instruments, but it was the arrival of electronic techniques that allowed them to impress, anger and confound audiences. This was electronic music – the hard stuff! The beginning of uneasy listening.

The initial palette of Luigi Russolo included:

1 Roars, thunderings, explosions, hissing roars, bangs, booms.
2 Whistling, hissing, puffing.
3 Whispers, murmurs, mumbling, muttering, gurgling.
4 Screeching, creaking, rustling, humming, crackling, rubbing.
5 Noises obtained by beating on metals, woods, skins, stones, pottery.
6 Voices of animals and people. Shouts, screams, shrieks, wails, hoots, howls, death rattles, sobs.

With that line up, how could his idealism of noise in music not succeed? When performed in 1913 and 1914, the majority of audiences were shocked and afraid, leaving just the super intellectuals to marvel at the out-there-ness of it all. Was it the emperor's new music? Or the future?

Fragments of recordings of this nature still exist today, and the CD 'Musica Futurista: The Art of Noises' is an intriguing collection of music and spoken word from 1909-1935, including vintage 'free verse' readings by Marinetti as well as sound pieces performed on the Intonarumori (noise intoners) created by Russolo. The set also features many piano pieces that show stark regard to melody, plus spoken pieces by Marinetti, often interrupted by noises of one description or another, the most striking of these being the thirteen minutes or more of 'Cinque Sintesi Radiofoniche', a slice of voyeuristic futurism that took their art to new extremes.

Also included are two early electronic sound pieces from Russolo, his evocative but very short journey through a city, 'Risveglio Di Una Citto', and the longer 'Esempi Sonori Di' with staccato gargling and humming with treated pitch shifting notes. The disc also includes an early cut-up piece from Russolo's brother Antonio that transposes military and romantic orchestrations with bouts of noise.

These precious noises from the past are, and were, truly different, and Russolo's thinking for his manifesto was elaborate and, importantly, carried through. He reasoned in a letter to fellow Futurist composer Balilla Pratella that "Musical evolution is paralleled by the multiplication of machines, which collaborate with man on every front. Not only in the roaring atmosphere of major cities, but in the country too, which until yesterday was totally silent, the machine today has created such a variety and rivalry of noises that pure sound, in its exiguity and monotony, no longer arouses any feeling".

Russolo was fascinated by the juxtaposition of sound, reasoning that the "limited circle of pure sounds must be broken, and the infinite variety of "noise-sound" conquered". Revolution was in the air and his disappointment at the very "acoustic" nature of modern orchestrations of the day further ostracised his concept. Like all good provocateurs, he wanted to go to extremes, but his concept did not require the simple addition of noise, tacked on for the sake of it. Instead, he declared that "It seems pointless to enumerate all the graceful and delicate noises that afford pleasant sensations". Russolo's manifesto openly demanded action. He described the noises in his head that he envisaged being performed with or without orchestra:

"Every five seconds, siege cannons gutting space with a chord ZANG-TUMB-TUUMB. Mutiny of five hundred echoes smashing, scattering it to infinity. In the centre of this hateful ZANG-TUMB-TUUMB area, fifty square kilometres of leaping bursts, lacerations, fists, rapid-fire batteries".

He went on: "Violence, ferocity, regularity, this deep bass scanning the strange shrill frantic crowds of the battle. Fury, breathless ears, eyes, nostrils open! Load! Fire! What a joy to hear, to smell completely the taratatata of the machine guns screaming breathless, under the stings, slaps, traak-traak, whips, pic-pac-pum-tumb weirdness leaps two hundred metres. Far, far in back of the orchestra pools, muddying, huffing goaded oxen wagons pluff-plaff horse action, flic flac zing zing shaaack, laughing whinnies, the tiiinkling, jiiingling tramping three Bulgarian battalions marching croooc-craaac [slowly]".

Intriguing; and on it goes: "Shumi Maritza or Karvavena ZANG-TUMB-TUUUMB, toc-toc-toc-toc [fast], crooc-craac [slowly], cries of officers slamming about like brass plates pan here, paak there, BUUUM ching, chaak [very fast], cha-cha-cha-cha-chaak down there up around high up. Look out your head beautiful! Flashing flashing flashing flashing flashing flashing footlights of the forts down there behind that smoke Shukri Pasha communicates by phone with twenty seven forts in Turkish in German, "Allo! Ibrahim! Rudolf! Allo! Allo!" Actors parts, echoes of prompters, scenery of smoke forests, applause odour of hay mud dung. I no longer feel my frozen feet. Odour of gunsmoke, odour of rot Tympani, flutes, clarinets – everywhere, low-high birds chirping blessed shadows, cheep-cheep-cheep, green breezes, flocks, don-dan-don-din-baaah".

He carries on at some length, for, as any great artist should, Russolo spoke with coloured steam, expressing emotion and breaking boundaries. He sensed the enormous possibilities of creativity whilst also, of course, pre-naming Trevor Horn and Paul Morley's record label ZTT (ZANG-TUMB-TUUUMB) and their first creative vehicle, The Art Of Noise, who debuted in 1983. Was it Horn and co who expressed their intentions so graphically when they said "We want to attune and regulate this tremendous variety of noises harmonically and rhythmically"? Actually, it was Russolo, but the sentiment, seventy years after the Futurists demanded that acoustic music was not enough, still resonated.

original recordings by
GUILLAUME APOLLINAIRE
JEAN COCTEAU
MARCEL DUCHAMP
LUIGI GRANDI
RICHARD HUELSENBECK
MARCEL JANCO
WYNDHAM LEWIS
FILIPPO TOMMASO MARINETTI
ANTONIO RUSSOLO
KURT SCHWITTERS
TRISTAN TZARA

TRISTAN TZARA, MARCEL JANCO AND RICHARD HUELSENBECK
L'Amiral Cherche Une Maison A Louer
Original recording: 1916
Available on 'Futurism And Dada Reviewed'
SUB ROSA RECORDS

'L'Amiral Cherche Une Maison A Louer' didn't further the cause of electronic music like the Futurist's 'Art Of Noise' manifesto – in fact, it didn't provide a scientific breakthrough in any way - but it was undoubtedly the inspiration for the freedom that the development of new technology would embrace. As the Futurists had looked towards sound to seek tomorrow's art, the Dadaists looked there to send their ideas even further left of the leftfield they were already camping in.

Tristan Tzara was a Romanian artist who found his way to Zurich, where he established the Dada movement and opened the notorious club Cabaret Voltaire (whose name would be adopted as a moniker for the experimental recordings of Richard Kirk, Stephen Mallinder and Christopher

Watson in the early '70s). Here Tzara met with fellow Romanian painter and engraver Marcel Janco and German literary and poetic innovator Richard Huelsenbeck. They all frequented the club, where minds would wander and stand-up experimentalism was the order of the day, and would perform 'L'Amiral Cherche Une Maison A Louer', a tonal Dada poem. People would wince agreeably.

Sadly, the club is no longer there but, in the alleyways of Zurich, there is an inscribed toilet seat hung on the wall where it used to be. Somewhat fittingly, this symbolic plaque displays the club's contempt for normality.

In the history of electronic music, the concept of the tonal poem seems to fit well, due to the creative mixture of sounds and how they were overlaid. In the instance of "L'Amiral...", the trio of performers seem intent on performing different pieces, with whistles, duck calls and explosions interrupting their spoken or sung parts. Like a primal four track recording of unrelated events, it's a live version of the anarchy that Russolo and the Futurists predicted; a multi-layered sound bed that allows the listener either to hear snatches or moments of sound or take the whole episode as an engaging whole, much like the "jazz" or avant garde moments that were to invade the work of Can in full jam mode on their 'Monster Movie' LP many decades later. It was challenging stuff, the living embodiment of Russolo's diatribe, and was a complete statement that would never be the same twice. It was "proper" art.

However, both the Futurists and the Dadaists were given short shrift by Phil Sutcliffe in Q magazine in 1994, when the 'Futurism And Dada Revisited' album was dismissed as "Cacophonous experimental music", a "historical document (unlistenable) from when the wheels fell off art and Hitler got a flying start".

GEORGE ANTHEIL
Ballet Mécanique
Original performance: 1924

If Dada tone poems delivered the idea of multi-tracking and the Futurists destroyed romantic classical music with their war on acoustic sound and the addition of noise, George Antheil's 1924 soundtrack to Fernand Léger's experimental, Dadaist, film Ballet Mécanique, with its shape shifting forms, blurred edges and kaleidoscope effects, took film - and its accompanying soundtrack - to a whole new dimension.

Léger's film was looped and repetitive and Antheil's soundtrack employed similar techniques, with regimented piano pieces augmented by airplane propellers, sirens and electric bells. The modal sounds and intruding noises are like nothing that had happened before, being so wild and different. But it had some order, unlike the Futurists and Dadaists. There was some discernable structure, a form that resonated through the work of Stockhausen, Terry Riley, Steve Reich and of course Philip Glass and Michael Nyman many years later. It was music bent out of shape to accompany images bent further, and Antheil became legendary as a self-styled "bad boy of music", taunting audiences in his native USA and in Europe during the 1920s with wild sounds and writing provocative music columns, and even a novel, as well as his work on Léger's film. It was extreme stuff done in extreme situations.

The truth is, though, the two parts of the 'Ballet Mécanique' were created totally separately - the soundtrack and the visuals were never even married together until the 1990s, where Antheil's offbeat approach became bizarrely at home with Léger's similarly madcap visions. The music alone is analysed in frightening detail on Wikipedia, where the following statement acts as a foreword to some complex probing: "The Ballet is hard to surmise from just looking at the score - one must hear it to get a real sense of its chaos. It moves frighteningly quickly, up to 32nd notes at tempo (quarter = 152). It sounds like an onslaught of confusing chords, punctuated by random rings, wails, or pauses. The meter rarely stays the same for more than three measures, distracting from the larger form of the music and instead highlighting the driving rhythms". Scary, indeed.

'Ballet Mécanique' was created to illustrate a modern dance carried out by machines rather than people, the frenetic sound acting as a foil for the footage of rotating machinery and moving parts. Long after Antheil's original soundtrack was created, he revisited the piece in 1953, shortening and toning down the concept using four pianos, four xylophones, two electric bells, two propellers, timpani, glockenspiel and other percussion. The result was more approachable, more ordered, more Pink Floyd.

Intriguingly, before Antheil and Léger's work were reunited, film composer Michael Nyman re-scored the film in 1986 and, in 2005, a robotic orchestra named The League Of Electronic Musical Urban Robots was created to deliver an even more bizarre version of the piece. Great name.

The Léger movie with Antheil's original score is easily found on the internet, and various versions of the piece can be found on CD. 'Ballet Mecanique' is a truly oddball experience, a very scary thing as Antheil would later recall: "It had various performances in Paris during 1925 and 1926, and was performed in Carnegie Hall on April 10, 1927, for the first time in the United States. All the concerts were riotous in some way, the Paris performances having fistfights in the audience. The New York performance less so, but nevertheless it is said that the concert was as scandalous as the city has witnessed. It became a very notorious piece, much talked about but little played".

People were engaged and confused by the piece. They asked why Antheil used propellers, to which he replied they are part of modern day life. He compared the piece to architecture, to abstract art. He wasn't helping any, insisting that, "If one has a mind to understand it, let him listen with new ears". The method of construction, the everyday objects littering the sound and the intrigue with technological developments were all part of music's blossoming and the early development of electronic sound. Initially, it took artists and extremists to challenge the norm, but in 1920 the string quartet or classically trained pianist was further eroded when Leon Theremin developed the Theremin.

After demonstrating his device to fascinated audiences in Europe, Leon Theremin arrived in the United States in 1927 where his invention was put into production by RCA. Working with fellow Russian émigré Clara Rockmore, a child prodigy violinist, Theremin refined the instrument whilst Rockmore became a respected virtuoso.

CLARA ROCKMORE
The Art Of The Theremin
Original release: 1977
DELOS RECORDS

Tracklisting:
Rachmaninoff - Vocalise, Rachmaninoff - Song of Grusit, Saint-Saens - The Swan, De Falla –
Pantomime, Achron - Hebrew Melody, Wieniawski – Romance, Stravinsky – Berceuse, Ravel
- Piece en forme de Habanera, Tchaikovsky – Berceuse, Tchaikovsky - Valse sentimentale,
Tchaikovsky - Sérénade mélancolique, Glazunov - Chant du ménestrel.

Although Clara Rockmore became a key part in the development of the Theremin, her recorded
output was never considered until she was tempted out if retirement in the 1970s. Her live
performances and radio appearances with the instruments' inventor were hugely popular
throughout Europe and the United States during the '30s and '40s, where her customised
instrument allowed her to deliver the classical works of many of the great composers with a
sound that was truly like nothing else.

'The Art Of The Theremin' was commissioned and released in the '70s at the request of Moog
inventor Robert Moog, who'd originally worked to develop the Theremin. His sleevenotes
praised Rockmore and the instrument itself: "She has shown the Theremin to be a valuable
musical resource, capable of producing beautiful music and worthy of the dedication of talented
performers. No other artist has ever come close to Ms Rockmore's level of achievement;
no other Thereminist has ever produced music of such beauty and aural appeal".

Later, Moog would turn up in a 1998 documentary about Rockmore, where he shared a dinner
party with her, her sister, pianist Nadia Reisenberg, and other members of her family. Set in the
suitably surreal setting of the Rockmore family home, with a particularly distracting space age
table as its centrepiece, the footage is nothing short of bizarre. Dinner abandoned, and after
briefly discussing her first meeting with Louis Theremin, Rockmore performs, with her sister on
piano, and the amazing control she has over what is deemed to be a truly difficult instrument to
master is amazing. Looking like a B movie out-take, accentuated by a bad hair day, she makes no
contact with the machine, and her intense hand movements create the illusion she is playing air
violin. The sound too is staggering, containing as it does all the melancholy of a suicidal Chaplin
set piece. It's reminiscent of vintage saw players in parts, surely another instrument where the
haziness of a precise note adds to the charm of the sound. It is filled with classical romanticism
and remains an artefact of an instrument and an era long gone.

While 'The Art Of The Theremin' remains true to Rockmore's tone and sound circa the '30s
and '40s, there has been, more recently, the discovery of her 'Lost Theremin Album' (Bridge
Records), which was released in 2006.

The mood is inevitably sombre, but the Theremin is set against violin and guitar in places, creating new and fresh dimensions in sound. In fact, the guitar interplay proves amazingly poetic on a truly moving version of 'Esterellita', which, along with her version of 'Humoresque' (accompanied by piano), has the Theremin sounding like a mutant opera singer with a fantastic range. The stand out track on 'The Lost Theremin Album' is a glorious version of Billie Holiday's 'Summertime', where the down chords of the piano allow the Theremin's melody line to reach new heights of moribund desolation.

At the end of the 1930s, a host of new inventions were being unveiled. The Sonorous Cross was a version on the Theremin, while electro-acoustic keyboards like the Electrochord and the Novachord were beginning to emerge. And while the Theremin was being developed further in the States, in France the Ondes Martenot had become the electronic instrument of choice, especially for composer Olivier Messiaen.

OLIVIER MESSIAEN
Trois petites Liturgies de la Présence Divine
Original release: 1943
ELEKTRA (1993, conducted by Marcel Couraud)

Tracklisting:
Antienne de la Conversation Interieure, Sequence du Verbe, Cantique Divin, Psalmodie de
l'Ubiquité par Amour.

Olivier Messiaen was a much-admired French composer of the 1930s, a man obsessed with sound and the structure of music. An ornithologist, he would incorporate birdsongs into his pieces and the construction of his work, including a penchant for serialism, became an influence for minimalists like Philip Glass and Terry Riley, while many of his pieces have been acclaimed as touchstones for both Boulez and Stockhausen.

"In 1937," according to an online resource, "in response to a commission for a piece to accompany light and water shows on the Seine during the Paris Exposition, Messiaen demonstrated his interest in using the Ondes Martenot, an electronic instrument". This early move into electronic sound was to stay in his thinking for years to come, and, although the original commissioned piece 'Fêtes Des Belles Eaux' remains unpublished, 'Oraison' a seven minute piece from the same year is available on both 'An Anthology Of Noise And Electronic Music, Fourth A-Chronology 1937-2005' on Sub Rosa and the excellent 'Ohm: The Early Gurus Of Electronic Music' on Ellipsis Arts.

Both of these versions were recorded by The Ensemble D'Ondes De Montreal in 1998 and feature the instrument with all its melancholy allure. However, a Portuguese student recently unearthed a reported 60 CD set owned by her university which traces the history of electronic / acoustic music from 1937 onwards and includes a 1937 Ondes Martenot version of 'Oraison' by Messiaen himself. Richer and deeper in tone, the piece has more of a haunting Hollywood feel, with the rumbling of the Martenot's machinery adding to the tension.

The sleevenotes of the 'Ohm' set include a note from John Schaeffer, the host of 'New Sounds' on the New York radio station WNYC-FM, who notes that the addition of the Ondes Martenot to the orchestral palette in the 1920s and '30s was "exactly as its inventor Maurice Martenot intended it to be". It was a supplementary sound rather than an alternative to existing instruments. Schaeffer continues: "It was Messiean, the mystic and organist, who heard something unique in the instrument and decided to write a piece for a whole ensemble of Ondes Martenots, without trying to meld it to pre-existing acoustic instruments". The result is amazing, and 'Oraison' floats with spectral beauty.

Six years later, in 1943, Messiaen employed the instrument again on 'Three Short Liturgies', a religious concert work that he wanted to be able to play in places that weren't traditionally religious but were still able to create a sense of spiritualism. The instrumental passages see piano and solo violin set against the Ondes Martenot, the first movement including an electronic sound swirling behind the proceedings, whilst the second passage has the Martenot churning above the choir. But it's the lengthy tone poem of the third part, which has a pulsing Glass-like repetitiveness in places, where the "metallic timbre" that Messiaen loved about the Ondes Martenot is allowed to dictate.

Jean Hughes, who wrote the sleevenotes to the copy of the album I have, concluded that Messiaen "respects tradition but sees nothing in it that inhibits innovation. He mixes notions of the profane and sacred love. There are times when he seems to have the perfect expression of his ideas; for him the Ondes Martenot is an instrument remarkably suited to his melodic ideal, which can produce loud terrifying effects and contrary-wise, halos of sweet unreality".

Much like the Theremin, the Ondes Martenot carried unique melody possibilities that were quite unlike traditional instrumentation, and it wouldn't be long before both of them filtered into contemporary music. The Theremin was perfect for anything with a hint of the inexplicable, and Dr Samuel J Hoffman was the master of capturing such things.

DR SAMUEL J HOFFMAN
Music Out Of The Moon
Original release: 1947
CAPITOL RECORDS

Tracklisting:
Lunar Rhapsody, Moon Moods, Lunette, Celestial Nocturne, Mist O' The Moon,
Radar Blues

According to the sleeve of the 1947 album 'Music Out Of The Moon', which features Dr Samuel J Hoffman on Theremin, backed by an orchestra conducted by easy listening guru Les Baxter, the whole album is "in reality, an exploration using exotic harmonies, timbre and composition to play upon the more remote realm of human emotions. It is music that has been outstandingly successful as a mood-creating background for motion pictures dealing with the macabre, the fantastic".

Hoffman would go on to release 'Perfume Set To Music' a year later, then 'Music For Peace Of Mind' in 1950, having already lent his sound-bending techniques to movies like 1945's Spellbound (among others), all of which feature the eerie, otherworldly vibrato that the Theremin delivered at the flick of a wrist. Hoffman would later contribute Theremin to the 1951 film The Day The Earth Stood Still.

The Theremin sound of Hoffman is different to Rockmore's classical approach. It sounds like nothing else. The two protruding antennae from the instrument are controlled by moving each hand, one controlling the volume, the other the pitch of the sound and is considered "easy to learn but notoriously difficult to master, Theremin performance presenting two challenges: reliable control of the instrument's pitch with no guidance (no keys, valves, frets, or finger-board positions), and minimizing undesired portamento that is inherent in the instrument's microtonal design".

Hoffman, like Rockmore, became synonymous with the instrument, and the re-issue of his three themed studio albums came with an explanatory booklet that compares the Theremin to "the phenomenon related to the squeals old radios gave off when the hand approached the tuning dial and interfered with the antenna's electrical field". The resultant audio from such a device was always going to be shaky and, perhaps because of these problems, the Theremin's use remains minimal on 'Music Out Of The Moon'. The mood is, of course, otherworldly, but that's really down to the multiple harmonies and lush strings. The Theremin slots into the easy groove quite comfortably.

The Theremin's place as an electronic innovation that influenced and changed music is unquestionable, but, in truth, most bent and eerie waveforms that we think are Theremin-created are variations or developments. The Beach Boys' life-changing 'Good Vibrations', for example, doesn't feature an original Theremin, but rather a mechanical development, The Electro-Theremin, built by Paul Tanner. More recently, the Theremin led track 'Mysterons', on Portishead's 'Dummy' album, turns out to have been created by a monophonic synthesiser.

So, apart from adding drama to movies, is this almost uncontrollable dream weaver able to command emotions and carry a tune? 'Music Out Of The Moon', with its half dozen tracks suggests it can. Remaining within the realms of melodic music, the Theremin was the development in contemporary electronic sound that was acceptable and accessible. But while America was being treated to melody, lush strings and emotional wallpaper, the European's experiments with sound were about to enter a whole new phase. Musique Concrète couldn't have been further from Les Baxter's silky orchestrations, Rockmore's classical variations and Hoffman's swirling soundtracks.

PIERRE SCHAEFFER
Etude aux Chemins de Fer, Original recording: 1948
INA-GRM (France) EMF (US)

Available as part of the three CD set 'L'Oeuvre Musical' featuring Schaeffer's 1948 recordings plus his collaborations with Pierre Henry from 1949 to 1958.

Clocking in at just under three minutes, 'Etude aux Chemins de Fer' is a monumental moment in audio history. It sounds like nothing else that had come before, but a hell of a lot that came after.

Pierre Schaeffer was a radio engineer responsible for field recordings at Radiodiffusion Française. Having taken a recording truck out to Batignolles, near Paris, to record the sound of a railway yard, he returned to the studio and began editing the recordings to make a semi-rhythmic piece which used moving trucks, train whistles and various sounds that he had captured to make a short symphony of "found sounds". Why he did this, no one is particularly sure. But thank God he did! It was the first of several recordings he would create that year and call 'Musique Concrète' (real music) - a symbolic title that's constantly back referenced today. Was it 'music'? Was it any different from what we might have heard if we'd travelled to those same railway yards on the same day?

'Etude aux Chemins de Fer' became an inspiration for composers from Stockhausen, Cage and Varese through to Zappa, Nurse With Wound and way beyond. The concept of Musique

Concrète insured that music didn't have to retain any sense of order or shape; a quantum leap in thinking that led to the development of the mixing desk, reverb units, octave filters, sound loops, and sampling. Its arguable too that its sense of juxtaposition and disorder inadvertently foresaw the dance revolution of the 80s and 90s, not to mention triggering numerous lawsuits and a whole lot more. Schaeffer, having discovered that a 'normal' audio experience could be recorded and manipulated, opened the floodgates for creativity. Melody was still sought after, but its creation became complicated.

After he'd completed 'Etude', Schaeffer adapted other everyday objects in his quest to create further super real sounds. Using thin-metal instruments, wooden percussion, and whirligigs, he delivered 'Etude aux Tourniquets' which sounds like the invented instruments of Harry Partch or an acoustic version of The Residents. That was followed by the shocking but strangely understated 'Cinq Études de bruits: Étude Violette' and 'Etude Noir', which sound like out-takes from a dubstep album.

All five compositions from 1948 were broadcast from Paris on October 5, billed as a 'Concert Of Noises', and people were stunned. Following the broadcast, Schaeffer was lauded as a visionary and given an assistant, namely one Pierre Henry. The duo were to work for almost a decade extending the boundaries of the genre. These were serious guys, and their first collaboration, 'Symphonie Pour Un Homme Seul', an exploration of a "lonely" man told in 22 sound pieces, was staggering. It was cut-up and challenging. A real murder one.

At the same time that Schaeffer's sound experiments were destroying conventional song construction, one John Scott Turner was building a composition machine for popular music, whilst Hugh Le Caine was perfecting the electronic Sackbutt, which sounded very much like an electronic cello, and the mysterious H Bode was inventing the Melochord. Innovation and experimentation was rife, and the first computed sounds were just a heavy-handed click away.

THE CSIRAC COMPUTER
First computed music
Original performance: 1949

Over the first half of the Twentieth Century, music had been forcibly re-ordered. Simplicity was replaced by cerebral thinking, traditional shape was questioned and nothing was at it had been as the 1940s drew to a close. What better time than to completely simplify everything again and to use so many whizzing parts to attain minimalism that the irony of it all was lost for the sake of the most naïve song.

Late in 1949, the CSIRAC computer, an enormous forty square metres of technology, was developed by Dr Trevor Pearcey and his colleagues Maston Beard and Geoff Hill. Looking like something out of a sci-fi movie, It performed rather rudimentary functions and was also able to synthesise monophonic music which, when heard now, sounds amazingly like a Stylophone played by a hungover stooge rife with the DTs. Weird.

"These were the electronics of the time and they weren't terribly reliable." declared Melbourne University many moons later. "Indeed, compared to computers available today, CSIRAC's grunt seems laughable" comments their website dedicated to 'The Machine That Changed The World' (visit it at www.abc.net.au/science/slab/csirac/default.htm and listen at www.abc.net.au/science/slab/csirac/csirac2.ram). "It ran at 0.001 megahertz, with 2000 bytes of memory and a mere 2500 bytes of storage. By comparison, a typical desktop PC today has a processing speed of 500 megahertz, with 64 megabytes of memory and a hard disk containing 10 gigabytes (10,000 million bytes) of storage."

"CSIRAC's first programmer, Geoff Hill, came from a musical family and programmed the computer to play popular musical melodies which could be heard through a loudspeaker originally installed for a quite different purpose - to indicate with audible "beeps" when particular points of interest in the program had been reached".

Such is the stuff of accidental legend. An obscure precursor to the electronic bleeps that became music, the CSIRAC's brief tenure at the Top Of Tomorrow's Pops was nevertheless short-lived, and, only two years later, all things futuristic were summed up on the soundtrack to the Hollywood sci-fi epic The Day The Earth Stood Still.

BERNARD HERMANN
The Day The Earth Stood Still
Original release: 1951
ARISTA

Tracklisting:
Twentieth Century Fox Fanfare, Prelude Outer Space Radar, Danger, Klaatu, Gort The Visor The Telescope, Escape, Solar Diamonds, Arlington, Lincoln Memorial, Nocturne The Flashlight The Robot Space Control, The Elevator Magnetic Pull The Study The Conference The Jewellery Store, Panic, The Glowing Alone Gort's Rage Nikto The Captive Terror, The Prison, Rebirth, Departure, Farewell, Finale.

You've got to love Tyler Bates' soundtrack for the 2008 remake of The Day The Earth Stood Still, Whatever you think of the movie with Keanu Reeves, Bates' echoey booms and enormous melody lines are something else. Back in 1951, the Bernard Hermann soundtrack for the Robert Wise directed original, which came with the tag line 'A robot and a man hold the world spellbound with new and startling powers from another planet' and a plotline that involved world peace or death, had everything the state of art studio could offer. And two Theremins!

Hermann was an advocate of composer Charles Ives, who'd worked with Wise on both Citizen Kane and The Magnificent Ambersons, both Orson Welles movies from the '40s where Wise had been head of editing (indeed, he won an award for the former). In 1950, he was brought in to provide the ethereal sounds for one of the earliest big screen science fiction epics, a film so out there that, like the Futurists' early musical experiments, it had audiences fleeing from cinemas.

Hermann's score predates his work with Alfred Hitchcock, but much of the tension he was to capture in that work was already evident, as was the haunting use of reverb he was to master. The Theremins, alongside electric violin, cello and bass, vibraphone, glockenspiel, Hammond organ and some lush strings, add an element of the unknown. But Hermann's inventiveness didn't stop there - tape dubbing and reversed playback provided moods of isolation, loneliness and despair, as well as the kind of ambience that would become omnipresent in the trail of sci-fi exploitation films that followed.

HERBERT EIMERT
Klangstudie I
Original recording: 1951
Available on 'Ohm: The Early Gurus Of Electronic Music'
ELIPSIS

Bernard Hermann may have been dabbling with changing and reversing tapes, but Herbert Eimert, a founder of the WDR studio in Cologne in the early 1950s, had other goals in mind. According to notes by composer Konrad Boehmer in Ohm, Eimert wanted to "synthetically continue the musical achievements of the late Anton Webern".

Working with Robert Beyer, Eimert spent months creating two short pieces, namely 'Klangstudie I'. and, a year later, 'Klangstudie II'. They sounded like orchestral compositions delivered with purely electronic sounds. There was traditional composition in these pieces, and little in the way of effects. The sound, which came from miles of edited tape, was unique.

Boehmer, interviewed on the Perfect Sound Forever website in 2000, noted of the Beyer/Eimert partnership that they were very different in their approach, Beyer being more dreamlike, while Eimert was more ordered. Even though they worked together, there were definite leaders in each piece.

"There was a piece called 'Sound in Indefinite Space', which shows more the impact of Beyer, while 'Klangstudie' shows more the impact of Herbert Eimert. It is a little bit more rigid, orientated on models of instrumental composition, not on compositions. It has a more rigid structure than certain of their other early pieces".

Amazingly, the primitive WDR Studio were able to produce such versatile and grand music. Eimert was testing the boundaries of composition and sound seemingly travelling wherever their creation propelled them.

"In the beginning they had the melochord, designed in the 1940s. This could produce sounds nearly as clear and clean as sine waves", Boehmer recalls. "This was an instrument with a keyboard, so they had to take every sound from the keyboard, put it on a tape and then start the synchronisation and the montage work. That was mainly what, and just about all, they had. Even when I came to the studio seven or eight years later, they only had two primitive sine wave generators, not even a noise generator, and some very primitive filters. All these instruments were loaned to them from the technical department at Cologne radio. These instruments were not built for the purpose of composing music, but for measuring and things like that".

Even a brief listen to 'Klangstudie' explains why Eimert and Beyer are so influential. This was music like no one else was producing, and 1952's collaboration 'Klang Im Unbegrenzten Raum', a ten minute plus creation that features an unearthly synthetic rhythm throbbing beneath its floating, disjointed "melody" line, plenty of space age bleeps and an almost down-home, spiritual keyboard flourish, really is the strangest of sounds.

As Boehmer pointed out, "The interesting thing is that these people made very fascinating compositions with very primitive tools. Every step they took, every button they turned, they had to think about what they were doing".

MICHEL PHILIPOTT
Etude Number One
Original recording: 1951

Like Eimert, French composer Michel Philipott was ensconced in more traditional work with orchestras and chamber music composition. Later, at the end of the '50s, he would work with Pierre Schaeffer. but in 1951 he was fascinated by the potential of tape editing and the sounds that could be created and re-ordered.

Philpot's 'Etude Number One' was an early exploratory work with tape manipulation. A pulsing, almost serial, composition that has real spirit of menace, with sounds arriving from nowhere and echoes and sustain hanging in the air and ringing like the internal workings of some ancient grandfather clock. It's almost as if you're stuck within the sound and, all the while, some madman is occasionally thumping as he moves around outside.

While Philipott managed to keep a constantly evolving structure to the five minutes of 'Etude Number One', there's a sense of echoed reverence. A religious experience of sounds from, well, almost nowhere. But, If Philpot was putting order into things, then John Cage had decided that the very opposite was the best way forward.

JOHN CAGE
The Williams Mix, Original performance: 1952
Available on 'Ohm: The Early Gurus Of Electronic Music'
ELIPSIS

In 1950, John Cage had decided to dispense with traditional structure altogether. By chance, he'd stumbled upon indeterminate music, that is sound created almost by accident. Cage and fellow members of the New York School, Morton Feldman and Christian Wolff, were expressing their desire for a lack of considered order, an idea which they'd fallen into after Cage had been overwhelmed by a performance of Webern's 'Symphony, Opus 21'. The story goes that he hurriedly left the auditorium, where a chance meeting with Feldman - also fleeing the scene - resulted in a decade of unscripted explorations.

'The Williams Mix', from 1952, was a masterpiece of unplanned excursion. The result of nine months of experiments with Forbidden Planet soundtrack pioneers Louis and Bebe Barron, it remains a challenging listen, but in 2008, in an effort to help people understand the work, the exceptional website Diagonal Thoughts (www.diagonalthoughts.com) analysed the piece and looked at its complex construction.

"The raw recordings, collected by the Barrons, were manipulated by Cage, who mixed categorised areas of sound; city sounds, country sounds, electronic sounds, manually-produced sounds, wind-produced sounds and small sounds which required amplification in order to be heard with the others. These groups were further split up into controlled and uncontrolled noise and again into even more segregated groups".

The razor blades were out. Cage took it all apart and reconstructed it in a process that "involved the precise cutting and splicing of recorded sounds to create eight separate reel-to-reel, monaural, 15-ips magnetic tape masters for the 4-minute 15-second, octophonic tape piece. The 192-page score is, as Cage referred to it, a kind of "dressmaker's pattern - it literally shows where the tape shall be cut, and you lay the tape on the score itself".

This was a man who suggested recording something / anything, getting the recorded tape, cutting it into strips and re-ordering it. A DIY symphony, where even the length of the edits was predetermined. Only the actual audio on the tape was not.

In an interview with author Richard Kostelanetz in 1985, Cage revealed that "someone else could follow that recipe, so to speak, with other sources than I had, to make another mix". It was all about random construction, although there was actually a plan to follow in order to be 'random'.
The 'Williams Mix' was created after Cage received a grant in the early '50s to examine the relationship between music and sound. It led him to expand on his 1937 statement: "If this word 'music' is sacred and reserved for eighteenth and nineteenth-century instruments, we can substitute a more meaningful term: organisation of sound".

Cage's experiments harked back to the 'Sonic Taxonomies' which were performed by Futurist Luigi Russolo, who organised sounds in six families of noises. It's something which Stockhausen would also study in 1966 when he made an even more complex classification of sixty eight sound types for the thirty three "moments" that comprise his piece 'Mikrophonie I'. These included groaning, creaking, grunting, clinking, jingling, crashing, screeching, choking (rattling in the throat), whining, whimpering and many, many more. Armoury comparable to Cage's 'William's Mix' material.

As Diagonal Thoughts revealed, Holger Czukay, who was once a student of Stockhausen and later a member of Can, wrote in detail about his teacher's piece: "Four musicians were standing at a huge tam-tam with some 'creation tools' and a microphone in their hand. The tam-tam was prepared at different parts with chalk or colophony (the resin which a violinist applies to his bow before he starts playing so that he is able to create a tone) so that a hard paper bucket, for example, could scratch upon the chalk or colophony field. An electric razor was another device which created a rich world of sounds when it was touching the surface of the tam-tam. Two microphones were scanning the different sound areas of the tam-tam, connected to two Maihak W49 radio play EQs, passive filters with a strong cutting characteristics. Stockhausen was sitting in the audience at a little mixer and created something like a 'tam-tam live dub mix'."

Stockhausen, like Cage before him, was rewriting the rules. But back to Cage. The question is, was, and is, the 'William's Mix' any good?

The jury is still out. In 2005, the JohnCageblog, a site which was created by "Nonmusician" Zac for the purpose of listening to Cage's entire (almost) recorded output, opined that "This is pretty much the most depressing work in the entirety of Cage's career. I say it's depressing simply because a huge amount of effort (Cage apparently gave instructions on how to complete if he died working on it) went into something that could now be replicated in a tiny fraction of the time.

"My experience in listening to it is pretty wild," continues Zac. "It's almost like some sort of incredibly fast out-of-body experience, as if you are rushing through all of human civilisation, with rapid blasts of highly distorted speech, rumbling noises of electronics, tiny snippets of music.... all that and a seemingly omnipresent frog. When I heard 'Revolution 9' by The Beatles, I thought it was a wild idea. Then I heard this from well over a decade before and the poor Beatles just weren't interesting anymore".

The 'Williams Mix' is a real oddity. As Chris Cutler of Recommended Records reports in Ohm's sleevenotes, "A piece making the same demands could be programmed now in less than a day. In 1953 this was groundbreaking and well as backbreaking".

So what does it sound like nearly 60 years later? The 'William's Mix' sounds like a pivotal moment caught in time - a turning point. An advance on the Dadaist multi-layers, and a prequel to scalpel happy fast edits from the avant-garde. It's not easy listening, or comfortable. It's hard work, but evocative, and easy to lose yourself in it. It feels random and threatening.

Following Cage's death in 1982, Q acclaimed him as "one of the century's maestros of avant-garde musical obscurity". Perhaps the 'Williams Mix', and certainly its legendary antidote '4'33"', show the two extremes of his art. Cage remains infamous for the silent piece from 1952, which has been copied and parodied over the years, resulting in many a lawsuit, but that ironic moment of solitude and clarity came as something of a respite amid many experiments with sound that employed radio receivers, taped music, found sounds and various treated instruments".It has three movements," Cage commented, "any number of players can perform on it, but at no point are they intentionally to produce a sound".

On the album 'Electronic Music', from the 1960s, there is further evidence of Cage's chance recordings. 'Fontana Mix' features on the release, and the sleevenotes include an interview with Cage where the "logic and cohesion" of indeterminate music is championed by the interviewer, to which Cage replies, "This logic was not put there by me, but was the result of chance operations".

As Brian Eno would much later confess, "Avant-garde music is sort of research music. You're glad someone's done it but you don't necessarily want to listen to it". However, if you do make it through the eleven minutes and thirty nine seconds of 'Fontana Mix', the truncated speech, the shaky, blurred noise and rumblings and the half-heard radio waves - interjected with clips of choirs, ancient rhythms and electronic sounds – make for a truly disconcerting experience. It's a natural, if synthetic by its creation, descendent of 'Williams Mix' with an even more cohesive hook. Everywhere, there are snatches of things which sound familiar, straining to get out.

So, is it genius or rubbish? Apparently Cage didn't care what people thought of it – from the sleevenotes for 'Electronic Music': "I consider my music, once it has left my desk, to be what in Buddhism would be called a non-sentient being... If someone kicked me – not my music, but me – then I might complain. But if they kicked my music, or cut it out, or don't play it enough, or too much, or something like that, then who am I to complain?"

Much earlier, in 1939, before the chance meeting with his NY School partners, Cage was already toying with unnatural instrumentation. The staggering 'Imaginary Landscape' revealed his skill for multi-layered sounds - a harrowing multi-level, multi-volume piece, it revolves around a swirling electronic pulse which is punctuated by piano crashes and occasional cymbal swirls that sound like they were recorded from within a mighty grand piano, while a plucked lead line sounds not unlike the hokey synthetic banjo that Silver Apples would much later use on 'Ruby' in the mid-'60s.

Unlike the random concept of 'Williams Mix', 'Imaginary Landscape' has an order and unity that predates Cage's search for the irregular. Nonetheless, it also has a strange charm. Cage continued the 'Landscape' series and, in 1951, 'Imaginary Landscape Number Four' was recorded. A staggering piece of chance recording, it catches snippets from talk radio, a piece of music here, and a crescendo there. It's a cohesive piece, almost accessible, and hardly hints at what was to come.

The following year, as 'The Williams Mix' was in preparation, 'Imaginary Landscape Number Five' took its lead from be bop and avant-garde jazz. The edits and retrospective loops, the strident piano behind the wild saxophone, the temporary silences, the gaps and the déjà vu of it all make for spectacular theatre. Cage was producing real visionary stuff by this point, and in doing so taking the theory of free jazz and releasing it into the wild. Something that his continued experiments made possible for all musicians going forward.

VLADIMIR USSACHEVSKY
Sonic Contours
Original release: 1952
Available on: 'Pioneers Of Electronic Music'
CRI

Tracklisting:
Vladimir Ussachevsky - Sonic Contours (1952), Otto Luening - Low Speed (1952), Invention in Twelve Tones (1952), Fantasy in Space (1952), Otto Luening/Vladimir Ussachevsky - Incantation (1953), Otto Luening - Moonflight (1968), Vladimir Ussachevsky - Piece for a Tape Recorder (1956), Pril Smiley - Kolyosa (1970), Bulent Arel - Stereo Electronic Music #2 (1970), Vladimir Ussachevsky - Computer Piece #1 (1968), Vladimir Ussachevsky - Two Sketches for a Computer Piece #1 (1971), Vladimir Ussachevsky - Two Sketches for a Computer Piece #2 (1971), Mario Davidovsky - Synchronisms #5 (1969), Alice Shields - The Transformation of Ani (1970)

In the early 1950s everything seemed to be ready for dismantling and reconstruction. The post-war years had conditioned people to reshape and re-use, and music was no different. John Cage had caused a stir, and there was talk of Stockhausen in Europe and stuff going on in Cologne. At Columbia University the arrival of an early reel-to-reel tape recorder was the catalyst for yet more invention.

In 2008, the blog Bravi Juju (bravojuju.blogspot.com) posted the story of the Columbia University Music Department. It told of how the team at Columbia "requisitioned a tape recorder to use in teaching and for recording concerts. In 1951, the first tape recorder arrived, an Ampex 400, and Vladimir Ussachevsky, then a junior faculty member, was assigned a job that no-one else wanted: the care of the tape recorder. This job was to have important consequences, both for Ussachevsky and the medium he developed."

By 1952, Ussachevsky was producing his own sound manipulations, which blossomed into the formation of the Columbia-Princeton Electronic Music Center. There his many collaborators became key in the development of electronic music - legendary composers were invited to use the facility, and the arrival of Luciano Berio, Bulent Arel and Edgard Varèse made it a hotbed of creativity. Ussachevsky's students at the Center included Jon Appleton, Alice Shields, Walter/ Wendy Carlos, Charles Dodge and Robert Moog, all key innovators as the movement began to gain momentum.

The 'Pioneers Of Electronic Music' album features contributions from Ussachevsky circa 1952, along with recordings from the next two decades from Otto Luening, Ussachevsky, Alice Shields and Oril Smiley. Between them they tackle a wide variety of sound experiments on an album that must have seemed startling when first released. Ussachevsky's 'Sonic Contours' features reverbed piano patterns, echoed effects and almost modal construction. It sounds like disturbed nursery music. His later works, like the awesome 'Incantation For Tape', with its ghostly ambience, and 1960's 'Wireless Fantasy', with its surging modular sound, are also suitably intense, the latter sounding like Radio Luxembourg's unfathomable tuning in peaks and troughs, tracing the ebb and flow of sound, the boom and bust of noise.

Also featured on 'Sonic Contours' are three pieces by Otto Luening, a contemporary of Ussachevsky whose snappily-titled 'A Poem in Cycles And Bells, Gargoyles For Violin And Synthesised Sound' and the revered 'Low Speed', which was commissioned for the opening of The Museum Of Modern Art in New York in 1952, are both startling pieces constructed by taping, re-taping and editing. 'Low Speed' especially, with its brooding echoey spaciousness, is a grumbling monster, scary, unnerving and jarring. You can easily imagine its premiere in the wide-open spaces of the Museum Of Modern Art. This was music as art; sound that didn't have to be explained.

"The sound source for this piece is the flute," Luening recorded in his notes from Columbia and Princeton Universities. It "used acoustic relationships and the tape recorder to modify the sound and to highlight certain overtones. This treatment brings out new characteristics from the instrument".

Electronic Music at this point was clearly about to change. Luneing, like Ussachevsky, had explored the possibility of editing, using the flute as his tonal starting place. It was the same starting place used for Bruno Maderna's 'Musica Su Due Dimensioni', but the outcome for Maderna was much different.

BRUNO MADERNA
Musica Su Due Dimensioni
First played: 1952

With so much happening in 1952, the barriers to creativity were quickly being destroyed. In Italy, composer Bruno Maderna had fallen in with the likes of Stockhausen, Boulez and Messiaen, the most important performers of the new music. His 'Musica Su Due Dimensioni' began with a gripping flute exploration holding the attention in an offbeat arrangement which at first grates, before succumbing to soothing melody.

The listening experience is calm and comforting, and, at around seven minutes, 'Musica Su Due Dimensioni' appears to be an expressive, flowing tapestry of sound – perfect for one of Dali's surreal movies, perhaps. But Maderna has lulled us into a false sense of security - all seems harmless enough and quite unchallenging until, around two minutes before its conclusion, the mood completely changes. Suddenly Maderna's vision is invaded by electronic dissonance, a puttering rhythm and synthetic melody line coming from nowhere, the flute discarded and the time signatures going haywire.

Roughly translated as 'music from two dimensions', 'Musica Su Due Dimensioni' made a huge impact on the audiences it confronted. Maderna shook them out of their daydream and forced them into uncharted territory. These were sounds from another planet, never mind sounds from another dimension.

Maderna went on to produce movie soundtracks, but not before more experimentation with the possibilities of electronic music. The sharp edits of 'Notturno', from 1956. showed that in his struggle to make sense of the possibilities of the genre he was also dealing with personal demons. Ridding himself of their evil, if you will.

Maderna journeyed yet further in 1958, when he revisited 'Musica Su Due Dimensioni' and made a clearer, better defined edit with state of the art equipment. At the same time, he also produced the Poltergeist-like 'Continuo', a harrowing, layered piece wherein the listener feels like he's being sucked into the white light, with pulsing noise puncturing a floating, reverb-drenched blanket of sound every bit like the used music to accompany an arrival into an underground lair in any B-Movie of the decade.

KARLHEINZ STOCKHAUSEN
'Electronic Musiche (1952-60)'
Original release: 1952
Available from Stockhausen Verlag www.stockhausen.org/cd_catalog

Tracklisting
Etude (1952), Studie I (1953), Studie II (1954), Gesang der Juenglinge (1955-56), Kontakte (1959-60): Struktur I – XVI

If Cage, Maderna, Ussachevsky and co were re-inventing music and leaving the ends bare, then Karlheinz Stockhausen put the proceedings into reverse and put back some semblance of order. During the key period of the late 1950s, while American rock 'n' roll was destroying light orchestral dance music and John Cage's New York School were destroying the structure and natural rhythm of song itself, Stockhausen was manipulating sounds, first in Pierre Schaeffer's studio in Paris, then in his native Cologne, a setting and culture that would add discipline and order. His work was complex, as Erich Boehm reported in Q magazine in February 1995 after a rare meeting with the man. "Understanding Stockhausen," mused Boehm, "isn't easy, and he's not overtly bothered in being understood".

Stockhausen's early experiments in the Western German Radio Studios in Cologne, where he worked as a technician, were paramount to scientific studies. He would loop and splice tapes, and made use of an early sine wave generator. The sound was electronic in places, and incredibly sharp. But the edits made it rhythmical and compulsive. While Cage's free form avant-garde composition style was truly determined by chance, Stockhausen's electronic experiments had simple structure using manipulated sounds to create whole new pieces.

"I spent most of the year in the studio for electronic music at a radio station in Cologne or in other studios where I produced new works with all kinds of electronic apparatus," he recalled. "In particular, what is most important to me is the transformation of a sound by slowing it down, sometimes extremely, so that the inner sound becomes a conceivable rhythm".

Both 1952's 'Etude' and the ten minutes of the following year's 'Studie 1', as well as the shorter, more ambient 'Studie 2' from 1954, have an unreal feel; a repetitive sound, rhythmic, but almost impossible to place. Footage from the '50s of spinning cabinets and Stockhausen with his head almost submerged in the washing machine-like vortex, positioned for maximum sonic effect, gave a sense of the extremes he would go to for the right sound, and indeed the perfection he would seek to get the perfect tone. In explaining the importance of position in the receipt of audio, he explained, "I have projected the sound in a cube of loudspeakers. The sound can move vertically and diagonally at all speeds around the public".

Next came the editing. "I compress longer sections of composed music, either found or made by myself, to such an extent that the rhythm becomes a timbre, and formal subdivisions become rhythm," he explained to one magazine. The hypnotic 'Gesang Der Juengline', which was completed in 1956 as Bill Haley was rocking around a clock somewhere, set the template for the kind of experimentalism that came from the Dada and Futurist movements and so carried on through to disparate bed partners The Beach Boys, The Beatles, Can and Nurse With Wound.

With music being produced by people who were trained technicians as well as musicians, the results seemed like 'Which?' reports on technique rather than the beauty of sound. Stockhausen's role as overseer, coupled with his sense of order, became key to his compositions, and from there an electronic revolution began. "I was free to make my music - or a new music which I didn't know myself," he told Q. "It was a revolution from mechanical performance practice to electronic sounds".

After Stockhausen, the beauty of music was replaced by the art of music. This became most apparent on the sixteen part 'Kontakte', where the cut and paste technique was given added muscle through the deconstruction of electronic as well as natural sounds. With reverb and echo giving further presence amid the ambience, 'Kontakte's range of tones, sound levels and semi-silence, plus the unorthodox nature of some of the electronic blips, acted as a precursor to the psychedelic bubble which would inflate in the '60s.

On visiting the States, Stockhausen's music became the cause celebré of the '60s counter culture. The Grateful Dead and Jefferson Airplane attended his lectures in California and both John Lennon's 'Revolution Number Nine' and Brian Wilson's experiments in sound showed traces of Stockhausen.

But already, Stockhausen himself had moved on, and his initial experiments became larger and more consuming. 1966's 'Telemusik', which was based on tape recordings from South

America, Eastern Europe and Asia mixed with his own electronic sounds in a unique meta-collage, moved even further 'out there'. The pieces featured shortwave radio solos and strange opera arrangements set to electronic music, and inspired a phalanx of followers including Can, Kraftwerk and Amon Duul to ignite their own creative flairs.

Stockhausen created possibilities and opened doors. He underlined that different was good. Chance meetings and casual acquaintances led to further tangents. No one went away empty-handed.

KAREL GOEYVAERTS
Komposition Nr. 5
Original recording: 1953

Violin concertos and chamber music was the stuff of Belgian composer Karel Goeyvaerts during the 1940s, and sonatas for piano much later. But in the early 1950s he met Karlheinz Stockhausen, with whom he shared a devout belief in Catholicism that led to a spiritual influence on both of their works. The two met at the Darmstadt New Music Summer School, where they found methods of integrating religious numerology into their serial compositions. Goeyvaerts is often acclaimed to be the first serial composer, but the disputes on that particular argument could lead to a whole other book!

The fact is that, during 1952, Stockhausen had access in Paris to a generator of sine waves. Goeyvaerts' developments in composition and his interest in sound and its possibilities had led him to the conclusion that sine waves were the most important discovery in music. He was convinced that they created the purest sound possible. Stockhausen listened intently.

By 1953, Goeyvaerts made manifestations of his theory with 'Komposition No. 5' and 'Komposition No. 7', two varispeed manipulations of sound featuring slowly simmering bleeps that lived as much on expectancy as actual substance. They were a stripping away of all previous knowledge. A rebirth. Featuring a portamento keyboard blurring into nothing then returning with a more continuous wobbling focus, they are an early kind of disorientated drone music, a stuttering wall of sound that had a strangely hypnotic spirituality to them.

PIERRE HENRY
Le Voile d'Orphée
Original release: 1953
PHILIPS

While Goeyvaerts' drones captured a kind of pure, minimal sound, Pierre Henry emerged in his own right, following his collaborations with Pierre Schaeffer, with a more complex electronic sound. In 1953 he recorded 'Le Voile d'Orphée', a remarkable mix of electronic sound, looped samples, dialogue and effects. Often acclaimed as the first symphony of Musique Concrète, the original piece runs for a staggering 27 minutes plus and makes for a claustrophobic and unnerving epic. Eventually, a second, more widely heard fifteen minute version was created by Henry as the original was felt to be just too much for people to take in. But, for the dedicated listener, the Avant Garde Project website features the lengthy version of 'd'Orphee' in its complete form, as was released on Philips in the 1960s (www.avantgardeproject.org/agp43).

35

In that original piece, vocal tracks of whispered dialogue are mixed with reverberated pulses and throbbing, shuddering sounds whilst, amid the chaos lay melodic interludes, wayward lullabies made by seemingly dismantled grandfather clocks. The whole piece never relaxes, with varispeed tampering and distant conversations blended into one sonic landscape.

"These two versions are difficult to choose between," commented Jacques Lonchampt on the sleeve of the late '60s release of both pieces. "The shorter version conserves all the essential elements of the longer and sounds as perfectly unified as if it had originally been written in this form. But the first version breathes more easily, and the feeling of mystery is more poignant, more profound, for the slowness of tempo corresponds to an essential characteristic of the composer's personality".

The sleevenotes also offer some explanation as to the mindset in which Henry created it; "At the time it stood out from among the many experiments as finished and significant; it sounds as valid today despite the great progress made by the technical evolution upon which electro-acoustical music so closely depends. Pierre Henry profoundly individualises instruments and instrumental (or choral) ensembles, as would classical composers, without adopting classical moulds. What is astonishing is that here in the infancy of concrete music he had already reinvented everything: a mysterious quality in the orchestral fabric, a large, complex rhythmic structure, a polyphony of rhythms and sound planes obeying no known rules and nevertheless achieving a unity, an internal logic, that cannot be gainsaid.

"The point is that this music is dominated, organized and drawn onwards by a vision that does not show itself until the final stage of its development. All of Pierre Henry's major compositions are attuned to his personality. In the 'Veil of Orpheus' we already recognise his two main 'ideas', in fact two aspects of the same problem: the mystery of religion and the mystery of death".

As with all great artists, Pierre Henry, like his mentor and working partner Pierre Schaeffer, didn't shirk from the challenge of the new electronic opportunity. 'Le Voile d'Orphée', like so many soundtracks to imaginary films during the 1970s, changes tack and moves through musical themes abruptly. There was seemingly no need to explain how each part fitted together. Like listening to cartoon music for Tom And Jerry without the visuals, the impact of each audio action becomes a terrifying leap into the unknown.

"From the outset," the sleevenotes continue, "Pierre Henry establishes an atmosphere both lyrical and tragic by the use of wide, slow-moving, rich-textured brush strokes upon which he embroiders violent percussive effects and evil-sounding motifs. This grandiose tumult is followed by a liturgy of distant voices above an enigmatic pulsation like the beating of a heart; then the orchestration of the noises becomes less harsh, lighter, and the work builds up extremely slowly, with out-of-focus images, to an Elysian height where the voices and 'instruments' finally fade away, as if passing into a paradise of ultra-sounds".

Remember, these sleevenotes, with their talk of "ultra sound", were written in the 1960s and, as they also refer back to the simplistic rhythms of the heart, they marry the vision of the future with the common understanding of natural rhythm. Nevertheless, 'Le Voile d'Orphée' sounds like the soundtrack to the Dada and Futurist experiments that littered the early beginnings of electronic music.

HUGH LE CAINE
Dripsody
Original release: 1955
Available on 'Ohm: The Early Gurus Of Electronic Music'
ELIPSIS

One of the unsung heroes of electronic music, Le Caine hailed from Ontario in Canada and, during the 1940's and '50s, studied atomic physics and nuclear physics, which somehow allowed him to continue his life-long interest in electronic music. In the 1940s he developed the Electronic Sackbutt, often perceived as the first synthesiser, and composed numerous experimental pieces to accompany his forehead scratching day job.

"By the end of 1955, I had produced 'Dripsody' on my variable-speed multiple tape recorder," Le Caine recalled on the sleeve of Ohm. "I had been working for months on a composition using three sounds: the breaking of a pane of glass, the sound of a ping pong ball on a paddle, and the sound of a single drop of water".

The question of why such disparate sounds should have been chosen remains unanswered. The result of extensive editing is, however, absolutely bizarre. Le Caine allows the drips of water to become a synthetic lead melody played over a lower, deeper sound that acts as a bass part. The two inter-mingle perfectly, and against them the crash of breaking glass and the rhythm of a ping-pong ball provided an unnatural rhythm. 'Dripsody' was about the rhythm and melody created by the synthetic dripping of the tap. Sped up, slowed down, taken down and octave or up into a melody line, the whole thing took on a shape of its own. A shape that shifted structure before heading off to some far-flung water-free galaxy.

Le Caine remains a footnote in the electronic story, but he sits among a wealth of lesser-known experimentalists whose stunning revelations, and in many cases oddball recordings, straddle art and the avant-garde. Each of them had their place in the mid-'50s. One experiment wonders, destined to change people's perceptions, then never to be heard from again.

Collecting our thoughts, at this stage, in the developing story, the thing that strikes you most is that the genre of electronic music was embracing not only scientists, nuclear physicists, artists and eccentrics but also classically trained composers, conductors of chamber music, cerebral thinkers, film composers, well-educated collegians and a host of radio engineers. Crucially, electronic music was still in the hands of the outsiders.

MICHAEL KOENIG
Klangfiguren I
Original release: 1955

Having studied church music, composition, piano, acoustics, music representation techniques and computer technique, Michael Koenig was in the right frame of mind at the right time. He was destined to pull everything together into something that was going to challenge the boundaries of music.

From 1954 to 1964, Koenig worked in the electronic music studio of WDR in Cologne with Stockhausen and Gyorgy Ligeti. Quite early in that period he started producing electronic works of his own including the short and almost ambient 'Klangfiguren I' in 1955 and 'Klangfiguren II' during the following 12 months. The latter piece follows a similar route to its predecessor but demonstrates a more aggressive, panoramic use of sound that adds depth and a thundering echoey presence, along with what sounds like the very earliest use of glitch sound effects that became so prominent during the 1990s and 2000s via Aphex Twin, Autechre and the emerging dub step scene.

ERNST KRENEK
Pfigstoratorium (Spiritus Intelligentiae Sanctus) soprano, tenor e tape
Original recording: 1955

Like Koenig, Krenek was part of the WDR set up in Cologne from 1955. Having previously written works for solo vocalists, choral pieces and scores for ballets, as well as several symphonies, Krenek was intrigued by the possibility of electronic music and recorded 'Pfigstoratorium (Spiritus Intelligentiae Sanctus)' a long piece for soprano and tenor voices and tape. 'Pfigstoratorium' also featured spoken word, rising oscillations and plenty of reverb.

During the piece, the melodies remain intact but searing sound and snatches of sampled songs acts as odd sonic punctuations, wandering between the simple structure, adding ever more levels of seeming madness, transposing barber shop harmonies with the sound of someone letting their fingers do the walking over endless blips and scattered dew drops of noise. At times it feels like the action is taking place just out of earshot, and there's a great sense of the random. The overall effect is that of a church organist having been drugged and the resultant pipe organ solo being performed whilst people talk among themselves in the aisles and a transistor radio plays opera next door.

Three quarters of the way through this sixteen minute piece, the joyful play off between tenor and soprano are melded into an echo-laden vibrato that sounds like the audio used in '60s movies to soundtrack characters succumbing to drugs. There's more than a hint of wanton psychedelia and, without doubt, when these kind of sounds were revisited by the lysergically-challenged a decade later they were allowed visionary status.

JOHN PRESTON (NARRATION)
The Sounds And Music Of The RCA Electronic Music Synthesizer
Original release: 1955
RCA VICTOR

Tracklisting:
The Synthesis Of Music - The Physical Characteristics Of Musical Sounds, The Synthesis Of Music - Synthesis By Parts (Part 1 and 2), The Synthesis Of Music - Excerpts From Musical Selections (Part 1 and 2), Music Produced By The RCA Synthesizer - Bach Fugue No. 2, Brahms Hungarian Dance No. 1, Oh Holy Night (Adam), Home Sweet Home (Bishop), Stephen Foster Medley, Nola (Arndt), Blue Skies (Berlin)

Whilst tape manipulation and sound collages were hinting at the possibilities of electronic music, it took two engineers to move the genre into a more traditional direction with the invention of an early synthesiser. In 1955, Olson and Belar, both working for RCA, invented the Electronic Music Synthesizer, aka the Olson-Belar Sound Synthesizer.

"This synth uses sawtooth waves that are filtered for other types of timbres. The user programs the synthesizer with a typewriter-like keyboard that punches commands into a 40-channel paper tape using binary code," claimed the sleeve of their demonstration record set. It was the perfect accompaniment for an instrument that RCA hoped would eventually arrive in every parlour across America.

What better way to tell people about this ground-breaking development than to release recordings where it was put through the motions. 'The Sounds And Music Of The RCA Electronic

Music Synthesizer' is the stuff of record collector's dreams, a beautifully packaged set with four seven-inch singles explaining the whys, wherefores and what have you of The RCA Electronic Music Synthesizer as very dryly recited by John Preston.

"How has it become possible for us to create all musical sounds by electronic means?" asks Preston, "The answer lies in the nature of sound as a combination of clearly defined physical characteristics which are shared by all tones of effects".

The subject of this monologue laboriously switches to random frequencies, the proper envelope, rapid growth and slow decay, very high frequencies and other such terminology, all of which is punctuated by various bleeps before a selection of music is played on the thing, always getting its full title in reference.

Unlike the electronic artisans and inventors, RCA had decided that this machine would replace all of your instruments that were littering the lounge, and the recordings featured a synthesised set of sounds, from piano to a "low sounding effect", which Preston claims has been "created by various RCA engineers".

"In the future, synthesis can bring us a totally new experience," Preston sums up on side one of disc three, before hammy fugues and well tempered claviers are brought into action. But, even before the fourth disc had spun to a fitting climax, competitive inventions were sneaking out of their laboratories, Martin Klein and Douglas Bolitho were using a Datatron computer called 'Push-Button Bertha' to compose music, and David Seville showed that tape manipulation couldn't merely stay in the hands of the artists and deep thinkers by using varispeed and various other electronic techniques to create The Chipmunks. Yeah, thanks for that.

OSKAR SALA
'Concertando Rubato'
Original release: 1955
from 'Elektronische Tanzsuite'
Available on 'Ohm: The Early Gurus Of Electronic Music'
ELIPSIS

If the Chipmunks were a side product of the electronic revolution, then so were the soundtracks for Hitchcock's early movies and the tension created by their electronic construction. Oskar Sala's scary keyboard flurries were part of Hitchcock's off kilter vision, and his earlier 'Concertando Rubato' still has a direct lineage to today's electronic sounds.

In fact, the intriguing website Pretty Goes With Pretty even spotted the influence of Sala on the superb 2009 album 'Merriweather Post Pavilion' by Animal Collective. "Something about the intro to 'Daily Routine' — maybe it's just those first tentative, random hits of the keyboard, not to mention the tonal similarity", and with one listen to 'Concertando Rubato' you get their drift.

There are versions of 'Concertando Rubato' produced as early as the late 1940s, but as part of the German composer's 'Elektronische Tanzsuite' from 1955, the piece has a sound base that's every bit the exploitation synth sound of a decade later, as performed by the likes of Jean Jacques Perrey and Gershon Kingsley.

There was a chirpiness and upbeat style to Sala's sounds on a keyboard that he'd developed himself. His Trautonium, and the later Mixtur-Trautonium, had a huge impact when it was used on the soundtrack for Hitchcock's The Birds.

"'Elektrinische Tanzsuite'," Sala told Ohm for the sleevenotes of 'The Early Gurus Of Electronic Music', "is still one of my most important works. When I look at the electronic scene today I am proud to be one of the first ones who worked with this 'simple' technology".

LOUIS AND BEBE BARRON
Forbidden Planet
ORIGINAL RELEASE: 1956
MGM

In the mid '50s, electronic music still remained outside of the mainstream. But as the need for creative sound in the movies grew, Sala's contribution to The Birds, the soundtrack to The Day The Earth Stood Still and Louis and Bebe Barron's effects and tape manipulation for the 1956 film Forbidden Planet began to spark interest in who and what made that sound.

Some years ago, the RE/Search book Incredibly Strange Music Volume One interviewed the curator of the strangely titled Unknown Museum, Mickey McGovan. There, in his strange wonderland where lost TV monitors, plastic squirrels, storefront Santas and 15,000 records congregate in an alternative Smithsonian scenario, the Barrons took their rightful place.

"Another major influence was science fiction film soundtracks, especially the ones featuring Theremin. I was addicted to 'Forbidden Planet' which has a great soundtrack by the electronic pioneers, Louis And Bebe Barron," Mickey enthused when quizzed about why he'd collected so much 'stuff'. "I have a 1948 recording of them in San Francisco performing background music for a lecture by Anais Nin at the SF Art Institute". Now that would be something to hear. "I was fascinated by the tonalities the Barrons generated – the Forbidden Planet soundtrack is still one of the most imaginative electronic music creations of all time. They did tape manipulations, generated tones of their own, and basically wrote the book on what outer space sounded like".

The Barrons also worked closely with John Cage. According to filmmaker and electronic composer Dean Santomeieri, in the second volume of Incredibly Strange Music, "They made hundreds of recordings of raw sound and, in a nine month splicing marathon, helped John Cage edit them into the hurricane of sound known as 'The Williams Mix'".

Pre-Cage, the Barron's recording relationship began when Bebe married Louis Barron's brother and received one of the earliest tape recorders as a wedding present. At the time, Louis was deciding whether to pursue a career in electronics and Bebe and him began to experiment with the new machine.

"Immediately we became aware of the possibilities," Bebe recalled when interviewed for Incredibly Strange Music Volume Two. "We did the usual experiments, slowing the tapes down, running them backwards and adding echo. Louis started building circuits to make sound – ohmigod, every move took forever, but it was so exciting!"

When John Cage and David Tudor were given a grant to explore the links between music and sound in the early 1950s, they called on the Barrons to come and work with them. As Louis told Keyboard magazine in 1986, "You realise you don't have to be restricted by the traditions or the so-called 'laws' of music". The new partnership certainly wasn't.

Around the same time, the Barrons were involved in creating unique soundtracks for the films The Very Eye Of Night and Crystals, before embarking on the groundbreaking soundtrack for Forbidden Planet. After meeting MGM film supremo Dore Schary, they were invited to LA to show what they could do, and, after much to-ing and fro-ing, ended up scoring 20 minutes of the film.

"For Forbidden Planet," Bebe told Incredibly Strange Music, "we just tossed convention aside, forgot about all that, and just did what we wanted to do. And it worked".

The Forbidden Planet soundtrack was developed on the most basic of equipment. Tapes were slowed and slowed again. Then again. Love songs were requested with lush strings, sound effects were asked for. And the low-tech machinery meant that everything took forever to finish.

"I thought what we achieved was remarkable, considering the technology of the day," Bebe recalled, "Those circuits really could express a full range of emotions, and we treated each little theme like a character rather than a musical theme, because that was how we liked to work".

TOM DISSEVELT AND KID BALTAN (The Elektrosoniks)
Song Of The Second Moon: The Sonic Vibrations Of...
Original release: 1957
LIMELIGHT

Tracklisting:
Song of the Second Moon, Moon Maid, The Visitor From Inner Space, Sonik Re-Entry, Orbit Aurora, Pianoforte, The Ray Makers

The possibilities of space exploration seemed to be at the heart of much of electronic music as the '50s drew to a close. Forbidden Planet had set the benchmark, but over in the NATLAB in Eindhoven, Holland, several similarly skyward gazing enthusiasts were at work.

The NATLAB was beginning to experiment with electronic sound in much the same way as WDR in Cologne and Columbia University in the States were. The first fruits of their recorded output arrived in 1957 under the name 'Electrosoniks', who consisted of Tom Dissevelt and Kid Baltan and proved that some form of regular melody could be introduced to swirling synthesised sound, and that people might also like it.

The duo, along with Henk Badings and Roelof Vermeulen, recorded between 1956 and 1968 at the Philips funded research laboratory, where Baltan (real name Dick Raaijmakers) and Dissevelt completed the 'Song Of The Second Moon' set and garnered great reviews for their forward looking use of technology. The fact was, they didn't even have a keyboard to use - they did everything with tone generators, oscillators and spliced and manipulated tapes. This was a labour of love that, like the Barrons before them, took months to complete. Interestingly, during this same period of technical and commercial breakthrough, the Philips NATLAB (Natuurkundig Laboratorium) was also involved in the development of effects such as chorus, delay, echo, reverb, surround sound and Dolby noise reduction. It was a hotbed of futuristic solder.

Once complete, the title track, composed by Raaijmakers, was even released on seven inch vinyl, becoming a cult item – you can even see it being spun on YouTube, it's that rare. The album was also re-issued in 1968 under the duo's name, and 'Song Of The Second Moon: The Sonic Vibrations Of...' was subsequently slowed to half its normal speed and used as a soundtrack for Boris Karloff to read over on the album 'Tales Of The Frightened'.

Amazingly for 1957, 'Song Of The Second Moon' managed to capture that inter-planetary vibe perfectly. You'd be forgiven, when looking at their meagre armoury of sound sources, for thinking that there would be a lack of melodic intent, but the album had it all there. It's a spectacular album, a thought-provoking set that was way ahead of its time and still sounds relevant today.

VARIOUS ARTISTS
The Sounds Of New Music
Original release: 1957
FOLKWAYS

Tracklisting:
Bahnfahrt, Symphony of Machines - A (Aleksandr) Mossolov, Dnieprostrot - Julius Meytuss, Dance - John Cage, Ionization - Edgard Varèse, Aeolian Harp - Henry Cowell, Banshee - Henry Cowell, Sonic Contours - Vladimir Ussachevsky, Fantasy In Space - Otto Luening, Symphonies In Sonic Vibration -Spectrum No 1 - Halim El-Dabh, Transposition - Vladimir Ussachevsky, Reverberation - Vladimir Ussachevsky, Compositionion - Vladimir Ussachevsky, Underwater Waltz - Vladimir Ussachevsky, Natural Pipes - Roger Marin and Fredric Ramsey, Jr, Natural Pipes - Roger Marin and Fredric Ramsey, Jr, Natural Pipes - Roger Marin and Fredric Ramsey, Jr, Sonata For Loudspeakers

Taking their lead from the manifesto for Folkways, the same team travelled the world in search of new music sourced from different cultures and environments. Their mission was to collect unique electronic sounds that they felt people needed to be introduced to, and their move into this arena created this, one of the maddest albums I've ever heard.

The closing track, 'Sonata For Loudspeakers' is in fact a dialogue from Henry Jacobs at Radio Station KPFA-FM. Its an "experiment in synthetic rhythm", wherein he introduces manipulated sounds, that included the looping and slowing of tabla rhythms to make a completely new piece of music. Jacobs' deadpan tone was much later replicated by Todd Rundgren on his classic 'Something/Anything' album, when he runs through all the distortions that can happen in the recording and pressing process, right down to the vital scratch in the vinyl.

Jacobs' actual pieces were recorded in '53 and '54 for the Folkways' set and include a great cut-up vocal rhythm that's rife for sampling. The nine-minute recording provided an awkward but illuminating insight into what had been happening in experimental spaces everywhere during the 1950s. The album itself, in true Folkways style, also laid down a variety of techniques alongside an array of the most celebrated perpetrators of the time.

Opening with the unaccredited 'Bahnfahrt', a collage of sounds and effects over a jazz tune in the style of the legendary Spike Jones, which the sleeve underlines the piece pre-dates, 'The Sounds Of New Music' was an amazing trip which showed how this emerging genre was growing all over the globe. Alexander Mossolov's recordings came from a steel foundry in 1928, his 'Symphony Of Machines' featuring a host of rattling rhythms like latter day industrial music percussionist Z'ev. The heady mix of John Cage's treated piano, Edgard Varese on siren, Henry Cowell's "tone clusters", plus scratching and plucking techniques, tape manipulation of piano pieces by Ussachevsky and tonal music from his contemporary Otto Luening positioned the album between frightening and incendiary.

The first side closes with El-Dabh, an Indian percussionist relocated to the US, who straps bongos to a piano to produce vibration within the piano's strings – almost the perfect cultural crossover for a true Folkways experience. Side two of the original album offers different musical tape techniques from Ussachevsky, along with three gamelan-style explorations of pipe work from Roger Marin and Fredric Ramsey Jr, all of which is presented for the user to use in future compositional pieces, a concept that was revolutionary at that time.

The sleevenotes conclude with an essay by Marin, where he talks about the revolution of "Concrete Music" in France that had, in 1957, not yet troubled the general public in the States. During the lengthy explanation, he reveals that "the concrete experiment discovers that within the ear is a sense having almost no connection with the musical ear – a sort of sonorous eye, sensitive to the forms and colours of sounds and to the effect of relief". Something that this Folkways album tries to stimulate with its extraordinary track listing.

IANNIS XENAKIS
Diamorphoses
Original recording: 1957
Originally available on 'Electronic Music' (Electronic Music Foundation)
Also on 'Anthology Of Noise And Electronic Music First A-Chronology 1921-2001' (Sub Rosa)

Iannis Xenakis was an old school renaissance man, a Greek-born French mathematician, architect and experimental music pioneer. He was also an old fashioned artist, seeking a moral and social statement for his work, which was more than evident in his music. If Marin's 'sonorous eye' analogy on the Folkways' album sleevenotes suggested that the electronic storm of Musique Concrete was the space for true creativity then Xenakis was right there, holding aloft a tape recorder.

Working with abstract percussion and strings, he had fallen into using recordings of natural events, re-arranging them, adding effects and completely changing the sound and structure of the original recordings, creating a music-based piece in its own right. In 1957, he worked alongside Pierre Schaeffer and others at the Groupe de Recherches Musicales in Paris, where he composed various electronic tape pieces, including 'Diamorphoses' which features the sounds of earthquakes and car crashes. The edit's complexity created an unnerving soundbed that flowed like an ethereal orchestral piece, hanging in the air at times or thrusting upward like an uncontrollable, untraceable source of noise. At one point it actually sounds like he's holding a microphone inside a jet engine as it took off.

His 'Concret PH' from the following year used the sounds of burning charcoal to create the impression of a million shards of glass tinkling into the atmosphere, every one seemingly en route to a different part of the listener's audio spectrum. It's an intense sound that completely freaked my fourteen year old out when she heard it, forcing her to flee the room as the music intensified! The piece was performed at the Brussels World Fair in an environment designed by Xenakis, where Varese's 'Poème Electronique' was also performed through hundreds of strategically positioned speakers. The system inevitably gave both pieces even more impact, and undoubtedly people ran for cover when the piece fully exploded.

Xenakis continued to deliver intense musical scores into the '90s, most notably with 'Hibiki-Hana-Ma', which was designed for The Osaka World's Fair in 1970. Using recordings of a Western orchestra and Eastern traditional instruments, including a biwa and a snare drum, the piece acted as a bridge between cultures, and a statement on the Japanese worldview post World War II. The result is strangely reminiscent of the beginning of The Beatles' 'A Day In The Life' from 'Sgt Pepper'.

"Xenakis explores how sound can portray the emotive qualities of an absurd world where racism, ethic strife, and the betrayal of compassion have created conditions of horror," noted musician and producer DJ Spooky in the sleevenotes to 'Ohm'. Talking about 'Hibiki-Hana-Ma', Xenakis himself added, "These sounds have been co-ordinated in an electric studio in space so they whirl around and around or follow a labyrinth in a plaintive glass box". That really nails it, I think.

LUCIANO BERIO
Perspectives
Original performance: 1957

As ever, the progress of electronic music was taking place in decidedly different situations during the late 1950s. While Xenakis was destroying the template, Luciano Berio was intent on using his previously gained compositional skills to head down another route. Unlike Xenakis, the Italian composer had been working with string orchestras, wind quintets and various other configurations since the late 1930's and, renowned for his experimental approach to writing, he embraced electronic techniques.

After studying with Luigi Dallapiccola in the early '50s in America, Berio had developed an interest in serialism – a form of music composition that, like so many things, has many interpretations by the various people who are singled out as being part of such a genre. In simple terms, serialism is a form of composition wherein pre-determined, fixed values are used to dictate the elements of a composition. Berio was fascinated by such limitations, and the emerging interest in taped music and the possibilities of electronic sound further influenced his opinion that, without doubt, the most exciting and innovative ideas were happening in such spheres.

Attending the Internationale Ferienkurse für Neue Musik at Darmstadt, he met other challenged and challenging idealists including Pierre Boulez, Karlheinz Stockhausen, György Ligeti and Mauricio Kagel, following which he co-founded the Studio di Fonologia, an electronic music studio in Milan, with Bruno Maderna. He also began to meet Henri Pousseur, John Cage and many others and, in the style of underground movements that have existed ever since, created his own fanzine (as it were), Incontri Musicali, which translates as "Musical Encounters", to tell people about what they were doing.

The mood soon became decidedly experimental. Electronic sounds had endless possibilities, and in 1957 Berio's 'Perspectives' was one of many bleep and swirl-friendly pieces that set chins stroking the world over.

Already, Studio di Fonologia had been the stamping ground of Pousser's 'Seismogrammes I+II' (1955), which challenged the boundaries of new music, and the intelligent thought that went with it. But not everyone was convinced by the emperor's new music. Franco Evangelisti, another Italian composer, was aghast at what the studio created. Part of the respected school of successes from the studio, along with Boulez, Stockhausen, Maderna, and Luigi Nono, Evangelista accused some of their followers and copyists as being "dodecaphonic police". He was shocked at how their struggle to master new techniques and ideas, and the chance of extending music, had been simply imitated. Undoubtedly, he would be apoplectic at some of the criminal acts that have taken place in the last 50 years in the name of electronic music.

Evangelisti's 'Incontri di Fasce Sonore' followed similar patterns as Pousser and Berio, but the work was more abrasive, deeper. The impression given is that the notes have been displaced by the echo, reverb or sustain that they leave in their wake, and these sounds have been suitably treated to add even more menacing presence in all their rumbling glory – akin to the soundtrack of Evil Dead, but even scarier!

EDGARD VARESE
Poeme Electronique
Original performance: 1958
Available on 'Ohm: The Early Gurus Of Electronic Music'
ELIPSIS

By the late '50s, "Electronic Music" had become a broad and seemingly boundary defying title. The experimentalists rubbed shoulders with those in search of additions to existing orchestral possibilities, and those who were in search of music from a far off galaxy. Namechecked by Frank Zappa, whos love of the man's music reached almost stalker-like proportions, Edgard Varese was an intriguing character.

So the story goes, Zappa, at the tender age of thirteen, was inspired by an article in Look magazine that claimed that the Sam Goody's chain store was such a great place to buy records that it could even sell copies of 'Ionization' by Edgard Varese. Zappa reasoned that, if such a record was so obscure and challenging to chain store mentality, he had to have it. When he eventually located a copy he played it three times a day to anyone who'd listen.

"I didn't know what timbre was," he's quoted as saying in the book No Commercial Potential, "I never heard of polyphony. I just liked the music because it sounded good to me".

Aged fifteen, and armed with a $5 gift from his mom, he decided to invest it all in a long distance call to Varese. Zappa noted in Stereo Review magazine: "His wife answered. She was very nice and told me he was in Europe and to call back in a few weeks. I did. I don't remember what I said to him exactly, but it was something like: "I really dig your music". He told me he was working on a new piece called 'Deserts' - this thrilled me quite a bit since I was living in Lancaster, California then. When you're fifteen and living in the Mojave Desert and find out that the world's greatest composer, somewhere in a secret Greenwich Village laboratory, is working on a song about your "home town" you can get pretty excited. It seemed a great tragedy that nobody in Palmdale or Rosamond would care if they ever heard it. I still think 'Deserts' is about Lancaster, even if the liner notes on the Columbia LP say it's something more philosophical".

By 1957, Zappa was heading to New York where Varese was resident. He called ahead and demanded an audience, receiving this note on his arrival:

Dear Mr Zappa,

I am sorry not to be able to grant you your request. I am leaving for Europe and will be gone until next Spring. I am hoping however to see you on my return.

With best wishes
Sincerely,
Edgard Varese

Zappa had the handwritten note framed, and remained a fan. Indeed, his last album, before he succumbed to cancer was 'The Rage And The Fury', inspired by and dedicated to Varese.

"I never got to meet Mr Varese. But I kept looking for records of his music. When he got to be about eighty I guess a few companies gave in and recorded some of his stuff. Sort of a gesture, I imagine. I always wondered who bought them besides me. It was about seven years from the time I first heard his music 'til I met someone else who even knew he existed. That person was a film student at USC. He had the Columbia LP with 'Poeme Electronique' on it. He thought it would make groovy sound effects".

A French-born composer who relocated to the US, Varese had a dalliance with the Dadaists and was acclaimed the "Father of Electronic Music", while author Henry Miller described him as "The stratospheric Colossus of Sound". His 'Poeme Electronique' certainly confirmed both nom de plumes.

"'Poeme Electronique' is so visceral it's almost vulgar," opines David Toop, musician and writer. "It's fantastic. It's an extension of what he was trying to do with the orchestra – great chunks of physical sound, undiluted by using electronics".

Professor Chou Wen-Chung, composer and Varese collaborator: "'Poeme Electronique' was one of Varese's only purely electronic pieces, and it represents the culmination of years of work in trying to capture sounds and ideas that couldn't be communicated with traditional instruments. He imagined the sound being set free in space and was concerned with how sound can move, interact, collide, and integrate with other sound".

At just over eight minutes 'Poeme Electronique' is a strangely alluring rhythmic piece with bells, sirens, piercing and grating noises making way for chirps, honks and low, rumbling electronic sounds. There is rhythm in places, along with chimes and the rumbling of an aeroplane, an organ, snatched speeches, slowed tapes, varispeed sounds and distant voices. Pop music it is not. More a brooding stew of sound; a filmic, visionary moment that scratches at the psyche. There's a nod to the Futurists' list of sounds, but this is forty five years on and perfected for a more developed ear.

The original piece was commissioned for the 1958 Brussels World's Fair and was played through four hundred and twenty five loud speakers in a space with architecture and lighting under the direction of Le Corbusier. By the nature of the number of speakers, the piece sounded different depending on where the listener was standing, allowing them to perform their own mix of the mix.

As an opportunity for inclusion in a magnificent piece of art. electronic music was becoming everybody's. This was more than evident in the UK, where the BBC had established the Radiophonic Workshop and infiltrated TV and radio with sounds that seemed to emanate from nowhere. The electronic experience was coming to the radio, and even TV.

BBC RADIOPHONIC WORKSHOP
Quatermass And The Pit
Original recording: 1958
From The BBC Radiophonic Workshop (1958-1997) – A Retrospective
MUTE/GREY AREA 2009

The haunting sound effects for Quatermass And The Pit, a BBC television series from the end of the 1950s, were spectacular and, indeed, scary. The electronic squawk of sound created by Desmond Briscoe for the scenes where the "thing" did its evil mind-manipulating were suitably abrasive, but their grating simplicity only really came to my attention when the thirty second piece was used as part of The Goon Show's classic 'Scarlet Capsule' episode, which made up one side of 'Best Of The Goon Show Volume 2'. The Goons were way ahead of their time - their half hour shows were filled with effects, tape manipulation, orchestral interludes and even the sound of Major Bloodknock's stomach, which was also created by the Radiophonic Workshop.

In the 1950's, Dick Mills, along with Desmond Briscoe and studio manager Daphne Oram, were given license to produce interesting sounds that radio and TV producers could use. The Goons were immediately inundated with effects, but the workshop also set about supplying other programmes with effects and signature tunes. The department also created electronic sounds which would fill space between programmes, and one such piece, 'Time Beat' by Maddalena Fagandini, would later become a groovy instrumental 45 by Ray Cathode – a pseudonym for Parlophone's comedy producer, the George Martin.

"In 1963 came Dr Who," composer and BBC Radiophonic Workshop archivist Mark Ayres wrote in the sleevenotes to Mute's 2009 retrospective, "with a theme written by Ron Grainer and realised by Delia Derbyshire". It was that hugely memorable tune that put the Workshop on the map, and the subsequent series of the science fiction drama allowed the team to further experiment.

While the realms of outer space were being channelled weekly, the team were also creating electronic-based melodies for other signature tunes, including the pulsing 'Choice' and 'Hard Luck Hall' by John Baker, the overlayed vocals and melody of 'Talk Out' by Delia Derbyshire and the almost Rococo ambience of 'Science And Health', an electronically-created metallic harpsichord melody that was neglected by the show's producer for being "too lascivious".

The dusted off recordings on the Mute release are mainly taken from a couple of vinyl albums that emerged over the years, and Mark Ayres' efforts to deliver some unheard gems and give full versions of some pieces that have gone neglected have created a wondrous journey into electronic sound. John Baker interprets traditional songs, as well as delivering futuristic weirdness, which is set alongside Delia Derbyshire's short, strange and fanciful introductions to programmes that may now, in many cases, have lived up to their musical prompt.

There were groundbreaking firsts too, with Delia Derbyshire employing the EMS VCS3 synthesiser on 'Dance From Noah', a drama workshop production. Dick Mills' surreal 'Martian March Past' and Paddy Kingsland's dabbling with the EMS Synthi 100 and sitar also create fantastic psychedelic moments. Without doubt, the Workshops non-commercial brief allowed them to create beautiful and imaginative scores - 'The Comet Is Coming', from a 1980 programme on Halley's Comet, is truly gorgeous, while Dick Mills' 'Macrocosm', recorded for a play on Radio 4 from the following year, is spacious and enveloping.

Ironically, technical developments overtook the Workshop, and some of the later pieces seem quite pale by comparison to the inventiveness of their earlier work, which was brazenly different and hugely influential. Throughout, the Workshop's understanding of melody and song construction allowed their use of the latest equipment to retain an accessible edge, and Q magazine, in May 1997, acclaimed the Workshop as 'Unsung Heroes Of Rock 'n' Roll' as the team fell victim to the BBC's cost-cutting (sound familiar?). The feature explained that as, with all early electronic material, much of their work had to be recorded one note at a time, something you'd think might stunt any fluidity. But as new technology was unveiled the BBC was one of the few places that could afford it during the 1950's.

"We admired rock musicians," stated Peter Howell from the Workshop. "We admired Rick Wakeman, but some of us felt that he never quite mastered the tuning before he started playing".

The feature concludes with the department's Elizabeth Parker, on the verge of redundancy, wistfully saying that, "Anyone can have access to the technology, but it's not just technology, it's how you use it that counts".

GYORGY LIGETI
Artikulation
Original release: 1958

While the BBC's Radiophonic Workshop made everything easy on the ear, it might be said that Gyorgy Ligeti didn't suffer listeners gladly. His work is not easy listening, and he uses music in ways that, well, you might not imagine possible. Or sensible. Take a look at footage of any of his piano concertos hosted on YouTube. It's almost as if he wanted the intensity of the piece to be reflected in the difficulty level and subsequent damage to the pianist.

It's all about timing, and the force applied to create the notes. It's a kind of demand on the senses that few have the ability to master and in some cases even fewer have the desire to understand. Whereas John Cage and The New York School craved the results of chance happenings, of directions found by the almost irrational, Ligeti's work is pinprick sharp. Absolute. There are no half measures - "He means it, man!"

Ligeti's work is something of a mystery to most, but enthusiastic support from the late Stanley Kubrick ensured that his pieces were heard, from 2001: A Space Odyssey and The Shining through to Eyes Wide Shut. Anyone who's seen the hovering menace of The Shining will get a reasonable idea of where Ligeti's oeuvre resides.

His 1962 piece 'Poeme Symphonique For 100 Metronomes' gives some idea to the eccentric boundary-pushing nature of his ideas, and in the late '50s his brief dalliance with electronic music produced two similarly succinctly choreographed pieces, 'Glissandi', from 1957, and the explosive echofest of 'Artikulation' from a year later. Like one of his orchestral or piano pieces, 'Artikulation' is precise, abrasive and deep. Sounds overlap, and noises explode, implode and rumble. Cauldrons bubble and the fast edits move you from reverberation to glitches that move through the air, drop out, then re-appear in a split second.

Within the electronic genre of the 1950s there are a lot of constructed collages of this style, but 'Artikulation' is a truly magnetic experience. It's uncompromising and demands attention. Somehow the structure makes it truly emotional, like a scurrying set of clicks and whirls that could be experienced on numerous occasions, spinning off into many possibilities. Somehow it made sense in its structure, and the underlying slight melodies seem to have some kind of rhythmic tradition. It scratches, it glitches and, as I sit listening to its conclusion spinning off into Lightnin' Hopkins' 1948 recording 'Baby Please Don't Go' – purely by the mechanism that is my iTunes library – there seems to be a strange correlation between natural sounds of the time and this seemingly unnatural creation.

THE IBM 7090 COMPUTER AND DIGITAL TO SOUND TRANSDUCER
Music From Mathematics
Original release: Late '50s
DECCA RECORDS

Tracklisting:
Frère Jacques, Fantasia, Variations in Timbre and Attack, Beat Canon, Bicycle Built for Two, Molto Amoroso, Stochatta, Five Against Seven - Random Canon, Melodie, Numerology, The Second Law, Theme and Variations, May Carol, Study No 1, Study No 2, Pitch Variations, Noise Study, Joy to the World.

It's quite frightening to think what Gyorgy Ligeti would have done if he'd been able to compose music using a computer. At the end of the 1950s, they were basic to say the least. But, given a screwdriver – or probably a sledgehammer....

And so we move on to the IBM 7090. In Ted Hering's article 'A brief history of Electronic Music' published in a 1997 issue of Cool And Strange Music magazine, he revealed that "Bell Telephone Laboratories experimented with synthesised sounds in the late '50s, using IBM punch-cards for data input. Their 7090 computer and digital sound transducer singing 'Bicycle Built For Two' is quite clear".

Prior to the arrival of the Moog Synthesiser, 'Music For Mathematics' was released on Decca and presented something quite alarming. Mixing traditional songs with musical exercises, the synthetic sounds that the IBM made was something completely different. The album has a futuristic strangeness, but mostly revolves around tunes you know, done in a very strange way.

But there were some different strokes. The track 'Numerology' synthesised the Theremin and sounds like Pink Floyd or Tonto's Expanding Headband, while 'Bicycle Built For Two's voice simulation is straight out of the movies, a precursor to Robbie The Robot mixed with a touch of Cher's synthesised 'Do You Believe?'. Part of 'Music From Mathematics' is about putting the machine through its paces - 'Themes And Variations' throws together melody lines, effects and modulation quite nicely, whilst the enigmatic 'Pitch Variations' sounds like it could have come out of rehearsals for an analogue Prodigy session, and 'Noise Study' is straight from Tangerine Dream's moodier spacescape. The music was always out there.

RAYMOND SCOTT
BC 1675
Original release: 1957
Available on 'Manhattan Research, Inc.'
BASTA

While, the IBM 7090's vinyl debut with 'Music For Mathematics' was more about the process than the finished result, Raymond Scott was embroiled in the development of new sounds and the hardware to make them with the goal of using these sounds as the soundtrack for all manner of new innovations at a time when post-War America was beginning to look to space and its mysteries as a national goal. Scott was the king of jingles and he saw the developing technology as the perfect way to make sounds to make money.

Scott met Robert Moog in the 1950s when both were busy developing instruments and techniques for performing electronic music, and Moog was suitably inspired to further his work upon seeing the success that Scott was having recording electronic pieces mainly for use in 'futuristic' ad campaigns. One such piece was 'BC1675', which was also known as the Gillette conga drum jingle. Popular Mechanics magazine reported in 1959 on the techniques used in its creation: "Among the instruments which Scott has developed is a device that automatically finds a selection in a particular recording tape and continues to repeat it as long as he wants (US Patent 2998939)".

This primal form of sampling and looping was used by Scott in the early '60s as his chirpy upbeat jingles were employed by the Baltimore Gas Company, Vim, Bendix, Sprite and many more. The Basta released album gathers together a fine selection of Scott's material, including excerpts from his soundtracks to early Jim Henson movies The Organized Mind and Ripple, along with adverts for Nescafe, Twinkies and Ford. The release also features insights into Scott, and the music's creation, as well as details on his many inventions, including the Clavivox, Circle Machine, Bass Line Generator, the Rhythm Modulator, Karloff, the synthetic bongo creation Bandito The Bongo Artist and the Electronium, as well as his revolutionary '60s LP series 'Soothing Sounds For Baby' that utilised electronic melodies to lull infants to sleep.

"Astoundingly ahead-of-their-time," was the Billboard reaction to the 'Soothing Sounds' albums' re-issue in the late '90s, "Predating by a decade such innovators as Brain Eno and Kraftwerk, Scott's work exhibits impressive sophistication".

"These minimalist electronic discs," added the CMJ New Music Monthly, "are at once instructive historical documents (pre-figuring similarly minimalist works by Fripp, Eno, Glass and Riley) and eerily sanguine lullabies that might turn the sweetest babe into a little Damien".

As the '50s were about to become the "swinging" '60s, Scott was hard at work developing his ideas and inventing the sequencer, which would revolutionise electronic music and, in turn, everything we listened to as that decade rolled on.

"The concept for my musical pitch sequencer," Scott recalled in the '80s, "was triggered by the introduction in 1959 of a Wurlitzer Drum Machine called The Sideman – a rotating mechanical disc switching device that produced an electronically generated sequence of drum sounds. It immediately occurred to me, "Why not build a device that would automatically sequence through a string of musical pitches'".

Scott began inventing studio equipment following the Second World War, when he would pick up discarded electronic equipment on Canal Street in Manhattan. There he acquired an early tape recorder and began developing various electronic pieces of machinery. By 1957 he had set himself up as 'The Jingle Workshop' and produced an audio album to advertise his availability to create musical soundtracks for any kind of product. The accompanying photograph with the album features Scott and wife Dorothy Collins swamped by a bank of electronic dials and spools, lounging in front of a room-size computer.

Robert Moog, who was at the time developing the Theremin, visited the Scott's house with his father in the late '50s and saw the first very early keyboard that Scott had created.

"He showed us a prototype of a keyboard instrument," Moog recalled in the sleevenotes of Basta's 'Manhattan' release, "There was a very light vane, an inch wide and about a foot and a half long, positioned across the backs of the key levers. The vane was pivoted at the high, right hand, end of the keyboard. When you pressed a key, the vane went up. The higher the key, the more the vane would rise. He'd attached a small metal electrode to the free end of the vane, and had wired in our Theremin so that the vane electrode would 'play' the Theremin".

Scott's invention also added vibrato to the sound, and with this new development and his existing creations he was quickly carving out a career as a commercial composer while funding his exploration into new instruments and futuristic sounds.

"The house where Raymond Scott and Dorothy Collins and their two children live is not a home," reported Alan D Hass in Popular Electronics in 1959, "it is a thirty two room electronic labyrinth".

As the '60s unwrapped, Scott released a series of 'Fascination' machines, a "group of sound happening devices" that would provide a new kind of "chic background sound", including "the sound of bongo drums, softly playing, softly swinging", or "puzzlingly beautiful sounds – strangely confusing yet lovely harmonies, slowly mixing and emerging from each other", plus a version that delivered "nature-like 'sound happenings', water, birds, wind, insects".

Scott was nothing if not prolific, and from series like the Fascination machine he seems to have been a gifted marketer too, although some of his other concepts – electronic jewellery for ladies, vending machines that play the product's jingle, an electronic desk set for men – were perhaps less grounded. The 'Fascination' machines sound no different to today's 'Buddha Box', and are just as essential.

There was more. The much-touted and long worked on Electronium was seen by Scott as a versatile machine that could be miniaturised and used in all environments, but rivals were beating him to the production line as the decade rolled on. Alan Entenman, an engineer who worked with Scott on the project, recalled in the sleevenotes for Basta's release that, "The Electronium would never be finished. He was always changing and modifying it. What it did one day was not necessarily what it would do the next".

The end of the '50s was in sight and electronic music seemed to be ripe for exploitation. The developments were coming thick and fast, the possibilities, away from the wildcard artists and composers, matched the need of an emerging consumer-friendly generation who'd never had it so good. Scott's commercialism was infectious but there were still people at the close of the decade who sought a simple purity in Sound. Richard Maxfield was one such.....

RICHARD MAXFIELD
Sine Music (A Swarm Of Butterflies Encountered Over The Ocean)
Original recording: 1959
Available on 'Ohm: The Early Gurus Of Electronic Music'
ELIPSIS

Richard Maxfield originally worked in a neoclassical style, but after studying with Ernst Krenek and being exposed to the experimentation of John Cage he began to develop an interest in electronic music and to compose unique pieces of his own. One such was 'Sine Music', a recording of sine waves re-edited to capture the rhythmic wings of the song's title.

In Maxfield's work, there's more than a hint of the emerging hippie worldview, and as he entered the '60s he became involved in the Fluxus art movement, curating live music events and happenings with Yoko Ono. He also became one of the first teachers of electronic music, and his editing prowess became the stuff of legend.

'Sine Music (A Swarm Of Butterflies Encountered Over The Ocean)' is one of the earliest surviving electronic compositions by Maxfield. Its simple patterns and resonating humming sounds making it hugely different from some of the extreme cut ups that the decade had witnessed from the likes of Berio, Cage and Stockhausen, and it has a comforting, ambient feel.

"It was always very beautiful," commented La Monte Young, a student of Maxfield's, in the notes for 'Early Electronic Gurus'. "The piece features a constellation of sounds that are treated to time fields of different organisation," Young continues, comparing the structure to that of Webern, a composer whose work has been inspiration and a jumping off point throughout this chapter. "I can imagine this static pitch constellation," he concludes, "to represent a swarm of butterflies in which each sine tone corresponds to a single butterfly". Electronic music and the emerging music scene of San Francisco were about to collide.

As the 1950s drew to a close, electronic music was in the hands of a wide variety of people. Purely experimental sounds were beginning to make way for more ordered compositions, and electronic effects and taped pieces were beginning to be used in conjunction with more traditional instruments. From the early Futurists' wild ideas, through aeroplane propellers, sirens and the whirring tapes and blinking lights of gigantic early computers, the stage was set for the electronic revolution.

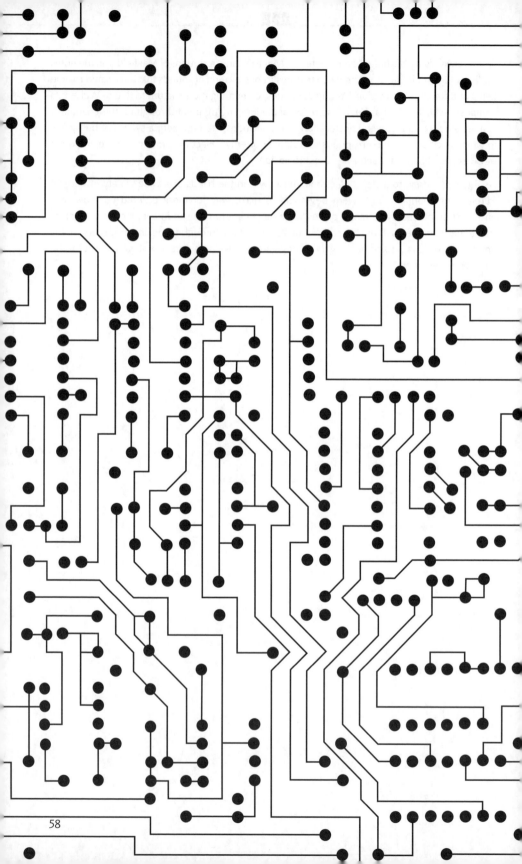

THE SIXTIES - FROM INVENTION TO EXPLOITATION

The dawning of the '60s allowed people to throw away a good deal of post-war austerity. The decade was destined to be a cultural and musical turning point and to announce a whole series of new arrivals. There would be new heroes in Kennedy, Martin Luther King Jr, The Beatles, Che, Uri Gagarin and, eventually, Armstrong, Aldrin and Collins. Elvis returned from the army a changed, be-leathered man and the new decade saw the cold war slip into slow motion overdrive as the Berlin wall was erected. The sense of separatism became claustrophobic, and its soundtrack was electronic.

Musicians by this time included savvy jingle composers, classical performers on the turn and crazed artists prone to adopting the all new vacuum cleaner into their arsenal - they were all at it under the guise of "experimentation". But, unlike the previous half century, they were now in competition with the emerging Motown sound, the British invasion led by The Beatles and the Stones, Dylan, The Beach Boys and the increasing availability of recreational drugs that resulted in the summer of love, baby boomers and what would become the Woodstock generation.

People lightened up. Anything went. Austerity made way for the Swinging Sixties and, as access to instrumentation became easier, it wasn't just the eccentrics who were allowed to dabble outside of the 4/4 time signature and the crowd pleaser. Sci-Fi movies and TV series began to capture the imagination and The Outer Limits suggested that stuff just "happened", set to a soundtrack seemingly created inside the head of malfunctioning robots. Experimentation with sound was, of course, to continue, but the seriousness and complexity of earlier concepts was replaced by a new freedom and an appetite for new technological invention.

Despite the freedom, questions still needed to be answered. "Can computers compose?" begged the sleeve of the Nonesuch release 'Computer Music'. "Electronic music" as a concept was being bent out of shape.; meanwhile, some people were still happy to edit and re-edit what they had in the hope of putting all the right noises in the right places.

LUCIANO BERIO
Visage
Original recording: 1961

For Italian composer Luciano Berio, the 1960s was a time of challenge. Having worked through various combinations of instruments, orchestral pieces and compositional intricacies, he would ultimately find fame and international respect for 1968's 'Sinfonia For Voice And Orchestra' and also for 'Sequenza', a series of numbered solo pieces.

But it was in 1961 that he conceived and recorded 'Visage', a 20-minute plus piece for tape, based on the voice of the stunning Cathy Berberian. If early experiments in sound had been a series of stolen words and snatched esoteric effects drawn together to make new symphonies, 'Visage' was a never-less-than-scary progression, where Berberian's vocals were edited in such a way that she sounded like the proverbial tortured artist... actually being tortured. If ever the phrase 'uneasy listening' were apt, then this was it, and 'Visage' was Berio's last work before he left the Studio Di Fonologoa in Italy to live in the USA.

"If language is not made of words on one side and concepts on the other but is rather a system of arbitrary symbols through which we give a certain form to our way of being in the world," he quipped on his departure, "so music is not made of only notes and established forms of relations among them but is the way we are able to select, shape and relate certain aspects of the sound continuum".

He went on. And on, but concluded, quite tellingly, in the style of everyone from Pink Floyd to the latest abstract conceptualist: "'Visage' is purely a radio-program work. A soundtrack for a drama that was never written".

'Visage' doesn't make linear sense in some respects. The words that Cathy Berberian sings are interspersed with cries and howls and noises delivered at obtuse angles. Electronic sound rumbles, cascades, throbs and dissolves. There are crescendos and climaxes, carefully placed ambient segments that lull the listener into a false sense of security. But what could this imagined drama be about? It sounds Goons-esque in places, it sounds Shakespearian elsewhere. Getting through the twenty one minutes and four seconds is a trial, but it's absorbing as it unfolds, sponging into the atmosphere like the hum of a fridge.

As Berio's feedbacking finale rises like a demon from the deep, reverberating into melody, the recording morphs into perfect out of body experience music, a séance of souls that vibrates and rattles before spiralling to nothing. Imagine the pot-smoking fraternity in the mid-'60s wowing to its excess. It was only a matter of time.....

FORREST J ACKERMAN
Music For Robots
Original release: 1961
SCIENCE FICTION RECORDS

Tracklisting
Tin Age Story, Tone Tales From Tomorrow

While Berio sought an artistic release from his projects, Forrest J Ackerman, a respected American science fiction and horror writer and editor of 'Famous Monsters Of Filmland' among many other publications, was very much in the right place at the right time. As America became obsessed with the possibility of a leisure-driven utopia aided by robotic servants, the sci-fi enthusiast was lured into a recording studio to exploit this new found intrigue. Film sound effects and music editor and part-time composer Frank A Coe was drafted in and teamed up with Ackerman for an album which the trade ad described in hugely enthusiastic terms:

"Ackerman time-travels to the 21st century to bring back 'Music For Robots'. FJA talks to YOU for 18 minutes in a thrilling narration about RUR, Tobor, Gort, Robby.... the automatons of Jules Verne, Edgar Allan Poe, Isaac Asimov, Leonardo Da Vinci... the metallic Frankenstein... Hear weird vibrational multisonic effects, electronic melodies created for the ears of androids. ONLY $1.98".

A bargain. Side one's 'Tin Age Story' features Ackerman unloading the stories of various robots and the creation of the RUR, and describing how pesky scientists destroyed it. The story is soundtracked by bleeps and the occasional hum, and is quite fascinating for 30 seconds, a real period piece, but, ultimately, it's eighteen minutes you're unlikely to want to live again. Side two, by contrast, features the joyful 'Tone Tales For Tomorrow'. By now, Ackerman is long gone from the studio, off to see some B-movie somewhere undoubtedly, and Coe is left alone, electronic effects humming and a side to fill. The result is a 15-minute futuristic piece of sound manipulation that's just wild. Lashings of echo and reverb accentuate the multi-layered swirling sounds which the educated mind might have considered suitable for robots to wig out to in future days.

Coe's brief flirtation with electronic music led him to record the score for the1968 film 'Like It Is', also known as 'Psychedelic Fever 'or 'The Enormous Midnight', a documentary on the "youth movement" of the late 1960s which focused, somewhat unoriginally, on the hippy, pot smoking. free love culture rampant in the San Francisco's Bay area. Included are discussions of the drug scene and, naturally, several examples of the hippy philosophy of peace, love and gratuitous nudity.

A niche for exploitation movies was all Coe's, and he later scored 1971's 'Blood Shack', 'Talk Naughty To Me' from 1980 and 'Sounds Of Sex' from 1985. Ackerman, probably wisely, opted to avoid.

That said, 'Tone Tales Of Tomorrow' is quite a startling swoop of sound. It's rampant and pulsing in its extremity – way off the beat for 1961. The initial impression, that Coe just knocked it off to fill the side, seems almost ludicrous. The technology at the time wouldn't allow just anybody to take on such a textured piece, so he must have laboured for many hours to create this primordial, wildly avant-garde gem which follows no natural rhythm whatsoever. Indeed, Frank Coe may have been a visionary precursor to Tangerine Dream at their most scary. We'll never know, but we can dream.

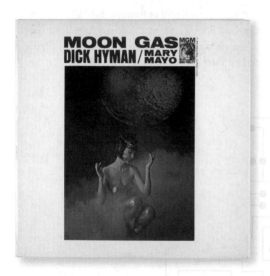

DICK HYMAN
Moon Gas
Original release: 1963
MGM RECORDS

In the early '60s, the race for the moon was just beginning in earnest. In 1962 the US's SA-3 rocket achieved a "maximum burn" time of just over four minutes and the far-fetched concept of inter-galactic life seemed to be just around the corner. Electronic instruments and sounds to express such concepts were thin on the ground, but the Lowery Organ, at the hands of seasoned keyboard player Dick Hyman, was the weapon of choice for a generation whose previous lunar audio had been created by tape manipulation, the Theremin and difficult to control wave oscillators.

The sleeve of his intriguing 1963 album 'Moon Gas' featured notes by Leonard Feather, who sang the praises of Hyman, his Lowery and vocalist Mary Mayo from the off...

"A lot of electronic music has been created by making marks and cuts on the actual recording tape – the musique concrete technique – as well as by using machines that make synthetic tones, or by recording various sounds and then changing them by tricks such as altering the tape speeds, playing the tape backwards, adding echo and so forth. By the time you get the final product this way, it was the result of a great deal of editing and splicing.

"The same results," he continued, "can be produced by playing electronic instruments live, with Mary's voice over a swinging rhythm section".

The key to this new futuristic sound, apart from some mad lyrics and otherworldly contexts, was the Lowery organ, which allowed Hyman to add reverb from built-in settings, to bend the notes using a 'glide pedal' and by use of the AOC switch, which allowed an orchestral chord for each single note played. The result was, perhaps surprisingly given the limitations of the organ in comparison with a scalpel wielding Pierre Henry, pretty damn good, and buzzers, oscillators, sound effects, wordless vocals, quasi-Hawaiian guitar effects, glide pedal madness, synthetic clarinets, some interesting time signatures and plenty of reverb made the album a real bachelor pad space age must.

Hyman later went on to record several Moog albums for the Command label, adopting the developing instrument most notably on 1969's 'Moog: The Electric Eclectics Of Dick Hyman', which includes the monumental 'The Minotaur', an eight minute plus piece of electronic genius featuring multiple layers of tinny drum machine, swirling oscillating synth rasps, modal bass and a lead melody line that makes the whole piece positively howl as it swings across the stereo range. Hyman later composed film scores for Woody Allen as well as 'Moonstruck', 'The Mask' and 'Billy Bathgate', his virtuosity and early experience with swing, spy and lounge music proving to be incredibly useful as new instrumentation appeared. But it's 'Moon Gas' and it's plucky electronic sound, created on the most basic of not strictly electronic equipment, and the monumental 'Minotaur', that single Hyman out as a key part of the development of electronic pop music.

THE TORNADOS
Telstar
Original release: 1962
DECCA RECORDS

In the early '60s people were just as fascinated by the idea of space and the arrival of new technology in the UK as they were in the States. But studio techniques were relatively standardised, and there was a tradition of such things that allowed contemporary song to have a threshold suitable for radio. It was, in retrospect, inevitable that a maverick would come along and change all the settings.

Joe Meek worked through hits for EMI and Decca, managed bands, promoted tours and, famously, set up his studio above a handbag shop in Holloway Road, North London. A spiritualist in a suit with an ear for a tune and a bank of primitive recording equipment, he eventually succumbed and shot his landlady and himself, convinced that his studio was bugged by Phil Spector and others, desperate to steal his secrets.

In the early '60s, Meek was managing Billy Fury's backing band The Tornados, who also played in a variety of guises behind touring rock 'n' roll legends and any passing celebrity that Meek felt could carry a tune and deliver a hit record. Keen for them to have their own signature tune and, so the legend goes (perfectly delivered in the Telstar movie of 2009), a melody line came to him in the middle of the night, "from the other side", which he delivered on the monophonic Clavier.

The single was a massive global hit but, devastated by an unsuccessful lawsuit for plagiarism, Meek went into financial decline, working longer hours and further exasperating his chances of success and his own health.

In the early '60s his hits for John Leyton, 'Johnny Remember Me' and the Applejacks 'Have I The Right' and a string of novelty 45s were just part of a huge output of inventive and playful ideas. In the late '50s, he had prepared the truly off kilter 'I Hear A New World – An Outer Space Fantasy', a concept album about the moon which mixed Chipmunk-styled vocals, varispeed and echo feasts and strange rhythms. The album was scrapped, but released in part in 1960. The whole conceptual madness and electronic tomfoolery would have to wait until the early '90s, when the RPM label restored and issued it.

JEAN JACQUES PERREY
Musique Electronique Du Cosmos
Original release: 1962

Contrary to Joe Meek's vision of the outer nebulous being inhabited by high-pitched space creatures, Jean Jacques Perrey's was a more ambient and eerie proposition for the main, but the rampant 'Intercelestial Tabulator' is undoubtedly cut from the same cloth. Created for TV and radio background music, 'Musique Electronique Du Cosmos' is one of the rarest Perrey albums, the original pressing being limited to just 500.

A huge inspiration for his later collaborator Gershon Kingsley, and indeed a significant contributor in his own right, Perrey left his native France in the late '50s and moved to New York. A friend of Robert Moog, he became a key figure in the development of electronic music and 'Musique Electronique Du Cosmos' allowed him to mix the pioneering early exotic sounds with swathes of echo to create an album that is eminently sample-able. Like his later work, the mood is always upbeat, indeed 'Saturnian Bird' borders on the plain ridiculous.

LEJAREN HILLER AND ROBERT BARKER
Computer Cantata
Original release: 1963
CRI

Tracklisting:
Computer Cantata: I. Prolog to Strope I; Strophe I, Computer Cantata: II. Prolog to Strophe II; Strophe II, Computer Cantata: III. Prolog to Strophe III; Strophe III; Epilog to Strophe III, Computer Cantata: IV. Strophe IV; Epilog to Strophe IV, Computer Cantata: V. Strophe V; Epilog to Strophe V

Like Joe Meek, Lejaren Hiller was a busy man. In the '40s he studied piano, oboe and composition and attended Princeton University, majoring in chemistry and minoring in music. In the '50s he worked as a chemist and, while still composing music, became intrigued by the possibilities of electronic sound. So much so that, in1958, he organised the Experimental Music Studio of the University of Illinois.

Hiller had started experimenting with the ILLIAC computer at the University in 1957 and, with the help of it and Leonard Isaacson, they created a composition for string quartet called the 'Illiac Suite'.

"In 1962, Robert Baker and I started MUSICOMP and the COMPUTER CANTATA," Hiller recalled on the sleevenotes for 'Computer Cantata'. "MUSICOMP was an expandable set of programs for composition that was written in SCATRE (an IBM-7094 assembly language)". The program consisted of various "sub routines" that aided compositions, and in 1963 Hiller and Baker wanted to show what the program could do, writing 'Computer Cantata' to demonstrate its power.

"The five main strophes are stochastic settings of five successive approximations of spoken English," Hiller continues. "These texts were generated as an experiment in speech research. The music is correlated to these texts and goes from a state of great disorder in 'Strophe I' to some degree of order by 'Strophe V'. The Prologs and Epilogs, in contrast to the Strophes themselves, are concerned with rhythmic organisation for percussion, total serialism and scales of nine to fifteen tones per octave realised by a simple sound synthesis scheme devised for the CSX-1 computer. We deliberately left this synthetic sound crude".

Are we following this? Was the chemist in Hiller ruling the sound? The music itself is strange, like The Residents played at a faster speed. Regiment and rhythm seem to wander in and out, and an opera singer takes on the appearance of an oscillating next door neighbour signing in the shower. An explosion of drums interrupts. The computed sounds and their order seem random in places, elsewhere driving in a new direction. Was Hiller mixing the systematic certainty of his scientific background with the "chance" ruminations of the new fangled computer?

"Much nonsense has been written about computers 'thinking' and 'creating'," Hiller concluded, "After all, a computer is really nothing more than a complex array of hardware".

ILHAN MIMAROGLU
Le Tombeau d'Edgar Poe
Original recording: 1964
Available on the album 'Electronic Music'
TURNABOUT

Ilhan Mimaroglu was a Turkish music critic who became besotted with the idea of electronic music and moved to New York to study with Varese and Ussachevsky, among others. In the musique concret style of inspired editing, his early '60s work included 'Le Tombeau d'Edgar Poe', an exceptional tape cut up of a poem by Stephane Mallarme, read by Erdem Buri, a Turkish broadcaster.

In the piece, Mimaroglu applied the techniques of classical composition to make new music based around his preoccupations, which he listed as "Hitchcock and Godard, Rauschenberg and Dubuffet, Ives and Ornette Coleman". Traditional structures are dissolved, and Coleman's free jazz styles and the Hitchcock inspired tension hold court, leaving the new sound far removed from the old sound that had been fed into the machine.

"All of the musical ideas (or sound images) are meant to reflect those of the poem," Mimaroglu stated, "Believing, however, that once a sound image acquires its properties it should be experienced in its own terms".

The end product is far removed from the spoken original. As effects whizz past the ears and the mood is heightened by primal scratching effects and blurred dialogue skipping in and out of focus, there is a feeling, as one word disappears in a hail of noise, that the listener is reaching, almost craning to understand what is going on. For all the surface sound, the effect is amazingly accessible. The whole experience is remarkably tight and seemingly ordered, its four minute duration giving it a tension that's perfectly tangible.

Mimaroglu's material was well received too. "Incredibly inventive," said Alfred Frankenstein in Hi Fidelity magazine. "Fascinating aural beauty," opined Howard Klein in the New York Times. And his source material set him aside, from Debufet to the abstract art of Arshile Gorky, which he took as the inspiration for 'Agony' from the following year, a nine minute, more extreme romp which examined the rivalry between musique concrete and electronic music,. For Mamroglu the electronic medium was imperative, as he explained on the sleeve of another Turnabout compilation which featured the piece.

"The sound sources here are purely electronic," he noted on the sleeve, "although the piece may give the impression of having utilised natural sounds". Mimaroglu's belief was that, whatever sound was made, the re-arranging, dissection and re-ordering of what was on the original tape transformed it into something new, and that utilising electronic sounds – already synthesised content – you were already once removed from anything non-electronic. Such re-editing took it further into new territory, and into a sound field entirely of its own.

TZVI AVNI
Vocalise
Original recording: 1964
Available on the album 'Electronic Music'
TURNABOUT

In 2001, German-born Tzvi Avni was the laureate of the Israel Prize Of Music. A former follower of Vladimir Ussachevsky at the Columbia-Princeton Electronic Music Centre in the '60s, in 1964 he recorded 'Vocalise', a mixture of his wife on vocals and electronic melodies, both spliced and twisted and run together so that, in places the two meld into one strange echo-infested, scratchy piece wherein the vocal and electronic sound trade positions.

"It is an attempt to create electronic music of an expressive, emotional nature," Avni revealed on the original sleeve. "Two elements are juxtaposed, the human voice and sounds from an electronic source. The two elements are drawn closer and closer to each other until it sometimes becomes almost impossible to distinguish which is which".

COLUMBIA-PRINCETON
Electronic Music Center
Original release 1964
COLUMBIA RECORDS

Tracklist:
Stereo Electronic Music No 1 – Bulent Arel, Leyla And The Poet – El-Dabh, Creation – Prologue
– Vladimir Ussachevsky, Composition For Synthesizer – Milton Babit, Electronc Study No 1 –
Mario Davidovsky, Gargoyles – Otto Luening

By the early '60s, Columbia-Princeton had become the place in the States for people to experiment. As early as 1961, the McMillan Theatre of Columbia University played host to a program of the two universities' electronic music. By 1964, Columbia Records had released the album 'Electronic Music Center', the sleeve of which opined how young people had, in fifty years, broken free from the confines of Stravinsky to accept new sounds, either at the circus or in Disney films. In introducing six lengthy pieces of music it begged the question, "Do we find the substance rich, evocative, capable of subtlety and strength?". It goes on to apologise for the shortcomings of the pieces on the album - even the supporters of the electronic revolution, it seemed, were nervous at the outcome. This was not Sinatra! Or even jazz.

On the 'Electronic Music Center' album, the techniques and their idiosyncrasies are still limiting what can be done, but creativity is born of this. Turkish composer Bulent Arel goes for texture, "which the composer likens to the branches of a tree". Go figure. Halim El-Dabh adopts the cut up too, but as his piece is based on the vocal interplay between a madman and a poet and, as the sleeve claims, is still work in progress, it's just plain weird. Like William Burroughs' cut-up dialogue, it's hard work at times. The side closes with a chorale piece every bit Frank Zappa meets Philip Glass, an opera from Ussachevsky that uses polyphonic choral effects and the interruptions, both rhythmic and melodic, of early synthesizers.

Milton Babbitt, on side two, claims to be more interested in "the control and specification of total rhythms, loudness rhythms and the relationship and flexibility of pitch succession," while Davidovsky utilises sinsuidal and square wave generators along with some good old fashioned white noise, and Luening closes the side with an experimental play off between synthetic sounds and a violin.

At a time when The Supremes were begging the question 'Where Did Our Love Go?' and Johnny Cash was hailing the plight of the American Indian on his album 'Bitter Tears', the collegiate it seems, was treading water. Contemporary artists were addressing huge issues and trying to solve the riddle of life and love, whilst the alumni at Columbia and Princeton, it seemed, were re-editing the edits. Perhaps the question now was, "Does electronic music have to be the be all and end all of everything?". Could a simple moment of electronic trickery thrown into a traditional form have more of a startling effect than an entire eighteen minute exploration into reformatted ruler twanging? And don't get me wrong, I love a good ruler twang fed through and echo chamber.

Enter, almost by accident, Graham Bond.....

THE GRAHAM BOND ORGANISATION
Baby Can It Be True?
Original release: 1965
Available on the album 'There's A Bond Between Us'

At just around the two minute mark on this cocktail jazz croon from The Graham Bond Organisation, the Hammond gives way to a futuristic swirl that constitutes the mainstream's first recorded Mellotron salvo. A rudimentary sax honks behind Bond's blue-eyed soul vocal, but it's the unearthly synthesis of sound that takes over the song as it flows to its conclusion which marks it out as a noteworthy recording. In no way does it have the presence and overpowering electronic feel that the likes of King Crimson would muster on 'In The Court Of The Crimson King' a few years later, but the new fangled machine certainly adds a new dimension to an otherwise standard musical form.

The Mellotron had been developed in Birmingham in the UK at Streetly Electronics, where The Moody Blues' Mike Pinder was working prior to taking up music full-time. Having shown Paul McCartney and John Lennon around the factory, he sold Lennon the Mellotron which would come to global attention when it's hypnotic sound formed the basis of 'Strawberry Fields Forever', the video for which even showed the strung out Fabs playing the huge instrument outdoors.

Before the prog rock boom of the '70s, when the instruments string settings were choired to produce what became the distinctive sound of King Crimson, Caravan and many more, David Bowie was another early adopter, using the instrument on 'Space Oddity'. Traffic also made it the signature sound on 'Hole In My Shoe', The Stones dabbled on '2000 Light Years From Home', and The Bee Gees' 'Word' was driven by its bewitching sound. Tracks by Donovan, Procul Harum and The Pretty Things also all switched on to this fresh breakthrough.

BEAVER AND KRAUSE
The Nonesuch Guide To Electronic Music
Original release: 1966
NONESUCH/ELEKTRA

Tracklist:
*Peace Three / Signal Generators: Sine Waveform: Slow Motion Audible Example
/ Signal Generators: Sine Waveform: Composition / Signal Generators: Sine Waveform:
Harmonic Synthesis / Signal Generators: Sine Waveform: Non-Harmonic Synthesis
/ Signal Generators: Sawtooth Waveform: Slow-Motion (Negative - and Positive - Going)
/ Signal Generators: Sawtooth Waveform: Composition / Signal Generators: Rectangular
Waveform: Slow-Motion Audible Example (1/8-1/2) / Signal Generators: Rectangular
Waveform: Composition (using 1/8, 1/7, 1/3, 1/2) / Signal Generators: Triangular Waveform:
Slow-Motion Audible Example / Signal Generators: Triangular Waveform: Composition / Signal
Generators: White Sound Composition / Control Generators: Transient Generator, Amplitude,
Frequency, and Timbre Modulation in Slow-Motion / Control Generators: Sequential Voltage
Sources, Composition /*

*Frequency Modulation: Keyboard Control: 12-Tone / Frequency Modulation: Keyboard
Control: Quarter-Tone (One Real Octave=2 Keyboard Octaves) / Frequency Modulation:
Keyboard Control: Ditone (Four Real Octaves Played in Keyboard Range of One Octave) /
Frequency Modulation: Keyboard Control: Portamento / Frequency Modulation: Ribbon
Control / Frequency Modulation: Periodic: Vibrato (S) (Speed Increases as Pitch Rises) /
Frequency Modulation: Periodic: Sine-Higher Frequency / Frequency Modulation: Periodic:*

Sawtooth – Swept / Frequency Modulation: Periodic: Rectangular 1/2-Swept (L2) / Frequency Modulation: Periodic: Triangular-Swept / Frequency Modulation: Periodics Combined: 3 Square Waves at Different Frequencies / Frequency Modulation: Periodics Combined: 3 Triangular Waves at Different Frequencies / Frequency Modulation: Periodics Combined: 4 Different Frequencies (2L, 2N, 2V, 2S) at Different Frequencies / Frequency Modulation: White Sound / Frequency Modulation: Transient: /_____ Up an Octave, Back to Pitch / Frequency Modulation: Transient: /_____ Up a 3rd, Back to Pitch / Frequency Modulation: Transient: Down an Octave, Back to Pitch / Frequency Modulation: Transient: Down a 3rd, Back to Pitch / Amplitude Modulation: Keyboard / Amplitude Modulation: Ribbon Controller / Amplitude Modulation: Periodic: Tremolo / Amplitude Modulation: Periodic: Sine-Higher Frequency (S Sweeping S) / Amplitude Modulation: Periodic: Sawtooth (Negative- and Positive-Going Sweep) / Amplitude Modulation: Periodic: Rectangular (L2 Sweep) / Amplitude Modulation: Periodic: Triangular-Sweep / Amplitude Modulation: Periodics Combined: 4 Square / Amplitude Modulation: Periodics Combined: 3 Triangular / Amplitude Modulation: Periodics Combined: 4 Different (S, N, L2, V) / Amplitude Modulation: White Sound / Amplitude Modulation: Transient: Slow / Amplitude Modulation: Transient: With Rising Pitch / Amplitude Modulation: Transient: /| /| /| /| / Ring Modulation: Sine Waves: Series of Sub-Audible Constants / Ring Modulation: Sine Waves: Tune in Parallel / Ring Modulation: Sine Waves: Tuned in Opposite Direction / Ring Modulation: Sawtooth / Ring Modulation: Rectangular (L2) / Filtering: White Sound - with Fixed Filters Selected 3rd Octave / Filtering: White Sound: Broad / Filtering: White Sound: Sharp / Filtering: Low Frequency Sawtooth - Tuning Through Harmonics / Filtering: Composition - Tuning Through 2nd, 3rd, 7th and 16th Harmonics / Filtering: Sweep with Ribbon Controller / Filtering: Periodic: Sine-Timbre Vibrato Effect / Filtering: Periodic: Sine-Variable Rate and Depth / Filtering: Periodic: Sawtooth (Descending and Ascending) / Filtering: Periodic: Rectangular (L2) / Filtering: Transient (Sawtooth with Transient Controlled Filter): Descending / Filtering: Transient (Sawtooth with Transient Controlled Filter): Ascending / Filtering: Transient (Sawtooth with Transient Controlled Filter): Ascending and Descending / Filtering: Transient (Sawtooth with Transient Controlled Filter): Descending and Ascending / Tape Delay: Single Repeat / Tape Delay: Multiple Repeat / Peace Three (recap).

In 1966, people were still fascinated by the emergence of synthesised sound. Listeners and technicians alike were excited but, in most cases, couldn't see where this new palette could fit in with established musical ideas. How should work ?

The Nonesuch label was an offshoot of Elektra, its series of classical and world music being sold en masse and very cheaply across the States.

"On Nonesuch we could bring the musical and cultural past back to life in the present, and we could project music and culture into the future". recalled Jac Holzman, Elektra's headman, in his book 'Follow The Music'. "It didn't take much genius to figure out that the record was the ideal medium for electronically generated music".

Holzman, it turned out, had been exposed to homemade tape manipulation through the recordings of his father's friend Abe Frisch, who'd manipulated tapes by applying magnets to them, so when he introduced former Weavers' banjo played Bernie Krause to a collector of early electronic instruments, Paul Beaver, he knew that the result would be, er, different.

"Paul had a place in LA," Bernie Krause recalled, "he had the largest collection of Novachords, the first synthesiser, built by Hammond in the '30s". According to Holzman the machine had 169 tubes and weighed a quarter of a ton. Beaver also had an early French Ondes Martenot and several self-built machines which he'd been using for sound effects on soundtracks such as 'Creature Of The Black Lagoon' and, eventually, 'Invasion Of The Body Snatchers'.

Beaver and Krause started working together and bought an early Moog synthesiser, but Hollywood wasn't interested in their scores and effects. Fortunately for them, Jac Holzman was.

"Jac gave us a contract to record a guide to electronic music as a boxed set LP with a detailed booklet," Bernie Krause remembered. "The album was on the Billboard Chart for twenty six weeks, one of Nonesuch's best-selling records to that time!"

The album introduced electronic sounds to films and the emerging music scene and set Beaver and Krause on their way to producing some of the most offbeat albums of the '60s and '70s. However, as a listening experience, be warned, 'The Nonesuch Guide To Electronic Music' is not easy going. The stellar tracklisting has few tunes but plenty of technique, more of a calling card for what the duo could do given half a chance than an 'album'.

'Peace Three' is an actual song though, an early multi-layered groove which starts and ends proceedings, while the intervening 66 tracks, many of which clock in at under ten seconds, examine all manner of electronic swirls and grunts – it's a draining experience but one that pre-historic tape loopers and samplers must have marvelled at. Indeed, the set has been re-issued in the States on the Collectables label.

In the name of research, I've listened through the album in several settings, and can report that 'Amplitude Modulation' and 'Ring Modulation', even when the latter is cut reasonably short, are challenging, to say the least. In fact, when the twenty two seconds of 'Filtering: White Sound - with Fixed Filters Selected 3rd Octave' (track 52 to those without a copy) arrives, it's with a sense of euphoric release, a flowing wash of sound that's followed by the glorious ''Filtering: White Sound: Broad'. Having said that, this is the perfect set to iron to. The proceedings become mindless as noises collapse into each other, sounds disappear and the ambience becomes everything. Whatever the social conditions, 'The Nonesuch Guide To Electronic Music' is not a family listen.

PERREY AND KINGSLEY
The In Sound From Way Out
Original release: 1966
VANGUARD

Tracklisting:
The Unidentified Flying Object, Little Man From Mars, Cosmic Ballad, Swan's Splashdown,
Countdown At 6, Barnyard In Orbit, Spooks In Space, Girl From Venus, Electronic Can-Can,
Jungle Blues From Jupiter, Computer In Love, Visa To The Stars

"Atoms of pop music exploded into fresh patterns by bold Moog-ists. Squonk!" shrieked the heading on MOJO magazine's online selection for disc of the day in May 2009, and in Ian Harrison's review of said disc, he wonders just what flavour the acclaimed Perrey and Kingsley oddity might be. 'The In Sound From Way Out!' must be "very nutty, with added plastic fruit, elastic bands, helium and bracing electric shocks every five seconds".

According to the RE/Search book 'Incredibly Strange Music Volume I', "Electronic music pioneers Jean-Jacques Perrey and Gershon Kingsley created two of the most original LPs of the '60s, 'The In Sound Of Way Out' and 'Kaleidoscope Vibrations: Spotlight On The Moog'. Using only tape recorders, scissors and splicing tape they pieced together a humoristic vision of the future which has not dated".

Perrey, the piano protégé, and Kingsley teamed up in the US in 1964 and began rewriting music history using musique concrete techniques and early synthesisers – such as the Moog ur-synth – to produce the oddest sounding confection, something lovably twee and strangely Disney-esque with its honking duck calls and pedestrian rhythms. As Ian Harrison enthused: "'The Unidentified Flying Object'," which opens the album, "sends burps, bubbles and trills ricocheting around the interior of your skull, whilst the literally honking 'Swan's Splashdown' matches 'Cosmic Ballad's electro-dub for leisure-suited suburban swingers".

"I met a musician of great talent, Gershon Kingsley," recalled Perrey in the 'Incredibly Strange Music' book, "Together, using my new process of rhythmic sequences of musique concrete, we elaborated the material to produce 'The In Sound From Way Out' and then 'Kaleidoscope', where we added Ondioline and the Moog synthesiser".

According to CD Now's esteemed reviewer, "Perrey and Kingsley's brand of pop mixed live instruments with proto-synths and sound effects (duck calls, monkey noises), and if it all sounds goofy today (which it does) it should be noted that it was made, on some level, with tongue in cheek. Probably the best--and certainly the most elaborate track--is 'Little Man From Mars', which sounds like the sort of music they play on a TV game show while the contestants are writing down their answers".

Uncut noted on both albums' re-issue (as 'The Essential Perrey And Kingsley') that, "this is chipper stuff, snap and crackle pop… the duo enjoy simulating animal noises and ditzy melodies". while Down Beat acclaimed the two albums as "wild, joyfully silly," an "antidote to `serious' electronic music". Exactly what the genre needed.

Perrey and Kingsley extended and lengthy production process to make 'The In Sound From Way Out' and in doing so undoubtedly influenced many acts who, by the end of the decade, had everything and more at the touch of a finger tip.

The construction of 'The In Sound From Way Out' owed much to Perrey's roots in French tape manipulation, which allowed the duo to play off commercial America and austere Europe when they were let loose in a recording studio with a pair of scissors. "The secret of my loops," Perrey revealed to 'Cool And Strange Music' magazine in 2002, "is a little bit of leader tape between the loops so that nothing runs into anything else".

The results on the quirky and offbeat 'Cosmic Ballad' and the likes of 'Little Man From Mars' presented the future as a disturbingly childlike place inhabited by robots of the classic Smash: Instant Mash kind who, as the original advert displayed, simply laughed at the inadequacies of the human race. Perrey and Kingsley seem to be laughing too. Electronic music had at last discovered irony.

THE BEATLES
Tomorrow Never Knows
Original release: 1966
PARLOPHONE

Without doubt, The Beatles' 'Revolver' album, from 1966, was a revelation of their newfound freedom and intent, with the cartoon pop of 'Yellow Submarine', the beautiful ballad 'I'm Only Sleeping' and the pure pop of "Got To get You Into My Life' and 'Eleanor Rigby' all sitting quite comfortably next to each other. Even the garage band groove of 'Taxman' showed how versatile they'd become, but it was the set's closing track, the throbbing, fourth dimensional 'Tomorrow Never Knows', with its pulsing Krautrock rhythms, tape loops, backward guitars and quotes from Timothy Leary, that was the seismic glide into new and as yet uncharted territory that western pop had been waiting for.

With Lennon's vocal utilising automatic double tracking and fed through a Leslie speaker cabinet over Ringo's incessant beat and a gorgeous bass pulse, the mood is exotic and other worldly. Added to this, McCartney's pre-prepared bag of tape loops, inspired after listening to Stockhausen's 'Gesang der Jünglinge' and including sitars, seagulls, orchestral chords, a mellotron and the guitar solo from the aforementioned 'Taxman', make for a real reconstructed oddity. The groove was suitably accompanied by Lennon's line: 'When in doubt, relax, turn off your mind, float downstream' - a fitting sentiment that has led the track to be covered by a host of drug fizzed generations since.

"I was into tape loops at the time," Paul McCartney is quoted as saying in The Beatles' Anthology book, "I brought in a little bag with about 20 tape loops and we got tape machines from all the other studios and with pencils and glasses we got them all to run".

"That was a weird track," recalled George Martin, "Once we'd made it we could never reproduce it. All over EMI Studios there were tape machines with loops on them, with people holding the loops at the correct distance with a pencil. So the mix we did then was a random thing that could never be done again. Nobody else was doing records like that at the time".

EMIL RICHARDS
Stones
Original release: 1966
UNI

If The Beatles had finally arrived at a melody-driven state of druggy inventiveness, others were heading further out there. Emil Richards was one such spaced-out traveller. One man, on vibes, and some shuffling rhythms which sounded like they were played on a metal kitchen surface resulted in the album 'Stones', which also headed down the concept route with all twelve tracks named after birthstones.

From the opening 'Garnet' (January, of course) and 'Amethyst' (February), the album's sound has a strange queasiness, the synth sounding like it's just trying to keep up with the groovy drummer on a setting that lets the tone slip and the melody wander in and out of tune. Timing, as the album unfolds with 'Moodstone', 'Diamond', 'Emerald' – you get the picture - is not on the agenda, and in places the synthetic blur sounds like a four year-old let loose with a crazed jazz combo, in shades of course, playing on regardless. The jazz-fusion of October's 'Opal', however, sounds like Psychic TV playing human thighbone trumpets over Rolf Harris with a wobble board, all on eleven.

Emil Richards was a jazz session player who ended up being part of the Zappa camp for 'Lumpy Gravy'. 'Stones' with Paul Beaver on synthesiser, in all its efforts to be strange and mystical, was part of a trend for thematic star struck concept albums. Beyond music to read by or the sounds of some distant island, this was music created specifically for people obsessed with the gemstone of their birth sign. At a time when free love was on the agenda and a new kind of spiritualism was in the air, it all made perfect sense. And it wasn't just Emil who was tuning in and turning on...

MORT GARSON
The Zodiac Cosmic Sounds
Original release: 1967
ELEKTRA

Tracklisting:
Aries – The Fire Fighter, Taurus – The Voluptuary, Gemini - The Cool Eye, Cancer – The Moon Child, Leo – The Lord Of The Lights, Virgo – The Perpetual Perfectionist, Libra – The Flower Child, Scorpio – The Passionate Hero, Sagittarius – The Versatile Daredevil, Capricorn – The Uncapricious Climber, Aquarius – The Lover Of Life, Pisces – The Peace Piper.

Any album whose back sleeve bears the legend "Must Be Played In The Dark" has to be good, and Elektra Records' 1967 gem 'The Zodiac Cosmic Sounds' by Mort Garson (Cancer), with words by Jacques Wilson (Leo) is just that. If Emil Richards' zodiac and gemstones concept failed because its timing was wonky, Mort Garson had no such problems, and this album has become a real high-priced rarity.

Garson had co-written Ruby And The Romantics' gorgeous 'Our Day Will Come', and played on records with Doris Day, Glen Campbell, Mel Torme, The Sandpipers and many others before recording 'The Zodiac: Cosmic Sounds - Celestial Counterpoint with Words and Music', a legendary slice of exotica set out as a concept piece intended to express the central core values of each of the twelve zodiac signs. Crazy? It was the '60s. With spoken passages by Cyrus Faryar (Pisces) and instrumentation by the eclectic Paul Beaver (Leo), this is an album of glorious madness, laced with traditional instruments, including sitars, that's undercut by some fantastic Moog.

According to the Elektra Box Set, 'Forever Changing', the idea came from the labels' Jac Holzman, the set's accompanying book concluding that "Everyone had a ball, and the album turned out to be much more than just a summer-of-love period piece that drew on all things fashionably new age and mystical".

Cyrus Faryar was a baritone folkie signed to Elektra and Alex Hassilev (Cancer), who produced the album, suggested him for the recording. Faryar recalls: "Reading those lines was quite something. The musicians had a lot of fun and it was a lively set of sessions. I walked out of the studio at one point and there was the legendary jazz flute player Bud Shank practising his part on the bass flute".

"There were some remarkable people involved in that project, such as Paul Beaver," Holzman commented in the Box Set book. "That was one of the earliest uses of the Moog and Alex had quite a time taping it. It may have been a frivolous idea but the execution of it was taken very seriously".

A year later, everyone was at it. "After the huge success of 'Switched On-Bach' in 1968, a torrent of synthesiser albums hit record stores in an attempt to cash in on the public's fascination with this strange new instrument," claimed Julian West in Cool And Strange Music, decrying the volume of cash-in albums that followed, and concluding that, "In the late '60s and early '70s, Mort Garson created a series of phantasmagorical electronic LPs, many with occult themes that are highly prized today".

Garson's roots in songwriting and arranging came full circle in 1967 with the deep funky groove of the 'See The Cheetah' single by The Big Game Hunters. It was a cool slice of exotica that led to his association with Elektra and the 'Zodiac' project which, in turn, introduced him to wordsmith Jacques Wilson, with whom he'd work on his next project, the truly off-the-wall 'The Wozard Of Iz – An electronic Odyssey'. As its name suggests, this masterpiece used the story of The Wizard Of Oz as its basis, but was laced with a hippy ideal, including talk of being 'busted', as Dorothy tries to find 'Where It's At'. The dialogue is bizarre, and Garson's soundtrack beautifully accents this socially aware, tongue in cheek political stab at Nixon era America.

Next up for Garson was the album 'Electronic Hair Pieces' which I originally came across when I was piecing together a book on the strangest concept albums ever. I'd amassed a whole host of versions of 'Hair', the hippy musical, in a number of styles, including those performed by original casts here and there and general oddball am-dram takes that should have been destroyed immediately after recording. Among the detritus was Garson's A&M album, which featured comedian Tom Smothers' sleevenotes and the immortal line "Mort Garson's obvious comprehension, love and understanding of what 'Hair' is about, although not in the contemporary soul bag, has imparted a crystalline clarity to its music". Yeah, we can all agree with that. Even though it was an instrumental album, and a tad exploitation in nature, 'Electronic Hair Pieces' still has an edge on most of the other 'Hair' albums that were around at the time, trying to make a fast buck on a bit of on-stage full frontal. Garson's electronic pedigree adds a surreal feel that's like nothing else out there.

During the late '60s, Garson had become fascinated in the occult, and his music was heading to the darker side. In 1971, under the name Lucifer, he released the phenomenal 'Black Mass' album. Gone were the subtleties of pop music - this was a deep, dark, haunting album, with synths wandering off on weird tangents, multi-layered melodies escalating the pressure and a general feeling of foreboding dominant throughout. In a virtually black sleeve (of course), the set lets the synths produce an eerie netherworld of sound, on occasion underpinned by rampant rhythmic patterns and with crazed funky soulful segments thrown in to the general miasma.

"The music summons forth an unearthly world in shimmering layers of sound, conjuring up visions of moaning spirits and howling demons," enthused Julian West in Cool And Strange Music. Quite.

Garson was back again in the land of the strange in 1975 with the release 'The Unexplained – Electronic Musical Impressions Of The Occult' by Ataraxia. Weighing in at just over half an hour, it feels like a natural extension of 'Black Mass' although in some respects the mood is darker still. The opener, 'Tarot', retains the mix of rhythm and melody, but the likes of 'Sorcerer' and 'Séance' are Tangerine Dream-like – with a touch of Jean Michel Jarre – and 'Déjà vu' sounds not unlike a modal brother of Mike Oldfield's 'Tubular Bells'.

Garson was also making other synth-powered albums during the '70s, but it's the likes of 'Lucifer' and 'Ataraxia' that sound the most potent and provocative all these years later, whilst his earlier releases, 'Zodiac' and 'The Wozard Of Iz', still sound like the work of mad men let loose with a cache of new technology and a bag of screwdrivers. Synthetic sounds, whooshes of space dust, electronically generated spooks and the sounds of rockets taking off to far off places were suddenly everywhere.

PINK FLOYD
See Emily Play
Original release: 1967
PARLOPHONE

As a younger man, I think if I'd seen the film which Pink Floyd made to accompany 'See Emily Play' before I'd heard the record, I'd have been left irretrievably more confused than I was by the sound alone. Seek it out on YouTube and marvel at the black and white footage which features the quartet playing imaginary cricket with drumsticks for stumps and Roger Waters' bass guitar for a bat, Nick Mason's air drumming and Syd Barrett mouthing the words while keyboard player Richard Wright (the key to the whole song) gingerly stands around doing nothing.

On first listen, the Floyd's second single was, and still is, like something from the stars. Before it, only the Dr Who theme had provided non-earth soundscapes in the furthermost reaches on

the north where I grew up. In Carlisle, near the Scottish borders, aged a solid ten years old, drugs and drug culture would be several years away, and any out of body experience, musical or otherwise, was strictly at the hands of eating too many highly coloured sweets. Prior to that first exposure to 'See Emily Play' in the twisted summer of '67, Cliff Richard's lip curl had seemed almost a criminal offence. His music was threatening. Dangerous. But this? This was music from people who were from another dimension altogether. Using many of the techniques which were rapidly becoming standard in the year since 'Tomorrow Never Knows' had broken the mainstream mould (tape loops, masses of echo, pitch variation and so on), Pink Floyd opened the doors of possibility even further - the floodgates were breached and their wacked out tale of Emily, laced with the kind of keyboard flurries that had only previously been the territory of the BBC's sound department, seemed just at home in a three minute song as did the traditional structure of verse and chorus.

Years later, of course, I'd learn about Syd Barrett, the hallucinogenic, the girl he saw in a half awake state, the stories of clothesline thieves and the mantra of bikes and a mouse called Gerald. I'd even be consumed by 'Set The Controls For the Heart Of The Sun' for one glorious summer. But, at that point in time, the wildest party was in my head when I dislodged the arm on the record player to put the single on endless repeat, allowing its hypnotic multi-layered keyboards to waft me to anywhere but my tiny bedroom. 'See Emily Play' with its background noise and effects was the most exciting thing I'd ever heard.

PIERRE HENRY
Messe Pour Le Temps MoDerne
Original release: 1967

If Pink Floyd's electronic beginnings were over in a swirl of feedback and echo, Pierre Henry was already heading beyond simple formula and straight into the underground of groovy musical hybrids, bringing together the Hammond-dominated sound of jazz and soul over an RnB backbeat that allowed his blips and bleeps to sound like an almost natural robotic addition.

Henry had worked with Pierre Schaeffer in the '50s and been part and parcel of the development of 'Symphnoie Pour Un Homme Seul'. Involved in the development of Schaeffer's concept of musique concrete, he also composed the first such piece for the short film 'Astrologie Ou Le Miroir De La Vie'. His audio arsenal and ability to mix natural and wholly unnatural sounds led him to what, in retrospect, is something of a masterpiece in electronic music. As the funky rhythms, pop song constructions and electronic madness unravel, its cut with opera out-takes, tape manipulations and what sounds like someone trying to start a wheezing synthesiser with their keys. Everything which had gone before seems to have been incorporated into the creation of 'Messe Pour Le Temps MoDerne', an experimental piece that formed the soundtrack for a ballet by Maurice Bejart.

From the outset, the mood is managed by a succinct pop structure that acts as a solid backbone from which Henry twists and turns his electronic sounds and cut up raw recordings. The result is magnificent and, of course, much sampled in more recent times. Indeed, the second track, 'Psyche Rock' was used as the basis for the theme tune to the cartoon series 'Futurama' and was also released as a single under the name Les Yper Sound, featuring Henry and Michelle Colombier. Norman Cook, in his Fatboy Slim guise, also milked the material, releasing a pair of remixes in 1997.

Within the album, the percussive elements are allowed to wane during the lengthy multi-edited 'Marche Du Jeune Homme , La Reine Et Les Insectes', which sounds at turns like Tonto's Expanding Head Band, the very first ambient recordings (something that is revisited on the lengthy, minimal piece 'Le Couple') and the kind of fast splice pieces that would litter the underground in the early '80s prior to the arrival of synth pop.

'Messe...' becomes increasingly less accessible as it rolls on - there's more ambience on the nine minute plus 'Divinites Paisibles', with offbeat interludes that sound like electronic doors being forced cutting in as it draws to its conclusion, but, in its mixing of styles and genres, the early parts of 'Messe Pour Le Temps MoDerne' are truly inspirational. Indeed, the blues rock turned heavy psyche pop outfit Spooky Tooth decided to take Henry's marriage of the electronic and the more structured rock pop song to the next extreme and worked with him on the album 'Ceremony', albeit an experience which put pay to the original line up of the group and received mixed reviews from critics.

With the band's doleful blues interspersed with gothic chords of eerie keyboards, hammered steel blocks and what sounds like uncontrollable drills, not to mention heavy breathing solos, the album is a brooding oddity that, on its release in 1970, set a benchmark for the off-the-wall prog rock that would come into fashion during the next decade.

But if Henry had begun to illustrate what was possible in the electronic medium, it was Terry Riley who realised that the medium could be moulded into systematic series and truly uplifting symphonies of sound.

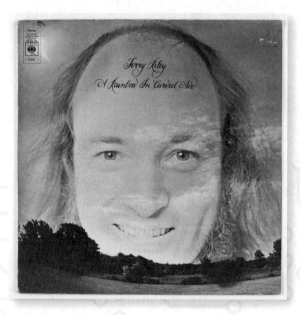

TERRY RILEY
A Rainbow In Curved Air
Original release: 1967
CBS RECORDS

The piece that originally established Terry Riley as the king of minimal, modal playing was 1964's awesome, pattern-shifting 'In C'. As Crawdaddy editor Paul Williams notes on the sleeve, "'In C' will certainly happen to you, possibly as many times as you choose to play it, certainly as a fresh experience each time. It will transfix, arouse and awaken you".

Riley's 'In C' was a mesmerising, multi-layered, repetitive performance that inspired co-conspirators at the San Francisco Tape Center, like Martin Subotnick and Steve Reich, plus their student La Monte Young, to change their thinking on electronic sound. Riley's own inspiration had come from one of his teachers, Pandit Pran Nath, a master of classical Indian voice, who'd introduced him to the music and culture of that nation, something that had a profound effect on the writing and arranging of his material.

Riley had slipped neatly into a unique mantra feel, something which he utilised for lengthy all night concerts where he'd play an organ harmonium powered by a vacuum cleaner and saxophone, recording elements and looping them back. This technique gave rise to the influential circular nature of 'In C', which was handed down to 'A Rainbow In Curved Air', on which he played electric organ and harpsichord, the rocksichord, dumbec and tambourine, looping them to create a slowly modulating piece that flowed mesmerically for close to 20 minutes.

As Paul Williams noted, "every nuance of the performance brings new possibilities, the cerebral effect like the best kind of ethereal journeys, way above the charlatan new age copyists that would follow". Riley had attained a new spiritual level through music, a hypnotising, electronic momentum that in turn gave 'A Rainbow In Curved Air' its own real beauty. When the album was originally released with a sleeve featuring the scary, larger-than the sky, bald head of Riley peeking from the horizon, it was like nothing else, both musically and visually. It inspired the band Curved Air of course, and also struck Pete Townshend of The Who, who used the concept on both 'Won't Get Fooled Again' and the opening of the glorious 'Baba O'Riley', which was named after Terry Riley and Meher Baba, another of Townshend's influences.

The flipside of the original album featured a similarly breathtaking piece, 'Poppy Nogood And The Phantom Band', which emanated from Riley's all night concerts and mixed saxophone and electric organ, which are "Spatially separated mirror images adapted for studio recording by Glen Kolotkin to resemble the sound Terry gets in his all-night concerts".

The mood is again hypnotic, the sound builds attacks and decays, adding further tension to the mood and giving the feeling of motion within the music; an exotic and tantalising journey. And his contemporaries, Reich, Subotnick and a host of others dutifully followed.

MORTON SUBOTNICK
Silver Apples Of The Moon
For Electronic Music Synthesizer
Original release: 1968
NONESUCH

Tracklisting
Part One, Part Two

I bought 'Silver Apples Of The Moon' by mistake years ago, thinking it was by the Damon Albarn-approved group of the same name. Determined to like it because I'd spent money on it, I played it a few times but always been non-plussed. The sixteen minutes plus of side one were slow and, like labelmates Beaver And Krause's 'Nonesuch Guide To Electronic Music', it seemed to be pieces of fragments of ideas, almost unformed in places. The record gave the impression Subotnik had started it and been distracted making coffee, or something. Then one day, after I'd gone through the usual "Well, people talk about it, and I like things it inspired, it can't be all-bad" line of thought, I played side two. It was genius!

If you take into account the time of its creation, what was around at the time and the lo-fi version of the desired hi-tech that was available, side two of 'Silver Apples Of The Moon' really is quite astonishing. Somewhere, the cognitive brain had been switched on. There is attack, onslaught, melody, rhythm and a hypnotic sense of release. Like side one, it's also lengthy, but even after it succumbs to blips and bleeps, the afterglow of the side's earlier form seems to hold everything together, no matter how obtuse things become or whatever tangent Subotnick decides to travel.

As already mentioned, Elektra's Jac Holzman had started the Nonesuch imprint and filled it with classical music, exploitative baroque versions of The Beatles and Joshua Rifkin's Scott Joplin rags and, when electronic music reared its head, he'd brought in Paul Beaver and Bernie Krause to record the 'Nonesuch Guide To Electronic Music'. Next, he commissioned Morton Subotnick to produce the first completely electronic album. The result was 'Silver Apples Of The Moon'.

According to the sleeve, Subotnick was the co-founder of a chamber group, The Mills College Performing Group and the San Franciscan Tape Music Center which, when the two amalgamated, bagged a $200,000 grant – a huge amount of money in the '60s!

Subotnick had worked with tape and its manipulation since 1960, providing soundtracks to plays and performances, and having his own 'Play No 4' written about in the Seattle Times: "Play No 4 embraces not only music, but also theatre and cinema and game-playing and light-shows and assorted ritualistic phenomena suggestive of contemporary society and institutions. The experience it creates is similar to a happening...". He seemed to Holzman to be the ideal person to deliver the first all electronic platter. The Seattle Times concluded, "And beneath, underneath and through all these sights and sounds is the scream and whine and blurp and krontch of some of the most affecting electronic music I've ever heard".

In Jac Holzman's essential book about Elektra, 'Follow The Music', he recalls that he "decided to take a leaf out of 17th and 18th century musical life and be the patron of an electronic album. After talking it over we decided that Morton Subotnick would be the ideal recipient of the first-ever commission of a piece to be created for the medium of home stereo. Subotnick was not only a gifted composer, he also helped develop the Buchla keypad on which 'Silver Apples' was created. It was honoured with numerous prizes".

'Silver Apples' takes its name from a line from a poem by Yeats, and as Subotnick concluded on the sleevenotes, the process of creating it was very much akin to "a kind of chamber music, 20th century style". He also explains that "The modular electronic music system," that was used to make the record, "was built by Donald Buchla for Ramon Sender and myself. The three of us worked together for more than a year to develop an electronic music machine".

The "machine" allowed Subotnick to create his piece through a series of patches, but on the sleeve he also, somewhat spookily, notes that "it is also possible to produce sound events that are predetermined by generalities…this means that one can "tell" the machine what kind of event you want without providing the specific details of the event… and listen". In a nutshell, Subotnick and his team realised during the creation of 'Silver Apples' that you could actually switch the machine on, nudge it in a general direction and it would create music almost of its own volition and invention. Crazy.

Bearing all of this in mind, 'Silver Apples Of The Moon' is still one strange slice of sound. Totalling 33 minutes, it's far reaching and, in 1968, a time when pop music was everywhere, it couldn't have been further out somewhere else. The Seattle Post-Intelligencer reported that Subotnick's live work prior to the album's release was, "A total concept in music that integrates theatrical media and destroys audience inertia". Without doubt, 'Silver Apples Of The Moon' left many a musical pundit dumbfounded, but as an inspirational piece and a source of audio mystery, it's an album that still sounds magnificently different.

SILVER APPLES
Silver Apples
Original release: 1968
KAPP RECORDS

Tracklisting:
Oscillations, Seagreen Serenades, Lovefingers, Program, Velvet Cave, Whirly-Bird, Dust, Dancing Gods, Misty Mountain

And so to the other, more familiar, Silver Apples. Like a delicacy found in some far flung corner of the musical planet, these Silver Apples were one of those great secrets in the UK until well after their original throbbing groove had faded away. According to Simeon Coxe III, half of the group along with drummer Danny Taylor, they were a "five –piece band working in New York's Café Wha?" with Simeon on vocals, three guitarists and the heady Taylor all combining to sound like a mix of Motown backbeat and Krautrock shuffle, way back in 1967.

"Being as we worked four sets a night and took a lot of extended guitar breaks," Coxe recalls, "I had nothing to do. One night I plugged in an old oscillator that a friend had lent me, and started swooping the room with electronic sound".

The guitar players hated it and left one by one leaving only Coxe and Taylor, who decided to change their name to Silver Apples after the poem by Blake and add more (and more) oscillators. Slowly the "Simeon" emerged, linking a number of oscillators which Coxe could play with hands and feet. The cumbersome beast was mounted on plywood, and with Taylor's insistent rhythms and lyrics supplied by a poet friend, Stanley Warren, Silver Apples developed a sound that was like nothing else before or since. With six notes available, each song had a gorgeous repetitive edge to it, added to by Taylor's enlarging barrage of percussion. With some cosmic lyrics, the whole experience was completely off the wall.

Through luck the band's first show was in front of 30,000 people in Central Park, New York on a bill with The Steve Miller Band, The Chamber Brothers, The Fugs and The Mother's Of Invention. They were allowed to play six songs – which was all they had – and woke up the next morning with plaudits aplenty in the local press. The duo were snapped up by Kapp Records and recorded two albums, their exquisite self-titled debut and the following year's similarly eclectic 'Contact', which features the hokey banjo goes electronica of 'Ruby', Their cult status was confirmed as they dissolved from view, becoming a footnote in the emerging US hippy scene.

Name-checked over the decades, the albums were eventually bootlegged in the '90s, before the duo reconvened and played a few live shows. Taylor dug out the unreleased third album 'The Garden' from his attic, which was released along with a series of his drum loops cut to Simeon's more recent electronic "noodles". These less formed tracks were alternated with the original third set and took on oddball titles like 'Tabouli Noodle', 'Cannonball Noodle', 'Cockroach Noodle', and so on. The latter tracks were some way from the spirit of 1968, and their cover of the soul classic 'Mustang Sally', which underlined the strange place the duo originally occupied, confused matters even further.

Back in the day, Silver Apples supported Atlantic soul legend Wilson Pickett and caught Jimi Hendrix's attention after he saw the band live. "Later, after Silver Apples was a known entity," Simeon recalled for Robert Young on the website Junk Media, for whom he was interviewed in 2001, "Jimi would come to our recording sessions and stuff. He was always getting me to try out some new piece of gear or another. I always loved his music, and he had to have been an influence, consciously or not".

The Silver Apples remained a buried treasure for well over 40 years and, they remain rather a cult item now. Alas, the album that really brought electronic music into the home of the masses didn't come from new dandies with uncontrollable instruments or old jazz heads looking for a fast buck, it came from one of Robert Moog's team of instrument developers, whose mastery of the instrument allowed him to reconfigure the classics and make them appeal again to a fascinated audience.

TRANS-ELECTRONIC MUSIC PRODUCTIONS, INC. PRESENTS
Switched-On Bach
Original release: 1968
CBS RECORDS

Tracklisting:
Sinfonia To Cantata No 29, Air On A G String, Two-Part Invention In F Major, Two-part Invention In B-Flat Major, Two Part Invention In D Minor, Jesu, Joy Of Man's Desiring, Prelude And Fugue No 7 In E-Flat Major, Prelude And Fugue No 2 In C Minor, Chorale Prelude 'Wachet Auf', Brandenburg Concerto No3 In G Major

It's impossible to listen to 'Switched-On Bach', billed as containing "virtuoso electronic performances" of the great man's music, without summoning up images of A Clockwork Orange. That movie's cultural effect and the the stark electronics created by Walter Carlos seem to be married forever, but, three years before the movie's release, in 1968, this extraordinary album changed things as much musically as the film did socially.

"By 1968," the book Experimental Pop reports, "'Switched-On Bach' served to popularise electronic music for mass audiences. The Bach inventions, preludes, and concertos were realised by Carlos on a Moog 55, set up in modular units connected together with cords". So basic was this initial unit that the monophonic notes had to be multi-layered on tape to get their orchestral-style effect, something that was hugely time consuming and, you might think, hugely limiting in terms of allowing the music to flow.

"Carlos and Rachel Elkind, along with the baroque specialist Benjamin Folkman and Robert Moog, worked on the recordings through most of the Spring and Summer of 1968," wrote Wilhelm Murg in the June 2002 issue of Cool And strange Music. "The album received critical acclaim, but also 'switched on' a nation of bad Moog recordings that will haunt Goodwill stores forever".

'Switched-On Bach' was a serious work which came from one Carlos experiment on the 'Invention In F', which Elkind recounts on the sleeve: "This completely electronic realisation seemed so right and natural that we immediately made plans for a whole album of 'electronic Bach'. Three months later, the first movement of the 'Brandenburg Concerto No 3' was finished. It completely exceeded my expectations".

An enthusiastic Robert Moog was flushed with excitement. "Walter Carlos' realisations on this album are a dazzling display of virtuosity in the electronic medium. But Carlos has gone further than mere virtuosity. He has shown that the medium of electronic music is eminently suited to the realisation of much traditional music, and in doing so he has firmly brought the electronic medium into the historical mainstream of music. The album is the most stunning breakthrough in electronic music to date".

The effect of 'Switched On Bach' resonated for many years that followed, and it was adopted by thousands of music appreciation classes in the USA as a central stuffy piece. "Carlos opened the way for hundreds of other electronic music recordings to be released," recalled Dean Santomieri, an electronic composer at the California College Of Arts And Crafts, when interviewed in Incredibly Strange Music back in 1994. Music would never be the same again and classical music would never be perceived in the same way.

Simultaneously, Syd Barrett and Pink Floyd had dismantled traditional songwriting with 'See Emily Play', adding swirls of noise and taking the traditional structure into new realms. By the time they recorded their second album, 'A Saucerful Of Secrets', even the novelty of verses and choruses had been discounted on its key tracks.

PINK FLOYD
Set The Controls For The Heart Of The Sun
Original release: 1968
from the album 'A Saucerful Of Secrets"
PARLOPHONE

John Peel referred to 'Set The Controls Of The Heart Of The Sun' as a religious experience, and the NME called the album it came from "long and boring," with "little to warrant its monotonous direction". It certainly split opinion, as the Floyd took their playful psychedelic rootsy sound and re-examined and re-evaluated everything. The whole album was complex, with a myriad of studio techniques helping to make the sound larger than life and twice as scary, and the five minutes and twenty seven seconds of 'Set The Controls.....", all timpani, echoing keyboard salvos and repetitive bass patterns, summon up the sense of a black mass ritual, no less, as the chanted title proves to be an evocative foil for the mellotron and keyboard lines which spin off in synthetic shards.

Unlike the title track's more outlandish structure, 'Sun' has a kind of ritualistic feel, as though it's escaped from the rest of the record like an intoxicating gas, ready to be inhaled and drawn in. The mix of sound blends into a single tone, which bends and weaves like a virus intent on infecting the ear. The shape of 'See Emily Play' was long forgotten, and made to look rather quaint little more than a year after its release.

But, if the Floyd were blurring the edges and rewriting the rock songbook by combining the sounds they made into one homogenised feel or 'vibe', rather than a classically-structured piece, then La Monte Young was stripping the layers of composition away even further.

LA MONTE YOUNG
Drift Studies
Original performance: 1968

There exists a bootleg of 'Drift Studies', easily located online amid a whole collection of rare Young recordings, that features members of the early Velvet Underground. Roaring Fork Press, of New York, wrote informatively that the piece was: "Frequency and amplitude ratios tuned by the composer, and a moog synthetiser utilizing it's sine wave oscillators, mixer and lowpass filter". Is that clear?

Young's association with John Cale and original Velvets' drummer Angus McLise produced a number of structured avant-garde recordings, but 'Drift Studies', on listening to the two pieces, seems to have no time at all for rhythmic gamelan or crazed Welsh violin. The copy I have of 'Drift Studies' is a FLAC digital file, which means you can watch the needle roll over a bright green sound mass that looks like Mark Rothko has painted it in one brush stroke. It explains a lot - it's mid-tone, gently humming, pulsing like you're locked in a room with an operatic air conditioning unit. Part one's nine minutes is reminiscent of the purring of a cat, sped up but rhythmically harmonious, while the second piece, clocking in at around twenty nine minutes, has more varied highs and lows... but only just. It's lower in tone but still a consuming hum, an engaging electronic buzz.

There's something altogether visceral and emotive about 'Drift Studies'. It impregnates you. It fills the room. Like an art installation or the engaging tinnitus-strewn buzz moments after your favourite band has departed the stage, leaving their guitars feeding back. It has a hypnotic feel, a life of its own. Even switching it off seems to have an effect. It leaves a clean palette, like an earful of fresh air.

La Monte Young was the originator, and king, of drone music; an undisputed groundbreaker who beget – after many moons - the likes of Sun O))))))))), Om and many more. His minimal compositions out-simplify his contemporaries such as Terry Riley, Steve Reich and Philip Glass. An American composer who dallied with the Fluxus art movement and ended up, in 1964, writing creative musical works about the dreams of tortoises among other things, Young is an enigma.

He did the whole Gregorian chant thing, he channeled Indian music and everything between, and by the mid to late '60s, Young had dismissed conventional structure and was using electronic instruments to create minimal drone pieces that, like abstract paintings we can never really understand as the artist intended, had suitably deep and questioning titles. 'Drift Studies' may have lacked something in its probing nom de plume, but as an electronic piece it was a vintage reduction of Darwinian proportions.

STEVE REICH
Pendulum Music
Original performance: 1968

While La Monte Young managed to study and dismiss sounds, one of his contemporaries began to work with sound created by accident. The piece 'Pendulum Music' avoided conformity and dismissed tradition, and laughed in the face of time signature. Comprised of the feedback created by a microphone and speaker passing each other, it was dictated by the microphone swinging to and fro to create other worldly swirls of noise. A second microphone with a different length of lead to swing from or set off at a different time provided a counterpoint and the two pieces of feedback overlapped and separated to create an ever moving piece, very much in the style of the series music that another contemporary, Philip Glass, was developing in more formal ways.

Reich's pendulum technique made sounds that were completely different and constantly changing. No two performances were the same, and a performance by a different person, or two people, would yet again change the work completely. For example, Sonic Youth revisited the idea and created their own version of 'Pendulum Music' for the 'Ohm' box set that I referred to in chapter one, their set up differing to Reich's and sounding unique because of that. Reich's conceptualisation allowed Sonic Youth and others to make the pendulum their own, and the end results are suitably out there.

THE LOVE MACHINE
Electronic Music To Blow Your Mind By!
Original release: 1968
DESIGN ALBUM

Tracklisting:
Mindblower, Zenquake, Clockburst, Bells For Eternal Zoom, Inner Ear Freakout, The Shadows Of
Vibrate, Prism On Prism, Lunar Sea, Ashbury Trippin', Coming Down

Somewhere amongst the rewriting of classical music, the experimentation and musique concrete, the dismantling of traditional song and the re-recording of original music played by new technology of the late '60s, there was also an emerging free and easy drug culture, which aided this musical growth in providing many creative people even stranger ideas.

"A pot full of psychedelic pop by the Love Machine" heralds the sleeve of 'Electronic Music To Blow Your Mind By!', and the album is just that - a Hammond-led freak out, with a madman on synth freely interjecting layers of sound over the funky soul grooves that hold it all together. Inadvertently, perhaps, this is something of a work of genius. As essential Moog site 36-15 Moog tells us, "This is '60's library beat music with Hammond organ, and they put all the effects on it they could get their hands on. Like Jimmie Haskell did on his exotica 'Countdown' album, and Belgian band The Free Pop Electronic Concept did on 'A New Exciting Experience'".

Acclaimed elsewhere on the web as a "'60s mod Moog soul psych funk exotica opus with fuzz and acid guitars, good groves and loads of psychedelic sound effects", 'Electronic Music To Blow Your Mind By!' is something of an oddity in as much as its highly accessible, whilst packed with grumbling disaffected noises always ready to swerve the vibe. Undoubtedly put together to capture sales on the back of the new 'hippy' acceptance and the interest in the synthesiser, it actually sounds superb.

And, as the 35.16 website quite rightly pointed out, "The last two songs are so disturbed, I can't believe this was on the original record". 'Ashbury Trippin' is suitably bizarre, with its upbeat jazzy groove seeming to evaporate in favour of haunting Poltergeist-styled noise, whilst the final track, 'Coming Down' is a jolly enough closing tune, almost finger snapping at times, but is interrupted throughout by the closing of metal doors (with plenty of reverb), a haunting shudder which sounds not unlike to someone being locked in the freezer section at the local mortuary! Add to that creative use of sound effects records and a buzzing sound that could quite conceivably be the paranoia setting in or someone revving up a handheld saw to sever a limb, and this is music to scare your neighbour with.

The final slammed door closes twenty three minutes and thirty five seconds of truly momentous psychedelia. It proved that the new electronic sounds could find a middle ground where they weren't heavily cerebral pieces of art or over twee, chilidish interpretations for the sake of the Moog. If you ever see this record, snap it up.

RUTH WHITE
7 Trumps From The Tarot Cards/ Pinions
Original release: 1968

Tracklisting:
7 Trumps From The Tarot Cards, Wheel Of Fortune, Magician, Hanged Man Sun, Tower, Lovers/ World, Pinions... a choreography about symbolic flight Beginnings (Prototypes), No Wings (without imagination/no desire for flight), Wings clipped (too many external involvements/flight stopped), Wanting wings (limited capacity/no flight possible), Love Gives Wings (with wings)

If The Love Machine closed their electronic funk grooves with almighty slam, then Ruth White's supremely strange '7 Trumps From The Tarot Cards' took the idea of a truly psychedelic vision way further. Her explanation of how she got to where she did is matter of fact, almost blasé. The sounds she made, however, were a different story altogether.

The site Mimaroglu Music Sales offers this CD with the note "Notably absent are Ms White's terrifying deer-in-headlights vocals, but this only leaves room for all kinds of late '60s psychedelic electronic treatments, ranging from atonal clavinet stabs to all kinds of home-brew and modular synthesiser glorp, and even a bit of proto drum-machine... of course with tons of tape echo and reverb on everything, yielding a murky fog of dissonance that's just right for your evening seance". It doesn't get better than that.

This '60s slice of weirdsville comes with great liner notes from Ruth too. For instance, of her studio she says, "It is my own personal place. No-one else works in it. I spend from 10-12 hours in it daily, approximately nine months out of the year. It is fairly well equipped - several multi-channel tape recorders (including two new Ampex AG 440 machines), a Moog synthesizer, oscillators, modulators, electronic organ and electronic clavichord, two pianos, a harpsichord and variable speed and reverberation devices are only a part of the list of machines that I have gathered".

Ms White makes her living making educational records; however details of these aren't particularly forthcoming, but her move from classical composition into electronic music is explained in great detail:

"I was curious but did not consider using electronic music - the medium seemed too far from the ideas of composition I had. One day (in about 1960), it occurred to me that I was really hearing pure experiments with noise or unorganised sound. The break-through of the noise concept was very important. I began to realise the fantastic potential for expanding our musical vocabulary if we could draw upon the new techniques for capturing and making noise. If we could find ways to manipulate these materials, it seemed we could bring them into the musical language in a meaningful way".

And Ms White got deeper than that; her analytical approach allowed her into new ways of thinking and new sensations to link to music.

"The largest common and basic idea I could discover was that of tension. This is the force, which grows out of the pull between opposites, or contrasting elements. It is the great regulator. In music, tension is the pull between tonic and dominant chords or the contrast of melodic line against melodic line".

On paper the theory makes sense. On the ear, the result is simply staggering. The Tarot pieces are clashing, extraordinary, and really disturbing, and because of these bold statements White was commissioned by choreographer Eugene Loring, from the University of California, to supply a soundtrack to the dance piece 'Pinions'. The result is equal parts 'Phantom Of The Opera' and 'Scary Movie'. However, the dance piece, which was first performed in February, 1968 was warmly received.

"In every sense the central work was 'Pinions', set to a really exciting, organically musical, electronic score by Ruth White," claimed The Los Angeles Times. "Not only the soloists, but all the participants, seemed to draw heat from this score, wedded to Loring's fluent choreography so convincingly one could not guess which came first".

There's something of the Harry Partch about Ruth White's music, in its timing and it's echoey rhythm, which at times sounds like two people hitting tennis balls. It seems to travel from eccentric ruler twanging to attack decay Legretti-style on the keyboard., and remains nightmarish and disturbing, despite its structure and direction. It is uneasy listening.

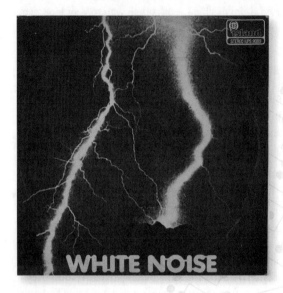

THE WHITE NOISE
An Electronic Storm
Original release: 1969
ISLAND RECORDS

Tracklisting:
Love Without Sound, My Game Of Loving, Here Come The Fleas, Firebird, Your Hidden Dreams,
The Visitation

"Many sounds have never been heard by humans:- Some sound waves you don't hear, but they reach you. 'Storm Stereo' techniques combine singers, instrumentalists and complex electronic sound. The emotional intensity is at a maximum". So claimed the back sleeve of 'An electronic Storm' by White noise, an album released by Island at the end of the '60s. An experimental electronic outfit put together by American composer David Vorhaus, along with BBC Radiophonic Workshop composers Delia Derbyshire and Brian Hodgson, their debut album was created by using early synthesisers and various tape loops and cut up tapes, all of which generates some Floydian moments and some melody, but it's the snatched speech fragments and sound effects – not to mention the heavy breathing solo on 'My Game Of Loving' – which make this album stand out as a little "odd".

The album's reception was sufficiently muted at the time, but disciples from Julian Cope and The Orb to Broadcast have acclaimed the set in the interim. Derbyshire and Hodgson left the band and Vorhaus, reputedly hid away in his studio in Camden where he produced the monumental 'Concerto For Synthesizer', which was released on Virgin in 1975. Based on the theory of Bartok's 'Concerto For Orchestra', the album found Vorhaus dismantling sound using the trusty tape recorder but relying more heavily on The Kaleidophon Synthesizer, which included "a couple of VCS 3s," according to Vorhaus, which were used to create a console of electronic modules. The result is a throwback to much earlier sounds without structure, which Vorhaus willingly allows to take over. The sleevenotes of the original album report that, "It even composed and created its own music in a few minutes of mechanical madness". The end of the second movement see the synthetic take over the physical as it rolls on into its own oblivion, expiring into eternity. For all its decomposition, Vorhaus then embarks on the final movement of his 'Symphony', which sounds like a cross between the theme for Star Wars – with all lasers guns to stun - and Bladerunner, as if to prove just how on the money he was. Sadly, few listened.

After this moment of Man vs Machine creativity Vorhaus embarked on further more atmospheric releases. Hugely influential, but as he himself concluded, "It means I won't be getting on Top Of The Pops". A sentiment that some contemporaries just couldn't agree with. Enter the decade ending world of electronic exploitation......

WALTER SEAR
The Copper Plated Integrated Circuit
Original release: 1969
COMMAND

Tracklisting:
Integrated Circuit, Jazz Waltz Circuit, Where's Prince Brilliant?, Circuit Breaker, Hey Jude, Resonant Circuit, Love Child, Relay Circuit, Feedback Circuit, Revolution / Where Have All the Flowers Gone?

A celebrated tuba player, Walter Sear met Robert Moog in the '60s while he was building his own studio and Moog was developing the Theremin and his early synthesisers. Sear began using the Moog, and contributed the soundtrack to the Dustin Hoffman film 'The Midnight Cowboy', among other things, whilst also maintaining a contract with the Command label, famous for their instrument-specific selections – bongos, strings, percussion, etc. During the '60s Sear began to deliver several synth-exploitation albums, including the truly bizarre 'The Copper Plated Integrated Circuit'.

Mixing self-penned titles like the suitably strange 'Feedback Circuit', with all its baroque regency, alongside super fluffy takes on The Supremes' 'Love Child' and the Fabs' 'Hey Jude', 'The Copper Plated Integrated Circuit' failed, for the most part, to live up to its grandiose title. That's until the closing medley of The Beatles' 'Revolution' and 'Where Have All The Flowers Gone?' which sees a hippy dippy version of the former invaded by aliens equipped with exploding rayguns and who hold court until it dissolves into a completely underplayed, almost funereal version of 'Where Have All The Flowers Gone?'. It's as if the band waited until everyone had gone home before they got weird and delivered the good stuff.

MARTY GOLD
Moog Plays The Beatles
Original release: 1970
AVCO EMBASSY

Tracklisting
Eleanor Rigby, Norwegian Wood, Day Tripper, Yesterday, Get Back, Penny Lane, Lucy In The Sky With Diamonds, Michelle, Hey Jude, In My Life, The Fool On The Hill, Good Night

William Sear's space age confusion take on 'Revolution' must have set brains ticking and cash registers flying. If the classics could be synthed and made into something that was new, different and, most importantly, saleable in the market place where traditional classical music was on a downward sales spiral, then the possibilities of contemporary music being re-interpreted and selling bucketloads a second time around was a no brainer.

Marty Gold was quick to cotton on. A typical super-busy composer, band leader, arranger, songwriter and musical everyman who dabbled in movie scores, easy listening and seemingly anything else that could keep him in work, Gould, according to Easy Listening site Space Age Pop Music, turned out everything from "syrupy strings, rocking walls of sound to hale and hearty vocal choruses for various albums".

Having been part of Korn Kobblers in the 1930s, he'd become a writer and arranger for The Three Suns' easy listening albums before co-writing The Four Aces' number two single 'Tell Me Why' in the '50s. Gould never missed an opportunity, releasing a string of albums including tributes to Rodgers And Hart and Hank Williams, alongside groovy bachelor pad sets like 'Skin Tight', 'Hi Fi For Fun' and 'Classic Bossa Nova', before he hit on the none too taxing equation that

The Beatles + new synthetic sounds >= cash

100

After the swinging '60s, the synth had become a futuristic tool that, when played over a tight rhythm section and embellished with a Hammond or suchlike, could be soulful and appeal to people in need of futuristic vibes. The Beatles' clever melody lines and succinct arrangements in all their household familiarity, however, didn't really lend themselves to such a synthetic setting. In truth, the likes of 'Eleanor Rigby', 'Day Tripper' and 'Yesterday' sounded like little more than a homogenised robot fed on a diet of Lennon and McCartney.

The end result is pedestrian in places, but the likes of 'Penny Lane' – played just about straight until a space ship seems to soar overhead - sound wonderfully bizarre, especially as the main melody is played out on a setting that sounds not unlike a Hammond sent through a reverb unit.

The sleeve boasts the use of "whistling effects", "Automatic octave slurs", along with all manner of futuristic sloganeering. With such explanations written in capitals throughout, it's clear Marty and co are trying to underline how offbeat they are. Sadly, for the most part, it's just nowhere near offbeat enough.

"I wanted more than anything else," says Gold, "to retain the musical values of these great Beatles' songs, and certainly not to sacrifice them to any machine. The Moog is a magnificent instrument, but I was interested in creating something beyond another pure Moog album. Rather I wanted to create a musically valid electronic album".

When the simple harpsichord-lite sound meets a vibrato melody line on 'Michele' it almost works, the sub-melody and Gold's arrangement moving the track away from the twee and into the land of the offbeat, but the following 'Hey Jude' and its trembling intro only makes you fear how they will handle the final chorus, the song's haunting singalong ending. Of course, your worst fears are realised as the fade is turned into the kind of hellish daydream you might expect to have if you dozed off doing 75 miles per hour on a snow bound motorway. Complete white out. Still, as Beatles' exploitation records go, the sleeve is a classic, and the record's agenda alone makes it a worthwhile experience.

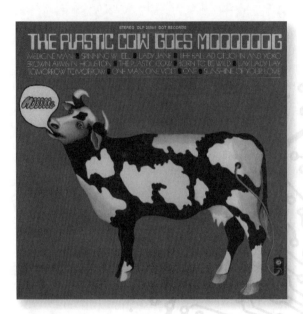

MIKE MELVOIN
The Plastic Cow Goes Moo
Original release: 1970
DOT RECORDS

Tracklisting:
Medicine Man, Spinning Wheel, Lady Jane, The Ballad of John and Yoko, Tomorrow Tomorrow, The Plastic Cow, Born to be Wild, One Man, One Volt Brown Arms in Houston, Lay Lady Lay, One, Sunshine of Your Love

Everything from the sleeve of 'The Plastic Cow Goes Moooooog' to the run out groove of the cover of Cream's 'Sunshine Of Your Love' feels strangely impossible, like 'The Spy Who Shagged Me' and Austin Powers' "ironic" take on the '60s curdled to the top of a homogenous pot of unnatural sounds. Amid the excitement, synths warble and fart in a way they shouldn't, and groovy jazz licks are sought on an instrument that just isn't up to the task for the most part.

The swinging '60s rhythms add a further veneer of dad-cred, and the whole shebang arrives at a place where it's a short hippy hippy shake to summon up images of pedestal-raised dolly birds frugging wildly throughout the whole proceedings. Maybe the world was expecting too much of synthesis, of future music? Or maybe Melvoin and the other exploitation experts were delivering exactly what the public wanted- with a wry smile too.

In places, 'The Plastic Cow...' sounds like background music for a dodgy sitcom where kinky boots and ageing landladies fail to come to terms with the changes in modern society. A true reflection of how the world actually was away from Carnaby Street or the West Coast American free lovin' pot parties. 'The Plastic Cow Goes Mooooooog' is not hip, and it struggles with just about everything.

By 1970, swinging '60s exploitation was in the hands of "the man", whilst the groovy hepcats had probably already psyched out on Woodstock peace and not stayed away from the brown acid as they were told. The world and his wife deserved 'The Plastic Cow Goes Mooooog', and the reaction, according to the sleeve, was: "Hey, man, I'd like to hear a little more of that phased rubber band". This was music for acid-dads high on Martini and heading for a midlife crisis and a spell living back at their Mum's.

The long lost Basic Hip website, which perfectly rounded up and provided warmth for all kinds of dysfunctional music, had a place in its heart for 'The Plastic Cow Goes Moooooog', even claiming that it was "a pioneer effort in many ways, an entirely new language".

According to them, composer, arranger and performer Mike Melvoin was ready to right the wrongs perpetrated about the Moog synthesiser, claiming that, "The public misconception of the Moog synthesizer, in my opinion, is that it's a bloodless, body-less sound-producing machine. This came to be the case because so many Moog albums, in the past, have relied on Moog effects rather than communicative musicianship for their foundations. This album is based on musicianship, performances, and repertoire more than effects. I think it's the first pop electronic album with a soul. It's a very human electronic album".

The track selection pretty much backed that up with a gentle take on the Stones' 'Lady Jane' and Dylan's 'Lay Lady Lay', but the analogue amps must have been overheating on 'Born To Be Wild', and 'The Ballad Of John And Yoko' makes a vaudeville poke at authority sound like a cabaret carthorse.

Technical assistance for the set was provided by Bernie Krause and Paul Beaver, both of whom have featured elsewhere in this book. For now, let's just marvel at the album's sleeve and it's description of this strange music.

"Listen, if you will, for such onomatopoetic sounds as a "phased rubber band," a "glass shower," "damped bells," and a "soprano with a gurgle". They're there. You've never heard them before, but you will hear them again!"

Really ?

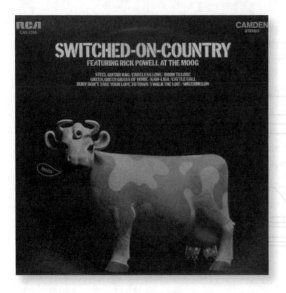

RICK POWELL AT THE MOOG
Switched-On-Country
Original release: 1970
RCA

Tracklisting:
Steel Guitar Rag, Born to Lose, Cattle Call, Careless Love, Ruby, Don't Take Your Love to Town,
Watermelon, Green, Green Grass of Home, Kaw-Liga, I Walk the Line

If easy listening classics, pop radio staples and classical overtures struggled when performed
by the slowly developing synthesisers, you'd think that country music and its distinctive lilting
frame, or souped-up bluegrass interpretation, would be a none starter. But, in the race to exploit
the synth before the novelty value wore off, anything was fair game.

Perhaps as homage in some crazed way to 'The Plastic Cow Goes Moooooog', the sleeve of
'Switched-On-Country' features a horned bovine, with valves emanating from its udders, uttering
a single, speech bubble encased, word - "Moog". Of course.

But from the opening bars of 'Steel Guitar Rag', as the notes are bent, you start to think Rick
Powell just might get away with this unnerving clash of styles. Free rolling, heart breaking
country and technophobic electronic make for odd bedfellows, for sure, but does Powell know
something we don't? Banjo settings are utilised on 'Born To Lose' and the strangely syncopated
'Cattle Call' even has a tinny dobro setting which just about works.

But sadly much of the album sounds laboured though, and the synthetic setting created for
parched lips doing dry whistling on 'Ruby Don't Take Your Love To Town' takes the set to a
comedic nadir that can only be surpassed by the robotic "voice" which struggles for words on
'I Walk The Line' and the stoned version of the same which tackles 'Green, Green Grass Of Home'.

'I Walk The Line' closes the set in fine psychotic style, begging the question 'Whatever happened to Rick Powell?' The sytnth police are undoubtedly still out there looking. But, perhaps more poignantly, have all the years of development led us into an ultrasonic cul-de-sac now that the decade is coming to a close?

CLAUDE DENJEAN
Moog!
Original release: 1970
LONDON PAHSE 4

Tracklisting:
Na Na Hey Hey Kiss Him Goodbye, Nights In White Satin, Sugar Sugar, Raindrops Keep Falling On My Head, House Of The Rising Sun, Everybody's Talkin', Venus, Come Together, Bridge Over Troubled Water, Lay Lady Lay, United We Stand, Proud Mary

There's very little known about Claude Denjean, other than that he was French and could expertly produce a synthetic version of, well, almost anything. Some Moog exploitation albums are way too twee for their own good, simply replacing the melody line with a blipping foray, and on occasion Claude is as guilty as the next man, but in places he multi-layers, arpeggios and adds the odd squeal of darkness which keeps you on your toes in a way others just don't.

Frank's Vinyl Museum website praises Claude for his Moog skills on this Phase 4 Stereo Spectacular – the Decca group's hi-fi enthusiast's demo disc to show just how good your new fangled stereo could be.

"Some guys take a traditional record, throw in a few notes from their Moog Synthesizer, and call it a Moog album. Not Claude Denjean," fizzes Frank, "The Moog takes center stage in this 1970 London Records release, in all its raw beauty. Electronic music never quite "made it" into mainstream culture - that's probably because it took so much work to produce these albums. For all its wizardry, the mainframe-sized Moog could only produce one sound at a time. Artists like Claude Denjean recorded track after track, probably sitting up late into the night hunched over Moog keyboards and sixteen-track tape machines".

It's a romantic image indeed, and when you hear the pedestrian version of 'Raindrops Keep Falling On My Head' in all its hokey mid-tempo finery, you wonder if all that candle burning was worthwhile. The song was never much good anyway, so why bother bringing it up to date?

Frank's comments forum does reveal true fandom for the album though, and amid the comparisons to other Moog exploitation albums, one Andy M recalls: "I spun this LP as a kid, shaking the house when my parents were gone. The bass tracks are great, I remember loving 'House Of The Risin' Sun' and 'Come Together' in particular". He's spot on too, 'Risin' Sun' follows 'Raindrops' and blows the speakers clean. The groovy drummer's backbeat and the rolling synth layers over what sounds like Animal from the Muppets playing jazz bass on uppers make it a formidable thumper.

'Come Together' is slower but maintains the beat derived power and, almost amazingly, Dylan's 'Lay Lady Lay' has a surreal life all of its own. Claude Denjean would go on to further investigate the car crash of electronic instrumentation and pop music, most notably on 'Open Circuit', where murder is committed on 'I Can See Clearly Now' and 'Big Yellow Taxi' among others. However, 'Kiss This' is a real treat, a funky groove with a laidback swing to it, and stands out as Denjean's coolest cut by far. That it took so many tries and undoubtedly endless late nights to get there is beside the point, the mix of electronic grinding funk and a proper human vocal cheekily intoning the title make it well worth the mountain of vinyl that's been created along the way in looking for something good to come from the thrift store synth albums that, amazingly, command ridiculously high price tags.

The '60s ethos of peace and love, of experimentation and opening up to new experiences, should have been the launch pad for great musical innovation. Instead, slowly developing equipment, traditional music standards and the fact that the only people really trying to experiment came from academic or artistic backgrounds meant that the public heard only the most inoffensive and strangely twee versions of electronic music, the ratio of groundbreaking and exciting ideas being set well against them.

At the end of the '60s, most people's idea of electronic music was coloured by 'Switched-On-Bach' or the Stylophone. Many marveled at the tape loop mastery of The Beatles or the strangeness of the Floyd, but synthesizer music, aided by the Stylophone's, arrival was nothing more than a novelty. Things weren't helped by George Harrison's 'Electronic Sound' on Zapple. The Beatle, inspired by a meeting with Bernie Krause recorded two lengthy pieces filled with squeaks and swirls, banging and no little lack of melody from the composer of 'Something' among other things. 'No Time Or Space' was recorded with Krause is California, 'Under The Mersey Wall' was recorded with Rupert and Jostick in Esher. The sleeve bears the immortal words "There are a lot of people around, making a lot of noise, here's some more." from Arthur Wax and "It could be called avant garde, but a more apt description would be 'Avant garde clue'." from Harrison himself which is much closer to the truth.

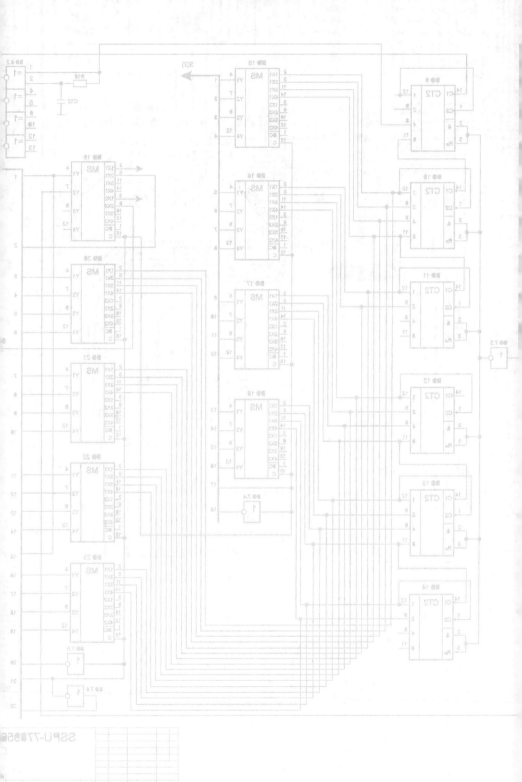

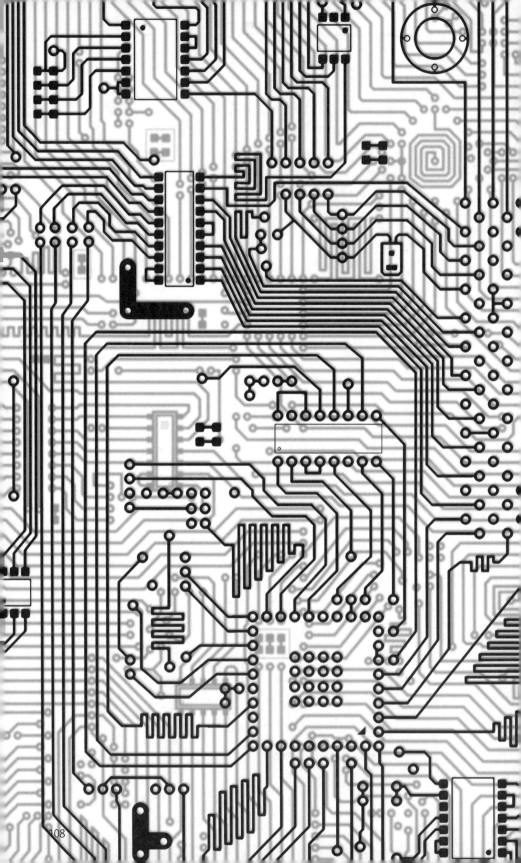

THREE

MOOGS, HEADS, THE INVENTION OF AMBIENCE AND A MOVE TO BERLIN

As we've seen, the journey from avant-garde experimentation to exploitation and commercial saturation during the '60s brought the synthesiser into the home via people's growing record collections. They marvelled at classical music being re-interpreted, they heard new meaning in Bacharach, The Beatles and Beethoven, all of whom were given a modern pristine sheen. By its very nature, this was just another new beginning for electronic music in an ever-shifting musical world where consumerism was now firmly in charge.

Home synthesising wasn't yet a reality, but Bob Moog's "Mini Moog" had made the possibilities of electronic composition more readily available to those beyond the world of super wealthy pop stars and studios, and soon less familiar but far more inspired people like noted Italian '60s experimentalist Pietro Grossi were engaging the concept further and destroying what had quickly become the norm. In Grossi's case, he developed telematic concerts, wherein two performers would play one concert separated by language and distance. It was all mind-boggling as Grossi twinned Pisa and Paris and delivered the first concert simultaneously played in two different places, connected by telephonic connections.

The live electronic music of Robert Ashley and David Tudor further pushed the boundaries, if not by location by their very method. Ashley created 'Perfect Lives' in the '70s, a television opera riddled with electronic techniques and ideas that took in closed circuit TV flashbacks and all kinds of futuristic and up to the minute technology, mixed with an everyday narrative. Electronic music had infiltrated all forms of music by the time 1970 rolled around, and the decade was to become a staggering adventure into what could be done with sound. Some of these early(ish) adopters would make electronic music anthemic, and some of them would make it downright accessible, whilst others would eventually turn it into a pivotal part of a revitalised dancefloor scene.

Long before the anarchic re-thinking of music in the mid '70s, the wavering crescendos of Tangerine Dream would take the ethereal elements of Pink Floyd into completely different, previously undiscovered dimensions. Their 'Electronic Meditation' set was the kind of album that fellow schoolmates would recommend to be played in the dark, noting that it was one of those things that you "really had to live with"; you just wouldn't like it straight away. The opening 'Geburt', with its far out flute and droning loops, certainly lived up to the legend. Uneasy listening littered electronic music as the '70s began, a fantastic time before it would, inevitably, all become commercially minded and much, much more accessible.

TANGERINE DREAM
Electronic Meditation
Original release: 1970
OHR/VIRGIN

Tracklisting:
Geburt, Reise Durch Ein Breennendes Gehirin, Kalter Rauch, Asche Zu Asche, Auferstehung.

Personally, I bought 'Electronic Meditation' for the sleeve alone. It looked weird and threatening and dangerous. Featuring what seemed to be a doll's headless torso with wires cascading from its back, it was just wonderfully strange, and the inside gatefold's brain diagram and song title explanations only served to make it even more exotic. It encapsulated life, from birth to death, and asked, "Does A Brain Burn You?". How could this not be the work of men with genius in their hearts?

Edgar Froese, Claus Schultze (later Klaus) and Conny Schnitzler played a selection of acoustic and electronic instruments - cello and guitar were both among their armoury - but the sounds were skilfully deconstructed and reinterpreted as never heard before. Keyboards roared, sound effects rumbled and the end result was something hypnotic, genre defying and supremely different.

So the story goes, the whole thing was recorded onto a Revox two track in a rented factory in Berlin. That alone made it a slice of vintage music history, and the sound that ensued merely extended the legend. Sure, it's arty, freeform in its construction and there are no words. Sounds emanate from vaguely recognisable instruments and a host of tape manipulated found sounds feature, along with backward passages of music and vocals. But how else could you bring to life 'Reise Durch Ein Breennendes Gehirin'? That's 'Journey Through A Burning Brain,' to you and I.

"In times of electronic experimental music, everything's possible. When you unfold the record cover you'll see a dissected burning brain. When you hear the record a dissected human life will pass in front of you. One among a billion."

Well, that's what the sleeve said, and who could argue? This was music of the greatest intensity. There was the tub thumping repetitive rhythm that held Can together, a strident guitar that's all Michael Rother without the effects pedal and Schulze sparring with the hugely under rated Conrad Schnitzler. It builds slowly, to wild crescendos, confidently art rock, free jazz, and wild abandon. The bright light of a simmering fuse has built the mood for what feels like forever.

This three-piece incarnation of Tangerine Dream never performed together again, but this truly mind-blowing album is a superb legacy, which manages to mix religious melancholy with industrial momentum, eerie symbolism and an incomplete and abstracted view of life's rich agenda. The closing track's sleevenotes, by Hans Ulrich Weigel, conclude:

"And since the brain wasn't quite satisfied with this little bit of life and this little bit of life and this little bit of luxury, one finally promises it a 'piece of candy'. It may rise again. Back to the start. The Circle closes".

What better way to conclude an experimental milestone that, at the time, confused the hell out of most people? Play it again, for it's a work of multi-layered beauty, a tidal wave of cultures clashing, a melting pot of experiments and a meeting place of tangents. Tangerine Dream were flamboyant creatives and this, their earliest flurry, is truly staggering.

In August 1974, Zigzag magazine chatted with Edgar Froese and Peter Baumann of TD. The magazine had originally dismissed 'Electronic Meditation' as "sub Pink Floyd 'Saucerful Of Secrets'". Their re-evaluation admitted that, whilst it may not be the best place to start with the band, it really was "a bold, uncompromising debut, well worth investment".

Froese recalled that the album was "only a tape of rehearsal", it was never really intended for public consumption. That said, it's an archival treat that was never to be repeated. By the time of their second album, 'Alpha Centauri', Klaus Schulze and Conrad Schnitzler had left the band and Christoph Franke had joined, along with Peter Bauman. The subsequent 'Zeit', 'Atem' and the soundtrack to 'Phaedra' fully established the band, underlining their ethereal sound that would inspire generations and genres in the years that followed.

THE FIRST MOOG QUARTET
The First Moog Quartet
Original release: 1971
AUDIO FIDELITY

Tracklisting:
In The Beginning, Miracles, Have It- Or Grab It- Or Go, Images, Sounds Of Silence, Eleanor Rigby, Did You Ever Take A Journey, Rebirth

While Tangerine Dream were developing a uniquely German ambience, German-born Gershon Kingsley was heading for far different territory. But, their musical ideas did cross with the monumental First Moog Quartet. Having previously teamed up with French composer Jean Jacques Perrey in the late '60s, Kingsley also worked closely in electronic music and with the developing synthesiser. He made huge, bold statements, but also trifled with the re-imagining of existing commercial music. His output was prolific and unique, and with albums like 'The In Sound From Way Out' and 'Kaleidoscope', recorded with Perrey, having tested new ground in the previous decade, he now moved into his own series of recordings and became a champion of synthesised sound.

Evidently, impresario Sol Hurock who would later bring the Bolshoi Ballet to New York, was keen to hear the synthesiser in a live setting and, in 1970, Kingsley's First Moog Quartet were booked to play the Carnegie Hall before embarking on a tour at Hurock's request. It was the first set of live performances to feature such instruments, and a year later Audio Fidelity released this live album culled from the dates. By all accounts the audience reaction to the quartet, which consisted of Eric W Knight, Howard Salat, Kenneth Bichel and Stan Free, with Kingsley directing the proceedings. was mixed. By track two, you know why.

An eerie, Tangerine Dream styled intro opens proceedings, before the truly bizarre 'Miracles', which features the Moog in fine form, enters like a debuting ambient Kraftwerk. But it's the trippy, 'pyschedelic beat' poetry – an action painting in words, no less – which pitches the whole thing onto a wonderfully surreal level which, undoubtedly, anyone outside of the art set wasn't going to get. That said, the track is pure genius, a real oddity with great electronic surges lurking behind oddball, disjointed, and almost operatic vocals which border on the folky in places.

Kingsley, or course, didn't stop there. Even stranger is 'Have It - Or Grab It - Or Go', which sounds like a hippy diatribe, with a throbbing funky bass holding firm behind lines read by a Jim Morrison-styled hell for leather preacher. Again, it's just bizarre – especially as it breaks into a hokey American anthem three quarters of the way through, with drum rolls that conjour memories of The Doors' 'Unknown Soldier'. So, less than 14 minutes in and The First Moog Quartet's only album is without doubt one of the most evocative electronic experiences ever. You really do have to hear it to believe it.

The album's middle section features the downbeat 'Sounds Of Silence', before an explosive version of The Beatles' 'Eleanor Rigby,' which rides high on a greasy funk groove. The following 'Did You Ever Take A Journey?' pushes the envelope of strangeness yet further, disguised as it is as a light, sunshine pop tune with close harmony vocals of the kind that's piped into lifts, before it's hijacked half way through by a psychotic Keith Emerson-alike, who throws his synthesiser around before being restrained so that the sunshine vibe can return.

The album, which clocks in at just over half an hour, closes with 'Rebirth', which sounds like a religious show tune, with the Moog players comfortably overshadowed by the chorus line. A fitting end to what must have been a bizarre evening's entertainment.

Audience members leaving these shows must have been completely bemused. A year previously, the world was awash with exploitation albums which saw every tune imaginable given uncomfortable, bleep-ridden makeovers, Kingsley had even provided similar on 1969's 'Music To Moog By', and he'd obviously also penned the hugely popular 'Popcorn', but The First Moog Quartet were made of more serious stuff.

"The inclusion of vocals and narrations from a cast of the whitest folks this side of The Lawrence Welk Show pushes this album well into the realms of the laughable and, in my opinion, the unlistenable," states one reviewer on the Discogs website, but I reckon there's something to this album. It's so far out there that it's coming back into focus.

To compound the confusion, Kingsley also released 'Switched On Gershwin' in 1970 (re-issued in 1973 as 'Switched-On Moog'), wherein he tackles 'Porgy And Bess', 'Rhapsody In Blue', 'Summertime' and so much more (a great stab at the Gershwin legacy, which was revisited several years later by The Residents, of course). His lengthy take on 'Rhapsody In Blue' is enthralling, but the driving, shorter tracks are startling, and demonstrate more than a hint of Keith Emerson's layered techniques in places. With Leonid Hambro on piano, the album, like The First Moog set, shows Kingsley as a serious musician ferociously trying to add credibility to the much-talked about electronic revolution. In places, it certainly works, but the madness of his supporting singers on First Moog, and of some of the arrangements on 'Switched-On

Gershwin' (or indeed 'Switched-On Moog', which warrants second mention purely for its mad sleeve), made it sound like it was produced on an old school fairground organ in part.

By the early '70s, Gershon Kingsley had already released a host of albums. The public's astonishment at some of them perhaps prompted him to concentrate on sound effects records and production work, while the endless stream of compilations featuring his 'Popcorn', not to mention a host of cover versions of the track, kept the bank manager happy. Perhaps his unpraised homage to Gershwin and the exceptional First Moog Quartet's lack of success, despite their lauded Carnegie Hall debut, made him think that mass exposure just wasn't the way forward. After all, it would take the release of a Stanley Kubrick movie to really drive home the possibilities of electronic sound, and a three in a bed romp set to a seemingly sped up electronic version of 'The William Tell Overture' to break all sorts of boundaries and take synthesised sound into a whole plethora of thus far unwelcoming homes.

ORIGINAL SOUNDTRACK
A Clockwork Orange
Original release: 1971
WARNER BROTHERS

Tracklisting:
Title Music from A Clockwork Orange, Rossini: The Thieving Magpie (Abridged), Theme From A Clockwork Orange (Beethoviana), Beethoven: Symphony #9 - .2 (Abridged), March From A Clockwork Orange (Ninth Symphony, Fourth Movement, Abridged), Rossini: William Tell - Overture (Abridged), Elgar: March #1, "Pomp & Circumstance", Elgar: March #4, "Pomp & Circumstance" - (Abridged), Timesteps (Excerpt), Overture to the Sun, I Want to Marry A Lighthouse Keeper, Rossini: William Tell - Overture (Abridged), Beethoven: Symphony #9 - .2 (Abridged), Scherzo, "Suicide", Beethoven: Symphony #9 - Mvt. #4 (Abridged), Singin' In The Rain

WENDY CARLOS
A Clockwork Orange Original Score
Original release: 1072
COLUMBIA RECORDS

Tracklisting:
Timesteps, March from a Clockwork Orange, Title Music from a Clockwork Orange, La Gazza Ladra, Theme from a Clockwork Orange, Scherzo, Ninth Symphony- Second Movement, William Tell Overture [Abridged], Orange Minuet, Biblical Daydreams, Country Lane

I quite clearly remember exiting the cinema in Carlisle one cold, wet evening after watching A Clockwork Orange. The reports had been all over the local paper, screaming about this "disgrace" and how it would upend society. And, indeed, as we walked out there was a distinct feeling of aggression; there was definitely violence in the air, ultra or otherwise. The film remains an intense experience, and was banned soon after we saw it following outbreaks of inner city trouble at the hands of Alex lookalikes.

Years later, when I first went to Sheffield to interview Cabaret Voltaire in about 1978, they had a copy of the film on video, which we watched in their Western Works studio. I'd forgotten the power of the music, the eerie ambience and Walter Carlos's haunting synthesiser. It was strikingly wired and seemed every bit as pertinent as the movie itself, especially in a part of the north that looked like it was on its last legs.

"That was probably the first time a lot of people heard electronic music," remembered Cabaret Voltaire's Richard H Kirk, "It made me forever associate classical music with people getting their heads kicked in".

I had the soundtrack at home and played it immediately I got back. The extremities of Carlos' compositions were exaggerated yet further by the fact that the album, like the movie, mixed those primal electronic sounds with classic orchestral pieces and, of course, Gene Kelly's 'Singin' In The Rain', a romantic closer to the set which will forever remain every bit as sinister as Steeler's Wheels' 'Stuck In the Middle' (as heard in 'Reservoir Dogs') for the context in which it was used.

"Wendy, or Walter," recalled Human League's Philip Oakey, about the music's famously sex changed composer, "was just amazing. It was the first time that we'd heard that absorbent synth sound. We just raved about it".

The album, like the film, with its futuristic references and traditional values was a totally different experience, but, according to various articles, Carlos had supplied much more music that ended up on the cutting room floor. Those remnants were gathered together by Carlos and released as the original score of the movie some months after the soundtrack itself had emerged, and seeking out that album offers some intriguing moments, including early use of vocoder on 'Country Lane' and a mechanical vocal delivery of 'Singin' In The Rain', and the full 13 minutes of 'Timesteps', which was drastically edited for the movie. A wild and expressive piece, it was actually in preparation by Carlos before Kubrick and he collaborated on the soundtrack, Carlos having been inspired by reading the original Anthony Burgess novel whilst completely unaware that the film was in production.

To further confuse matters, the Walter Carlos of the original music, by the time the complete recordings were put together, had become Wendy Carlos. Much later, when profiled in 'Cool And Strange Music' in 2002, the amount of work which had been done on the recordings, and their painstaking production process, were explained, and it transpired that, as with much work produced in the very early days of synthetic sound, everything had been done note by note! Still, Carlos continued to rework the classics for many years after, as well as supplying the soundtrack to the original version of Disney's 'Tron' and the haunting music from 'The Shining'. But, without doubt, it was for his gargantuan efforts for 'A Clockwork Orange' that we will always remember him as an early cornerstone of electronic sound.

BEAVER AND KRAUSE
Gandharva
Original release: 1971
WARNER BROTHERS

Tracklisting:
Soft/White, Saga Of The Blue Beaver, Nine Moons In Alaska, Walkin', Walkin' By The River, Gandharva, By Your Grace, Good Places, Short Film for David, Bright Shadows

Like Walter Carlos, the place of Beaver And Krause in the development of electronic music can't be underestimated. The duo were responsible for Elektra offshoot Nonesuch's 'Guide To Electronic Music' in the '60s, which asked people to sample it, refer to it and use it to develop the genre. They even had a booth at the Monterey Pop Festival in 1967 where they played their newly acquired Moog, evidently impressing Simon And Garfunkel, The Doors and The Byrds, all of whom dabbled with the instrument in the following year at their instigation.

Indeed, by then they'd also introduced such possibilities to Mickey Dolenz of The Monkees, whose 'Pisces, Aquarius, Capricorn And Jones, Ltd' featured the instrument, as well as a cameo from Beaver on 'Star Collector'. So excited were passing pop stars that George Harrison also had a crash course, which resulted in him recording his own, er, "free form" electronic album, 'Electronic Music' for Apple offshoot Zapple.

Beaver And Krause had come together at the suggestion of Jac Holzman from Elektra. Bernie Krause was a former member of The Weavers, and the more electronically-focussed Paul Beaver sported a melodic side which, according to Krause, "comes from more nightclub Hammond B3 jazz jam 1940s-50s gigs than he'd care to mention". That succinct description comes through loud and clear with the funky undercurrent that's present on 'Gandharva', but there's also so much more.

Both Gerry Mulligan and Mike Bloomfield appeared on the album, adding cool saxophone and blistering guitar respectively, and helping to make 'Gandharva' much more complex than the sum of its parts. Mixing traditional musical forms and instrumentation with synthetic sound cast Beaver And Krause some way from both the headier experiments of their contemporaries and the '60s exploitation scene. According to Krause, 'Gandharva' means "the celestial musician," which the set seems to have been almost magically created by in the form of the duo's eclectic selection of foils, Bloomfield, Mulligan, Bud Shank, the gorgeous vocals of Patricia Holloway and a choir that is straight from a spirituality sanctum. The record has all the hallmarks of a futuristic religious experience.

Side one offers an intriguing insight into the duo's creativity, reflecting work they'd done with everyone from Neil Young, Jimmy Webb, Andy Williams, Quincy Jones and Jack Nitzsche among many others, with Bloomfield and Ronnie Montrose supplying flamboyant guitar on 'Saga Of The Blue Beaver' and Patricia Holloway providing a moving vocal on 'Walkin'', which the duo later treated to various synthetic washes.

But, Side two is a whole different story. Recorded in Grace Cathedral, San Francisco over two days in February 1971, it mixed the church's pipe organ with Moog, harps and the sax and flutes of Mulligan and Shank. The whole side is a cascading masterpiece, intended, as Krause recalls, as "a score from a non-existent film". The spacious mix allowed them to add a new dimension in sound, something of an echoey precursor to Blade Runner, a chill out classic in the making. And the piece's reputation as a "make out" album cast it as a bachelor pad essential in the blossoming, permissive '70s. Indeed, such status was alluded to a decade later, at the end of the '70s, when a letter to Throbbing Gristle's Industrial Times magazine berated TG for their '2nd Annual Report' album. The lady in question had balked at having her romantic interludes soundtracked by the band when she'd realised what their early rhetoric was about, claiming that she and her partner would now return to 'Gandharva' when the moment was right rather than sully themselves with Throbbing Gristle's controversial subject matter, "even if it was just noise".

The sound on 'Gandharva' had been perfected on two earlier Beaver And Krause albums, 1969's 'Ragnarok', which mixed chirpy Perrey-styled instrumentals like 'Dill Piccolo' and 'Moogy Blues', with the brooding, deep ambience of 'Circle X' and 'As I Hear It', as well as strange vocal interludes like 'Dr Fox'. The album was followed by a more considered set, the gorgeous 'In A Wild Sanctuary', which mixed jazzy organ, eastern rhythms and classical influences as well as recordings made on the streets of San Francisco.

Billed on the sleeve by Krause as "Environmental impressions recorded with Moog synthesiser, Hammond organ, congas, cuica, tablas, tambourines, drums, piano, guitar, wooden and metal flutes, the sea, live voices, live lions, birds, monkeys, cable car tow cable clicks and San Francisco buses," the set was truly innovative and started Krause's interest in recording natural sounds, which was to become a key part of much of his work after the duo's demise and Paul Beaver's death in 1975.

'In A Wild Sanctuary' has an enormous sound. It's mix of neo-classical chamber music, thumping thunderous white noise and space age blips places it on an odd pedestal, but it's a very endearing sound, especially the winsome 'So Long As The Waters Flow'. The stunning, funky 'People's Park' is followed by on-street recordings, which mix with a slow groove for 'Walking Green Algae Blues',

a strange hybrid of new and old that seemingly rises from the pavements of SF. At over seven minutes, it's the centrepiece of a hugely creative album that undoubtedly fired the second side of their most famous work, 'Gandharva'.

The final Beaver And Krause album, 'All Good Men' was released in 1972, but public reaction was mixed. In recent times, All Music were particularly disparaging, but they did mention in their review that "an unwary listener coming to the album blind might assume it was an early example of the mixtape, such is its haphazard collision of styles and genres chosen seemingly to demonstrate its compiler's Catholic taste". I don't know about you, but that definitely makes me want to seek it out.

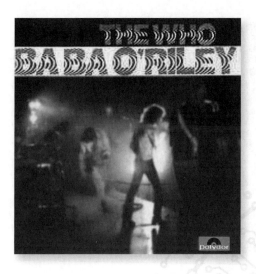

THE WHO
Baba O'Riley
from the album 'Who's Next'
Original release: 1971
POLYDOR

While Beaver And Krause were reaching for spirituality through electronic sound and clever studio cut ups, The Who's Pete Townshend was in the process of fusing his own mystical readings, after studying Meher Baba, and the modal sounds of Terry Riley. These two strands formed the basis for the band's 'Baba O'Reilly', which was originally featured on the classic 'Who's Next' album, having started life as part of Townshend's personal concept project 'Lifehouse'. The construction of the track was science in motion, as Townshend fed information about the life of Meher Baba into a computer and used it to produce a musical form. The result sounded like nothing else.

Following the riff-laden 'Live At Leeds', the opening bars of 'Who's Next', with its wavering, multi-layered synthesisers, was like nothing that had emanated from The Who before. It signalled an embracing of new technology and shook of the band's guitar-led image. The distinctive sound even inspired Kraftwerk, whose 'Elektrisches Roulette', released two years later, used a similar model.

Perhaps inadvertently, if anything, 'Baba O'Reilly' signalled the arrival of the synth into a traditional (and hugely successful) band setting. Electronic music had infiltrated the traditional rock sound.

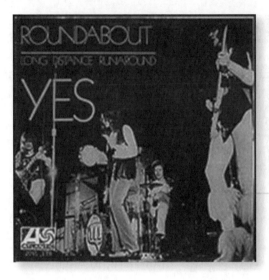

YES
Roundabout
from Fragile
Original release: 1971
ATLANTIC RECORDS

At the same time as The Who were delving into modal sequencing, the development of Yes as inspired, synth-handed prog pioneers reached new heights with the release of their fourth album, 'Fragile'. Early in 1971, the hugely significant 'Yes Album' had introduced them to a far greater audience as they fused classical music, rock, folk and jazz ideas to move out of the underground. The phenomenal 'Yours Is No Disgrace' was different, new, exciting and futuristic.

During '71, the band's original keyboard player, Tony Kaye, was replaced by Rick Wakeman, a flamboyant session player who'd famously provided keyboards for David Bowie's 'Space Oddity'. In Yes he came into his own. The play-off of styles and accomplished flurries from guitar, drums and percussion were the perfect foil for his multi-keyboard prowess, and in late 1971, 'Roundabout', from 'Fragile', saw him sparring with Steve Howe's guitar, allowing his Hammond to hold sway while his lingering synth lines added an eerie calm before the song's crescendo at around the six minute mark, the point where the effects pedals take control before the song's mighty climax.

Yes never did anything simple, and with Wakeman on board they were able to step further out there. In fact, the frenetic time changes of the closing track, 'Heart Of The Sunrise', which continued the interplay between Howe and Wakeman, gave them an even more epic sound, a calling card for what were to become some truly histrionic excesses on following albums. On 'Roundabout', however, the balance of vibed up new rock and the desire to rekindle excitement in classical and jazz forms was perfectly set. It has a hair-triggered pulse wracked with emotion, every part perfectly positioned to make a far greater finished piece that was truly groundbreaking.

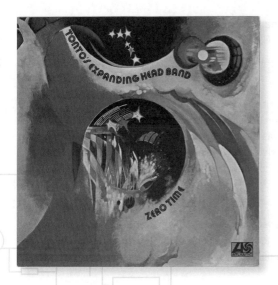

TONTO'S EXPANDING HEAD BAND
Zero Time
Original release: 1972
ATLANTIC RECORDS

Tracklisting:
Cybernaut, Jetsex, Timewhys, Aurora, Riversong, Tama

If Yes teetered on the edge of dramatic tunesmanship, elsewhere there were artists who'd already whole-heartedly embraced the cosmic possibilities of electronic music. In the early '70s, 'head shops' selling drug paraphernalia, incense sticks, cheesecloth shirts, Kaftans and posters of The Jefferson Airplane seemed like forbidden territories, overflowing with myth and mystery. After the moon landing, the possibilities of the future and the theory that Haight/Ashbury might finally come to Carlisle, where I lived, seemed almost tangible. If Yes had opened the doors of my mind, then acts like Tonto's Expanding Headband were beckoning everyone to corners far groovier than ever previously imagined.

The news that Mariner 9 was returning images from Mars and a new fangled "calculator" would soon replace our redundant slide rule – if we could afford the $400 it cost, that is - gave a feeling that anything was possible. In the early '70s it really felt like there was something out there, something to look forward to, and the Peel show, with its wavering signal, provided the soundtrack for dreams of an attainable future. Amid the poetic other worldly musings of Marc Bolan's Tyrannosaurus Rex, The Velvet Underground and the witty Loudon Wainwright III, the strange, ethereal rumble of Tonto's Expanding Head Band arrived unexplained. Nothing would be the same again.

I had to get a copy of 'Zero Time'. And, let me tell you, in the far-flung north it was not easy. ET Roberts, my local record shop of the day, admitted that it could be ordered, but conceded it may take some weeks to arrive. The only other option was mail order through Sounds, the weekly music tabloid. Postal orders were bought, filled in successfully and despatched to far off London,

and within the week this strangest looking album arrived, adorned in a sleeve that cried out to be immediately copied in poster paints.

John Peel had spun a couple of tracks, but this was the whole thing, an entire vision. Featuring lengthy, almost classical, pieces played on instruments that sounded like they might have been discovered by Mariner 9, 'Zero Time' was not recognisably of this Earth. The sleeve revealed that. "All sounds on this album are of electronic origin performed on an expanded Series III Moog Synthesiser." Spookily, the sleeve cover was a painting called 'Apollo On Mars' by Carol Hertzer. The whole thing seemed so wonderfully offbeat that it made perfect sense, even down to the song titles. The formidable 'Jetsex', in particular, summoned up Barbarella-styled visions.

The future of electronic music seemed perfectly rendered by this mysterious outfit. The Headband had hair aplenty, and the concept of a world littered with new inventions from Tomorrow's World seemed perfectly logical under their influence. Everything in the electronic garden seemed rosy, but then...

HOT BUTTER
Popcorn
Original release: 1972
PYE INTERNATIONAL

Without doubt, Hot Butter's 'Popcorn' could have finished synth music forever. It's incessant "popping" melody line and layered rhythms was state of the art when it was first recorded in 1969, by Gershon Kingsley (of Perry and Kingsley fame) for his exploitation synth opus 'Music To Moog By' but in '72, Stan Free's version as Hot Butter went global, becoming the first electronic-based (with the concession to drums adding momentum) piece to reach the US charts, peaking at number nine.

And, like a pre-computer virus, its mesmerising uptempo chirpiness soon topped the charts in territories as diverse as Australia, Germany and Scandinavia. Reaching number six in the UK, 'Popcorn' became the benchmark for synth pop, a mesmerising oddity that stuck in your mind like a precursor to 'The Frog Song', all novelty and of no value to anyone who'd only weeks before been awoken by Tonto's Expanding Head Band. In retrospect, it's incessant melody sounds marvellously twee, and it still retains that hook, much like a recurring hangover to an alternative future. Needless to say, it sold by the crate load.

BILLY PRESTON
Outa-Space
Original release: 1972
A&M

While 'Popcorn' lodged the synthesiser in everyone's psyche, there were more tempered performances that allowed the instrument to explore far cooler musical genres. Billy Preston's credentials as a souped-up keyboard player and master of the dancefloor-shaking rhythm were, and still are, well known. Apart from achieving the golden double of playing with both The Beatles and the Stones, he's also turned out over the years for Sam Cooke, Sly And The Family Stone and latterly The Red Hot Chili Peppers, as well as producing some of the greasiest Hammond instrumentals along the way.

Ensconced in the process of recording his own album 'I Wrote A Simple Song' back in 1972, Preston managed to wire his clavinet keyboard into a wah wah pedal and produce an almighty cacophony, complete with lunar ambience, which became the uptempo funk of 'Outa-Space', a dancefloor curdling gem that was originally issued as the flipside to the debut single from the album. However, when DJs started flipping the disc, the track took on a life of its own, and its hammer-handed rhythm became quickly copied as a funk staple, not to mention a sampler's delight.

Its success prompted Preston to repeat the formula with the slower 'Space Race' a year later, a similarly funky ride that was picked up as a background link for American Bandstand and inspired many a fellow musician with its exotic futuristic vibe. Soul and funk had found a way forward.

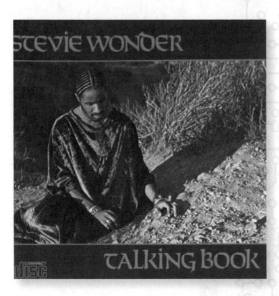

STEVIE WONDER
Talking Book
Original release: 1972
TAMLA MOTOWN

Tracklisting:
You Are The Sunshine Of My Life, Maybe Your Baby, You And I, Tuesday Heartbreak, You've Got It Bad Girl, Superstition, Big Brother, Blame It On The Sun, Lookin' For Another Love, I Believe (When I Fall In Love With You It Will Be Forever)

When MOJO magazine's Geoff Brown was asked to compile a guide to 'How To Buy Stevie Wonder', his top ten selections came with the proviso that any of his albums from golden period from 1971-'76 could have topped the list. 'Talking Book', 'Songs In The Key Of Life' and 'Innervisions' all contain the essential Stevie ingredients of soul, rootsy pop songwriting and an edgy dabble into the developing studio possibilities. Like Billy Preston, Stevie was keen to let his fingers do the talking, and these sharper new electronic sounds gave him the perfect foil for his soulful arrangements and vocals.

In his assessment of 'Talking Book', Brown celebrates the synthesised Stevie and his note-perfect band as they take on fresh material which "draws on soul, funk, pop, rock and jazz, from the still sensational 'Superstition' through the album's melody-rich ballads". An enthused listener, Brown concluded, "It's all gold". And, indeed, it is.

On its budget price re-issue in 1988, along with the following year's 'Innervisions', 'Talking Book' bagged five stars out of five (as did '73's follow up) from Paul Du Noyer in the UK's 'Q' Magazine. Both are acclaimed as "wonderful things," and display Stevie's "instinctive gift for entwining a song around a rhythm, in patterns of unpredictable intricacy". Re-issued again in 1992, both stood the test of time and remained as five star staples in Q, as Andy Gill marvelled: "His musical innovations were matched by a lyrical maturity that couched bitter political sentiments in their most palatable form," whilst recognising that this was the turning point in Stevie's career prior to 'Talking Book', when he teamed up with synthesiser duo Robert Margouleff and Malcolm Cecil, aka Tonto. "Their programming gave Wonder an individuality that set him apart from his peers," enthused Gill of the partnership that had initially explored the world of synthesised sound on 'Zero Time' by Tonto's Expanding Head Band in 1971. Stevie's Motown upbringing fused with what had been pretty out there two years previously made for something wholly unique.

By the early '70s, Wonder had toured with The Rolling Stones, and his move into electronic keyboards and a mastery of the studio's possibilities took him into new territory, crossing genre and racial limitations with this groundbreaking album. The rootsy Motown sound had moved on by Marvin Gaye's more expressive lyrics and arrangements, and Stevie's partnership and break up with Syreeta became his tipping off point, providing an aching backdrop for his lyrics, whether on cool ballads or the expressive fluid funk rhythms created with the help of Tonto, courtesy of Moog(s), an ARP synth and, on the thumping 'Superstition', a Hohner Clavinet. The brooding 'Maybe Your Baby', with its cartoon backing vocal and layered electronic melody lines, also creates a driving groove, and a chunky pre-amble for 'You And I', which pulses with wafting synth lines set behind a lost vocal, delivered somewhere near the end of time.

Stevie's synth funk on 'Tuesday Heartbreak', and the original side one closer 'You've Got It Bad, Girl', with its synthetic pulse and sumptuous melody, give the album a futuristic, otherworldly feel that's reigned in only by Stevie's gorgeously earthy vocal.

You don't need me to tell you that the repetitive riff of 'Superstition' became one of the most memorable sounds of the '70s and established Stevie as a genre-spanning creative force that would influence on a huge scael, while his political vision on 'Big Brother' underlined a decade of political activism that was almost unthinkable from the Motown stable in the '60s. Side two of 'Talking Book' closes with three gorgeous relationship songs, all utilising a softer electronic feel, which was to influence a soulful generation, and a whole substructure of slo-mo jazz funk grooves that threw the possibilities for black music open to all manner of twists and turns.

Released in October 1972, 'Talking Book' was followed within eight months by the similarly huge 'Innervisions'. Following an accident wherein a logging truck shed its load and knocked Wonder unconscious, his spirituality went up a notch and, in hospital with his trusty clavinet, he began to piece together that album, working full time after being in a coma for ten days.

"I would like to believe in reincarnation. I would like to believe that there is another life. I think that sometimes your consciousness can happen on this earth a second time around. For me, I wrote 'Higher Ground' even before the accident. But something must have been telling me that something was going to happen to make me aware of a lot of things and to get myself together. This is like my second chance for life, to do something or to do more, and to value the fact that I am alive," he offered as the album was released.

"Stevie Wonder's 'Innervisions' is a beautiful fusion of the lyric and the didactic, telling us about the blind world that Stevie inhabits with a depth of musical insight that is awesome", trumpeted Playboy magazine as the Tonto duo sparked the new electronic edge behind tales of romance and political finger pointing. Never was Wonder's social conscience more evident than on the album's centrepiece, the lengthy 'Living For The City', which packed everything, both lyrically and musically, into a seven and a half minute excursion into the reality of 1970's America and how it viewed the decade's more outspoken black worldview. A true masterclass in both music and humanity.

ROXY MUSIC
Virginia Plain
Original release: 1972
ISLAND RECORDS

Often ranked as one of the greatest singles of all time, 'Virginia Plain' was a collision of ideas from the art school band's original and highly competitive line up. Phil Manzanera created a simple riff around Bryan Ferry's lyrical stew of namechecks, which took in a Fred Astaire film, exotic cha-cha-cha dances and flamingos, whilst his sparring partner within Roxy, Brian Eno, added the "wobbly bits". "The best bit," claims Q Magazine, was at fifty nine seconds in, when "the first ever guitar and effects solo sound like Manzanera is beating a cow to death with his guitar". We can only hope he wasn't.

'Virginia Plain' dabbled with classic rock 'n' roll song construction and, behind Ferry's camp glamness, Eno was allowed to be just plain weird over the top of it all. His dipping swirls of sound made Roxy Music an immediate slice of offbeat futurism that gathered its inspiration from grainy Hollywood kitsch and an intrigue about the future. Roxy Music were, by the sum of their parts, making something completely different, and Brian Eno's almost nonchalant air and banks of wires and flashing lights made them all the more intriguing.

THE EDGAR WINTER GROUP
Frankenstein
Original release: 1973
EPIC RECORDS

If Roxy Music had discovered a new band structure, then across in the US The Edgar Winter Group had happened upon a similar glam persona almost as an after thought.

You've got to love Winter. His brother is blues guitar legend Johnny, and in the early '70s he'd hooked up with another guitar legend, Ronnie Montrose, and songwriter Dan Hartman, who would rocket to fame with both 'Instant Replay' (in 1978) and the Take That and Lulu covered 'Relight My Fire' – both Guilty Pleasures without a doubt.

In 1972, the be-glammed quartet recorded a chugging album called 'They Only Come Out At Night' – their fourth, in fact. On this offering though, they closed side two with a monster piece of synth-fuelled instrumental madness, named 'Frankenstein'. Why was it called 'Frankenstein'? And why was it so off the groove of the rest of the album, which was otherwise a good time MOR set with occasional nods to commercialism? We may never know. It did, however, showcase Edgar's considerable synth-powered playing and, set against a predominantly rock environment, it's release as a single gave the band far more interest than had happened before.

'Frankenstein; was a tour de force which allowed Montrose free reign and access to more than a few effects pedals. It also allowed some squealing keyboards to drive it forward amidst the math rock swagger, drum breaks, drum solo and spacey jazz rock. It also becomes more than a little funky as it progresses, almost melding into something akin to a latter day Sly.

Sadly, the album never lived up to the promise of the 45, and it ended up remaindered throughout the UK. The single, however, still remains a glowing piece of dancefloor electronica, way ahead of its time.

KRAFTWERK
Tongebirge and Tanzmusik
from the album 'Ralf Und Florian'
Original release: 1973
VERTIGO RECORDS

Clocking in at just under three minutes, 'Tongebirge' still feels like a turning point for Kraftwerk. Their previous album, 'Kraftwerk 2' had been an experimental and challenging set, the lengthy 'Kling Klang' testing the possibilities of electronic sound and the possibilities of bringing the studio to life as an instrument. Shortly after this almost eponymous offering, Ralf Und Florian's follow up album, and particularly the single 'Autobahn', catapulted Kraftwerk to global fame, somewhat overshadowing the music that this 1973 set offered.

Sure, there's plenty of off-kilter sound collision present on the album, but the short 'Tongebirge' begins to form the synthesised sounds into a layered cascade that suggests what was to follow, and the lengthier 'Tanzmusik' sets a rhythmic blueprint for the Kraftwerk who would dominate electronic music from the mid-'70s on. Sadly, the first few Kraftwerk albums are often left out of the band's history now, with 'Autobahn' being considered their year dot by many, but these two tracks definitely warrant seeking out for anybody with more than a passing interest in the group.

VANGELIS
Creation Du Monde
from L'apocalypse des Animaux
Original release: 1973
POLYDOR

While Kraftwerk were finding a pulse in their electronic experimentation, the possibilities of electronic sound as a more versatile machine were beginning to interest people who'd previously used orchestras as the sound sources for their work. TV and film companies were becoming aware that synthesisers were not only there for other worldly blips and squeals, they also had great potential for mood and place.

The French TV series, 'L'apocalypse des Animaux' studied the evolution of animals and their struggle with the planet. It was a very modern, searching examination of the world and needed a soundtrack capable of adding new dimensions to the images. Enter Vangelis.

'L'apocalypse des Animaux' was one of the Greek composer's earliest and most significant works. Put together while he was still in the seminal psychedelic outfit Aphrodite's Child, after having already been commissioned to score the film 'Sex Power', Vangelis' ethereal, echo laden keyboards were drafted in by director Frederic Rossif, and huge teasers and future flashbacks to his much later score for the seminal 'Blade Runner' litter the work, especially on the hugely evocative 'Creation Du Monde'.

Elsewhere on the album, huge soundscapes are created as synthesisers snugly layer on top of, and intertwine with, each other, and humming tonal resonance underpins brave crescendos climaxes. There are lighter interludes, chilled emotive signatures, but on the likes of 'Creation

Du Monde' there's that trademark thick and enveloping synthetic sound that quickly becomes quite intoxicating.

Where Aphrodite's Child had bent psychedelia out of shape, Vangelis was now dismantling sound and the structure of traditional music with an incredible creative flair, a perfect calling card, no doubt, for the array of stylish soundtrack offers that followed.

KEN FREEMAN
Infinity + One
Original release: 1973
OMEGA INTERNATIONAL

While Vangelis would go on to major accolades with 'Chariots Of Fire', 'Blade Runner' and some spectacular concept albums, there were also a host of other lesser known but equally significant people making landmark electronic sounds in 1973.

Ken Freeman's contribution to electronic music is substantial, and he's undoubtedly one of the lunsung heroes of the genre. That said, his 1973 single, 'Infinity + One' is emblazoned with the unmissable "Ken Freeman On Synthesizer" on the cover, and his subsequent input to albums by The Moody Blues' Justin Hayward, David Essex, Amii Stewart, Sally Oldfield, Baker Gurvitz Army, BA Robertson, Bob James and The Chequers showed his in-demand versatility, with disco, jazz and pop all falling under his remit and into his synthesised imagination.

During the '60s, Freeman had fallen under the spell of the mellotron, but without the funds to buy one he'd begun his electronic odyssey by creating sound by whatever means necessary. As Sound On Sound magazine reported in 2007, "The Selmer Clavioline wasn't intended as a string synth, but Ken Freeman found that playing it through a Copicat delay opened up new possibilities". The magazine went further into technicalities, "Used as preset synthesizers, these instruments and their spin-offs produced very distinctive timbres that became mainstays of the '60s palette of novelty sounds: witness the Beatles' use in 'Baby You're A Rich Man', Del Shannon's 'Runaway' and, of course, 'Telstar' by The Tornados. But they sounded nothing like strings — until Ken Freeman got his hands on one".

'Infinity + One' was just the start of the story. Freeman was nothing if not inventive, and much later, in1980, he was gainfully employed with Jeff Wayne on the soundtrack to the ambitious 'War Of The Worlds' project. Another seasoned synth expert named George Fenton was also on the project. Fenton had previously recorded a few library albums for the KPM and Bruton labels, and the duo, intrigued by the interest in everything that might gain interest from a Tomorrow's World-obsessed public, took the opportunity to record one of the classic KPM library albums, 'Handplayed By Robots'.

The album featured a series of "quirky", pulsing instrumentals, including the often-sampled 'Mobile Unit'. The drum machine may be pedestrian – especially the hi-hat setting - and the desire for a melody line and verse/chorus structure is always there, but there are enough bursts of white noise, echo, resonating sub-melodies and euphoric themes in evidence to make this a worthwhile listen. As with all KPM albums it came in the most basic of sleeves, but, if you can find it, it's well worth having to hand for your groovy homemade mixes, samples and even a 37 minute treat in itself as it slips from 'Tubular Bells' minimalism to Wendy Carlos classicism, laced throughout with ambient splurges like the restrained 'Datalink' and the truly off the wall 'Fission Chips', the album's penultimate freak out. The grumbling 'Time Warp' concludes the set just before it threatens to lose control of itself. A quick re-edit here and a loop there and I reckon there's a cohesive gem lurking among the more obvious upbeat commerciality.

Freeman went on to provide music for 'Casualty', 'Holby City' and 'The Tripods', among others, while Fenton worked on the soundtracks to 'Jewel In The Crown', 'Dangerous Liaisons', 'The

Fisher King' and 'The Company Of Wolves' as well as providing music for a whole string of Classic Chillout albums, before, in 2006, providing the soundtrack to the BBC's 'Planet Earth'. Two very British success stories, with a touch Blue Peter, from people who heard the magic of the synthesiser on the radio and went out to make their own versions with whatever they could find.

MIKE OLDFIELD
Tubular Bells
Original release: 1973
VIRGIN RECORDS

Tracklisting:
Part One. Part Two

Ken Freeman was expert at making both electronic sound with whatever means necessary and using the studio as the palette for his multitude of ideas, a very useful concept that multi-instrumentalist Mike Oldfield seemingly mirrored as he set about creating one of the most innovative albums of all time.

If the likes of Tangerine Dream and Vangelis were looking for a film to supply their synthetic textures to, and Philip Glass was re-examining his series minimalism to refine it yet further, Mike Oldfield was at another crossroads of musical conundrums entirely. Heading out of the UK folk scene, Oldfield found himself on the road with Kevin Ayers And The Whole World. The band were a more accessible and lyrical version of Soft Machine, with Machine veterans Robert Wyatt and Ayers joined by Oldfield on bass and David Bedford on keyboards.

The group's jazz rock and psychedelic prog allusions, combined with Ayers' clever psyched lyricism, allowed plenty of free thinking, and Oldfield was encouraged by Bedford to develop his own writing style as the band progressed. As The Whole World morphed onwards with the 'Shooting At The Moon' album, Oldfield had already created an early version of 'Tubular Bells'.

Rejected by record labels until, legendarily, Richard Branson decided to launch his Virgin label with the piece, it seemed unlikely that this lengthy composition would see the light of day. But with Branson's cash and the electronic wizardry of The Manor's 16-track studio to hand, Oldfield was able to play everything on the elongated piece, bringing in only Viv Stanshall from the Bonzo Dog Doodah Band for a touch of narration, thus ensuring that it was made quite comfortably and affordably.

The modal motif of the keyboard melody on 'Tubular Bells', which echoed Philip Glass, acted as a pivot from which Oldfield could meander to and from and play off. The result was startling. It was groundbreaking and completely unexpected success. It was also given extra attention and a significant boost when the main theme was used in 'The Exorcist' the same year – a controversial and much talked about movie that propelled the original album's sales into territories in excess of two and a half million.

The long promised possibilities of the studio as an instrument, with multi-instrumentalists now able to adopt all kinds of effects and editing techniques, were now becoming a reality. Anyone with enough money and time could create seemingly anything in this new synthetic world, and as technical developments came every day, the potential for new, different music was huge.

THE PEPPERS
Pepper Box
Original release: 1973
SPARK RECORDS

As ever, as the doors of creativity were being unhinged, there was a key moment where anything could, and in this case did, happen. In three minutes, the swirling synth of The Peppers' 'Pepper Box', with its clapalong chorus and cheesy bass synth. distilled the multi-track vision down into something you could whistle.

On the heels of the success of Hot Butter's 'Popcorn', this similarly faceless French group emerged a year later with a whole new level of synth magic. The Peppers were Mat Camison on keyboards, Pierre Alain Dahan on drums and Tonio Rubio on bass, and 'Pepper Box' was written by Apardys, who went on to be part of the Spacial French Disco scene in the mid to late '70s.

'Pepper Box' became a dancefloor fave in northern clubs during the '70s. Its drum beat and rolling synth line cast it too close to disco for purist northern soul clubs, but at the less idealistic local clubs of Carlisle, where 'Return To Sender' by Elvis could sit contentedly next to Trammps and Earl Van Dyke's '6 By 6', it was a shoe-in. The fully side-burned Feds who controlled the decks at the Twisted Wheel nightclub – as well as manning the counter, hungover, at the city's Pink Panther Records Shop - would never have stooped to 'Popcorn', but a year on, 'Pepper Box' had enough tempo to make the cut.

FRIPP AND ENO
(No Pussyfooting)
Original release: 1974
ISLAND RECORDS

Tracklisting:
The Heavenly Music Corporation, Swastika Girls

If 'Tubular Bells' showed the possibilities of the studio as an electronic tool to further the possibilities of what one person could do with a 16 track tape recorder and plenty of time, then Brian Eno and Robert Fripp's collaboration on '(No Pussyfooting)' dispensed with that record's need for structure and fused all of their efforts into two lengthy pieces that completely shook the formality of arrangement. Indeed, 2009's re-issue took matters even further into deconstruction by adding a second disc with 'The Heavenly Music Corporation' delivered at half speed and 'Swastika Girls' presented in reverse, as if to prove that neither speed or direction could alter the quality of these transcendental pieces.

Strangely, Island Records, who were attempting to launch Eno's solo career with the magnificent 'Here Come The Warm Jets' set at the same time, were suitably unimpressed. Fripp, who was also busy with the always-challenging King Crimson, whilst also developing the Frippertronics techniques which underpin both pieces on the album, acted as a staccato foil to Eno's droning tape loops, which dictate the tempo and pattern of the tracks as they seemingly shift throughout.

Reviewers were not impressed either, until Robert Christagu of 'The Village Voice' gave the album a B+ review and claimed that it was the most important electronic piece since Terry Riley's 'A Rainbow In Curved Air', an accolade that is absolutely accurate in my opinion.

Over thirty years after its release, the record has, if anything, an even more pertinent place in modern music. In fact, if any aspiring post rock band were to get anywhere near it today, they would undoubtedly be hailed from the rooftops. '(No Pussyfooting)' is drone music plus, with Fripp's introverted guitar shapes adding an almost sparkling lift to the ambient base on both pieces. The re-issue's lack of the obligatory sleevenotes or explanatory booklet with copious comments underlines that this was personal project that, like many of Eno's works, needs to be taken on its own merits set against the current state of the world. In 2010, it still sounds incredibly relevant.

TOMITA
Snowflakes Are Dancing
Original release: 1974
RCA RECORDS

Tracklisiting:
Snowflakes Are Dancing, Reverie, Gardens In The Rain, Clair De Lune, Arabesque No 1, The Engulfed Cathedral, Passepied, The Girl With The Flaxen Hair, Golliwog's Cakewalk, Footprints In The Snow

Isao Tomita's 'Snowflakes Are Dancing' was a brave work and, like the teetering early steps of Walter Carlos, his subject matter, the classics, gave him plenty of challenges as he interpreted Claude Debussy's tone paintings with his multi-wired Moog synthesiser. Subtitled 'The Newest Sound Of Debussy', the set is mellow and ethereal, suggestive even, like a sketchy Monet take on modernism. The multi-layered keyboards add a real sense of power that shifts from chill out soulfulness to spacey filmic segments with a dose of Todd Rundgren nursery rhyme-styled lifts. Indeed, the synthetic whistle on 'Arabesque' sounds like it could have come straight from a Disney cutting room floor.

By the time of its recording, technology had advanced enough for Tomita to realise Debussy's music with a sound that pulls from the classical inspiration but adds a whole new dimension to the original score. With Mellotron employed for the choral effects, 'Snowflakes' took on an extra dimension, a gorgeous set of textures on an album that was Tomita's first to be released outside of his native Japan.

A year on and Tomita had turned his attention to Mussorgsky's suite 'Pictures At An Exhibition', a piece originally written in 1874 before being re-imagined by Emerson, Lake And Palmer in

1971. In fact, ELP had released their version, a live run-through that utilised the perplexing skills of Keith Emerson's many keyboards, and the piece remained at the centre of their bombastic live shows through the '70s.

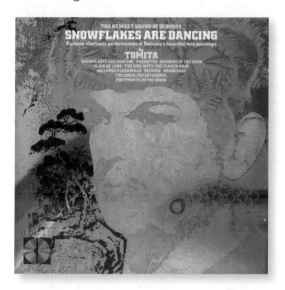

Tomita's reading, however, is far more restrained, although the motifs from the original piano piece are given added ferocity by the nature of his Moog armoury, something that Tomita recognised and used to his favour.

"Compared to traditional instruments with a history of many centuries," he wrote on the sleevenotes, "electric musical instruments have a history of only 50 years. In addition, their shapes are not yet established, so the player is apt to become disorientated". Many a listener, too, no doubt.

PHILIP GLASS
Music in Twelve Parts
Original release: 1974
NONESUCH

If the possibilities of disorientation were purely a side effect of playing electronic music then Philip Glass and his endless search for structure and order was developing an alternate view. Having won Golden Globes and been nominated for Oscars for his film scores, Glass is now regarded as something of an enigma, a hugely productive and eclectic composer who has worked with countless great artists and writers and been at the forefront of musical development, reconstruction and its deconstruction for many years.

During the '70s he was considered primarily to be a leading minimalist composer, along with fellow student Steve Reich. As if to dispel this idea, he concluded this period of his work in 1974 with 'Music In Twelve Parts', an ambitious four hour piece which summed up his musical development thus far. "I had broken the rules of modernism, and so I thought it was time to break some of my own rules," he commented of the work, an epic encounter that travelled through system and series pieces.

On 'Music in Twelve Parts', Glass indeed installed order and a sense of place to this electronic modal epic, but the effect of hearing the piece is as disorientating as anything Tomita must have felt in creating 'Pictures At An Exhibition'. 'Music in Twelve Parts' moves around the room, and its shape changes, like an ever-vibrating jelly of sound. Once you've engaged with it, it begins to carry you to new places, before returning unannounced. In itself it asks and answers questions about the possibilities of electronic music and places it as a fluid concept, something so askew to the commercial world where the likes of Roxy Music, The Commodores and Kraftwerk were discovering that synthesised sound could be dramatic and even funky.

THE COMMODORES
Machine Gun
Original release: 1974
TAMLA MOTOWN

Before The Commodores became synonymous with Sunday Love Songs and schmaltzy soul, they were a down and dirty funk band whose debut album for Motown rippled with dancefloor overtures. The debut single and title track from this set, 'Machine Gun', was a full-blooded instrumental that revolved around an incessant clavinet rhythm which Motown boss Berry Gordy recognised as having all of the subtlety of a machine gun going off – hence the title.

It peaked just outside of the Top 20 in the US and became a northern soul staple in the UK, the 45 being followed by another track from their debut album, the Kool And The Gang at their most funky-styled 'The Zoo (Human Zoo)' that kept the tempo up and the dancefloor shaking.

"This is the stuff that made the group great long before they lapsed into clichés and soft adult contemporary pap," the Dusty Grooves website enthuses, "and a number of tracks here have a fair bit of funk in the mix, something that will come as a surprise if you only know the group's later hits"

'Machine Gun' went on to be sampled by The Beastie Boys' on 'Hey Ladies', and was even played every day on Nigerian TV after the country's national anthem. Inevitably, it became a recurring chart topper. Lurking on the B side is the Lionel Ritchie-penned 'There's A Song In My Heart', a precursor of what was to come, but it's the keyboard frenzy of the late Milan Williams, with its insistent funky rhythm and rolling, spacey swirls of sound that made 'Machine Gun' the phenomenal record it was, trumpeting the arrival of all kinds of three minute gems that began to filter onto the radio in the mid-'70s.

SPARKS
This Town Ain't Big Enough For The Both Of Us
from Kimono My House
Original release: 1974
ISLAND RECORDS

After spending time creating pert pop under the wing of studio craftsman Todd Rundgren in the early '70s, the unsuccessful Halfnelson became Sparks and arrived in the UK at the bequest of Island Records. "(They) found a house for us in Beckenham, of all places. After 10.30pm you couldn't even get a train home," recalled Ron Mael.

Ensconced in the studio during the recording of their debut for the label, 'Kimono My House', amid power cuts and three day week shutdowns, the future must have looked pretty grim to the duo, but the album's debut single, 'This Town Ain't Big Enough For The Both Of Us', was a revelation. "It really took off when we appeared on Top Of The Pops," recalled Russell Mael in 'MOJO' magazine in 2002. "Nothing could have prepared me for the suddenness of the reaction. That was mind-blowing".

The reaction came courtesy of the band's sound, the oddball Ron Mael's moustache and the twitchy stage persona perfectly augmented by Russell Mael's pop star façade. This heady mix made for a bizarre and alluring vision, but their sound was a simple, stylish piece of primal synth pop, and with one song they launched a veritable cavalcade of incessant and exploratory pop bands.

Sparks would roll out their trademark tunes and chart throughout the '70s, with 'Beat The Clock' and 'The Number One Song In Heaven' among the more memorable of their radio-friendly tunes which were inspired by movies, show tunes and good old Brian Wilson's multi-layered visions. A cursory look at their record collections in the '90s, courtesy of 'Q' magazine, revealed the Ron and Russell Mael were far reaching in their influences both old and new. The dramatic storylines and epic Hollywood feel of their simple synth symphonies embraced the music of Serge Gainsbourg and Peggy Lee, while also delving into the experimental sounds of Steve Reich (his technique of looped vocals and the melody derived from them on 'Different Trains' being a latter day influence on the duo), and the soundtracks of Jacques Tati films, Orson Welles' 'War Of The Worlds', Bernard Hermann's soundtrack to Welles' 'Citizen Kane', a dash of opera from John Adams on 'The Death Of Klinghoffer' and, of course, the Beach Boys, who undoubtedly influenced their earliest thoughts as schoolboys.

Sparks revolutionised electronic music, bringing it to a mass audience and cementing their place in popular culture as a result. Their inspirations, from films music to modal sounds and back to pop gems, imbued their synth pop sensibilities and gave the genre a significant sunshine feel which carried on through Depeche Mode to The Pet Shop Boys and, more recently, the likes of La Roux.

EDGAR FROESE
Aqua
Original release: 1973
VIRGIN RECORDS

Tracklisting:
Aqua. Panorphelia, NGC 891, Upland

As Tangerine Dream prepared the soundtrack for 'Phaedra', Edgar Froese also embarked on a solo career that was to produce some hugely entertaining concept albums and themed releases. 'Aqua', with its title track running close to 17 minutes, was the first of these. Rhythmically driven by what sounds like a sampled running tap, it's a hugely engrossing idea that quickly developed into a multi-layered synthetic soundscape simply awash with effects.

A year later, after visits to Malaysia and Australia, Froese released the similarly engaging 'Epsilon In Malaysian Pale', another exotically-layered album with two lengthy pieces magnifying the natural environment of both countries, much like 'Aqua' is based on a purely liquid ambience. Both albums are inspired by natural resources and the environment, pulling the purely synthetic instrumentation into new settings and, like Tangerine Dream's 'Phaedra', painting pictures with sound that were like no other in 1974.

NEU!
Isi
from Neu! '75
Original release: 1975
EMI RECORDS

While Edgar Froese was sailing to new lands on wafting layers of synthesised sound, fellow Germans Neu! were all about the rhythm. It was their groove which inspired generations that followed, from Oasis and 23 Skidoo to The Gorillaz, Public Image Ltd and Bowie to Foals. That distinctive sound debuted on their 1971 album's 'Hallogallo', and in soon developed a life of its own. Klaus Dinger was a full time Kraftwerk member, and Michael Rother had been drafted in to play guitar before the duo began working together on Neu!.

"I thought the first Neu! album was gigantically wonderful," admitted David Bowie. "Looking at what could be the future of music and comparing it to punk, I had no doubt which way the future was going".

Music was indeed at a crossroads, with punk exploding in the UK and New York becoming besotted with disco. In the mid-'70s the German scene was split between the ethereal Tangerine Dream and the far more orderly Kraftwerk.

"Kraftwerk were more intellectual," Dinger once told 'MOJO' magazine, "totally undanceable. But Neu!'s music was not only for the head".

If Neu!'s first two albums were inspirational on release in the early '70s, their third brought everything together and leant heavily on those pulsing, repetitive and hugely hypnotic rhythms. The opening track on 'Neu! 75', 'Isi', was a culmination of all of their ideas, a bringing together of everything from the first two albums, and the subsequent technical changes allowed their rolling keyboard motifs and Rother's incessant guitar, a multi-layered motorised trip of echoey modulation, to propel the listener through time and space.

"To me they sound like joy," Thom Yorke from Radiohead also told 'MOJO', "like endless lines stretching forever in parallel, like a brand new motorway and you are the first person to drive along it".

Dinger was eventually to move on to wordier fare with La Dusseldorf, while Rother's distinctive guitar sound would be the central pivot to a string of album releases. Neu!'s tenure was short, but their effect on contemporary music, a bringing together of Kraftwerk's rhythmic travelogue, Philip Glass's modal vision and the electronic hue of their contemporary German bands, remains a hugely significant part of its development

PARLIAMENT
Mothership Connection
Original release: 1975
CASABLANCA

Tracklisting:
P Funk, Mothership Connection, Unfunky UFO, Supergroovalisticprosifunkstication, Handcuffs, Give Up The Funk, Night Of Thumpasoraus People

As Neu! were creating a motorised throbbing dance rhythm, George Clinton had fused rock and soul with Funkadelic and was bringing together space travel futurism, James Brown grooves and a new synthesised funk sound with its more dancefloor orientated sister group Parliament.

While Kiss rode around on super high heels and face paint, labelmates Parliament had developed from a close harmony soul group into a super visual ultra funky gang whose futuristic vision of a mothership, aliens and the beloved P-Funk was a synth-laden groove powered by James Brown's horn players Maceo Parker and Fred Wesley.

The band toyed with synthetic swirls and ran Bootsy Collins' bass through so many effects that it sounded like it was drowning in a super thick gloop of funk. As synths carve channels of echoey ambience, Bootsy blasts the most seriously effected bass raspberry on 6m 48s of the opening cut 'P Funk' and goes truly supernova on the synth-driven 'Supergroovalisticprosifunkstication'.

Describing the album, Parliament mainstay, George Clinton said, "We had put black people in situations nobody ever thought they would be in, like the White House. I figured another place you wouldn't think black people would be was in outer space. I was a big fan of Star Trek, so we did a thing with a pimp sitting in a spaceship shaped like a Cadillac, and we did all these James Brown-type grooves, but with street talk and ghetto slang".

Add to that a volumous set of effects, squelching bass and a synth cranked up to funky heaven on the closing 'Night Of Thumpasoraus People' and 'Mothership Connection' is nothing short of a sci-fi masterpiece. A soundtrack you can certainly shake a tail feather to.

TANGERINE DREAM
Ricochet
Original release: 1975
VIRGIN RECORDS

Tracklisting: Ricochet Parts One And Two

Not everyone was in the mood for dancing in 1975. No less so than at the cerebral moment that was Tangerine Dream live – or was there? There's certainly something strangely timeless about their 'Ricochet', a live album recorded in Europe in 1975. It didn't fare as well as predecessors like 'Phaedra' in terms of chart activity, and is often found languishing in the bargain bins of the slowly evaporating second hand record stores of the UK, but it has a hypnotic soul to it that undoubtedly laid the foundations for plenty of the ambient music, chill out and IDM (intelligent dance music) of later decades.

By '75 the band's line up included Edgar Froese, Chris Franke and Peter Baumann, and although Froese's neatly-effected guitar is in evidence, it's the trance-like groove of the thirty eight minute piece that truly impresses. There are no discernable drums as such to hold the proceedings in check, instead the rhythmic tonality comes from the combination of synthesisers which evolve as the piece progresses, moving the listener into new levels of consciousness. While minimalist composers hover over distinct areas and drag the proceedings out into lengthy explorations of micro music, 'Ricochet' manages to travel far and wide, building slowly, moving gradually, unwrapping itself before snatching up further layers of sound to create an almost vibrating central focal point.

Undoubtedly, The Orb and a host of like-minded heads lapped this up, and in the dark days when all of those copies of 'Ricochet' were confined to the second hand stores as such music for the mind became unfashionable, a whole generation began to feel the benefits of lying comatose to its comforting hum, invariably in states of recovery after a long night on far more energetic dancefloors.

KLAUS SCHULZE
Totem
from Picture Music
Original release: 1975
MAGNUM

Klaus Schulze had left the fledgling Tangerine Dream, along with Connie Plank, after their initial 'Electronic Meditation' set. He'd continued to experiment, but 'Picture Music' showed him in two distinct fields and at something of a crossroads of ideas.

Opinions are certainly split on the album too. Away from Tangerine Dream, Schulze had released 'Irrlicht', 'Cyborg' and 'Blackdance' before 'Picture Music' – although it's suggested that the album was recorded earlier in that sequence. Reviews at the time acclaimed it as a throwback to his rock roots, solely for its addition of rhythms, but it was also trumpeted as Schulze's first fully synthesiser-led album. The difference of opinion was based on two very different sides that contained lengthy pieces.

Schulze's armoury included an EMS VCS3 synth, an ARP Odyssey, an ARP 2600, a Farfisa Professional Duo organ, drums and percussion, the latter rhythmic elements harking back to his former days as drummer with Ash Ra Temple. The drums are unleashed on side two's 'Mental Door', but it's the monumental fluid rhythm of 'Totem' that provides the essential turning point here. With a pulse that's shifting around a click track rhythm holding sway, Schulze builds layers of sound like a mantra over the allotted twenty three minutes, the frenetic almost tribal feel gaining intensity at twelve minutes when the rhythmic driver doubles in speed. It's a remarkably complex piece, something of a ritualistic dance number, which is propelled by Schulze's unique sense of composition.

BRIAN ENO
Discreet Music
Original release: 1975
EG RECORDS

This first fully ambient album by Brian Eno was created while he was recuperating after an accident. Featuring the side long 'Discreet Music', as well as 'Three Variations Of The Canon In D Major' by Johann Pachelbel, much of the album was based on the idea of furniture music which Erik Satie had championed. Eno's use of synthesisers' recall systems allowed him to play and re-play sections of sound and change the timbre and focus of the piece using a graphic equaliser, resulting in a wholly understated looped sound that flows majestically, changing shape as it does so, like a slow motion, ever-changing take on minimal composition.

A natural development of the loop drones created by Eno for '(No Pussyfooting)', the piece was originally prepared for Robert Fripp to play over, but ultimatley became the starting place for Eno's Ambient label and further excursions into the simplification of music. Like Schulze's 'Totem', 'Discreet Music' has an almost religious feel to it, and the slowly changing atmosphere it creates adds to the wonderufl spiritual feel.

DIONEE-BREGENT
Et Le Troisieme Jour
Original release: 1976
CAPITOL RECORDS

Tracklisting:
...Et Le Troisieme Jour, L'Eveil Du Lieu

It's intriguing that the development of electronic music and the simplifying of instrumentation should lead both Klaus Schulze and Brian Eno to more ethereal sounds. The electronic genre by the mid-'70s, aware of Prog's pompous possibilities, seemed to be looking for a higher church. What could be done was now being examined further ,and the bringing together of disparate cultures, styles and sounds allowed electronic music to grow further, and to embrace different ideals.

The Prog Archives website claims that Dionne-Bregent, a stunning Canadian duo that managed but two albums during the '70s, were a hybrid of Krautrock and Electronic prog. Their debut album 'Et Le Troisieme Jour' is a gorgeous, multi-layered and effects-drenched gem that contains the motorised hum of Neu!, the eerie playfulness of early Tangerine Dream and more than a hint of Mike Oldfield's 'Tubular Bells' in its modal structure.

Michel-Georges Bregent was a seasoned keyboard player who'd begun to dabble with synths, Mini Moogs, claviers and so on in the early '70s when he and his brother formed a group that musically illustrated the texts of 20th century French-speaking poets like Baudelaire and Verlaine. Their sole album is the stuff of obscure legend, but it was Bregent's meeting with Vincent Donne that was to create a truly groundbreaking sound.

Bregent developed his keyboard flourishes, and Dionne's skills as a percussionist on tabla, glockenspiel, bells, Chinese gongs and a variety of Eastern-sounding instruments made for a stunningly different sound. Like gamelan music with an array of effects allowing the sound to create a sense of heightened awareness, their debut album sounded like a spiritual trip in more ways than one.

JEAN MICHEL JARRE
Oxygene
Original release: 1975
DREYFUSS

If electronic music was becoming a quicktime religious experience at the hands of ever-streamlining technology, it was to become a revelation some way into the career of Jean Michel Jarre. The French composer's debut single 'La Cage' was turned down by just about everybody before Pathe Marconi picked it up in 1971. Selling a mere one hundred and seventeen copies, it was quickly dropped from sale and the stock was destroyed. Jarre's electronic vision was just too new. Indeed, the trend continued until 1975 as Jarre patiently waited for the world to catch up in the comfort of his home studio.

The lengthy concept album 'Oxygene' looked to have similarly fallen on deaf ears until Helene Dreyfuss persuaded her husband to release the strange sounding but visionary album on his label. The effect was monumental, and the album scored global sales and a number four single in the UK with the infectious 'Oxygene IV'.

"All those ethereal sounds on 'Oxygène IV' come from the VCS3.... It was the first European synthesiser. I had to go to London in 1967 to get it," recalled Jarre, who, since the release of 'Oxygene' has taken electronic sounds to the most unlikely of places around the world, playing shows at Place De La Concorde (in front of one million people), in Beijing, at the Forbidden City, in Tiananmen Square and at the Gdansk Shipyard in Poland, to name but a few.

In doing so, Jarre inspired a generation of dance music producers and DJs with his unique mix of electronic sounds and his mastery of studio techniques. "The whole album was done on just one eight-track and you can hear that in the piece - it's quite minimalist, and I think that contributes to its timelessness".

Perhaps even more so than in Europe and the States, the studio and its limitations as a factor in the completed musical vision has always been very much a part of Jamaican music, from Lee Perry's Black Ark to the distinctive sounds created in various makeshift and often short lived environments. And thus the late Augustos Pablo, a seasoned melodica player, dub enthusiast and producer, produced a revolutionary side at the same time that Jean Michel Jarre was perfecting 'Oxygene'. Their sounds couldn't have been further apart, but their individual use of electronic techniques made them both groundbreakers in the mid 1970s.

AUGUSTOS PABLO
King Tubby Meets The Rockers Uptown
Original release: 1976
ISLAND RECORDS

The penchant for reggae producers to produce dub versions of their more polished commercial sides, often quickly and with a sense of freedom from commercial requirements, led to a whole sub strata of Jamaican music spiked with effects, manipulated tapes, reorganised vocals and additional flurries of echo and reverb and heard only by those who bothered to flip their records.

Thus Pablo, working in Jamaica's famous Studio One set up, prepared a wayward instrumental version of the Jacob Miller song 'Baby I Love You So' with the help of King Tubby and Errol Thompson, who mixed the side, and "King Tubby Meets Rockers Uptown" was born. Tubby was a studio and electronics expert whose visionary mix completely rewrote the Miller tune, making it far greater than the sum of its parts and giving the genre its first crossover single.

Legendary PiL bass player and all round heavy duty dub enthusiast Jah Wobble rated it the best dub track ever when interviewed in the Guardian back in 2004. "I first heard this as a pre-release in 1976. Love the sound of Augustus Pablo's melodica; I am also kinky for the sound of the dubbed-up timbale drums that feature on this recording. King Tubby was the king of pure, heavy-duty dub at that time," he enthused, "Hearing 'King Tubby' for the first time had a profound effect on me: it was like hearing music from another cosmos".

Elsewhere in his selection of ten dub monsters, Wobble listed Bob Marley's 'Concrete Dub', Burning Spear's dub version of his 'Marcus Garvey' cut, Trinity and Yabby You's 'Promise Is A Comfort To A Fool' plus tracks by Dennis Bovell, Culture, King Sunny Ade, Israel Vibration and Lee Perry with The Jolly Brothers. There are, of course, thousands more that have technique and appeal. In fact, Yabby You and Trinity's 'Jesus Dread' is one with added bite, but none have the completeness of 'King Tubby Meets the Rockers Uptown'. It's pressing, pulsing and evocative, clever, relentless and a swaggering dancefloor hit.

DONNA SUMMER
I Feel Love
Original release: 1977
CASABLANCA

Elsewhere, on another dancefloor and in another time and placec entirely, the mood had become rather more sensual at the hands of different people and different drugs. Taken from the concept album, 'I Remember Yesterday', which used elements of different decades set to electronic music, 'I Feel Love' was at the futuristic end of an ambitious Giorgio Moroder-produced set that allowed the already controversial Donna Summer, whose 'Love To Love You, Baby' had already raised eyebrows and filled dancefloors all over the world, to bring together diverse genres of music under an electronic umbrella.

"This is obviously Giorgio Moroder's record," claimed Human League's Philip Oakey when asked about his favourite single of all time in 'Q' magazine. "'I Feel Love' was the first kind of music that sounded like nothing had ever sounded before, and it's still vital today". Oakey would later collaborate with Moroder on 'Electric Dreams', one of the producer's many huge, movie-related records.

After 'I Feel Love', nothing would be the same again. Disco had become bogged down in silky strings and succinct orchestrations, and Moroder had dispensed with all of that.

"One day in Berlin," recalled David Bowie, who was ensconced there in his darker electronic period, "Eno came in and said, 'I have heard the future'. He put on 'I Fee Love' and said, 'This is it, look no further. This single is going to change the sound of club music for the next 15 years'". He was right.

GIORGIO MORODER
From Here to Eternity
Original release: 1977
CASABLANCA

Tracklisting:
From Here To Eternity, Faster Than The Speed Of Love, Lost Angeles, Utopia - Me Giorgio, From Here To Eternity (Reprise), First Hand Experience In Second Hand Love, I'm Left, You're Right, She's Gone, Too Hot To Handle

Moroder was industrious. While working on Donna Summer's 'I Remember Yesterday' opus, he was also creating the key electronic album 'From Here To Eternity'. Bearing the legend that "only electronic keyboards were used in the making of this album.", 'From Here to Eternity' clocked in at just over half an hour but it was side one's elongated mix, starting with the monumental title track that proved so influential, inspiring house music and generations of DJs, producers and artists.

Like 'I Feel Love', 'From Here to Eternity' was a moving, motorised rhythm that was purely electronic. It was revolutionary, and positivbely bulging with robotic vocoders and almost whispered lyrics, echoing signatures and squelching synthesisers, all propelling the Eurodisco beat onwards. In short, everything that must have pricked up the ears of hundreds of impressionable youngsters destined to take Moroder's ideas further and dominate the charts with their offspring in the coming decade.

Most revolutionary, however, and even more so than the title track mixing right into track two with its even more expressive take on the mechanics of robotic sex, is that the first side closes with a reprise of the title track, providing a fit ending to fifteen minutes that would be inspirational right down to the mixtape, and offering enough for serious musicians, from Eno and Bowie to Kraftwerk and back, to influence their future thinking.

DAVID BOWIE
Low
Original release: 1977
RCA RECORDS

Tracklisting:
Speed Of Life, Breaking Glass, What In The World, Sound And Vision, Always Crashing In The Same Car, Be My Wife, A New Career In A New Town, Warszawa, Art Decade, Weeping Wall, Subterraneans

In 1975, Bowie had famously announced that "rock 'n' roll is dead... it's a toothless old woman, it's really embarrassing". His gaunt expression on the legendarily druggy 'Station To Station', the fragility of the Thin White Duke and his intrigue at the growing German music scene and the differences it offered to popular music led him to decamp to West Berlin with Iggy Pop and Brian Eno. During their time there, they produced groundbreaking music, working with producers like Conny Plank in Cologne and Bowie veteran Tony Visconti.

Bowie's classic 'Berlin trilogy' was to include 'Low', 'Heroes' and 'Lodger'. Pop was reinvented with 'The Idiot' and 'Lust For Life', and Eno contributed and explored the local talent, absorbing the ambience and the German bands' unique take on things. While Tony Visconti produced Bowie's releases, Eno's input into the recording process went beyond the cerebral as he contributed chamberlain and mini moog, while Bowie himself supplied everything from xylophones to pump bass, ARP, brass synthetic strings and tape horn.

For 'Low', the studio set up was different. In a word, 'limited'. But the business was not about great rock epics. It wasn't even about singles. 'Low' was a journey somewhere else. The sleeve gave little information, and the song titles hinted at deeper thinking – 'Always Crashing In the Same Car' - and self examination – 'A New Career In A New Town' - along with a knowing mopping up the surroundings and the outpourings of popular culture in 'Warszawa', 'Art Decade', 'Weeping Wall'. Reaction was mixed.

"'Low' is neither danceable nor possessed of any genuine vision," reported The Record Mirror on its release, "It says nothing and goes nowhere. Bowie has fallen to earth with a resounding bump".

To add insult to injury, there were also few words. Gone was the poetry of 'Ziggy' or 'Aladdin Sane', replaced by awkward self-destructive one-liners and JG Ballard-styled observations.

'Low' was well received in less mainstream publications, and all three of the Berlin era Bowie albums were re-appraised favourably fifteen years after their original release when re-issued in 1991. Contrary to Record Mirror's view, and quite possibly due to the passage of time, Q's Colin Shearman said: "'Low', with its poppy tunes, remains the most accessible. 'Heroes' now sounds a trifle self-indulgent and the less than sophisticated use of the William Burroughs styled cut up technique on some 'Lodger' lyrics sounds dated, but, crucially, all three albums are an essential part of rock history".

CLUSTER AND ENO
Cluster And Eno
Original release: 1977
SKY RECORDS

Tracklisting:
Ho Renomo, Schone Hande, Steinsame, Wehrmut, Mit Simaen, Selange, Die Bunge, One, Fur Luise

While working with Bowie in Berlin, Eno began a cycle of work that would see him studio-bound and highly productive for some time. During the period, he added a masterful touch to hugely influential albums by Ultravox!, Talking Heads and Devo, and also took time to explore the possibilities of developing new music, working with Dieter Mobius and Hans-Joachim Rodelius of Cluster on 'Cluster And Eno' and 'After The Heat'.

The trio brought in Can bass player Holger Czukay and Asmus Tietchens on synthesiser for the initial sessions which spawned this album, the result being a spacious dreamscape, a futuristic electronic soundtrack underpinned by sporadic rhythms and beautiful piano motifs.

When Brian Eno was asked, 'What do you think has been your most enduring contribution to production?' in 'MOJO' magazine in 2001, he replied: "Ten years ago, I would have said 'Making people realise that the studio is a place where music is made rather than simply recorded'. But I'm so fed up with the process that I don't want it written on my gravestone".

But it was at Conny Plank's studio that Eno was destined to work with Cluster. The album's recent re-issue on Water Records included sleevenotes by Stephen Illife, who abstractly paints a picture of Cluster and their union with Eno:

"In a Zen-like way," Illife offers, "Cluster is the question, a consciously intuitive enquiry into the improvisational properties of electronic sound".

Asked about why Cluster were so attractive to him, Eno commented: "I liked the fact that I could hear in Cluster a sort of European alternative to the African root most other pop music had taken". It was a marriage made in the studio, in a pre-sequencer time wherein one of the ensemble would repeat a motif and the others would "jam" into it, hence the album's mantra-like feel and multi-layered textures, which move from early chill out to raga in construction. As with all Cluster albums, it sows a field of possibilities and reaps heavily.

As with all the greats, "Cluster may have only sold a few thousand albums," noted composer Tim story, "but it seemed like every listener wanted to start their own band".

KRAFTWERK
Trans Europe Express
Original release: 1977
CAPITOL/EMI

Tracklisting:
Europe Endless, The Hall Of Mirrors, Showroom Dummies, Trans Europe Express, Metal On Metal, Abzug, Franz Schubert, Endless Endless

With what seemed like the whole world congregating in Germany, and the roots and branches of Krautrock being so widely acclaimed, focus on Kraftwerk's next release in 1977 was intense. It had to be a grand gesture, a complete statement of both position and intent. 'Trans Europe Express' didn't disappoint.

Containing the immortal line 'From station to station and to Dusseldorf city / meet Iggy Pop and David Bowie', 'Trans Europe Express' was at the heart of a further step in the electronic revolution. Revered and rated for their austerity and invention, Kraftwerk had made Germany the destination of choice for Bowie and co, and their experiences there, along with the arrival of 'Trans Europe Express', were the catalyst for a wealth of new music.

The locale led to changes in sound and structure for contemporary music everywhere and, as Garry Mulholland pointed out in his book 'This Is Uncool', "Meanwhile, some black kids from the Bronx get hold of 'Trans Europe Express' and are beguiled by its glistening take on their own funk backbeats and so it becomes a fave on the emerging hip hop scene". Enter Arthur Baker and 'Planet Rock', and not only did Kraftwerk reshape European rock music and American garage rock, they also gave hip hop a leg up and signalled the arrival of beat-box electro, which led, of course, to house music and all stations west.

"At the same time," continues Garry Mulholland, "some kids in Chicago also fall in love with 'Trans Europe Express', but to them it's the sadness in the machine melodies, rather than the beat". The result, ultimately, was techno.

So great was the effect that 'Trans Europe Express' had, with favourable reviews being plentiful and ever more applause stockpiling in hindsight, it has now reached an enviable position as one of the most heralded records ever. Pitchfork's online panoramic view of contemporary music concluded that "the day will soon come, if it hasn't already, that 'Trans Europe Express' will join the ranks of 'Sgt. Pepper's Lonely Hearts Club Band' and 'Exile On Main Street'.

Orchestral Manoeuvres In The Dark's Any McCluskey was one of many youths inspired to form his own band after hearing 'Autobahn' and seeing Kraftwerk live. In a recent (2010) issue of 'MOJO' magazine, he enthused about 'Trans Europe Express', saying that it was "the apex, where the beauty and the machinery chimed together. It was the first really witty record. They were called showroom dummies by a journalist criticising their lack of mobility on-stage, but they took it on as a badge of honour".

Kraftwerk's live performances were the antithesis of burgeoning punk rock scene. While hails of gob and turbulent mosh pits had become the norm circa 1977, Kraftwerk remained static, emotionless, a caricature of themselves, a Gilbert And George painting with sound. But despite this stony outward appearance, the album in question contains some fantastic Kraftwerk humour, particularly in the countdown on 'Showroom Dummies', which parodies The Ramones' legendary '1,2,3,4' count-ins which had become a signature of the punk rebellion.

The music on 'Trans Europe Express' had developed a marvellous rigidity. The use of the Synthanorma Sequencer, a customised, 32-step, 16-channel sequencer, provided a perfectly balanced rhythmic core for the songs, around which their textured keyboards and ice cool vocals could sit confidently. The second side's suite of songs, taking in the title track, 'Metal On Metal' / 'Abzug' (Departure), 'Franz Schubert' and 'Endless Endless', are a rolling symphony, while the ironic 'Showroom Dummies' and the startling 'Hall Of Mirrors' had a strange, haunting film noir feel, which felt particularly unusual in their original late '70s setting. A strange hybrid of melancholy and robotic isolation pervades throughout. .

Within twelve months, Kraftwerk had stepped even further into self-parody with 'Man Machine', wherein robots would actually replace the four Kraftwerk players for a section of their live shows. "It seemed they'd created an alternative universe," enthused an inspired Moby recently. "The 'Man Machine' was an important image and idea," percussionist Wolfgang Flur told 'MOJO' journalist Ian Harrison, "We could have gone on to do many other things, but Ralf and Florian couldn't. Ralf was like something from Goethe, he became what he wrote and thought about".

Undoubtedly, the blurring of life and art is evident on 'Man Machine'. From the constructivist Russian cover image to the band's red outfits, 'Man Machine' was more than an album; it was a way of life.

"So – funsters – der veir fab Ubermensch," Sounds magazines review opined, "extend their humanoid boogie in what is probably the most completely, clearly realised packaging and presentation of a particular mood since the first Ramones album".

The effect of Kraftwerk was irresistible. However, not everyone thought so, as The Rolling Stone Guide reveals.

"'Autobahn' is a twenty two minute composition that encapsulates the hypnotic redundancy of a twelve hour drive. Valuable as both a musical oddity and background music for watching tropical fish sleep. The other albums ('Man Machine', 'Radio-Activity' and 'Trans Europe Express') repeat the latter's musical themes with varying motifs, and are hence unnecessary. Hmmmmm........

SUICIDE
Ghost Rider
from Suicide
Original release: 1977
RED STAR RECORDS

In 'Fear Of Music', Garry Mulholland gathers together the 261 greatest albums since punk, and Suicide's self-titled debut clocks in comfortably as one of its milestones for the late '70s. Mulholland reports in his pre-amble that Suicide "Formed in 1971, but were unsaleable until, in the mid '70s, CBGB's threw a spotlight on conceptual Manhattan sleaze". At the heart of the New York punk rock revolution, Suicide were the thorn in the side of the new, minimalist, guitar-led revolution.

"In those days it was like an insult to the audience not to have guitar and drums in your set up," recalled the band's Alan Vega. Suicide were not about brash one liners, they throbbed with wheezing electronic rhythms and used stripped down old school New York rock 'n' roll and doo wop melody lines to influence their simple score. Toying with the seedier side of street life, they sounded like a disjointed radio floating in over a humming, haunting hangover.

"Every synth pop duo owes something to Suicide," Fear Of Music reasons, whilst also pointing out that, famously, Bruce Springsteen drew a line between Woody Guthrie and Suicide for Vega's vocal style and his sparring partner Martin Rev's minimal approach. Suicide were in your face, and 'Ghost Rider', the opening track from their debut album, outlined their alienation, their innermost fears and exactly why they chose their name.

The track has since been covered by R.E.M., Soft Cell, The Young Gods and, more recently, The Horrors. It's poignant sense of emptiness illustrates what lies at the very heart of the band, and their reflection of the grubbier side of New York life had as much to do with The Velvet Underground at their most candid as it did their fellow punks. An electronic street opera played out with rumbling noises and evocative vocals.

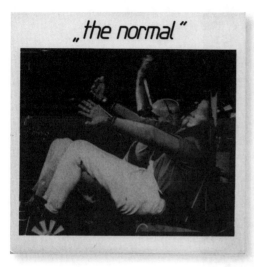

THE NORMAL
Warm Leatherette
Original release: 1978
MUTE RECORDS

When Daniel Miller, inspired by Krautrock, fascinated with synthetic sound and holed up in his bedroom at his Mother's house, decided to record a single, he'd no plans of what he would do with it. As so many people did, he arrived at Rough Trade and hung around until Geoff Travis had time to listen to the test pressing. Miller was thinking of pressing 500 copies, Travis insisted he should be looking at 2000.

"A journalist from Sounds called Jane Suck picked up the single from Rough Trade and apparently liked it so much she did a review calling it 'Single Of The Century'," recalled Miller. The review ran with a picture of the test pressing, Seymour Stein from Sire was inspired to release it in the US and Miller began to meet like-minded electronic fans like Cabaret Voltaire, Throbbing Gristle and Robert Rental. A journey had begun.

"Less a pop record," claims This Is Uncool, "more a visionary dipping a first toe in the water, The Normal's one and only single remains one of Britpop's most startling and accomplished records".

Almost out of necessity, Mute Records quickly became a home for electronic sounds. Miller's synth pop vision Silicon Teens followed with revamped cover versions, the mysterious Fad Gadget honed his performance art, German trio D.A.F. joined the label and, in 1981, Depeche Mode, with all their backwoods Basildon bravado were added to the roster. A new generation of electronic music had begun, and it all started with a homage to JG Ballard's 'Crash'.

155

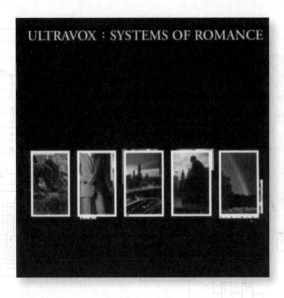

ULTRAVOX
Systems Of Romance
Original release: 1978
ISLAND RECORDS

Tracklisting:
Slow Motion, I Can't Stay Long, Someone Else's Clothes, Blue Light, Some of Them, Quiet Men,
Dislocation, Maximum Acceleration, When You Walk Through Me, Just For A Moment

Ultravox! (note the exclamation mark, which was dropped in 1978) arrived in the punk maelstrom
of late 1976, playing deep, cerebral pop. Their debut, self-titled album featured the tell-tale
hallmarks of futurist thinking in 'I Want To Be A Machine' and the robotic 'My Sex', which had an
alarming frigidity to its delivery. Their follow up album, 'Ha! Ha! Ha!', saw them embrace synth
melancholy in a more Roxy Music-inspired 'For Your Pleasure' way, as their sound was broadened
with drum machines and an ARP Odyssey. The single from the same period, the rambunctious
'Young Savage', was an exuberant piece of electronic punk, but it was their third album, 'Systems
Of Romance', recorded at Conny Plank's studio in Germany, which really singled the band out.

By this point, the group had become far more focussed, and the themes of alienation and the
proto-industrial feel to their sound, which was powered by Roland TR-77 and ARP-created
rhythms, gave them an enormously filmic sense of seriousness. It was a heavy experience, and
one which led to the band's splitting and singer Jonn Foxx working on completely electronic
projects. His debut solo album, 'Metamatic', takes the ideas of 'Systems of Romance' a step
further out there.

'Systems Of Romance' is often singled out as one of the key influences on the emerging new
romantic scene, which was to feature predominantly the new line up of Ultravox, with Midge

Ure, most notably on the huge electronic pop epic ' Vienna', the dramatic soundcsape of which was seen by some as a clinical reshaping of the themes and spine tingling bleakness of parts of 'Systems Of Romance'.

ORCHESTRAL MANOEUVRES IN THE DARK
Electricity
Original release: 1979
FACTORY RECORDS

As the decade drew to a close, electronic music had become an inspirational force that was poised to be radio-friendly, chart-topping and a sweet antidote to punk's muscular explosion. Punk had unleashed the new wave, allowing timely makeovers for pub rockers, old school folkies, recharged rock acts, stylish singer songwriters and bedroom synth players.

In 1979, the Nashville Rooms was a new wave friendly pub at the end of North End Road, serving Fuller's beer and hosting inventive bills from the burgeoning scene. In the punk heyday, Eddie And The Hot Rods, The Gorillas, northern soul legend Major Lance, the Pistols, Buzzcocks, Stranglers, Rezillos and a host of others had crammed the sweaty venue, but on August 13th 1979 there wasn't even room to breathe at an early Factory Records' night headlined by Joy Division, who were supported by a drummerless A Certain Ratio and openers Orchestral Manoeuvres In The Dark, a drum machine-powered duo who exuded quirky pop melodies over an austere but melodic set of tunes.

After the exuberance of the punk explosion, bands in '79 seemed intent on reinventing the wheel, plundering all that had gone before and making it speak to the masses in simple, three minute blasts. Gone was the pomposity of prog rock, and everything seemed to be fresh and new. Of course, hindsight tells us otherwise, but seeing OMD, bottom of a bill that was dark and powerful, simply reinforced the fact that this was the greatest time for music, and the band's perky, upbeat singer, Andy McCluskey had an innocence that made them seem all the more special.

McCluskey played bass and sang while his partner in crime, Paul Humphreys, played keyboards and a TEAC 4-track, christened 'Winston' after the character in George Orwell's 1984, delivered further layers and keyboard and drum machine flourishes. The duo had collaborated as VCL XI (named after something written on the back of Kraftwerk's 'Radio-Activity' album sleeve) after their original band, The Id (pure sci-fi stuff), had floundered. McClusky briefly left to front the short-lived, but much loved, Dalek, I Love You (Dr Who references, of course), before reuniting with Humphreys and changing their name to Orchestral Manoeuvres In The Dark. Quite plainly, their path to this point, and their debut single, 'Electricity', was steeped in electronic noise and futuristic visions, something that future releases would capitalise on as they charted big all over the world.

Their debut single for Factory failed to chart, but from the rolling modal synth beginning, driving rhythm through and McCluskey's easy vocal made for one of those new wave nuggets, wrapped in a typically austere Peter Saville sleeve, that made 1979 sound wonderfully new and innovative. Ultimately, OMD would sign to Virgin offshoot Dindisc and work closely with gifted producer Martin Hannett. However, the original Factory 45 featured the band's demo version of 'Electricity', a version that just pulses with a kind of euphoria seemingly at loggerheads with its setting.

"OMD were the runts of the runts of the post-punk Liverpool litter," Q's Danny Ecceleston reasoned when reviewing their best of… package in 1998, pointing out that the duo were "regularly scorned by the McCullochs and Copes for their blatant unrockness, but their longevity as a hit making entity demands respect". Indeed, it does, and the non-charting 'Electricity' still sounds decidedly awesome today.

THE HUMAN LEAGUE
Reproduction
Original release: October 1979
VIRGIN RECORDS

Tracklisting:
Almost Medieval, Circus Of Death, The Path Of Least Resistance, Blind Youth, The Word Before Last, Empire State Human, Morale… You've Lost That Lovin' Feeling, Austerity/Girl One (medley), Zero As A Limit

Additional tracks on the 1987 CD release:
Introducing, (original B side of the 'Empire State Human' single), The Dignity Of Labour part one, The Dignity Of Labour part two, The Dignity Of Labour part three, The Dignity Of Labour part four, Flexidisc (originally given away as a flexidisc with copies of 'The Dignity Of Labour' 12-inch on Fast Records), Being Boiled (original Fast Records 45), Circus Of Death (original Fast Records 45 B side)

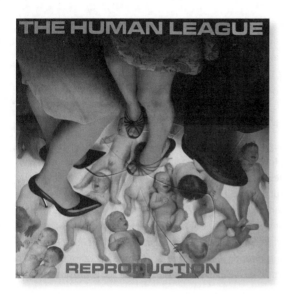

In the bleary, angst-ridden late '70s, the charts had been overtaken by the filth and the fury of The Sex Pistols, which opened the floodgates for a blizzard of DIY idealism that had offered the refreshing concept of everybody getting up and doing it themselves. By 1979, however, Johnny Rotten had morphed into John Lydon, and Public Image Limited, with its Krautrock hum and off-kilter lyricism, moved the goalposts yet further. Suddenly, the rules of engagement for the new wave began to embrace everything from power pop to wanton experimentalism.

Lydon's view counted, and when he guest reviewed singles for NME, his first impression of The Human League led to him dismiss the trio as "trendy hippies". His reaction came after hearing the band's debut single, 'Being Boiled', on Fast Records, an Edinburgh-based label that also boasted the Peel favourites The Mekons and The Gang Of Four. Unperturbed by Rotten's quip, The Human League soldiered on and found themselves supporting The Rezillos at The Music Machine in late 1978, a time and place which played host to new wave favourites as diverse as Killing Joke, The Only Ones, The Specials and The Cure as the decade drew to a close.

Living a short walk away in Kentish Town, The Music Machine, which later become The Camden Palace and more recently Koko, was a regular haunt of my unemployed, art school and would-be post-pop star mates at the time, and The Rezillos and their sci-fi '50s throwback sound was perfect party music. We were out in force, but completely unprepared for the awkward austerity of the support band. Phil Oakey's lop-sided haircut, two synth players in what looked like steel cages on either side of him accompanied by stark white lighting, flickering colours and strange images all made for a vision just as unique as the sound. Beer glasses flew, ricocheting off the scaffolding that surrounded Martyn Ware and Craig Marsh, but the sound was triumphant. After three years of three-chord nirvana, The Human League were truly unique.

A couple of months later, the trio were added as support to Pere Ubu's tour, and a second chance to see the band at the London College Of Printing at Elephant And Castle presented itself. Just days before Christmas, this was undoubtedly the place to be, and, having arrived early to ensure a good position, we encountered a fracas of major proportions at the door. The Human League had pulled out and several irate punters were furious with the organisers, having travelled from the group's home town for this difficult away fixture. David Bowie was luckier later in the month, encountering the band live and telling the NME that he had seen "the future of pop music", a remark that added new kudos to their status.

The Human League story had begun in 1977, when computer operator Martyn Ware and friend Craig Marsh saved up to buy a Korg 770S synthesizer. Dabbling with its swirls of sound they were asked to play at a mate's party, where, legend has it, they delivered a fine version of the Dr Who theme. Billed as The Dead Daughters, their different approach to music attracted a third synth player and, very briefly, another Sheffield native, Adi Newton. Demos were recorded and the Daughters were renamed The Future, but this incarnation proved short-lived and Newton quickly left to form the influential and much overlooked Clock DVA. His replacement was the unproven Philip Oakey. Another name change was deemed necessary, and The Human League was borne, the name coming from the game Starforce: Alpha Centauri. Early live shows in their native Sheffield were minimal in frequency and attendance, but one of Oakey's schoolmate's, Philip Wright, was added to the line up as 'director of visuals' in an effort to add some presence.

Oakey's first lyrics became their debut single for Fast, the evocative 'Being Boiled', and as presentation, style and the decade changed, the band set about recording a follow up EP. Several major labels had become intrigued by just how different The Human League might be, making this the perfect time, of course, to add further confusion to proceedings.

In April 1979, a second release, 'The Dignity Of Labour', materialised as a 12-inch single on Fast, with a free flexidisc in initial pressings. This was different, a much darker confection with an industrial grey cover depicting an image of Russian cosmonaut Yuri Gagarin on his return to earth. The four tracks were all instrumentals loosely related to the heroic space mission, while the flexidisc features the band members discussing what should be on the flexidisc, the conversation cantering around the John Carpenter movie 'Dark Star' and what they should do as a homage to it.

Through the passing of time since 1979, my original copy of 'The Dignity Of Labour' evaporated, but a few years back I picked up a copy in a record shop in Somerset for £3. The inner sleeve had a review glued to it, written by Oliver Lowenstein (founder and editor In Chief of 'The Fourth Door Review', a publication that concentrates on design, new media, music, art, philosophy and theatre).

"The Human League are very different from what preceded them. Another drummerless electronic showband, their equipment out on HP, from the bowels of Sheffield, they are a band with a fine perception of financial acumen. A passive and professional pop package, perhaps even a knowingly contrived, and thus ironical, stab at the supposed insular austerity of electronic music. The medium's very own Tubes? Who knows? The immediacy of their visual hardware – the Star Trek slide show; the glass cage for one of the synthesiser musicians, the lead singer's haircut, the immensely posed utilisation of their instrumentation – does lead one to suspect an amused but playfully subtle brand of satire at work... Krautrock with a smile? Of course, this could all be a serious thing. They may well believe that they're rather pretty, but an excessively derivative hybrid of post-Kraftwerk/Tomita electronic disco noise is as important as it is innovative".

The Human League in 1979 were an enigma. While cerebral comment was garnered from 'The Dignity Of Labour', the band's live shows were also attracting praise from a much more mainstream source. 'Smash Hits', which, back in the day, covered everyone from Costello and The Lurkers to the banal and the ridiculous, enthused in October 1979, "With their amazing slideshow, strong melodic songs, warm good humour and an intriguing all-synthesiser line-up, Sheffield's excellent Human League will certainly be among the leaders of the '80s. Greatness is inevitable – be the first one on your block, etc".

More recently, Q's special edition on 'The Story Of Electro-Pop' featured a number of essential albums, including The Human League's 'Reproduction'. Stuart Maconie's lengthy review acclaimed its eclectic mix of styles in the marker "it was steely, northern, witty... but marinaded in disco, glam and pop". The review goes on to name check Roxy Music, The Glitter Band's pounding rhythms and Abba, along with previous synth masters such as Tangerine Dream, Kraftwerk and the dabbling Bowie, and to recall that, on its release, latter day red top journalist Garry Bushell, then at weekly inkie 'Sounds', wrote a review where he pretended to be an alien. But, truth be told, no-one knew what to make of 'Reproduction' when it was first released. Britain was gripped in post punk rebellion, a Jackson Pollock-powered surge of free thinking and often stupid excitement. By contrast, The Human League were tempered, ironic, intelligent and dangerously witty. The play off of Oakey's naïve northern character set against the austerity of Marsh and Ware's electronic vision were the key to this debut set. It didn't sell well on initial release.

Maconie acclaimed 'Empire State Human' as a "Weimar cabaret nursery rhyme", while noting that the album contains no "futuristic guff" as it samples speech as diverse as prime minister Jim Callaghan and Hawaii Five-O's Steve McGarrett, mixing humorous asides with tales of dehumanisation and a call for the punk rebellion to lighten up on the churning 'Blind Youth'. The All Music Guide, however, dismisses 'Reproduction' as a "set of grim, rigid tracks that revealed a greater lack of humanity than even Kraftwerk," concluding that "It's a surprise that the Human league hit the British charts at all with the single 'Empire State Human', since this could well be the most detached synth pop record ever released".

The jury was out, but at least everyone was talking about The Human League, The Undertones' 1980 pop hit 'My Perfect Cousin' even lambasted their arty approach and different musical palette: "His mother bought him a synthesiser/Got the Human League in to advise her/Now he's making lots of noise/Playing along with the art school boys/Phillip's trying to attract his attention/But what a shame - it's in vain - total rejection".

'Reproduction' didn't make a huge impact at the time and, as we know, later incarnations of The Human league appealed to a far wider audience, but, without doubt, it is a seminal work, which listening to again over 30 years later is remarkably rewarding.

From the zoned out metronome fade-in to its pounding, primal chant, 'Almost Medieval' is a claustrophobic drive into alienation. The mood rolls through spacey synths and high end melodies, lifting Oakey's vocal while the drudging bass synth and incessant drum machine make the song an almost celebratory piece of time travel with a sense of Victorian melodrama creeping into proceedings. The following 'Circus Of Death' underlines the feeling of being third party, twice removed as the TV channel is switched to the intro of 'Hawaii Five-O' and the cascading synths pull on a futuristic news story that's as much a cold grey day in Sheffield as it is an out-take from The League Of Gentlemen's disturbed Royston Vasey, with it's freaky clowns powered by the deadpan rhetoric Oakey intones about the drug Dominion. Two tracks in, and the landscape is bleak, morbid and mesmerising.

There's a sense of austerity about 'The Path Of Least Resistance', but the lyrics are far more mundane, again harking back to their northern environment and a period where the government of the day was reeling from post-Jubilee hopelessness and the nation had become Londoncentric and directionless. It was grim up north and the sentiment that "self belief's the answer and not another drink" was everything that Alan Bleasdale's 'Boys From The Blackstuff' would reveal on TV in 1982. 'Blind Youth' follows, with its forced march pace and a stab at the "No Future" ethos of punk, throwing in one liners about high rise living and inner city living as the frog marching rhythm and simple synth melody prove an ironic foil for Oakey's "things ain't so bad" sentimentality. After these pop-paced beginnings, the original side one ended with 'The Word Before Last', a thoughtful monologue that reads like a diary entry from the last man on earth.

Side two begins with the single, the momentous 'Empire State Human', which didn't chart on its initial release in 1979 and only scraped in at 62 in the UK a year later when re-issued. But it is a great lost hit, as Garry Mulholland recalled in 'This Is Uncool': "Over a martial electronica inspired more by Ron Grainer's 'Dr Who' theme than Kraftwerk, Oakey regales us with a first-person child's story about wanting to be the tallest person in the land". The playfulness of the Human League is perfectly evident, as Mulholland continues, "Oakey drops to a bluff spoken word to tell us that he has willed himself to become "fourteen storeys high", and a set of chipmunk voices add: "At least!"". He concludes his review with the theory that 'Empire State Human' is "the best example of that old music-hack cliché: the huge hit in a parallel universe".

At over nine minutes, 'Morale... You've Lost That Lovin' Feeling' is an ironic fusion of an almost filmic description of hopelessness that collapses into a cabaret croon of The Righteous Brothers' 'You've Lost That Lovin' Feeling', interpreted as if it's being sung in a downtown bar on a minor Star Wars planet. Stuart Maconie acclaimed 'Morale...' as "a cracked, agonised interior monologue from an old man at the end of his tether". There's a forceful frankness to it, a sense of a tortured soul that's magnified by the blue-eyed soul of the Righteous Brothers' tune that's delivered over a tinny click track that sounds like a milk bottle's ring. The effect is haunting as the song builds to what is a crescendo of uplifting soulful power that is well known for its popularity as a drunken closing time howler mistreated by generations. The Human League, of course, underplay it and add as much pathos as possible.

If 'You've Lost That Lovin' Feeling' has all the twee innocence of a classic love song, as written by Phil Spector along with the Brill Building's Mann and Weill, then the League's self-penned tale of everyday awry lifestyles, parental pressure, youth and madness, 'Austerity/Girl One (medley)', is like an out-take from a seriously disturbed play for today, a confusing tale that leads neatly into the car crash slow build of the closing cut 'Zero As A Limit', which has plenty of the JG Ballard about its sci-fi content. Indeed, it's graphic storyline is almost a precursor to the emotive video shoot that would signal The Human League's eventual rival as a globally successful pop act with 'Don't You Want Me'.

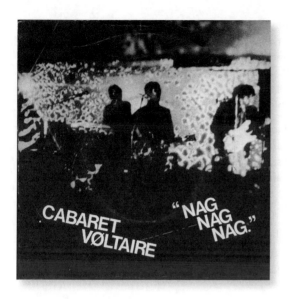

CABARET VOLTAIRE
Nag Nag Nag
Original release: 1979
ROUGH TRADE

The Human league painted an austere picture of their native Sheffield, which fellow steel city residents Cabaret Voltaire made much darker.

In an early correspondence to a German fanzine, the band's Richard H Kirk prepared a few notes about their beginnings. "CV came about by mutual interest in producing sounds rather than music, making very rare appearances from time to time. Now an interest has developed in the band, we are playing live more frequently instead of just recording. CV dislike the sick commercialism which pervades contemporary music".

I first met Cabaret Voltaire at Western Works in Sheffield, their cold studio set up above a sewing machine-powered clothes production warehouse. Richard, Mal and Chris Watson had managed to take their cultural reference points, 'A Clockwork Orange', Eno, reportage footage, old soul music, Kraftwerk and William Burroughs and fuse them into much more.

As the story was told, they'd wanted to play music like Motown but it came out completely different - they couldn't really play, and what little they had available to play on made them sound nothing like what they'd expected, and nothing like anybody else. Richard Kirk's exploratory echoed guitar and clarinet, Mal's heavy bass and effected vocals and Chris Watson's synth and tape loops created an eerie soundtrack. Their debut EP and early cassette-only recordings veered away from mainstream and, in many cases, traditional forms of song. Even when they covered The Velvet Underground's 'No Escape', the rhythms overtook everything, making for a throbbing and disorientating version.

Their first recordings arrived on Factory Records' 'Factory Sample' EP and on their own EP for Rough Trade, but their first single proper, the anthemic 'Nag Nag Nag', pulled all of their disparate elements together and crammed them into a glorious slice of industrial dance music – as long as the dance was pretty basic. Sounding like a wicked uncle's take on the nursery rhyme pastoral joy of Pink Floyd's 'See Emily Play', 'Nag Nag Nag' was brooding, brash and completely beguiling. Live, Cabaret Voltaire took things even further.

"At the moment we are working on a basis which involves two types of performance," Kirk told the German fanzine, "A "set" of songs, and a set which is completely improvised, lasting from 20 minutes to "x" number of hours. CV also use slides and films as lighting in live performance. A CV concert is like a bad acid trip. CV want to create total sensory derangement".

Memorably, some time after 'Nag Nag Nag', the band headlined a Rough Trade night - one of their last with the label - at Club Foot, which was above Hammersmith tube station. Earlier in the evening, pint glasses had been left on the tables that the PA sat on and when the band opened with 'This Is Entertainment', the thudding rhythm sent the glasses off the edge onto the floor with every telling beat, like explosive lemmings, the sound of breaking glass proving to be the perfect noise to accompany their tongue-in-cheek anthem.

Cabaret Voltaire were about extremes, but the Rough Trade singles, 'Silent Command' and 'Seconds Too Late', that followed 'Nag Nag Nag', and the magnificent trio of albums 'Mix Up', 'The Voice Of America' and 'Red Mecca' were magnificent collisions of three inspired ideas people. Following 'Red Mecca', Chris Watson left to work at Tyne Tees and concentrate on his own natural recordings, of which he has released many through Touch, even ending up on the cover of Wire magazine in 2010.

Richard and Mal picked up a Roland sponsorship while on tour with Japan, wound up on Virgin via Some Bizzare and produced a string of thumping electronic dance tracks that their new found technology allowed. They fashioned industrial dance music, dabbled in IDM and influenced, and were influenced by, various emerging US-generated dance genres. They never had a hit record, their subject matter and vocal embellishments never allowing, and their choice of rhythm over melody often made their output more esoteric than radio programmers might have liked. That said, they remain one of the most under rated electronic music acts to emerge during the '70s.

THROBBING GRISTLE
Hot On The Heels Of Love
Original release: 1979
INDUSTRIAL RECORDS

Cabaret Voltaire's early, more obscure and less rhythmic recordings appeared on the vast Industrial Records cassette-only release schedule, as did much Richard H Kirk solo material. The label also boasted '24 Hours Of Throbbing Gristle', a set of twenty four tapes of their live performances. The Industrial label flirted with all kinds of dysfunctional people, whether in bands or as enthusiasts, but the engine for the whole enterprise was Throbbing Gristle and their strange mix of personalities.

Genesis P. Orridge was a gruff vocalist and bass player who'd come from performance art circles with fellow student and latter-day exotic dancer Cosey Fanni Tutti, who played so-called "satellite" guitar. They teamed up with Abba-loving electronics whiz Chris Carter and Hipgnosis designer and tape and sound manipulator Peter 'Sleazy' Christopherson, to create early music which was extreme and challenging. The live arena quickly proved the perfect environment for the extreme reactions their mix of noise and anthemic rhetoric brought out in people.

By the end of 1977, alongside the slew of live cassettes, came their 'The Second Annual Report' set, comprised of live and studio recordings which would later be released with the tapes playing backwards. 'DoA', from 1978, included songs about the war wounded, disease and sexual tension. People were shocked, awed, amazed and confused by Throbbing Gristle, but everyone had a reaction.

With that in mind, their third album, the misleadingly titled '20 Jazz Funk Greats', was a staggering hybrid of Carter's tuneful keyboard melodies, a homage to Martin Denny, tales of the mundane and the erotic. The mood was accessible, the sound electronic and upbeat and the subject matter inevitably subversive. Again, it shocked people for its accessibility.

Side two's opening track, 'Hot On The Heels Of Love' was a rolling, melodic, sequenced melody, complimented by vocoder voices, synthetic whipping sounds and Cosey's sensual whispered vocal, and topped with floating melody lines. It sounded like Kraftwerk with a sense of humour and pre-empted a whole host of Euro dance music that would emerge as the '80s unfolded. Urgent, vital and a must hear.

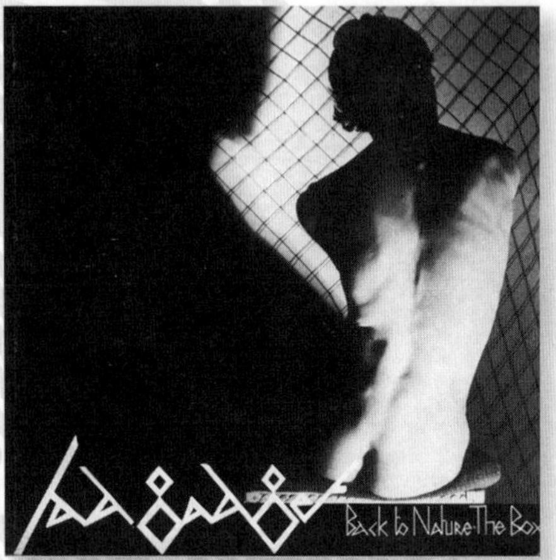

FAD GADGET
Back To Nature
Original release: 1979
MUTE RECORDS

After the success of The Normal's debut single, Mute received a number of demo tapes, including a cassette by Frank Tovey, aka Fad Gadget, who, armed with a Korg keyboard and Korg Mini Pops drum machine, had created a disturbing minimal swirl of sound laced with black humour and odd subject matter.

"Daniel wanted to turn my tape into an album, but I couldn't be bothered," the late Tovey recalled on his website, "So I let him do it".

The duo entered the RMS studio and re-recorded 'Back To Nature' and 'The Box', which became the first Fad Gadget single. Both tracks are filled with synthesisers, distorted keyboards and simple drum patterns, and the release, on Mute, became a huge inspiration for latter day Depeche Mode, Yazoo and Erasure songwriter Vince Clark.

The Fad/Frank sound was a hypnotic mix of analogue rhythms and keyboard flourishes, but it was his deadpan vocal delivery that really captured the imagination, and his lyrics added an offbeat view of the world. "They spoke for and against the little man," NME's Bib Kopf opined, "the ubiquitous civilian bewildered by the speed of events threatening to sweep him up or leave him behind".

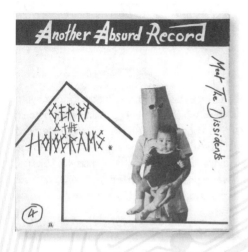

GERRY AND THE HOLOGRAMS
Gerry And The Holograms
Original release: 1979
ABSURD RECORDS

If Fad Gadget's worldview was a scary, rabbit-in-the-headlights super reality, then Gerry And The Holograms' self-titled electronic opus was its glass full-to-overflowing alter ego. When Frank Zappa was asked to play his top 20 songs on Radio One in 1980, he spun the disc – check it out on Youtube - it featured on Diplo's Santogold remix album and still sits on the internet as a thing of mystery, one site heralding the slowly pulsing, multi-layered tune, akin to having The Residents over for tea, and several people claiming that it sounds like the basis, when sped up, of New Order's 'Blue Monday'.

Gerry And The Holograms was created by John Scott and CP Lee of Alberto Y Los Trios Paranoias and emerged on Absurd with a string of hard to find 45s by similarly daft outfits such as Bet Lynch's Legs, The Dissidents and 48 Chairs. Undoubtedly created as a piss-take of emerging DIY synth music, it failed to ignite the world but remains a classic slice of simple sludgy electronic music, and an absolute gem.

SPIZZENERGI
Where's Captain Kirk?
Original release: 1979
ROUGH TRADE

While Gerry And The Holograms toyed with space age eclecticism, Spizz refined his frantic synth pop into the glorious 'Where's Captain Kirk?', a single which John Peel acclaimed as the best "Star Trek record ever", thrust him onto Top Of The Pops. Previously, as Spizzoil, he'd been a kazoo-toting vocalist with Pete Petrol on vitriolic guitar but as Spizzenergi he'd grabbed the nation's attention with this poignant 45. Spizz would later become Athletico Spizz 80, Spizzles, Spizzenergi 2 and just plain old Spizz but he'd never repeat the excitement of 'Kirk', a daft but loveable synth-powered slice of sci fi fanaticism that still raises a smile 30 years later.

THE FLYING LIZARDS
Money
Original release: 1979
VIRGIN RECORDS

Years after the fact, 'Q' magazine posed the question "Where are they now?" of The Flying Lizards. Martin Aston hailed them as creators of the "deadpan, art-pop reconstruction of classic covers before everyone's dad started having a go", and The Lizards were indeed that. They originally charted in 1978 with a version of Barrett Strong's 'Money', a squeaky and ultimately catchy take on the Motown and Beatles' standard, and their shtick was to place groovy tunes we all knew and loved into strange environments. But, as 'Q' stated, by the late '70s everyone was up to that same trick, and the Flying Lizards disappeared.

Main man David Cunningham revealed, "Some covers are done so badly, it gets me so annoyed". But the advent of samplers had moved the goalposts, and Cunningham decided to head off in new directions with former Henry Cow guitarist John Grieves, while sweetly monosyllabic and unshakeable vocalist Deborah Evans, who sang on much of the Lizards' oeuvre, fell out with Cunningham and suffered the ultimate insult of having her unique vocal mimicked by a replacement Deborah on the band's final album.

Were they just a clever art joke? Early incarnations included contributions from music experimentalists Robert Fripp, David Toop and Steve Beresford, but the likes of 'Money' were something completely different, and, as the band slowly diffused, their 1981 album 'Fourth Wall' arrived with even more exotica intact. The single from the set, a cover of Curtis Mayfield's 'Move On Up', was quirky enough, but the likes of 'Glide' showed that The Flying Lizards had life way beyond novelty.

STEVIE WONDER
Journey Through The Secret Life Of Plants
Original release: 1979
TAMLA MOTOWN RECORDS

Tracklisting:
Earth's Creation, The First Garden, Voyage To India, Same Old Story, Venus Fly Trap And The Bug, Ai No Sono, Seasons, Power Flower, Send One Your Love, Race Babbling, Send One Your Love, Outside My Window, Black Orchid, Ecclesiastes, Kesse Ye Lolo De Ye, Come Back As A Flower, A Seed's A Star/Tree Medley, The Secret Life Of Plants, Tree, Finale

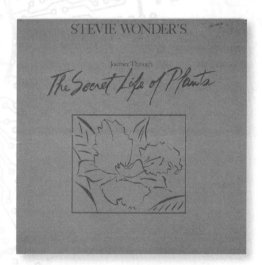

After a hugely successful run of albums, Stevie Wonder accidentally confounded fans and critics alike with the release of this staggering album. Created as the soundtrack to a documentary about plants, it was a double album of instrumental music that delved deep into the studio, utilising strange combinations of synthesised music. Sure, there's not a hit single here, but there never was intended to be one. Instead this is a much overlooked buried treasure, an electronic album that is, of course, an oddity in the discography of Stevie Wonder but no less a classic in all its multi-layered beauty.

Stevie was well versed in the complexities and possibilities of the studio, and he'd used electronic effects and keyboards on many of his groundbreaking cuts from 'Talking Book' and 'Innervisions', but 'Journey Through The Secret Life Of Plants' was something else altogether. Allowed to create a mood for visuals, which he'd obviously never be able to see, the pieces here are filled with gorgeous textures and magnificent flourishes in sound. Freed of the limitations of song structure, 'Journey Through The Secret Life Of Plants' has a unique sound that still retains some of the Motown groove in places, and the use of the first sampling synth, the Music Melodian, added new possibilities to the set and gave it a truly different sound.

YELLOW MAGIC ORCHESTRA
Solid State Survivor
Original release: 1979
ALFA

Tracklisting:
Technopolis, Absolute Ego Dance, Rydeen, Castalia, Behind The Mask, Day Tripper, Insomnia, Solid State Survivor

Conceived as one-off studio project by bass player Haruomi Hosono in 1978, with the idea of producing an electronic version of the rich exotica sounds of tiki-inspired band leader Martin Denny, The Yellow Magic Orchestra became a going concern following the excitement surrounding a Fuji cassette ad and the music they supplied for it. With Ryuichi Sakomoto on keyboards, the trio (completed by drummer and vocalist Yukihiro Takahashi) became as big as The Beatles in their native Japan, inspiring everything from record sales to the haircuts of respected businessmen.

Their second album filtered out to the rest of the world but never gained a full release at the time, and the hipper electronic fans who came upon it were suitably enthused by 'Solid State Survivor's Kraftwerk-styled inspiration and Roxy Music-paced wit.

"At their best," Q's Sam King pointed out in reviewing the 1982 re-issue, "they represented the genre's earliest attempts to reinvent itself, blending a wicked sense of irony with music that goes beyond simply playing rock on a keyboard. This is a highly inventive band using cheap new technology to create a novel form of music".

Throughout the album, there are effects aplenty, as the focus remains on sequenced dance beats, and on probably the most famous track from the set, 'Rydeen', there's a bizarre interlude that sounds like an underwater army marching, with a middle-eight that's straight from a Star Trek laser shoot out. Elsewhere, there are disjointed vocals and multi-layered melody lines, and the slower 'Castalia' is a beautiful piece of Sakamoto playing, while their cover of 'Day Tripper', with its chopped up construction, sounds not unlike Devo's assault on 'Satisfaction'.

THOMAS LEER AND ROBERT RENTAL
The Bridge
Original release: 1979
INDUSTRIAL RECORDS

Tracklisting:
Attack Decay, Monochrome Days, Day Breaks, Night Heals, Connotations, Fade Away, Interferon, Six AM, The Hard Way In, The Easy Way Out, Perpetual

ROBERT RENTAL AND THE NORMAL
Live At West Runton Pavilion
Original release: 1979
ROUGH TRADE

Long before Thomas Leer became half of Act with Claudie Brucken of Propaganda, he'd been a fledgling punk, then a born-again Krautrock fan who released obscure electronic nuances, first solo on the Oblique label, then in partnership with Robert Rental, a displaced Scot who'd released a distorted Stylophone single, 'Paralysis' on his own Regular label.

The duo were brought together under the "guidance" of Throbbing Gristle's Industrial Records label, a visionary collective helmed by Genesis P. Orridge, who lent the duo and eight track which they utilised to record 'The Bridge', a slow, brooding electronic masterpiece that said as much about inner city Britain circa 1979 as the photographs of the duo on the reverse of the sleeve, fag-handed in a tower block, looking like they'd been up all night. At least.

At the time of its release, everything on Industrial seemed to possess added menace and bravura. The duo used primal analogue sources like the WASP synthesiser and delivered music of the post-technical revolution, a heady brew of doom-laden scenarios that reflected inner city life post Jubilee in Thatcher's flagging Britain.

While Leer moved on to more accessible approaches, Rental seemed troubled, releasing a single for Mute and teaming up with the label's founder and driving force Daniel Miller for a truly staggering twenty five minutes in 'Live At West Runton Pavilion', a one-sided album released on Tough Trade that goes from Throbbing Gristle-styled noise to Cabaret Voltaire layered sound to schlock tea dance jazz before returning to the kind of pulsing electronic new wavery that Miller's only 45 release as The Normal hinted at.

'The Bridge' remains a fantastically-well observed, but reasonably disturbing, sketch of inner city dysfunctionality and drug-addled hopelessness, while 'Live At West Runton Pavilion' sounds like a slice of multi-tracked psychedelic mayhem laced with half heard conversations, occasional accessible melodies and vocal interplay that could have come from the sketchbooks of The Human league, Cabaret Voltaire or even Kraftwerk born into a post-Pistols Britain.

DR MIX AND THE REMIX
I Can't Control Myself
Original release: 1979
ROUGH TRADE

Out of the revolutionary Metal Urbain, who imploded in 1979 through a general lack of interest in their native France, Dr Mix And The Remix came armed with distorted guitars and vocals mashed into a muddy synth and drum machine rhythm. They had some original songs, but it was their dissemination of the music of The Stooges, Bowie, Velvet Underground and, particularly,

The Troggs' 'I Can't Control Myself' that set them aside. Sounding like they were recording their material in a garage with a tumble dryer providing the rhythm, they were certainly different.

Metal Urbain's reputation in the UK was such that, in 1979, on the back of this single's release, they seemed like a good launch vehicle for a monthly music venue at the London Film Collective on Gloucester Avenue, near Camden's Parkway. My promoter pal and I had met the band through their friend JC, who had worked in Vivienne Westwood's Seditionaries shop on the King's Road, and despite our obvious language barrier – they spoke little English – the four piece turned up and the doors opened on what turned out to be something of a fiasco.

Metal Urbain's cult status had not been passed on to Dr Mix and Co, and the attendance was small. The band performed with all their vim and vigour nonetheless, but the sound man's attempt to perfect their drudging rhythms put him at loggerheads with them, and when they ran over time as the crowd thinned even further, he shut off the sound, which Dr Mix celebrated by trashing a couple of microphones. Separated by a generation and a musical idealism that clashed like Iggy and Rick Wakeman, the sound man took exception to their antics, causing Dr Mix to remove his studded belt and use it to pummel said sound man into submission as a shocked crowd headed for the hills.

The sound of sirens approaching brought the fracas to an end. The incensed Dr Mix and JC demanded immediate payment for the show before fleeing, and the sound man vowed to never entertain a show with mindless punk dimwits again. We decided to can the club night before ts reputation for violence and poor sound quality began to outshine it credentials for delivering new music.

Many years later, I was re-introduced to "the good doctor" at SXSW, where he was at the French Music Export stand hawking re-issues of Dr Mix And The Remix's complete recordings on Acute Records. He still had the air of a leather-jacketed, glass-rolling garage rocker. His hair was much greyer and thinning on top. The studded belt wasn't in evidence.

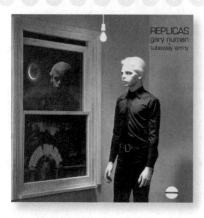

TUBEWAY ARMY
Replicas
Original release: 1979
BEGGARS BANQUET

Tracklisting:
Me! I Disconnect From You, Are Friends Electric?, The Machman, Praying To The Aliens, Down In The Park, You Are In My Vision, Replicas, It Must Have Been Years, When The Machines Rock, I Nearly Married A Human

'Q' magazine's 'History Of Synth Pop' special concluded that Gary Numan "had the perfect reference points, from futurist pop (Kraftwerk, Bowie) to post-modern sci-fi (Philip K Dick, William Burroughs), and the right personality – awkward, disconnected and fearful of the modern world".

Originally, Gary Numan's Tubeway Army had been a more orthodox punk outfit, but, searching for something more when in the studio recording their debut album in 1978, the story goes that they happened on a Mini Moog and the sci fi references, and a general feel of alienation in the songs soon began to underpin the band's sound.

The second and last Tubeway Army album followed a year later, and by then the clinical austerity of Numan's electronic sound had been perfected. "Musically, 'Replicas' was Numan's synth-pop symphony," enthused John Aizelwood, re-evaluating the album for 'Q', and even Smash Hits was suitably impressed in 1979 with the set's lead off single 'Are Friends electric?', which went to number one in the UK: "The single is a good example of what you'll find here. Strong, futuristic imagery, simple but catchy melodies and riffs, haunting synthesiser work – all strikingly delivered in distinctive fashion. Intriguing and definitely different – a good one".

Based almost entirely around the Mini Moog sound, 'Replicas' is riddled with self-doubt, bedsit angst and futuristic unease. It's effect on electronic music, on the emerging industrial scene and on thousands of student homes was enormous. The bleak worldview and the gaunt, robotic image of the sleeve became a look that was copied all over the globe, and Marilyn Manson and The Foo Fighters both covered one of the standout tracks, 'Down In The Park', in subsequent years.

Released in January 1979, 'Replicas' was followed within months by 'The Pleasure Principle', this time under the name Gary Numan. This set included the huge selling single 'Cars', a song inspired by road rage according to Numan. The album itself added Polymoog to the sound, as well as some strings, to further enhance the band's sound and the drama of the songs .

M
Pop Muzik
Original release: 1979
MCA

As the decade drew to a close, New Year's Eve parties resonated to truly different sounds to those of only a couple of years previously. Robin Scott's big hit from '79, 'Pop Muzik', seemed to sum up the mood as electronic music became mainstream. Sure, there were obscure underground elements, but the sound of synthetic strings was no longer seen as threatening and edgy, except by the musician's union.

"From its Radio Euro organ fanfare opening, through its chunky electronics and buzzing.... it makes joy out of cynicism," enthused This Is Uncool when analysing M's euphoric tune, the genesis of which was even simpler, according to Scott.

"I was looking to make a fusion of various styles which somehow would summarise the last 25 years of pop music. It was a deliberate point I was trying to make," M's mainman admitted. "Whereas rock 'n' roll had created a generation gap, disco was bringing people together on an enormous scale. That's why I really wanted to make a simple, bland statement, which was, 'All we're talking about, basically, is pop music".

Three months prior to the heralding of the '80s, all had not been so simple up in Leeds, where the first Futurama Science Fiction Festival was staged in a huge cavern-like space, the Queen's Hall. The brainchild of local promoter and new music enthusiast John Keenan, it brought together disparate factions, from Hawkwind to Public Image Ltd, as well as proving to be a seminal point in the career of Joy Division.

"Joy Division was one of the big surprises for me," recalled Keenan when interviewed by Johnny Black about the event. "They were the least glamorous band you could imagine, basically just scallies. Ian Curtis was this spotty-faced lad with a bad haircut but, on the day, that big dark, doomy hall with the echo bouncing around, was just perfect for them".

Joy Division's 'Unknown Pleasures' was three months old when the gig took place; they were already in the process of changing people's perceptions of just what the future of pop music was.

FOUR

SOUNDTRACKS, SAMPLES AND THE FRACTURED DANCEFLOOR

By 1980, electronic music wasn't shocking any more. It had been embraced by the mainstream, and the chart were rapidly filling up with electronically charged 45s all all shapes and sizes. Of course, there were still those who purposefully sought to disturb, reaching for sounds that were grating, frightening and strange, but the world and his wife were very much down with the blips and non rock 'n' rollness of it all. Any semblance of shock factor had, for the most part, departed.

Electronic music still straddled the gulf between the arty free thinkers and the arty new wavers, but the latter were on the radio, with increasing regularity. They were on 'Top Of The Pops', in all the magazines and and controlling the singles market. Back then, 12" singles in big sleeves were the key format, and as the New Romantic movement checked its reflection and the electronic pop bands arrived in Smash Hits, they were pin ups as much as pop stars. Or at least they wanted to be.

Despite this, Anarchy was still threatening, at the hands of The Angelic Upstarts and The Dead Kennedys, and what would become hardcore was brewing in the States as a reaction to the soft underbelly of new wave music. For the most part, electronic music had become associated with a fey nonchalance to the state of the world, where the haircut spoke louder than the sentiments of the tune. For many, both in the UK and around the world, this hardly reflected the realities of what they saw from their bedroom window.

It was 1980 when Prime Minster Margaret Thatcher first began to dig her heels in in the UK. By the time of Conservative Party Conference in September, she was "not for turning", and damn the consequences. Punk's attention span had all but fizzled out, and the winters of discontent were set to continue for the whole decade, it seemed. Political rhetoric in electronic music was mostly left to the hard-core extremists, but there were hints of rational thinking in even the most catchy of new pop songs....

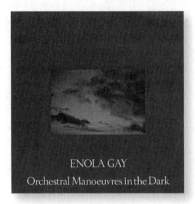

ENOLA GAY
Orchestral Manoeuvres in the Dark

ORCHESTRAL MANOEUVRES IN THE DARK
Enola Gay
Original release: 1980
DINDISC

Allegedly inspired by their former Factory labelmates Joy Division, OMD (who had, by now, been signed by Virgin subsidiary DinDisc) opened their 1980 debut album, 'Organisation', with the perfectly charming 'Enola Gay', an eminently hummable three minute song that saw singer Andy McCluskey dancing on 'Top Of The Pops' "like a happy Ian Curtis in jumpers", according to Danny Eccelston. His analysis in 'Q' of their re-issued catalogue, in 1998, recognised perfectly that every OMD song revolved around three things; "1) The theory that technology is brilliant, 2) The realisation that technology isn't brilliant, and 3) That the distance between individuals is often large". The result of the exploration of this formula was music of true melancholy, littered with three-minute slices of some of the happiest sounds ever recorded. The OMD formula in 1980 was beautifully simple.

"Enola Gay" was cheerful enough on the surface, but its lyrics were dark and ironic. A tale of remorse about the Enola Gay aircraft that dropped the first Atom Bomb – nicknamed 'Little Boy' - on Hiroshima at the end of the Second World War, this was a strange juxtaposition, posing some poignant questions on the nuclear threat, wrapped in sweet melodies. It wasn't head bangingly obvious like much of the band's leather-jacketed second wave punk competition, and OMD were roundly lambasted by the likes of Echo And The Bunnymen and A Teardrop Explodes for their lack of artiness. But, to their credit, OMD were out there putting in their ten penneth, and having a hit record into the bargain.

Later in the '80s, when Thatcher was dividing the nation further with her desire to spend more on nuclear deterrents while many were staring the three-day week in the eye, 'Enola Gay', in all its upbeat finery, was re-issued in an effort to focus people onto the issue of the day. Perhaps it was McCluskey's gyrations, or the seer numbers of the ever growing army of synthpop exponents that had arrived by then, but, whatever the lyrics and their social conscience, such a fine pop tune wasn't really going to change anything. Sadly, by that point the world just wanted to dance hypnotically and look a little like they were part of the newest wave of technologically savvy music fans.

HUMAN LEAGUE
Only After Dark
Original release: 1980
VIRGIN

While OMD had managed to break the charts, The Human League found themselves in a state of flux. Virgin were desperate to break the band, but the follow up to the 'Empire State Human' single from their debut album 'Reproduction', an EP called 'Holiday '80', was released to mixed reviews in April. Their cover of Gary Glitter's 'Rock 'n' Roll' seemed like their best stab at success, along with a cover of the Pop/Bowie Berlin period tune 'Nightclubbing', but it was another cover version, 'Only After Dark' – which was originally featured on Bowie guitarist Mick Ronson's solo album 'Slaughter On Tenth Avenue' - that was slated for release a month later, to let people preview their developing sound.

The track was taken from their upcoming second album 'Travelogue', but when Virgin did an about face and re-issued 'Empire State Human', with the first 15,000 copies coming with 'Only After Dark' given away free, relationships with the label and within the band began to dissolve. 'Only After Dark' added little to the Human League myth. Here was a band that just couldn't sell records in huge amounts. Live, they filled Hammersmith Palais at the end of May, supported by former Fast labelmates The Scars and special guests Athletico Spizz 80, but the mood from the stage was tense, and within months Craig Marsh and Martyn Ware left the band to form the British Electric Foundation and, in turn, Heaven 17.

CABARET VOLTAIRE
Three Mantras
Original release: 1980
ROUGH TRADE

If The Human League were aiming to cross over into the mainstream, fellow Sheffield experimentalists Cabaret Voltaire, with their vocodered vocals and echoey guitars cascading over primitive drum machines, were heading for somewhere else entirely. Following their Rough Trade single, 'Silent Command', they unleased 'Three Mantras', a 12-inch which, confusingly, featured just two songs, both of which clocked in at over 20 minutes in length.

'Eastern Mantra' was a Chris Watson powered cut-up of tapes and effects, some recorded in a market in Jerusalem, with added percussion by John Clayton – it was a bold, strange and exotic piece. By contrast, 'Western Mantra' was a frantic drum-machine driven piece of electronic dance music. Its incessant rhythm, Watson's synth melodies and Mal's pumping bass allowed the vocal and Richard Kirk's guitar to thrash and soar above the dense mix, which utilised an Eastern-styled motif as its anchor. With instruments feeding back, Mal's vocal panning across the stereo picture and overheard loops of dialogue dropping in and out of the overall texture, 'Western Mantra' was something close to the Cabaret Voltaire live experience, a trippy, psychedelic rollercoaster that sounded like Can on speed.

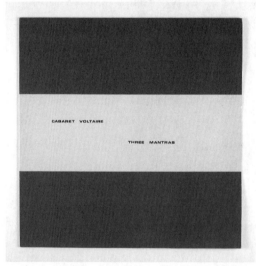

It was the sound of three people making a unified whole and, like a machine running its course, it could have gone on for hours. In twenty minutes, Cabaret Voltaire had successfully destroyed the very structure of traditional pop music. There were no verses, choruses and middle eights, just the multi-layered pulse of seemingly dozens of looped pieces coagulating into one, only to disappear again.

CHROME
New Age
Original release: 1980
BEGGARS BANQUET

San Francisco's Chrome had been around since 1976. Inspired by Iggy Pop And The Stooges
and fellow disenchanted speaker shredders, they'd originally juggled with feedback and noise,
but by the time they got to their third album, 1979's 'Half Machine Lip Moves', their gritty rock
sound was littered with the swirls and churning sounds of synths and sequencers seemingly left
running whilst the band wandered off to the bar.

Fortunately, the album was picked up for UK release, and the single 'New Age' was released as
a taster. It was a synthesised three minute slice of layered melodies, with dialogue and vocals
added seemingly as an afterthought to increase the sense of the unusual. Like Cabaret Voltaire's
'Three Mantras', 'New Age' had a throbbing groove, with proper drums and previously unheard
'stuff' going on that sounded damn strange to these young(er) ears.

In places,the mother album sounded as though someone had cut up some of the master tapes
and re-edited the thing to make it more disjointed. But it was the chugging guitar rhythms and
backbeat drums of 'New Age', all set behind a squealing guitar and a vocal performance that
sounded like it was being delivered by a man who'd swallowed the varispeed control as tape
loops passed through him, which caught the attention. What exactly was being said was hard to
define, and the general air of chaotic disharmony on 'New Age' certainly had a touch of the dark
side to it, but in that particular field, there were none darker than Throbbing Gristle...

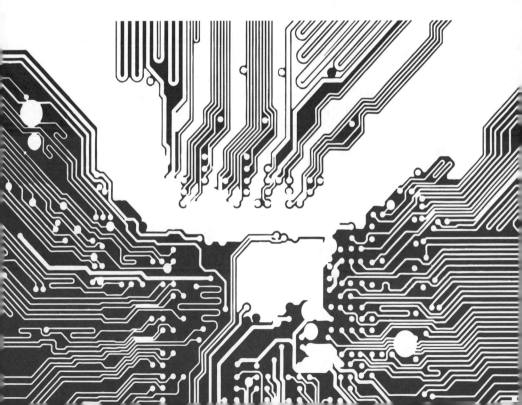

DISTANT DREAMS (PART TWO)
TG   IR0015
INDUSTRIAL RECORDS LTD.

THROBBING GRISTLE
Distant Dreams (Part Two)
Original release: 1980
INDUSTRIAL

If Throbbing Gristle had teased with 'Hot On The Heels Of Love' on '20 Jazz Funk Greats', then the follow up album, 'Heathen Earth', recorded live at their studio space, had offered yet another, still incomplete, insight into their personality. Featuring a live set that mixed ambient passages with some battered electronic assaults, 'Heathen Earth' was a stark counterpoint to '20 Jazz Funk Greats' and it's more accessible, sliced and diced tracks. This was TG off the leash, then, stepping out of the confines of order and traditional structure.

As ever, the quartet wouldn't follow it up in any kind of expected manner. Instead, the gatefold sleeve of 'Heathen Earth' was a precursor to two seven-inch singles housed in black and white bags with camouflage printed plastic covers. Both singles were released on the same day, with each track reflecting a different band member.

'Distant Dreams (Part Two)' was on the flipside of 'Adrenalin', and its predominant use of a synthesiser, with a gorgeous floating melody over a simple bass riff, was undoubtedly the work of Chris Carter, the band's electronic inventor. With the spoken words of Genesis P. Orridge heavily effected, there pervaded a sense of tension, offset by the joyous nature of the synthesised melodies. But, whereas Orchestral Manoeuvres In The Dark's upbeat tunesmanship negated their message on 'Enola Gay', Throbbing Gristle's claustrophobia was given added depth when set against the lush layered keyboards. Whichever way you cut it, there was something quite hypnotic about 'Distant Dreams (Part Two)'. Almost transcendental in places, and a vital reflection of the group's position at that time.

ROBERT SCHROEDER
Floating Music
Original release: 1980
INNOVATIVE COMMUNICATION

Tracklisting:
Floating Music, Divine My Future, Pastime, Out Of Control, Visions, Mediation For The Next Part, Shadows In The Night, Rotary Motion

German magazine 'Musik Express' described the second album by Robert Schroeder as "Music like a look into the deep black night, into the glowing blue eyes of a pretty woman, into a glass full of fiery red wine, for a jaunt through the countryside, for resting out in the open.....". They had a way with words, these journalists.

'Floating Music' was released on Klaus Schulze's Innovative, independent Communication label. "At least we are independent," Schulze explained on the sleeve. "I prefer it this way," he enthused, before he went on to explain that 'Floating Music' was Schroeder's second album, the first having been rated as one of the best albums of the previous year, where it was acclaimed as having a "harmonic transcendental sound".

Expectations were high for album number two, and Schulze openly admitted that, as the producer of the project, the new work was so complete that it defied the laws of real time recording, revealing that, "the album plays at 45rpm but, if you have the inclination you can play it at 33rpm with a different effect".

Schroeder, for his part, didn't impart any words of wisdom on the sleeve, but it's well known that he took the timeless nature of the piece and created the "artificial head" concept of recording music, which he utilised in 1985 on the soundtrack to 'Life's Abundance', producing a deep, hypnotic and extraordinarilyy spaced out sound. Two years prior to its release, in 1983, Schroeder played live at the inaugural UK Electronica festival in Milton Keynes, surely one of the most bizarre weekends imaginable.

Set in a conferencing facility in the new town, UK Electronica brought together disparate strands of a scene that was about to establish itself as the pivotal centre of heady uneasy listening. In booths, like some kind of WI convention, the likes of former Throbbing Gristle members' Chris And Cosey, Nocturnal Emissions, Attrition and several other post-industrial outfits plied their trade, while in the sterile main room new UK electronic experimentalists Ian Boddy and Ron Berry performed. On the Saturday, Schroeder headlined amid a wash of lasers, before vintage space travellers Hawkwind further confused matters by playing on the Sunday.

For Schroeder's part, it was a show without real connection. His mood music just didn't work live. In fact, one attendee reported in 'Word' magazine, still scarred years later, that it was "so dull, I actually fell asleep".

Schroeder may have lacked the dynamics of a Jean Michel Jarre, or indeed the edgy intrusions of a Klaus Schulze, but by 1983 he was enamoured by the emerging new age scene and his layered tapestry of synths was syrup-thick. For those in search of real 'Floating Music', the album was notably lacking in spectral whooshes and rhythmic passages which, if anything, highlighted how ahead of its time it was.

Listening back to it all these years later, Schroeder's two exotic suites, both of which last around eighteen minutes if played out at the correct speed, 331/3rpm, are masterful extensions of the earliest electronic music, performed as it might have been imagined by the great classical composers we skirted around in chapter one. Schroeder's interpretation was re-ordered into a symphonic sound with intricate overlaid melody lines, and 'Floating Music' was a truly evocative milestone of an album, being entirely one man's worldview, delivered only through synthesised sound.

JOHN FOXX
Underpass
Original release: 1980
METAL BEAT

Like Schroeder, John Foxx had, by 1980, become the sole survivor of his own futuristic vision. As part of Ultravox!, he'd played a part in the bringing together of numerous genres to create a unique electronic sound, but sales hadn't followed and, in 1979, the band were dropped by Island. A post-label US tour followed, but it proved to be their last in that guise and Foxx returned to the UK and a solo deal with Virgin under his own Metal Beat logo. According to Foxx, at the time he was reading too much JG Ballard and imagining himself as the "Marcel Duchamp of electro pop", a concept that must have been somewhat worrying, to say the least, to him and everyone around him.

His debut album under the new deal, 'Metamatic', was named after a painting machine designed by Jean Tinguely, and the Ballard influence was plainly evident on more than half the album's songs, which were based around cars or automation, as described by the author in his legendary book 'Crash' (the very same tome which had inspired the lyrics of The Normal's 'Warm Leatherette'). Foxx's take on Ballard's prose, as heard on the first single from the album, 'Underpass', had more than a hint of Gary Numan about it, and the minimal metallic beat of the Roland CR-78 drum machine and melody lines handled by an ARP Odyssey and an Elka string machine added complimentary dramatic depth to the single, which reached number 31 in the UK charts, one position higher than the follow up 'No-One Driving' (yet another car-related tune).

Like Numan, Foxx painted images of alienation in a future place that would be cold and decidedly grey. By contrast, within a year, Ultravox had dropped the exclamation mark, reformed with Midge Ure on vocals and released one of the biggest selling electronic singles of all time, embracing the New Romantic movement into the bargain.

ULTRAVOX
Vienna
Original release: 1981
Chrysalis

Released in January 1981, and packaged with a video that was shot on location in Kilburn, Covent Garden and, briefly, Vienna, Ultravox's signature tune became a huge turning point for synthpop. Midge Ure had replaced John Foxx and pulled the disparate parts of the band back together after a brief hiatus. When asked what he brought to the group, he legendarily quipped, "a smile", which, along with a well-coiffured moustache and an understanding of writing pop songs, he managed to turn into a multi-million selling single and album. "Midge didn't want to get too deep, and that I think was a positive thing at that time," recalled Billy Currie.

Working with Conny Plank in Germany, both band and producer decided to take the symphonic elements of some of Ultravox's earlier material and make the production even more dramatic. Bigger. Envisaging the collapse of Vienna in the 18th Century, they hit pay dirt with a grandiose coupling of violin and piano parts that had all the classicism of the old world coupled with a thumping and completely indiscrete metallic drum beat. A few ethereal, sometimes indistinct, synth lines echo in and out of the main melody, and a hit was born.

Perhaps it was by dint of the fact that 'Vienna' was, and is, one of the most played records on radio, aided by the memory of the beautifully overblown video, but the track remains an often maligned masterpiece. Slowly building behind Ure's vocal line, it's an incredibly carefully crafted slow burner, the swaggering bass synth and flashy white noise is all tempered as the song slowly moves into second gear, only adding strings to the doubled-up rhythm with just over one of its four and a half minutes remaining. As the strings soar, the bass rhythm seems hopelessly out of place and virtually evaporates before the labouring drum machine returns. For all that, as they intended, it was a monster of overblown pomposity that, unusually, seemed to spend so long arriving, just to disappear in seconds. Quite the opposite of fthe typical pop arrangement. And, of course, the range and the mix of acoustic strings and piano, combined with the electronic pulse and Ure's vocal performance, made it a goosebumps special.

Famously the song remained in the UK charts for an age (only kept off the top slot by Joe Dolce's 'Shaddapaya Face'), and topped the charts in many territories, but, ironically, only reached number eight in Austria.

DEPECHE MODE
Just Can't Get Enough
Original release: 1981
MUTE

"I had my synth for a month before I realised you could change the sound," admitted a fresh faced Martin Gore of Depeche Mode, and in 1980 the Basildon quartet were certainly wide-eyed and innocent. The huge success of 'Vienna' had instilled a sense of fashionability into synthpop, and Depeche Mode, named after a French fashion magazine, were, for all Dave Gahan's gruff Essex accent, poised to capitalise on the rise and rise of 'Smash Hits' and 'Number One' magazines and 'Top Of The Pops'' stranglehold on UK TV's musical output.
"Back then, Depeche Mode were all cherubic-faced and full of nervy swagger," former Doctors Of Madness and Cabaret Futurua organiser Richard Strange told Dave Thompson for 'Q''s Synth Pop special. But, while the glossy fortnightly publications searched for smartly attired youngsters, it was 'Sounds', the old inkie weekly. that was nurturing interest in these new futuristic sounds. The omnipresent electronic enthusiast, Stevo, was running clubs and supplying the paper with his Futurist Charts filled with the hottest new acts. Likewise, the magazine's attempt at a more music-orientated fortnightly, 'Noise!' - of which I was art editor - began to champion these new acts under the guidance of editor Betty Page.

Stevo's enthusiasm resulted in him launching the misspelt Some Bizzare Records, which debuted with a compilation that included tracks by Blancmange, The The, Soft Cell and Depeche Mode, who also bagged the support slot on an Ultravox tour and thus began to attract pop fans as well as the trendier Blitz club inhabitants.

186

At the same time, the band were touting their demo tape, ending up at Rough Trade, who suggested they talk to Daniel Miller at Mute, who was by that time developing the electronic covers band Silicon Teens. He wasn't immediately impressed, but changed his mind after seeing a live show in the East End of London. A deal was struck before the evening was out; an arrangement, in fact, that's been referred to as revolutionary in the intervening years, due to the control and percentage retained by the band.

Their debut single for Mute, 'Dreaming Of Me', peaked at 57 in the UK, while the positive, futuristic lyrics of 'New Life' thrust them onto 'Top Of The Pops', and reached number 11 in the charts. It seems inevitable, then, that the follow up, the radio-friendly 'Just Can't Get Enough', would crack the top ten, and indeed it did, reaching number eight. All three singles appeared on their debut album, 1981's 'Speak And Spell', of which 'Sounds' enthused, "These boys have a sense of humour, a sense of simplicity and a sense of what's good and natural... Synthetic textures and natural harmony make a highly vibrant whole. It's perfect, unprepossessing, unpretentious pop, but it's not so insubstantial that it just floats away".

Depeche Mode had arrived, and Paul Morley at the 'NME' took the opportunity to compare their debut with Orchestral Manoeuvre's second album, the more serious and intellectual 'Architecture And Morality', siding with the Basildon quartet's "bubbly fun pop".

ORCHESTRAL MANOEUVRES IN THE DARK
Maid Of Orleans
Original release: 1981
DINDISC

If OMD had lost out to Depeche in the weekly press, their knack of touching extremities and going highbrow with a pop beat never let up. Their second album, 'Architecture And Morality', housed in an austere Peter Saville sleeve, had hits for sure, but it also carried mountains of atmosphere, and so much depth of sound that it was a recognised as a monster of the genre. The play-off between Andy McCluskey's understanding of how pop music worked – he'd later go on to write for many pop bands in subsequent years - and Paul Humphreys' bank of instruments - synths, piano, Mellotron, organ, melodica, radios and a collection of percussive implements - made this odd couple unpredictable and always hugely rewarding.

'Architecture...' boasted commercial anthems, including the deadpan melody of 'Souvenir', but also featured 'Sealand', a lengthy, almost neo-classical piece that hinted at Tangerine Dream or soundtracks from documentaries about forlorn, barren European wastelands. The album also contained not one homage but two to Joan Of Arc, on the 550th anniversary of her death. If 'Enola Gay' had hinted at a social conscience, then OMD were now looking for historical context. Both tracks were released as singles, 'Joan Of Arc' reaching number four in the charts, with 'Maid Of Orleans (Waltz For Joan Of Arc)' hitting number five.

While 'Joan Of Arc' followed a more traditional song structure, 'Maid Of Orleans', set to a waltz rhythm, was a wash of layered synths, spread as thick as could be, with the Mellotron of Humphreys lending an air of classical drama. "It's not meant to "mean" anything specific," McCluskey was quoted as saying of the track, "(it was) just to set up a feeling, to let the track grow out of the strange noises." Unlike the original line up of the Human League, OMD had managed to fuse moody electronics with melody lines that appealed across the board.

THE HUMAN LEAGUE
Dare
Original release: 1981
VIRGIN

The League, now reduced to the duo of singer Phil Oakey and visuals man Philip Adrian Wright, had tour commitments set in place when Oakey famously met two girls at the Crazy Daisy Nightclub in Sheffield and recruited them on the spot. Joined by Ian Burden, formerly of Sheffield band Graph, on synthesisers, the revamped League toured before heading to the studio under the guidance of Martin Rushent. The result was 'The Sound Of The Crowd', which charted at number twelve and encouraged Virgin to persevere with the group, who were joined by seasoned Rezillos' songwriter Jo Callis for the recording of 'Dare'.

The very structure and rhythm of 'The Sound Of The Crowd' was everything that the new Human League would become remembered for, along with their image. Phil Oakey's lop-sided haircut was now supported by two teenage girls whose distinctive dance moves were straight from the new futurist clubs. After a memorable appearance on 'Top Of The Pops', it seemed that everyone danced like that and, had been for years. Nightclub cool was revamped overnight.

The mix of songwriting styles, Oakey's futuristic images, a touch of Hollywood-styled drama and the acceptance of the burgeoning New Romantic scene, as well as the band's newfound pin up potential at the hands of Joanne Catherall and Susanne Sulley, all seemed to fall into place at once. The album spawned four hit singles in 'The Sound Of The Crowd', 'Love Action (I Believe In Love)', which went top three, 'Open Your Heart', which peaked at number six, and the multi-million selling 'Don't You Want Me', which was originally considered to be a filler track by Oakey before it topped the charts in the UK and heralded a new British Invasion of America as it topped the charts there too.

The early days of MTV also coincided with the release of 'Don't You Want Me', and the cleverly-shot video, featuring a film set spoof that was plainly super real for some of the cast, placed The Human League head and shoulders above their contemporaries in a heartbeat. As would soon become the norm, the video for the already catchy single helped push album sales through the roof.

The band's pop success was phenomenal, but there was certainly much more to the album than the hits, as elements of the original band's sci fi ideas, and much of their Walker Brothers-meets-Dr Who sound, reached and delighted a whole new audience. As 'Q''s guide to essential Synth Pop cleverly observed, while 'Don't You Want Me' "turned them into new romantic pin ups, the likes of 'Seconds' and 'I Am The Law' harked back to the avant-garde chill of their first two albums".

HEAVEN 17
(We Don't Need This) Fascist Groove Thang
Original release: 1981
VIRGIN

After Martyn Ware and Craig Marsh split from The Human League, they first formed The British Electric Foundation, a smart throwback to '50s futurism. Their debut release, 'Music For Stowaways', was a cassette-only album, perfectly timed to coincide with the year's latest must-have gadget, the Sony Walkman. Following its release the duo recorded 'Music For Listening To', which came out on traditional vinyl, before they recruited photographer and old friend Glenn Gregory and formed Heaven 17, named after a chart act featured in the record shop scene of 'A Clockwork Orange'.

The trio's debut single, '(We Don't Need This) Fascist Groove Thang', broke free of much of the synth pop of the day and left behind Marsh and Ware's more tempered roots. The song seemed to be set in a superhyped club, with its combination of an upbeat, funky bassline and frenetic sequenced rhythm topped by electronic percussion seeming, at the time, totally new and different.

"It sounded new and fantastic, a tough new kind of electro funk," mused Garry Mulholland in his book 'This Is Uncool', "And it was pretty great dancing to a song that was right about Reagan and included a wry joke about Cruise missiles".

Filled with left wing one-liners, the single was banned by Radio 1, allegedly at the request of staunch Conservative Mike Reid. Whether as a result of this or not, the BEF/H 17 axis swiftly moved into more accessible territory. Their follow up was a significant departure, and a much-copied format in following years, wherein they invited a selection of people to cover favourite songs from their past, all lovingly fed into the BEF computer.

'Music of Quality And Distinction (Vol 1)', by the British Electric Foundation, was released in 1982, and featured songs that the Heaven 17 members had grown up with, re-interpreted in their funky electronic style by a gaggle of guest vocalists including former Manfred Mann singer Paul Jones, Sandie Shaw and Billy MacKenzie from The Associates, alomg with the "resting" Tina Turner, whose notable take on The Temptations' 'Ball Of Confusion' rekindled her career.

189

JAPAN
Tin Drum
Original release: 1981
VIRGIN

Japan had already gone down the covers route in 1980. Having lost much of their thrashier elements during the late '70s, they began to luxuriate in layers of synths, with Mick Karn's funky bass holding sway and vocalist David Sylvian coming across like Bryan Ferry on downers and seeming slightly removed from proceedings. It was a very European sound, and their cover of the Motown classic 'I Second That Emotion' was far from blue-eyed soul, more a re-awakening of the song in a completely different environment.

Sylvian had been exposed to The Yellow Magic Orchestra and all things Japanese, and when the quartet appeared on TV having dispensed with guitars and drums for completely synthetic sounds, their move into a completely different future seemed absolutely logical. Karn's bass always took a lead role in Japan, but on 'Tin Drum' it stood as the last remaining natural resource on a landscape which leant towards their newfound Eastern influences. After the departure of guitarist Rob Dean, 'Tin Drum' moved wistfully away from traditional rock music, and represented a stepping-stone for Sylvain, who was fast developing as a serious composer keen to experiment with sound.

"We worked really hard on the arrangements," recalled keyboard player Richard Barbieri, "Mick and Steve were creating this kind of jigsaw, not like a standard rock rhythm section, and David and I inserted electronic sounds, almost as if they were talking to the other instruments. It was slow, painstaking work".

ENO AND BYRNE
My Life In The Bush Of Ghosts
Original release: 1981
EG

Brian Eno was already making a reputation for himself for dismantling traditional music when he produced Talking Heads' second album, 'More Songs About Buildings And Food', in 1978. His interest in reshaping traditional songwriting began to come to fruition as old rules went out of the window, all things were considered and, without doubt, Talking Heads' place in modern music was insured by their collaboration, much in the same way that U2 and Coldplay have benefited in more recent times.

The partnership continued with 'Fear Of Music' and 'Remain In Light'. During a break in sessions for the former, Eno started playing with Talking Heads' David Byrne, stretching the envelope and moving out of traditional song constructions. He introduced the band to the music of Fela Kuti, a move which had influenced 'Remain In Light', and the sessions where Eno and Byrne played together took these influences much further, forming the basis of 'My Life In The Bush Of Ghosts', a set which drew heavily on world music, found sounds and the funky feel that Talking Heads had mastered to perfection under the former Roxy man's guidance.

190

MY LIFE IN THE BUSH OF GHOSTS
BRIAN ENO – DAVID BYRNE

Notably, the duo used dialogue from fundamentalist preachers, which was originally offset in places by Islamic chanting, although the section was eventually dropped from the recordings in an effort to appease disgruntled Islamists. But still, the electronic funk feel was allowed to sit behind the ruminations of various hellfire preachers and fundamentalists, and all manner of sounds were added, including gospel choir styled choruses as source music, along with disjointed vocals which were interwoven to produce a new, unique and quite different sound. The end result was a provocative mesh of styles, a hybrid laced with glimpses of different cultures, a studio-created piece of reportage which said more about its subject matter than any number of fly on the wall documentaries might have done. Together, Eno and Byrne painted a picture of frightening religion-based eccentricity.

LAURIE ANDERSON
O Superman
Original release: 1981
WARNER BROTHERS

Eno and Byrne's 'My Life In The Bush Of Ghosts' married the experimental with traditional song structures, and asked questions in a format that was understandable. It removed the safety blanket of the regular lineage of a verse/chorus structure, and their use of speech employed political/religious rhetoric as its base, exposing it in a new and different way, much in the same way that artist Laurie Anderson utilised the recording studio to deliver not only art but also a continuous commentary on politics and the American way of life.

Anderson's extensive eight-hour live performance, 'United States', examined the country, its ideals, its heroes and the people who lived there. Her use of electronic techniques and studio effects were transported to the live arena, and the subsequent five album box set – a truncated set of highlights from the piece – were like nothing else. Bizarrely, the set also spawned a number one single on both sides of the Atlantic in 'O Superman', an eight minute excerpt comprising vocoder, loops and the simplest of synth melodies.

The albums included Anderson-designed bowed instruments, where the bow was a piece of recording tape played over a recording head, sampled sounds and looped sequences, plus slowed and sped up dialogue, all delivered with a dark and haunting edginess. A 'South Bank Show' special on UK TV prior to her live shows at the Adelphi Theatre in Shaftsbury Avenue ensured that the art world understood that her performance was credible, while the public were agog at her storylines. Music fans, too, were amazed at her battery of self-made instruments.

'This Is Uncool' enthused about the single and its place in the unravelling commercial pop world; "What I hear in 'O Superman' is the slow death of America and America's calm acceptance of its inevitability". Perhaps most notably, Anderson had simultaneously managed to get an eight minute song on the radio, and get people to ask what the hell is going on in the world, take the possibilities of an electronic studio into a whole new arena and make what she'd called "Uneasy Listening". Few records can claim such impact, surely. Art and electronic sound were not only pop music, Anderson showed they were also a suitable backdrop for political pontification. However, she herself wasn't so sure; "I wasn't interested in pop music".

KRAFTWERK
Das Model
Original release: 1981
EMI

At the start of the '80s, electronic music had become the music of the masses, the sound of the future that was, for most, now bearable and understandable. Always forward thinking, Kraftwerk were still keen to be ahead of the game and were heralding and championing the arrival of gadgetry that would make everyday life simpler and more "accurate" with the album 'Computer

World' and its examination of the newest of new technology. Long before computers were in every home and the Internet was such an integral part of life, even pocket calculators, with their distinctive sounds, seemed almost dangerously romantic and the stuff of James Bond.

Their track 'The Model' had arrived in 1978 as part of their 'Man Machine' album, but it's re-issue as the b-side of 'Computer Love' in '81 brought Kraftwerk to a whole new audience. Radio DJs flipped the 45 and 'The Model' and the German version 'Das Model' enjoyed a second coming in a world now acquainted with electronic sound.

"The stark beats and beautiful melody," enthused 'Q', "were a timely reminder of Kraftwerk's pioneering status at a time when Depeche Mode and The Human League were dominating the charts." As Kraftwerk continued to innovate and take music inspired by their environment to the outside world, a bunch of brand new German acts were in the process of offering an even more incisive view of a country that was beginning to find itself some thirty years after the end of the Second World War.

DAF
Der Räuber Und Der Prinz
Original release: 1981
MUTE

The Deutsch Amerikanische Freundschaft (DAF) were an influential industrial band from Düsseldorf. Formed in 1978 they featured drummer/synth player Robert Görl, vocalist Gabi Delgado-Lopez, Wolfgang Spelmans, Kurt Dahlke "Pyrolator", Michael Kemner and Chrislo Haas, and played intricate sequenced music that came to the attention of Daniel Miller at Mute.

Gorl's whispered vocals on 'Der Räuber Und Der Prinz' had a haunting and disconcerted feeling, and the almost childlike nursery rhyme melody lines provided them with an unnerving juxtoposition. Gorl would later go solo and stay with Mute as they disbanded, their legacy in the electronic music scene of the early '80s remaining under rated alongside the developments of Einsturzende Neubauten, Abwarts and Die Krupps who, in a flash of aggressive abandon, added real metal percussion to electronic melodies and, in the case of Neubauten, played road drills on stage, a sight that guaranteed them significant column inches.

DIE KRUPPS
Wahre Arbeit, Wahrer Lohn
Original release: 1981

The Die Krupps' sound was at the heart of yet another emerging scene in Germany - Electronic Body Music was a dance orientated groove which fused metal percussion and repetitive synthesiser sequences, in Die Krupps' case those of Ralf Dorper, who would later go on to form the more commercially focussed Propaganda. In 1981, Die Krupps, like Neubauten and Abwarts, were an explosive mix of styles, but while Abwarts offered a punkier edge and Neubauten chose to experiment with all kinds of sound and rhythm, Die Krupps' brief flurry of activity was aimed at frenetically dancing teens who wanted to drown in sound. Consequently, their influence on an emerging hard dance scene was enormous.

COLIN POTTER
Here
Original release: 1981
MIRAGE

As the musical panorama evolved in the early '80s, the acceptance of electronic music led to further fascination in what might be possible. Further experiments were inevitable, but how would anyone hear them? At the opposite end of the spectrum from the chart topping single, a whole galaxy of bedroom composers congregated, many of whom had first emerged from the confines of their self made studios at the UK Electronica Festival in Milton Keynes, as mentioned earlier.

Colin Potter had begun his own tape label in the late '70s. Christened Integrated Circuit Records, or 'ICR', it began with a series of cassette-only albums which were central to the emerging cassette scene in the UK, a scene that also included live tapes of Throbbing Gristle and compilations like 'Rising From The Red Sand', which gathered together extreme and more complex acts like Attrition, Nurse With Wound and Current 93, all of whom were producing music that was decidedly complex.

The tape label Mirage also released music by this growing generation of experimental artists, as well as albums by more established old school electronic gurus. Colin Potter's 'Here' was released in 1981, sourced from a four-track tape which included the twelve minutes plus of 'Shallow Water', a slowly building, densely textured drone piece, and a side long electronic exploration called 'Gas', which infiltrated the senses as it grew awash with synthesised sound and sequenced rhythms.

Potter still continues today with IRC, and has worked closely on all Nurse With Wound releases since the early '90s, and his flair for nurturing modern electronic sound has transported him some way from the simple beginnings of ICR to a cult international following.

ESCAPE FROM NEW YORK OST
Original release: 1981

BLADE RUNNER OST
Original release: 1982

As well as a slew of intriguing new electronic acts, the early '80s also boasted two hugely significant films which cemented the public's interest in the future, in scientific technology and in how a future world might be run. Both also contained essential soundtrack recordings who's mass exposure and sheer brilliance were to inspire the growing electronic music scene.

John Carpenter, the director of 'Escape From New York', was an enthusiastic composer who, armed with an array of synthesisers, worked alongside Alan Howarth to provide the distinctive minimalist synthetic music for the movie. Using a Prophet-5, ARP Quadra and Avatar and an ARP sequencer, the pair produced a minimal but pulsing soundscape to accompany the story of Kurt Russell's attempt to save the President Of The United States, who had crash landed in New York, now a no-go fortified prison. The tension of the film and Carpenter's throbbing synth lines, plus some truly iconic one liners, made it a hugely popular movie, and the inspirational soundtrack proved its popularity by being roundly sampled in the years that followed.

Within a year, an even bigger sci-fi spectacular was released, again accompanied by a suitably ground breaking soundtrack. Vangelis provided the music for Ridley Scott's interpretation of Philip K Dick's 'Do Androids Dream Of Electric Sheep?', which became the slightly more High

Street friendly 'Blade Runner' by the time it hit cinemas. The movie itself featured ground-breaking technology, used by Harrison Ford's character in a story set in a futuristic run-down metropolis overflowing with whizzing space cars and plenty of robotic dialogue.

Luckily, I managed to see a preview of the film in Leicester Square one Sunday morning, and the stereo mix, with Vangelis' spacey, layered keyboards set off against the echoey sound effects and thrusting engines, made it a truly phenomenal audio experience. Of course, the action-packed drama made the whole thing even more memorable.

Since its release, a host of people have been inspired by the musical elements of the film, not to mention the never ending stream of samples of the film's dialogue which have appeared in numerous other recordings.

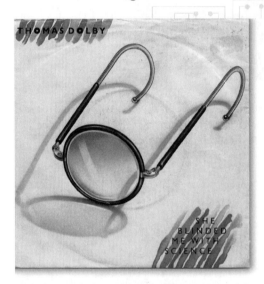

THOMAS DOLBY
She Blinded Me With Science
Original release: 1982
VENICE IN PERIL

In 1982, people were still as fascinated by what the future would bring as they had ever been, and none more so than Dr Magnus Pyke and Thomas Dolby. Dolby's debut album, 'The Golden Age Of Wireless', had set out his clever brand of interwoven synth pop, a more serious and considered sound which was reflected in the intellectualisation of the album, which concentrated on the possibilities of radio as well as new technology in the modern world.

Dolby was immediately cast as a boffin, and the 1982 single 'She Blinded Me With Science' was undoubtedly an attempt to underline this, as well as being a tongue-in-cheek crack at the kind of old school futurism that had pervaded '50s sci-fi movies and seemed, in some cases, to be prevalent in the unfolding decade.

The hugely catchy melody line, accompanied by guitar from XTC's Andy Partridge, drove a keenly observed examination of "love" between scientists, complete with sampled one liners from UK TV's scientific pundit and revered eccentric, Dr Magnus Pyke. Pyke's various theories and constant appearances on TV had set him up as a free thinking expert on the mystical future, and his series of cultural statements added fuel to his reputation.

"The main body of the citizenry, the 'workers,' are kept segregated from the drones, the women at home, the children, the old and the idle..." he enthused, "The necessary doctrine of the division of labour makes this regimentation necessary. But it has the effect of setting economic effort apart and dividing the day and the week into "work" and "everything else"."

Naturally, people were fascinated. "This way of thinking has so deranged our minds that we have come to accept that only when we are actually carrying out paid industrial work are we serving our purpose on earth," he continued.

"To minds so deformed, the things that 'retired' people do are not considered to be of value. They are empty, merely something to do. The leisure pursuits of the senior executive seem to be corroded with competitiveness, superficial sociability, display, and conspicuous consumption. He must own an automobile of a certain size and make, not necessarily to travel in, but to prove that he can afford it," he concluded.

Dolby was the perfect musical foil, and now, 30 years later we are at a point where Pyke's statements appear to have come true. Leisure is one of the biggest industries in the world, free time and how people value it has become big business and we are in a technological period where we are allowed more and more free time. Only our traditional guilt at being able to have such free time and our overpowering job fear, has stopped this generation from fully taking advantage of it.

Magnus Pyke's reputation ensured Dolby's eccentric reading of the value of science was a chart hit in several countries, and even though he continued to record and produce music, Dolby never came close again to nailing the world's amazement at the possibilities of the future. Much like Harrison Ford's character's array of new tech goodies that everyone leaving the 'Blade Runner' movie craved, Dolby and Pyke's image of a future brought on a platter by female scientists seemed as if it could and should happen.

TEARS FOR FEARS
Mad World
Original release: 1982
PHONOGRAM/MERCURY

Thomas Dolby's pristine sound on 'She Blinded Me With Science' provided clever novelty to a 1982 synth pop scene in which a host of very serious duos were emerging. Marriages made in the pages of the Musicians Wanted ads, where the technical geeky one, who could play keyboards, teamed up with a singer who could write lyrics, emote and provide passion to offset the mechanical beats when needed.

In 1982, Tears For Fears formed out of the mod band Graduate. Consisting of Roland Orzabel and Curt Smith, they mixed and matched Orzabel's melody lines with Smith's serious, almost deadpan vocals. That sound dominated their first two singles, but both 'Pale Shelter' and 'Suffer The Children' failed to chart. However, their third 45, 'Mad World', was altogether more sinister, demonstrating the correct blend of clicking rhythms and booming synthesisers behind Smith's troubled vocals, and a gorgeous piano motif on the chorus.

The duo were deadly serious about what they were doing, and interviewing them for the short-lived 'Sounds' glossy offshoot 'Noise!' wasn't easy. Deftly sincere, both Smith and Orzabel, who, for some reason, had to be spoken to separately, had a vision way beyond electronic music, seeing it as a stepping stone to much, much bigger things. They were electronic because those were the only instruments they had.

They would go on to have other huge hits, most notably 'Everybody Want To Rule The World' and 'Shout', but a musical hiatus between 1985 and the release of their third album 'The Seeds Of Love' in 1989 proved to be their undoing. The band had reached stadium size in the mid-'80s, but the simple keyboard interplay of 'Mad World' was to be replaced by a huge production and a fascination with the studio itself, resulting in a hefty timelag between releases, and even bigger bills. The tension of the four-year creation process proved costly, and the duo eventually split.

'Mad World', with its simple and evocative melody, was a long way behind Tears For Fears by the time they fell apart, but when makers of the movie 'Donnie Darko' needed a suitably offbeat theme tune to complement the movie's time and space hopping uneasiness, they looked no further. Re-recorded by Michael Andrews and Gary Jules, and concentrating on the vocal line rather than the original melody, it became a rather maudlin Christmas number one in 2003, a fact which still seems beyond belief to this day. But nevertheless, Tears For Fears were ripe for rediscovery.

SOFT CELL
Torch
Original release: 1982
SOME BIZZARE

If Tears For Fears weren't easy interviewees, Soft Cell were the exact opposite. Sharing a house in Leeds, the duo of Dave Ball (keyboards) and Marc Almond (vocals) had already recorded the pulsing 'Memorabilia' single when, as part of a piece about the city's music scene, which also included interviews with Dedringer, The Mekons and Delta 5, I arrived at their collapsing old building to talk synth pop. As it happened, Marc was out selling his album collection to raise a few quid, whilst Dave dabbled on a synthesiser in his room.

When Marc returned, he revealed that the whole process of Soft Cell was done in isolation. Dave would record synth lines onto a cassette and give it to Marc, who'd disappear into his room and work out some vocal ideas. It was poetry in motion. That evening, Marc DJ'ed at the Warehouse club and selected a few northern soul songs, including Gloria Jones' 'Tainted Love', a vibrant cover of which was to become their next single and take them to the top of the charts.

Soap opera tales 'Bedsitter' and 'Say Hello Wave Goodbye' both went top five, and their debut album, 'Non-Stop Erotic Cabaret', quickly established the pair as a truly offbeat partnership, with the seedy 'Sex Dwarf' completely at odds with ballads like 'Say Hello...'.

As if to add further proof of their dual personality, 1982 saw them release the haunting 'Torch' as well as a version of the their original album with the uptempo dance songs mixed into a cleverly segued piece. 'Non Stop Exotic Dancing', and its accompanying video, ensured them a sleazy left field following, and a lasting reputation with the dark side of clubland was enhanced.

As part of the Some Bizzare group of acts, their darker moments were perfectly acceptable to the label's freakier fans, but appearances on 'Top Of The Pops' also introduced them to a much younger audience and the world of 'Smash Hits', where their risqué antics provided a sense of danger for thousands of pre-pubescent girls.

Soft Cell were an enigmatic partnership. Dave Ball's mix of electronic sounds and washes of effects were the perfect backdrop for Almond's soulful and evocative vocal. As was the way in 1982, many of the tracks were released on 12-inch singles in extended mixes, but the concept of segueing them together was, at the time, something completely different, and a perfect reflection of their live antics.

"In one show, Marc stripped and smeared himself in cat food," Dave Ball once recalled of his partner in tune. Nice.

BLANCMANGE
God's Kitchen
Original release: 1982
LONDON

LIVING ON THE CEILING
Original release: 1982
LONDON

Like Soft Cell and Depeche Mode, Blancmange were featured on the original Some Bizzare album. A duo from Harrow in Middlesex, they subsequently released the 'Irene And Mavis' EP and eventually wound up on London Records, where, after the quizzical Talking Heads-styled synthpop of evangelical, Bible-bashing bubbler 'God's Kitchen', their third single, 'Living On The Ceiling', went top ten. Gangly front man Neil Arthur sounded like a deranged David Byrne, while Stephen Luscombe's layered keyboards added a touch of Arabic melody – in fact Luscombe would also play in the Asian-inspired West India Company later in the decade.

Blancmange continued to have hits into the mid-'80s, and their early success saw them catapulted into increasingly larger venues. Indeed, around '82 they played at Hammersmith Palais, but their lack of visual clout was evident and would forever limit what they could achieve.

In an effort to counter this, 'Living On The Ceiling' was released with an accompanying video, some of which was shot in Egypt. A neat piece of exotica, it helped chart the 45, but the duo were never really able to repeat the formula.

YAZOO
Don't Go
Original release: 1982
MUTE

By 1981, Vince Clarke had left Depeche Mode. The development of the synthesiser had convinced him that it was possible to do virtually everything himself, and, as Martin Gore was developing as the dominant songwriter in the band, Clarke felt that there wasn't room for him to do everything he wanted to. That said, he still needed a vocalist, and, after a Melody Maker ad was placed, RnB belter Alison Moyet was recruited. The mix of Clarke's clinical rhythms and catchy melody lines became the perfect foil for Moyet's huge vocal, as typified on their debut single, 'Only You', which went to number two in the single charts.

The follow up 45, 'Don't Go', upped the tempo and allowed Moyet room for an even more soulful delivery. With Mute now working with Sire Records in the States, 'Don't Go' picked up enormous radio play in the US and became a club favourite, sending it to the top of the Billboard Singles Chart for two weeks.

The accompanying album, 'Upstairs At Eric's', featured both singles, along with the 12-inch mix of 'Situation'. Every track revolved around Moyet's deep vocal and Clarke's knack for overlaying plush keyboard lines, and the opening salvo of the album, the distinctive riff of 'Don't Go', took on a similar role as the central riff of Gary Numan's 'Are Friends Electric?' and A Flock Of Seagulls' 'Wishing (I Had A Photograph Of You)', becoming a distinctive calling card for the band, and for synth pop itself.

A FLOCK OF SEAGULLS
Wishing (I Had A Photograph Of You)
Original release: 1982
JIVE

Praised by none other than Phil Spector as being 'breathtaking', A Flock Of Seagulls' 'Wishing (I Had A Photograph Of You)' has remained a radio staple all over the world since its release in 1982. From Liverpool, the band first came to the attention of former Be Bop Deluxe guitarist Bill Nelson, who recorded and released their first single '(It's Not Me) Talking' in the early '80s on his own Cocteau label. Subsequently signed to Jive, the band's electronic melodies and Mike Score's vocal – but probably more memorably his hair style – summed up a period of music which saw the combination of image and the huge amount of sway magazines like 'Smash Hits' held dictate the success of bands. That said, without doubt, the melody line from 'Wishing' is one of the most memorable riffs from the '80s, with or without the hairstyles and perfect smiles.

TRIO
Da Da Da
Original release: 1982
PHONOGRAM

If A Flock Of Seagulls were pandering to the new rules of pop, then German act Trio were plundering the novelty of electronic music. Performed using a Casio VL-1 in deadpan style, 'Da Da Da' was a repetitive slice of minimalism that was acclaimed as "New German Cheerfulness", in true ironic style.

It didn't further the cause of electronic music, but it brought a wry smile as it parodied German minimalism, almost suggesting that, with the arrival of Casio technology, the sound of Kraftwerk could be created at the flick of a switch. It was an idea that many people all over the world were indeed trying to perfect.

AFRIKA BAMBAATAA AND THE SOUL SONIC FORCE
Planet Rock
Original release: 1982
TOMMY BOY

Although Japanese technology was simplifying and demystifying the sound of Kraftwerk in the early 1980s, the Germans' status remained truly monumental, and their work was being blended into something completely new as 'Trans Europe Express' changed the shape of hip hop in New York. Producer Arthur Baker used the rhythm from 'Numbers', from Kraftwerk's 'Computer World' set, and the main melody line from 'Trans Europe Express', along with how own synth and vocoder elements, to make a funky middle ground between George Clinton and Baker's German inspirations.

"I liked the sound of Mr Gary Numan," Baker later admitted to 'Q', "but I wanted to add that funky end of James Brown and Sly Stone". Without doubt, Baker's influences were from the top drawer. The result of his experiments was also able to reside there, and, even though the single didn't sell in huge quantities, its effect on music was phenomenal, inspiring techno, house, hip hop and trance musicians for years, whilst becoming a club anthem in its home city and highlighting the groundbreaking work done in Germany several years earlier.

THE TWINS
Face to Face - Heart to Heart
Original release: 1982
HANSA

While Ralf und Florian were inspiring people in uptown New York, two other German composers, Sven Dohrow and Ronny Schreinzer, were becoming big news in Italy, and by doing so were spearheading what was to become Italodisco. Named 'The Twins', they'd already had some success in the States with 'The Desert Place', their sound being originally inspired by Gary Numan, OMD and Depeche Mode. But, their big European breakthrough came with 'Face To Face', which became one of the best-selling singles in Italy a year after its original German release. A mid-paced electronic shuffle with a repetitive melody line, it was far lighter than the sounds of Kraftwerk, leaning, as their original list of influences suggested, much closer to UK synth pop. This only served to make the track more accessible and an even bigger hit.

TUXEDOMOON
Divine
Original release: 1982
CRAMMED

In 1982, the majority of innovation in electronic music seemed to be taking place across Europe, and Tuxedomoon, who had started life in San Francisco playing post punk experimental sounds that were initially picked up by The Residents' Ralph label, relocated to mainland Europe, where they were asked to create the score for a new Maurice Bejart ballet, Divine (Bejart also features in this book in '67 when Pierre Henry was commissioned to work with him. He also worked with rock band Spooky Tooth).

For the piece, Tuxedomoon laid down a wash of multi-layered keyboards, vocoder vocals and sequenced passages, touching on diverse electronic visionaries as diverse as Klaus Schulze and Philip Glass in doing so. The track 'Ninotchka' was particularly crazed, sounding akin to William Burroughs editing a traditional Russian dance over a disgruntled drum machine. Elsewhere, dialogue mixed with string quartets and swathes of sound shifted into each other with discordant ease. 'Divine' was a challenging recording, proving that electronic music still had the much needed ability to shock and challenge, something the far tamer 14th studio set from Neil Young also did, inadvertently......

NEIL YOUNG
Trans
Original release: 1982
GEFFEN

Allegedly, by 1982, Neil Young was on a guaranteed $1,000,000 per album, and also retained full creative control. For him and his label at the time, 'Trans' was a controversial release whichever way you looked at it. Signed to Geffen after being with Reprise since his solo career began, he was eventually sued by the label for producing work - 'Trans' and the following non-electronic 'Landing On Water' - that was "unrepresentative".

Views were mixed on 'Trans'. Some fans felt it was a satirical message against the rise of electronic music, while others felt it was a homage to Kraftwerk. Nobody was quite sure what to make of it, although Peter Hook, of Joy Division and New Order, was a fan. "I loved the Kraftwerk influences, the mix of robotic discipline and dance feel. I never really liked Neil Young's guitary stuff all that much - too self-indulgent - but Barney (Sumner) got me into this," he claimed when once asked to list his ten favourite albums. The list also included Lou Reed's 'Coney Island Baby', the soundtrack of 'The Great Gatsby', The Birthday Party's 'Prayers On Fire', The Sex Pistols' 'Never Mind The Bollocks' and David Bowie's 'Aladdin Sane', among others. Hook is nothing if not eclectic.

'Trans' certainly had its moments. The vocoder use set against choppy guitars on 'We R In Control', 'Computer Cowboy' and 'Transformer Man' - the latter sounding like it's come straight from a Kraftwerk session - and the layered effects on 'Computer Age' are all engaging, although his version of his own Buffalo Springfield tune 'Mr Soul', with its vocoder-lite effect and thudding rhythm, was perhaps less convincing. That said, the effects-led solo-ing on 'Like An Inca', and its slowly fermenting rhythm, sounded like something Talking Heads might have attempted. In truth, as an album, 'Trans' doesn't hang together too well, but there are some really powerful moments there that still sound contemporary today. It's well worth a listen.

EURYTHMICS
Sweet Dreams (Are Made Of This)
Original release: 1983
RCA

Dave Stewart and Annie Lennox had been part of post-punk new wave outfit The Tourists before the electronic bug bit. They consistently made excellent melodic pop tunes topped by Lennox's fantastic vocal range whatever instruments they used, but it was on their fifth single as Eurythmics, 'Love Is A Stranger', that turned us all on to that fact. Not least because they were first attracted by a hugely memorable video featuring a cross dressing Lennox.

The 'Stranger' clip featured Annie at her notorious, androgynous best, sporting a blonde wig and fur before revealing a slicked back ginger coiffeur, and dressing in a traditional pin stripe man's suit. A classic visual, it even featured some stuttering robotic dance moves, further aligning the duo to the synthetic world.

The song itself focused on her phenomenal vocal range, which was allowed plenty of room over Stewart's spiky, but never too sweet, synth lines. The single also broke them in numerous territories, perfectly setting up the release of 'Sweet Dreams (Are Made Of This)', the title track from their second album and, of course, it's follow up, which further continued the visual storyline, 'Who's That Girl?'.

'Sweet Dreams' revisited the be-suited image, with Lennox also sporting newly cropped hair. The song itself featured an even simpler riff, with a synth-led string break and multi-tracked vocals adding a further devotional sound to the synthetic base. It became the band's biggest selling single and elevated them to arena status virtually overnight.

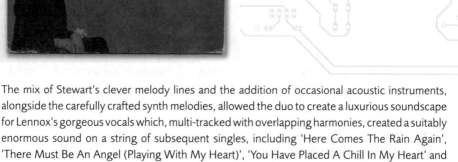

The mix of Stewart's clever melody lines and the addition of occasional acoustic instruments, alongside the carefully crafted synth melodies, allowed the duo to create a luxurious soundscape for Lennox's gorgeous vocals which, multi-tracked with overlapping harmonies, created a suitably enormous sound on a string of subsequent singles, including 'Here Comes The Rain Again', 'There Must Be An Angel (Playing With My Heart)', 'You Have Placed A Chill In My Heart' and the theme song for the movie of George Orwell's '1984', the vocoder-friendly 'Sexcrime'. By the mid-'80s, Eurythmics were set for massive crossover success all over the globe.

DEPECHE MODE
Everything Counts
Original release: 1983
MUTE

As Eurythmics employed the simple pop writing techniques they'd developed as an electronic duo on a wider canvas, Depeche Mode began recording the album 'Construction Time Again' and began to look around for external influences to colour their sound.

As Martin Gore began the process, a number incidents conspired to fashion both his thinking and how the set was created. The band's recent tour in Thailand had introduced them to the poverty of the country, Gore had witnessed Einsturzende Neubauten live and the band had been introduced to the Synclavier synthesiser and the concept of sampling. All three things affected both the sound and lyrical content of the album, and the single 'Everything Counts' touched all bases, with its sampled xylophone and melodica, industrial rhythms and lyrics telling of "grabbing hands".

The work with the Synclavier completely changed Depeche Mode's sound, and to thicken the mix, metal sheets were added to live shows. Their new found fascination with sound allowed them to stretch the envelope around Gore's highly melodic writing style. With Alan Wilder added to the line up of Gore, David Gahan and Andrew Fletcher, the Depeche sound began to embrace much wider source material, including the sound of industrial music and Gore's interest in any unusual musical form, from German experimentalists Der Plan to The Residents, adding even more variations to their music.

The single's flipside, the more spacious 'Work Hard', echoed their newly celebrated ethic. Its brooding ambience and thudding rhythms provided the inspiration for hundreds of admiring American bands with a penchant for the darker side, Trent Reznor from Nine Inch Nails and Marilyn Manson included.

Strangely, the video for 'Everything Counts', a new kind of calling card that was becoming increasingly important as MTV's influence grew, featured the band playing actual instruments. Wilder played xylophone and Gore blows a reed instrument, perhaps in an effort to show the natural textures that they were now adding to their arsenal.

HERBIE HANCOCK
Rockit
Original release: 1983
CBS

The prominence and influence of MTV in the States by 1983, two years after its launch, was becoming more and more evident to the music industry. Bands had to make videos, the quality had to be good and MTV had to want to program them. It seems strange now that one of the first videos to feature black artists on MTV came about with this single, some two years after launch.

An outtake from Hancock's 1983 album named after the influential Alvin Tofler book 'Future Shock', 'Rockit's funky electronic instrumental groove went big on UK radio, but it was in the US, particularly on MTV, where it had its biggest audience. Hancock himself, after masterminding Michael Jackson, digging the jazz scene and scoring some cool movies, played third fiddle in the video, with only his hand seen, rolling across the keyboard on a TV screen as robotic body parts gyrate and "normal people" fill the screen.

Whatever the concept of the impressive robotic engineering in the video, 'Rockit' was a great tune. It sounded like Jimmy Smith, dragged into a futuristic stratosphere. It had melody and natural funk, while the pulsing rhythm and programmed beats, mixed with at-the-time avant garde turntablist scratching, made it sound completely different. The video, directed by 10cc's Godley And Crème, brought the song to the masses, but it was the synth and drum machine programming of Michael Beinhom, and the heavy scratch techniques of GrandMixer D.ST, that really cut. They also proved to be a direct influence on DJ Shadow cohort Q-Bert and the similarly scratchy Beatie Boys DJ of choice, Mix Master Mike.

"The thing that we possess, that machines don't," opined Hancock when asked about his fascination with the future, "is the ability to exhibit wisdom". The developing electronic studio also made the possibilities of producing dance music all the more exciting.

EVELYN THOMAS
High Energy
Original release: 1983
RECORD SHACK

Ian Levine was one of the two key DJs at Blackpool Mecca's Highland Rooms in the early '70s (the other being Colin Curtis). They took northern soul and began to add hints of funk, moving away from the standard stompers and towards disco music with plenty of soulful edge. As the '80s rolled around, Levine was producing his own sides, and he enticed legendary soul singer Evelyn Thomas to the UK to record for his Record Shack imprint. Thomas had previously been signed to 20th Century and Casablanca and was equipped with one of the great soul voices. Levine's idea was to take a more repetitive, electronic rhythm and to build an upbeat groove that reflected the title.

And so a new genre was born. Hi-NRG went global and was embraced by the gay scene, the initial release, Thomas' 'High Energy' topping the charts for four weeks in Germany. Electronic music was indeed perfect for the dancefloor, and a string of Hi-NRG singles followed. Meanwhile, a few miles from the original Mecca, down in Manchester, New Order had become part owners of the Hacienda club and were in the process of releasing their biggest single ever, an electronic anthem that defied boundaries and reduced dancefloors everywhere to meltdown setting.

NEW ORDER
Blue Monday
Original release: 1983
FACTORY

"The future began here," say 'Q', "Two cultures meeting, the nightclub and the street corner, technology and laddishness," 'Blue Monday' was nothing short of life changing.

New Order had risen from the ashes of Joy Division, with Gillian Gilbert playing synthesisers alongside Bernard Sumner on guitar, Peter Hook on bass and Steve Morris on drums. Their previous single, 1982's 'Temptation', had hinted at a synth pop direction for the band who had, by now, fully embraced electronic music. By the time they recorded 'Blue Monday', traditional guitars and drums had gone and the Oberheim DMX drum machine was employed alongside Gilbert's synths and Hooky's "lead" bass.

Allegedly, Gilbert's synth was out of synch, but the band liked the structure it created and kept it in. "The textures were as repellent as they were gorgeous, the beats inhuman and Sumner's vocal spoke more about isolation than a shelf full of Penguin Modern Classics," claimed 'Q's Synth Pop Guide, and the track's effect on the club scene, and indeed the progress of what was previously called indie rock, became even more significant.

According to Sumner, the song was inspired by four key dance tracks, Sylvester's 'You Make Me Feel (Mighty Real', the rhythm of Donna Summer's 'Our Love', the arrangement of the obscure 12-inch 'Dirty Talk' by Klein And MBO and a sample of Kraftwerk's 'Uranium' from 'Radio-

Activity'. It was musically inventive and decidedly different, in fact everything about the record seemed to slip into immediate folklore.

So the story goes, the sleeve, by Peter Saville, was so elaborate that every time they sold a record it cost Factory Records money. That said, this unique mix of ideas merged two disparate cultures perfectly, dance music, which had erupted in the UK as an alternative to indie, and indie itself, which had become as homogenised as the rock music it set out to originally destroy, or at least to become an alternative to.

The idea had arrived after Sumner had been exposed to various kinds of dance music on the London club scene. "I started hearing this kind of dance music where people were trying to get these strict machine-like beats with tape loops and live drums," he told MOJO in 2001, "I thought that we could take our synthesiser and make the sounds that these people were after. We were consciously making music that people could dance to, even though we weren't going out dancing ourselves".

'Blue Monday' established New Order as a breakthrough act, not only in rock circles but with the dance fraternity too. They also wanted a song that they could put on instead of doing an encore at live shows, so it killed many birds with one beautifully-packaged stone. "We thought it would be a good idea if we could write a song that would play itself," recalled Steve Morris.

Famously, the hands-free tune also reduced Neil Tennant of The Pet Shop Boys to tears, being everything they were trying to achieve at the time. "New Order still have massive respect in the dance world," Pete Tong told MOJO, "The vast number of DJs still know and revere the track". Its effect was so widespread, it even enticed Kraftwerk to visit the studio it was recorded in.

CYBOTRON
Clear
Original release: 1983
FANTASY

Back in the States, a whole new sound was emerging in Electro, a kind of souped-up take on Kraftwerk, with robotic rhythms and melody lines sourced straight from the German Godfathers. The scene took root in Detroit five years before they developed their distinctive techno sound, and Juan Atkins and Richard '3070' Davis were key protagonists of the primeval techno sound.

Described by 'The Wire' magazine as a "groundbreaking first generation piece of pure machine music," 'Clear' was riddled with Kraftwerkian elegance and a superb driving rhythm. The duo were casting an all-seeing eye towards a possible future world, but Atkins' love of clinical accuracy didn't agree with Davis's desire to go into a more rock-based direction. Musical differences beckoned and they headed their separate ways, but not before leaving an indelible beat echoing around the dancefloor that would inspire generations to come.

CABARET VOLTAIRE
Fascination/The Crackdown
Original release: 1983
VIRGIN

In 1982, Cabaret Voltaire had released the startling 'Yashar' on Factory, a John Robie-produced blast of dancefloor electronica that took their 'Three Mantras' release to new pulsing heights. Robie had worked with Arthur Baker on 'Planet Rock', and the band's deal with Virgin also coincided with a sponsorship arrangement with Roland which gave them access to new equipment and a bigger sound, which enhanced their dysfunctional style.

"I don't think we'd ever lose that," Stephen Mallinder told me when we talked in 1984. "The rawness doesn't come from the equipment we use, it's part of us, it's the way we put things down on tape, the way we work. Technically we can upgrade, but we're not musicians, we don't think in that way".

"We know what we can do and what we want to do. I mean, no-one likes big guitar solos or anything like that, it's just something we don't go in for," added Richard Kirk. The duo, making a virtue of their inabilities which, on 'The Crackdown' and 'The Dream Ticket' (which also came out in '83 on Virgin), meant that their distinctive industrial edge was never over complicated.

"The simplest things are almost always the most effective," Mal concluded, "Proficiency is a danger that you've got to be careful not to slip into".

The departure of Chris Watson from Cabaret Voltaire as the band signed to Virgin may have reduced the amount of dialogue interrupting their grooves, but it also allowed them the chance to transform from industrial anarchists to dancefloor-friendly innovators, a process that SPK, were about to travel from Australia to the UK to undertake. 'Yashar' had started the process, as Kirk recalled, "It made us realise what you could do if you took this music apart and put it together again".

SOZIALISTISCHES PATIENTEN KOLLEKTIV
Leichensrei
Original release: 1983
SIDE EFFEKTS

Tracklisting:
Genetic Transmission, Post-Mortem, Desolation, Napalm (Terminal Patient), Cry from the Sanatorium, Baby Blue Eyes, Israel, Internal Bleeding, Chamber Music, Despair, The Agony of the Plasma, Day of Pigs, Wars of Islam, Maladia Europa (the European Sickness)

SPK were an Australian band whose extreme music and ability to dismantle sound was only matched by their extreme changes of name, scary sleeve images and mysterious line up. They produced abrasive electronic music, and Industrial Records released their first single in 1980, bolstering an already healthy roster of noise terrorists which included Non, Monte Cazazza and Throbbing Gristle, and giving SPK a cult following which they would steadily grow with a host of testing releases.

211

Their website - home.pi.be/~spk - recalls the story of that first UK 45: "The third Australian single, re-released on the legendary Industrial label (home of TG). There were around 2000 copies made; the first 1000 had the sticker pasted on the cover or as an insert, the next 1000 had the image printed on the cover. "Mekano" is listed as "Factory" on the record label, but as "Mekano" on the sleeve. "Slogan" is listed as "Slogun" on the sleeve and as "Slogan" on the label".

Confused? That's part and parcel of SPK, who played "synthesisers, elektronik rhythms, tapes, synkussion," and added vocals that covered the extremes of chanted despair, screaming or sexually active whelps or even, sometimes, spoken dialogues about all manner of social activities. You had to keep up to be part of the SPK experience.

Changing their name was only part of the process. They were Surgical Penis Klinik, System Planning Korporation and SoliPsiK on occasion. Even stranger, they became unlikely major label signings to Elektra when they turned their rhythmic tribal assaults into electronica spiked with metal percussion, and even some funky melodies.

Their main instigator, Graham Revell, had relocated to London by the early '80s, and his creativity knew no bounds. Raiding the British Library for insect recordings, he sampled the original sounds and made the truly exceptional 'The Insect Musicians' in 1986, pre-dating the extremes of Matmos sampling by some decades. But it's 'Leichensrei' and its documentary-styled construction, pulsing electronic rhythms, screaming sirens, stolen dialogue and crushing intensity that remains their most startling work.

Later incarnations of SPK may have simplified the sound for Elektra, but Revell was first and foremost a composer. He would later go on to deliver a startling series of big budget film soundtracks, including 'Collateral Damage', 'Aeon Flux', 'Sin City', 'The Hand That Rocks The Cradle', 'Tomb Raider', 'The Crow', the remake of 'Assault On Precinct 13', 'The Craft' and 'Freddy Vs Jason'. These were surely far more lucrative than his DIY roots.

When 'Leichensrei' was recorded in his homeland circa 1980, it was a physical attempt to change perceptions of recorded music – one of the side's ends with a lock groove that's as majestic and minimally rhythmical as Terry Riley – and the possibilities of electronics, tape editing and the theory that reworked found sound had many possibilities. Revell, an extremely approachable, well-read and hugely creative person, used the same theories of deconstruction and challenge as the Futurists of seventy years previous, the end result sounding like nothing that had ever been heard before, and rarely since.

FRIEDER BUTZMANN
Incendio
From Das Madchen Auf Der Schaukel
Original release: 1983
ZENSOR

Within electronic music there was always room to push the boundaries, always space for experimentation and, in some cases, opportunities for people to do stuff that really was different. Frieder Butzmann was one of those active performers who just had to find out what would happen if you stuck your finger in the circuit board. Just...... there. A former member of DAF, he recorded under the name Din-A Testbild, as well as under his own name, and veered towards Residents-styled eccentricity.

For his second solo album, he immersed himself in synthetic sound and made 'Das Madchen Auf Der Schaukel', which had more of an overtly soundtrack feel until the closing track, 'Incendio', an eleven minute piece that wafts in like Tangerine Dream before taking a leaf from early Cabaret Voltaire. Dialogue in German erupts as radio interference builds and collapses. He was really saying something – in a multi-tracked tormented artist kind of way - before a throbbing bass took up a gut-wrenching march to the end spiral.

Butzmann was one of many people who would never be part of the synth pop success story. But experimental music was alive and well in Germany, and also down on the farm where Nocturnal Emissions lived......

NOCTURNAL EMISSIONS
Drowning In A Sea Of Bliss
Original release: 1983
STERILE

Tracklisting:
Drowning In A Sea Of Bliss, Norepinephrine, How Groovy You Were, Hardcore, Gloppetta, Tongues Speak, Want To Die, Smoking Rat Machine, Wrongly Wired, Violence Is Love, Shan't Do That

Nocturnal Emissions were an odd looking duo. Nigel Ayers and Caroline K weren't ready for the world's press to examine their recordings, but in 1983 they agreed to talk to me for 'Sounds' magazine. It was a rambling discussion – mainly me rambling and them saying 'yes' or 'no' to my assumptions. Caroline and Nigel were lovely people but they couldn't explain their music. In some ways they didn't feel they had to.

According to Wikipedia, which I know is usually a no no, but occasionally throws up something definitive, their music concentrated on "the axiom of music being a form of social control", and indeed it did. 'Drowning In A Sea Of Bliss' shifts from a screaming opening moment to pulsing electronics and echoey noise which sounds like cheese being grated through the speakers, before segueing into recordings of scout troop singalongs and primitive drum machines as synths howl and helicopters land. This was extreme music.

Originally released on cassette on their own label, 'Drowning In A Sea Of Bliss' was a landmark recording, and remains a rare and sought after album that, along with Nurse With Wound, SPK and a host of other like-minded noise terrorists, began to attract a following in the early '80s. Many were featured in the Wild Planet column I wrote for Sounds around the time, which guaranteed a steady flow of strange tapes arriving at my office, occasionally accompanied by even stranger people, from all over the world.

At a time when synthpop was dominating the charts and everything was sweetness and light in terms of melody lines, hearing SPK, Nurse With Wound, Attrition, Portion Control or early 400 Blows was a challenge that was immensely rewarding. Like Cabaret Voltaire's early releases, the sounds from these releases shouldn't have made sense. But they did.

SEVERED HEADS
Since The Accident
Original release: 1983
INK

Tracklisting:
A Relic Of The Empire, A Million Angels, Houses Still Standing, Gashing The Old Mae West, Dead Eyes Opened, Golden Boy, Godsong, Epilepsy 82, Exploring The Secrets Of Treating Deaf Mutes, Brasserie, In Rome.

Another of the bands covered in my Wild Planet column was Severed Heads, the name alone immediately lumping them in with the anti-establishment noise manipulators. "We were called Mr & Mrs No Smoking Sign, because that was really ugly." Heads' mainman Tom Ellard revealed when he visited London from his native Australia, "Then, we wanted to fool people that we were Industrial and it worked. Severed Heads was a really dumb name, so that's what stuck. Forever. I hate it by the way".

The band had been part of the tape-swapping scene of the early '80s, a postal network which saw like-minded experimenters exchange their latest C60s, but the music they produced was far more competent than many of their rivals. Sure, it had weird noises and oddball samples, but it also possessed melody and a tongue-in-cheek sense of humour.

"People thought I was on drugs producing this music," Ellard explained, "I used to get the weirdest letters from people who were really off their heads. I never took anything, that was just the way the music came out".

The opening tape montage of 'A Relic Of The Empire', the first track from 'Since The Accident', sounded like the collapse of the record industry as swing jazz, dialogue and brass squeals are manhandled into a descending stew, but as soon as the rhythm kicks in it's plain that Severed Heads were moving outside of the industrial arena. Sure, loops are spun and noises interrupt, but these were songs with fantastic structure, and Ellard's remix of the 'Dead Eyes Opened' track, and the extended 12-inchers that followed on the Canadian Nettwerk label, were masterful edits that dipped into the sample bag to produce a whole new kind of electronic dance music, a shuffling off kilter sound long before the label 'wonky pop' existed.

On 'Since The Accident' the mood was reasonably heavy, but the edits and loops that Ellard pulled together, and the effects that riddle the melody lines, make it an accessible album, with more than a few Goons-like effects and the occasional rhythm that sounds like it was created by someone teetering on the edge of falling over.

OMD
Dazzle Ships
Original release: 1983
TELEGRAPH

Tracklisting:
Radio Prague, Genetic Engineering, ABC Auto-Industry Telegraph, This Is Helena, International, Dazzle Ships (Parts II, III & VII), The Romance Of The Telescope, Silent Running, Radio Waves, Time Zones, Of All The Things We've Made.

If Severed Heads were duping people into their reconstituted dance music by pretending to be industrial, Orchestral Manoeuvres In the Dark were heading down the same road but in the opposite direction. The hugely successful 'Architecture And Morality' album had introduced them to admiring pop fans and the world of 'Smash Hits' and 'Top Of The Pops', but their label, DinDisc, had folded and Virgin had taken up their contract, giving them their own label Telegraph in the process. But can you imagine the faces of the Virgin board when they heard the opening track of 'Dazzle Ships'? The gorgeous militaristic period piece 'Radio Prague' sounded like it was originally recorded in 1948, and as the album unfolded it was clear that OMD were in heavy concept land.

'Dazzle Ships' was nothing like their previous album. Featuring twelve tracks, it focussed on the cold war and contained half a dozen pieces of musique concrete, or short wave radio samples, with six "proper" songs between them. It was truly different and it sounded just amazing at the time, and even more so all these years later. The "weird" bits are still stunning, and the proper songs contain intriguing samples that give them a strange unreal feel, as the band utilised an array of electronic sounds in a boomy environment to exude a magnificently cold and serious feel.

Even though two tracks were released as singles, there were no hits here, and the whole album worked as a whole, unique piece of music. It created a quandary for anyone who was already an OMD fan, or an even tougher conundrum for anyone who had dismissed their singles as lightweight. The use of Mellotron and the E-Mu Emulator for samples, along with a Solina String Machine, gave 'Dazzle Ships' a marvellously melancholy feel throughout, and the minimal, instrumental title track (in several parts) was breathtaking.

THE ART OF NOISE
Close To The Edit
Original release: 1984
ZTT

The advent of sampling had added many new possibilities to all kinds of music in the first half of the decade, and a plethora of new and relatively affordable effects units in studios meant that anyone with the technical prowess to pull all of the elements together, combined with a vision for song construction and a sense of humour, could make pop songs that were far greater than the sum of their parts. Trevor Horn had been a member of Buggles, who hit the charts with 'Video Killed The Radio Star', a cheesy slice of pop fun which married vaudeville and vintage pop songwriting. He'd grown up in the studio and, in the early 1980s, was in a position to use his skills with a gang of like-minded individuals who would launch their own label.

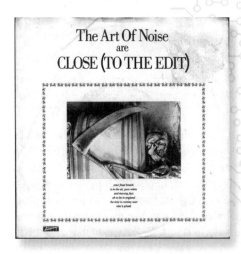

The Art Of Noise
are
CLOSE (TO THE EDIT)

ZTT, like the band name Art Of Noise, referenced the futurist ideas mentioned in chapter one, the initials standing for Zang Tumb Tuum. Its launch coincided with huge advances in digital sampling, and Horn worked closely with ABC and Frankie Goes To Hollywood, but also took time to develop The Art Of Noise, a studio-bound collaboration with Anne Dudley, JJ Jeczalik, Gary Langan and Paul Morley.

Echoing the heady ideas of the futurists, their first single, the mainly instrumental 'Close To The Edit', featured samples of Yes (who Horn had previously joined) and a VW Golf over a driving electronic melody line, complete with chorus flourishes and a dramatic sub-melody. It also boasted spoken word dialogue and enough twists to confirm its status as a piece of high brow genius. It was a state of the art big studio performance of the kind with which Horn's name would become synonymous.

HOLGER HILLER
Jonny
Original release: 1984
CHERRY RED

In the early '80s, the development of the home Portastudio by Tascam, and its availability at under £400, began to make home recording a realistic option. Like Apple's Garageband twenty years later, it opened the doors to huge spare room possibilities and let people try things at no specific further cost, other than their time. A whole industry of cassette-only labels and DIY practitioners were allowed to shape music in whatever way they wanted, free from the concerns of studio costs and third party producers and engineers. Songs could be developed and delivered in new, unique ways, and the device allowed them to work on songs by themselves, outside of the confines of a traditional group setting.

Holger Hiller had been the vocalist in the short-lived, but much praised, Palais Schaumburg. Inspired by the emerging variations of dance music and the possibilities that samplers could offer, he recorded 'Jonny', a succinctly sequenced three-minute slice of rhythmic pop which suggested that he'd hit on a new formula for pumping dance music that retained a tuneful edginess over metallic rhythms. His album 'Ein Bundel Faulnis In Der Grube' ('a bunch of foulness in the pit' to you and me), from where the single was taken, was an intriguing mix of styles veering towards the artier, experimental end of things, with 'Jonny' sitting somewhat uncomfortably in the midst of less formal material. Hiller may not have enlarged on the ideas of 'Jonny', but he had produced a truly magical three minute sidestep.

MANUEL GOTTSCHING
E2-E4
Original release: 1984
INTEAM

Tracklisting:
Quiet Nervousness, Moderate Start, And Central Game, Promise, Queen A Pawn, Glorious
Fight, H.R.H., Retreats (With a Swing), And Sovereignty, Draw

Another German-born composer, Manuel Gottsching's 'E2-E4' did change dance music. Forever.
At just under an hour, 'E2-E4' was one continuous groove split into cerebral thoughts about chess.

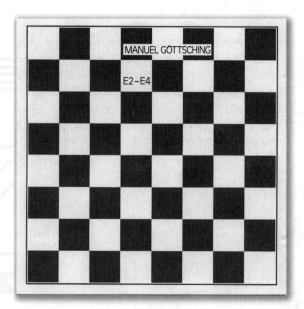

Named after the most common opening chess move, the album's technical prowess and complex
multi-layered electronic sequencing became the most coherent predecessor to continuously
mixed house music. Sounding like it was created on an echoey sound stage, 'E2-E4' is completely
hypnotising. Like a slowed and funkier version of Philip Glass, the 58 minutes make for one
continuous, ever-growing experience, a heady brew of over-lapping sound.

Manuel Gottsching was a former member of Ashra Temple, a guitarist known for his mantra-
like style. On 'E2-E4' he holds back on the riffology until late in the proceedings, adding some
choppy interplay to enhance the electronic flow, and sounding, in some ways, like Mike Oldfield's
'Tubular Bells' incursions. That said, 'E2-E4' has its own very unique sound, something that would
infiltrate the dance world and change it forever.

HAROLD FALTERMEYER
Axel F
Original release: 1984
MCA

The huge influence of Germany on the development of electronic music can never be over stated. None if its shape would have existed without Kraftwerk, Tangerine Dream and, to some degree, the likes of Can, Faust, Ashra Temple, Neubauten and, of course, Gottsching. Even Trio had captured a certain unique sound that was part of the electronic tapestry, a distinctive melody that was their own.

Another German composer, Harold Faltermeyer, and his theme tune to the hugely successful 'Beverly Hills Cop' movie ensured that the sounds of the Linn Drum and Roland and Yamaha synthesisers were implanted deep into the public psyche as the Eddie Murphy film played to enormous audiences. The distinctive riff became a radio regular, and its global appeal became more than apparent years later when it formed part of the 'Crazy Frog' ringtone, a ubiquitous, and frankly irritating, take on the riff which people have tried to erase from memory since it arrived. But lest we forget the glorious, masterful original, a slice of perfect 80s instrumental pop.

SILVER POZZOLI
Around My Dream
Original release: 1985
MANY RECORDS

In the mid-'80s, European dance music and its many variations were beginning to blur the boundaries of electronic music. European record distribution was linked to the Cartel-run independent network in the UK and, alongside alternative and indie releases, dance 12"s were beginning to get greater distribution across the continent.

It had become possible to record and release tracks and for them to pick up attention and airplay in a host of far off territories where they could be bought in a variety of specialist shops. In the mid '80s every major town across Europe seemed to have a variation of the Rough Trade shop.

The Italo-house sound of Silver Pozzoli's 'Around My Dream', a kind of mid-tempo electronic shuffle with a Bryan Ferry-styled vocal, topped the charts in Germany, it's simple rhythm also gaining some interest in the UK. It didn't have the memorable melody of 'Axel F', but it was set to inspire others to go out and start making their own records.

Sitting alongside the suave and a little scary looking Silver Pozzoli, there were electronic dance singles from Belgium's new beat scene, the States' Wax Trax label from Chicago, electro and techno sounds from Detroit, Germany's more austere metallic rhythms, the UK's hard industrial outfits like Portion Control and Nitzer Ebb plus releases from the Canadian Nettwerk label that included ethereal dream pop, Severed Heads and the thumping rhythms of Skinny Puppy. A blissful time for anybody with an ear for a sound they'd never heard before.

SKINNY PUPPY
Assimilate
From the album Bites
Original release: 1985
NETTWERK

As a result of this international availability and awareness, Canadian band Skinny Puppy had been influenced by the brash industrial music they'd picked up in their own local record stores. In fact, they decided to form Skinny Puppy after hearing Portion Control, a London-based power electronics outfit whose aggressive synths and pounding rhythms were topped by some gritty growled vocals. Portion Control had released a string of 12" records that had attracted a strong European following for their Illuminated Records releases, and their reputation had spread to the US and Canada through Rough Trade's distribution network there. By return, Skinny Puppy's two EPs from 1984 had given them a UK following, and their debut album 'Bites' opened with the superbly gruff and pounding 'Assimilate', with its sample from 'Marathon Man', "Is it safe?", adding a scary touch of realism and humanity to their sci-fi sound. Portion Control had made crunching rhythmic mixes and lengthy hypnotic salvos, but it was Skinny Puppy who added a touch of theatre, and a gothic sense of danger that elevated them to bigger, more fashion-conscious audiences.

PORTION CONTROL
Psycho Bod Saves The World
Original release: 1986
DMC

By '85, Portion Control had already moved on from the bludgeoning riffs of their early material and were feverishly searching for a new sound. The distinctive 'Psycho Bod Saves The World', laced with samples from 'Blade Runner' and a host of similarly bleak future movies, was a bedroom epic; a drama played out to a backdrop of computer games, comics and post-Space Invaders excitement.

The album proved more melodic than the group had been before. Sampled dialogue played off against the vocals, synth lines underpinned the main melodies and the tapestry of sound was riddled with found sounds, samples and sound effects. It was a spectacular concept album, as clever in its construction as The Art Of Noise, as wide ranging as the soundtrack to any of the movies that had inspired it.

'Psycho Bod Saves The World' became the band's most successful release, but the music scene had diversified whilst it was being made. There had been a split between tuneful three minute blasts of synthesised pop and the lengthier, hard edged dance beats which had been the band's stock and trade twelve months earlier. Portion Control had delivered a new visionary sound, but it languished in no man's land, remaining a cult item for the years that followed.

ERASURE
Sometimes
Original release: 1986
MUTE

After the release of the first Erasure album, 1985's 'Wonderland', Vince Clarke's earlier decision to disband the hugely successful Yazoo seemed somewhat ill-advised. Alison Moyet had gone on to much bigger things, yet Erasure's first three singles even didn't dent the Top Fifty.

"We wouldn't have a deal any more if we'd been on a major label," singer Andy Bell told 'Underground' magazine on the release of the next single, 'Sometimes', from the upcoming 'Circus' album. "We were getting worried at certain points, but Daniel (Miller) has always been really supportive, and never let us get discouraged about the lack of success".

Miller's faith paid off - 'Sometimes' took the duo to number two in the charts and, perhaps more importantly, to number four in the US Dance chart, which was fast becoming the barometer of electronic music.

MARSHALL JEFFERSON
Move Your Body
Original release: 1986
TRAX

While Erasure were appealing to a distinctive section of club land, over in Chicago, Marshall Jefferson, a record producer and DJ, had created the perfect house rhythm, spiced up by a fusion of piano and an intoxicating rising melody line. It was electronic music with soul and a swing feel, a deep and hypnotic vibe, topped with call and response vocals and an infectious good time feel.

Chicago had become the home of house music, and this track cemented that status, but the electro sound that spiked Detroit earlier in the '80s was developing a harder edge and a darker, more consuming beat.

RHYTHIM IS RHYTHIM
Nude Photo and Strings of Life
Original release: 1987
TRANSMAT

According to Frank Tope in MOJO's 'How To Buy Detroit Techno' feature in 2001, it was northern soul DJ Neil Rushton, and his Kool Kat label, that were first in the UK to pick up on house music. Whilst visiting Detroit he met up with "high school chums" Juan Atkins, Derrick May and Kevin Saunderson, who were "making bare-boned but wildly futuristic jack trax".

"'Nude Photo' still sounds like the future, all sleek lines and nagging irritants, melancholy melody, factory-piston percussion and a whiff of decay in its queasy, trebly synth-string sirens," claim 'This Is Uncool' of the Derrick May track. "'Strings Of Life' was released around the same time, but wasn't a mass market hit until a couple of years later when it was picked up by a major. The original is perhaps the only disco milestone that occasionally lurches out of sync and didn't even have a bassline, just an initially modest piano riff, whistling, tentative synthesised strings.... and then wave upon wave of churning rhythm and melody".

'Strings Of Life' is an odd record. The long intro was slightly misleading, but once the main rhythm and layered synths and effects arrived it became a bubbling brew of sound that gyrated around the central rhythm. An insistent dance track, with more than a hint of Manuel Gottsching's 'E2-E4' in the modal sequencing, the feel was more dancefloor-orientated than 'E2', the drum machine adding a more regimented, thumping urgency. It was "probably the most unlikely dance track ever, almost heart breakingly beautiful" Moby told 'Q', "but it still got thousands of ravers to throw their hands in the air".

PHUTURE
Acid Tracks
Original release: 1987
TRAX

While Rhythim Is Rhythim were employing the sequencer to the limits of it's possibilities, and Marshall Jefferson was heading to a deeper place, the Trax label in Chicago had hit on yet another setting on their synthesisers that would provide a host of wide-eyed club goers with the sound of MDMA being released.

DJ Pierre, Spanky and Herb J were had designed what is widely acknowledged as the first acid house track, "based almost entirely on the squelching B movie sci fi sound of the Roland TB-303," as Garry Mulholland correctly recalls. "There were many other Trax label records out doing roughly the same thing, but 'Acid Tracks' was the longest, the deepest, the headfuckingest".

The Roland TB-303 Bassline synthesiser, an awkward little unit with a mind of its own, was indeed key to the sound, and soon a host of others were turning on and freaking out to its endlessly tweaked resonant filter. From Fast Eddie, Adonis and Bam Bam in the USA to The Shamen, KLF, Baby Ford and A Guy Called Gerald in the UK, this was a new generation of musicians, amongst whom the idea of melody had been reduced to a rasping purr.

The acid house scene was to become a staple of Manchester's Hacienda by 1988 as the UK caught up with it's neighbours, but in '87 the sounds infiltrating the UK club scene were Detroit and Chicago imports, body beat from Belgium, courtesy of Praga Khan and The Lords Of Acid, plus the harder edged electronic body music of the likes of Front 242....

FRONT 242
Master Hit
Original release: 1987
WAX TRAX!

In the Spring of 1987, I persuaded the publishers of 'Sounds', which sold around 100,000 copies alongside 'NME' and 'Melody Maker', to launch 'Underground', an indie fanzine/mag, which they saw as an offshoot potentially on a par with 'Kerrang!'. The publishers hoped they might repeat the metal magazine's sales and ad base, but the indie sector didn't have the money to buy ads on the same level as the metal world, and after a year the title was folded.

However, during that time the strangely designed magazine managed to champion acts as diverse as The Mekons, Coldcut, The Wedding Present and The Band Of Holy Joy, as well as being part of an emerging dance scene, mainly thanks to future Chill Out DJ Chris Coco, plus the strange world of primal "Intelligent Dance Music" which, at the time, included everything from the industrial Cabaret Voltaire to the precursors of new beat in Belgium, Skinny Puppy and Ministry from the States and bizarre outfits like Front 242, again from Belgium.

The magazine's debut issue was given away free with 'Sounds' ("Over my dead body," had insisted the editor) and included a taster of what was to come, including, on page eighteen, an intro to Front 242 by Jean Marc Lederman, from The Weathermen. It opened with the classic quote from frontman Richard Jonckheere: "As far as Front 242 are concerned, most rock bands are still in the stone age". To which Patrick Codenys, their Emulator operator, added, "We're the result of our time. There's so much information about... radio, TV, the media has such presence these days. Front 242, takes it all, processes it and feeds it back again".

Jean Marc listed the band's influences as Kraftwerk, Yello and Depeche Mode, pointing out that the end result, the Front 242 sound which Richard K had described as "Electronic Body Music", was entirely unique and that their live use of paramilitary images, plus mentions of Edgard Varese plus found percussive objects proved that Front 242 were pretty damn different.

At that time, the band's catalogue had just been re-issued, and Richard K, now Richard 23, had become part of the lovingly named Revolting Cocks, along with various members of Ministry. Their goal appeared to be the addition of even more "demonic muscle" to electronic music.

By issue eleven of 'Underground', almost a year later in February 1988, Front 242 were back in the magazine with a new record, 'Master Hit', and a new masterplan, as reported by industrial specialist Alex Bastedo, who was fascinated by Richard 23's "sawn-off Mohican" haircut. By then the band had turned professional and just come off a lengthy tour with Depeche Mode, and the new single had established them as a throbbing, floor shaking band whose dark dancefloor roots suddenly appeared all the more enticing and accessible following a reworking of the tune.

Bastedo quizzed: "Were you happy with the 'Master Hit' reworking?

Richard 23: "No, not really. What happened was that we recorded a new 12" for release in the autumn but scrapped it. Then, for the first time in our careers, we compromised and went back into the studio and remixed 'Master Hit'. But none of use were 100 per cent happy with it. That's why it's only available in North America and on import in Europe".

The remixed rarity became a must-have/must-hear item, and the seven minute plus two-parter, with its throbbing rhythmic synths and multi-layered screeching, complete with 'master and servant' lyrical interplay and a touch of opera-lite in the background, made 'Master Hit' into a dance hit too. Of course, it didn't trouble the charts, but as an inspirational slice of industrial dance music, it worked an absolute treat.

NITZER EBB
Join In the Chant
Original release: 1987
MUTE

The electronic body movement had also spread to leafy Essex, where Nitzer Ebb's crunching rhythms and shouty sloganeering was heralded as "speedy Euro dance for the delirious disco age," in 'Underground'. On interviewing the band in June 1987, they noted that they looked like three members fresh from the Panzer Corps who were employing irony at the top level.

"Our method is sarcastic," they enthused, nonchalantly, "Almost all of our influences were German – Malaria, DAF, Die Krupps. We saw them as a new dance direction in the early '80s.

It had punk, it had funk, but it petered out. Now the evolved sound is spreading through Europe with the likes of Front 242, Neon Judgement and The New Gods".

Nitzer Ebb's sound was harsh, cold and pedantic. It was energetic and upfront, snagging at your heels on the dancefloor. "The other day," they continued, "Radio One said that Donna Summer's 'I Feel Love' was too fast to dance to, which sums up the state of things and the mentality we're up against. The reaction to us is that we are too alternative for mainstream clubs and too mainstream for the alternative clubs. We were very impressed with such a reaction but It won't stop us. We aim to kick apathy off the dancefloor".

With Nitzer Ebb upsetting the status quo and providing music to dance to, albeit frenetically, it was another pair of ironic East Enders who were about to break the mould and take intelligent electronic music to the masses.

THE PET SHOP BOYS
Actually
PARLOPHONE
Original release: 1987

Neil Tennant's aforementioned distress at the release of 'Blue Monday' proved short lived, as he and Chris Lowe's debut 45, 'West End Girls', soon defined their sound of trained keyboards and deadpan vocals and elevated them to instant star status. The duo made an art of disinterest, and the sleeve of 'Actually', with Tennant caught mid yawn, said everything about their attitude.

"Their expansive sounding second LP," Q's 'How To Buy Synth-Pop' claimed, "defined their do-no-wrong imperial phase, with anti-Thatcherite satire, Catholic guilt, a stunning cameo from Dusty Springfield and hits galore". Featuring 'It's A Sin', 'Rent', 'King's Cross' and, of course, 'What Have I Done To Deserve This?', 'Actually' married Lowe's melodic ear with Tennant's subdued delivery, the whole thing set off with the liberal use of an Emulator, which allowed them to add a touch of classicism to the sound with plenty of lush, sampled strings.

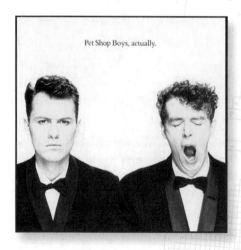

Pet Shop Boys, actually.

Atypically English, and jam packed with tongue in cheek references, The Pet Shop Boys' lyrics took on life, shopping and parties with an incisive wit. "Marc Almond wrote about sexual extremes," noted Tennant, "but we'd hint at those things instead". The result of his storytelling providing the perfect foil for the record's lush sound.

Inspired by producer Bobby Orlando and a single by The Flirts, Lowe and Tennant began to fuse their various influences to create the distinctive Pet Shop sound. "We liked Oralando's brutal electronic edge," recalled Tennant to Martin Aston in 'Q', "Bobby came from another lineage, from Kraftwerk to Giorgio Moroder to Patrick Cowley and Sylvester to Bobby O, which was the specific gay lineage. He (Chris) was copying Trevor Horn and New Order as well. But I liked early hip hop and Afrika Bambaataa too, which was very electronic".

The amalgamation of so many influences, Chris Lowe's classical training and Tennant's deadpan delivery gave The Pet Shop Boys instant access to the charts. A string of singles followed, revisiting ground trodden by Elvis whilst also penning anthems for the newest bath of bored teenagers off the construction line.

JEAN MICHEL JARRE
Revolution Industrielle
From Revolutions
Original release: 1988
DREYFUSS

Whilst The Pet Shop Boys were igniting dancefloors and infiltrating clubland, Jean Michel Jarre was taking electronic music onto the streets on a huge scale. In 1988, the Destination Docklands performance brought him to the banks of the River Thames for a spectacular, firework-spiced show in front of 100,000 people.

Set to coincide with the release of the album 'Revolutions', which became his biggest seller since 'Oxygene' on the back of such showmanship, the set was spectacular, and the inclusion of the overture and three parts of 'Revolution Industrielle', the album's key piece, allowed Jarre to introduce echoey ambience and layered Roland synthesisers, choirs and vocoders, suggesting another time and space entirely.

The very nature of Jarre's shows were, like his recording career, carried off outside of the norm, the show at the Docklands providing a typical example of his ability to present quite startlingly different music to a huge audience and achieve sales figures more commercially minded acts would have killed for in the process.

YELLO
The Race
Original release: 1988
FONTANA

Yello also appealed to a clientele outside of synthpop's core followers, having begun life with rather humble and small-scale ideas only to shed their experimental explorations and launch into the production of a startling hybrid of musical styles. Originally signed to The Residents' Ralph label, where they perfected tightly structured, short electronic pop songs with whimsical titles and bizarre storylines delivered over sequenced and phased passages from Boris Blank, the band eventually ended up with the far wider reaching Fontana label.

Hailing from Switzerland, they slowy grew into a more intense and intelligent mix of sounds, an oddball, atmospheric kind of schlager music, cleverly embroidered with intense rhythmic and sequenced confections and employing melody lines that could have originated decades earlier. Eventually, several albums into their career, they produced 'The Race' for their high brow opus 'Flag'. It proved to be a tune with such driving connotations that it would become a repetitive sports programme soundbed to this day, and their most synched offering still. It was a riff which instantly summed up motion, and they profited largely from it as a result. Yello, like Sparks, were a strange duo, making music that was acquired taste. When they were good they were great, and 'The Race' was them at their best.

A GUY CALLED GERALD
Voodoo Ray
Original release: 1988
RHAM!

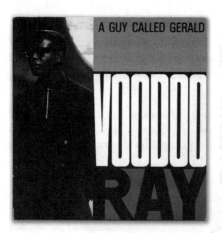

Like Yello, A Guy Called Gerald's name will always be synonymous with one killer song. Sure, he went on to score a book ('Trip City'), produce a host of killer 12"s and become a renowned DJ, but when 'Voodoo Ray' was first spun at the Hacienda in 1988, it was immediately apparent

228

he'd forged something entirely new and instantly classic. The track broke away from the Juan Atkins and Derrick May techno mould that he'd been well known for contributing to, and added something British and fresh to the emerging acid house scene.

A homage to Ray Charles, 'Voodoo Ray' took Gerald's Roland TB-303 and TR-808 drum machine into new acid-tinged territory, topped by a vocal loop praising the legendary soul crooner. It was already beyond Phuture, and had a stab at the charts as a result of the catchy blend of squelching, bulling acid bass, the vocal hook and an offbeat steel drum-sound used for a counter melody. It all set the single apart, and remix upon remix followed, and will probably continue to do so.

HUMANOID
Stakker Humanoid
Original release: 1988
WESTSIDE

By mid 1988, Acid house and rave culture was beginning to become an obsession with the British tabloid press, who were full of Middle England threatening sensationalist headlines and scaremongering LSD and E based horror stories every Monday morning. Nevertheless, the scene grew and grew at a rate not seen since the punk explosion of '76, and, alongside the rash of imports and Gerald's 'Voodoo Ray', 'Stakker Humanoid' proved to be one of the must have tunes of the year. A beguiling piece of robotic weirdness, the track went yet further to break the fast changing boundaries of the new sound.

Stakker was a collaboration between video artists Mark McClean and Colin Scott, who, inspired by the recent barrage of complex video singles with pulsing patterns set to music, set about creating exactly that. But in their case, the video would exist first, with the music to be added later. It was an idea that was also at the heart of several Godley and Crème visual experiments at the time, but something new in electronic music.

To bring the visuals to life, Stakker enlisted Brian Dougans to produce music to accompany their multi-coloured collage. Using the standard Roland set up of the day, Dougans inadvertently produced a driving acid house epic, the seven inch of which came adorned with a still from the video.

By this point, Acid House had taken root in the clubs of London, resulting in increased television coverage, and the Stakker visuals allowed punters to return home to their comedowns and watch a virtual TV replay of what had been snapping at their synapses earlier in the evening. The concept of visuals delivered with music in this way was complicated and short-lived, but the Stakker sound remains a classic. Dougans would eventually form the hugely influential Future Sound Of London, and more recently be part of the psychedelically-hued Amorphous Androgynous.

S'EXPRESS
Theme From S Express
Original release: 1988
RHYTHM KING

In the wake of Gerald and Stakker came a whole slew of acid-blottered squeaky 12-inchers and remixes. Illegal parties and the growing availability of Ecstasy had produced a loved-up generation on far greater scale than the 60s' Summer Of Love, and the scene's signature bass driven sound and smiley faces seemed to be everywhere almost overnight.

DJ and producer Mark Moore began with the basic building blocks of the genre, but added familiar sampled sections to create trippy, half-remembered moments of contemporary soul. His S'Express classic used the melody from Rose Royce's 'Is It Love That You're After?', the one-liner 'I Got The Hots For You' from a TZ record and a hi-hat sound sampled from an aerosol can to create the horn-blasted 'Theme From S Express', a strangely accessible, even 'poppy', take on the underground scene.

230

The various elements of the song were liberally sprinkled with further samples from Gil Scott Heron, Yazoo's 'Situation' and Sam The Sham And The Pharaohs among many others, demonstrating a high regard for music's history and some ingenious editing. The single topped the UK charts and led to a whole string of 45s from the band that reflected an old soul touring commune approach, augmented by dancing girls gyrating wildly around a smirking Mark Moore. As with many key cuts from this period, countless remixes, remodels and updates have abounded, but, as it the case ninety nine times out of a hundred, the original remains the best.

LIL LOUIS
French Kiss
Original release: 1989
LONDON

The free love and Curtis Mayfield groove of S'Express was central to the end of the '80s. It was no secret by now that electronic music was fuelled by Ecstasy and prologned, continous music. The concepts of live performance and the guitar had become secondary, and people were happily 'loved up', or at least they thought they were. During 1989 hip hop also was changing, with the arrival of De La Soul's Daisy Age and the harder yet still accessible sound of Tone Loc, among many others. Meanwhile, the primarily American funk rock scene, at the hands of Faith No More, Red Hot Chilli Peppers and Extreme was gaining momentum and reaching across the ocean to the UK. Everyone suddenly had a soul, and the London club scene elevated Soul II Soul to the top of the charts.

Madonna's 'Like A Prayer' was the biggest track of the year, but its gospel feel was too squeaky clean. S'Express were having a riotous party that spilled onto 'Top Of The Pops' but it was Lil Louis' 'French Kiss', with all its unorthodox arrangement and chic sounding title and band name, that provided the momentum for a far more sensual sound. "Dancers went bananas, and the

Balearic breakdown was born," recalled 'This Is Uncool' of the ten minute track, which made use of the simplest of notation, a sequenced melody line and an affected rhythm that slowed to a standstill as the sounds of a moaning orgasm were reached. 'French Kiss' was some way from Kraftwerk, it was fair to say. A distant cousin from a very different town.

808 STATE
Pacific State
Original release: 1989
ZTT

Having originally included A Guy Called Gerald in their line up, 808 State, named after the Roland drum machine that provided their backbone, was a throwback to classic, rock tinged structures, and any heavy breathing was from more likely to eminate from the horn man rather than a passing female admirer. While Lil Louis simplified things to the single note which held 'French Kiss' together, 808 State used the bass pulse that drove their brand of techno to provide a melodic lead, giving this particular track a completely different, almost free jazz feel, especially when topped by a uplifting saxophone line which provided the counter melody and, as proved by the endless remixes of the time, the hook.

The track became a dancefloor staple and was eventually picked up by Radio One, peaking at number ten in the charts. Gerald's former cohorts in the band, Graham Massey and Martin Price (who were involved with Eastern Bloc, Manchester and, for a time, the nation's most fashionable record shop), took their music from chart friendly techno to an ambient tinged Cafe Del Mar type sound over the following years, transporting their fans to all kinds of exotic locations along the way. Several hits ensued, including the classic 'Cubik'/'Olympic' double-A and some collaborations with fellow Mancunian MC Tunes.

In fact, the 808 State legacy is fascinating, and warrants further investigation for anybody with a passing interest in the period. A host of out-takes, live recordings, and even samples, can be found on their comprehensive site at www.808state.com

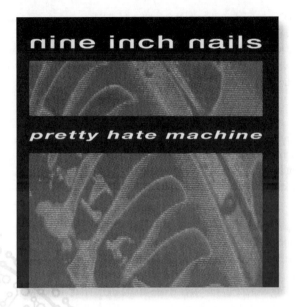

NINE INCH NAILS
Down In It
from Pretty Hate Machine
Original release: 1989
TVT

TECHNOTRONIC
Pump Up The Jam
Original release: 1989
SBK

The decade had certainly been one of extremes, and, in truth, far more anarchic and freeform than its predecessor. Inspired by technological advances, it was a time of a widely different variety of music, which split camps and attracted new disciples, igniting new sounds which imploded on themselves with a flash, only to be immediately forgotten and replaced with an apparent improvement. The dancefloor was unpredictable. So many genres and so many styles were battling for recognition, whilst so many sources were supplying the raw materials.

Jo Beogaert had spent the decade holed up in Belgium, eventually creating Technotronic's 'Pump Up The Jam', a chart topping descendent of the Belgian new beat sound that dabbled in slightly dated hip house territory. Simultaneously, Nine Inch Nails' Trent Reznor was locked in his bedroom creating tales of alienation and distrust. No finer example could exist of the quite staggeringly different sub-genres that electronic music and electronic musicians had split into. Technotronic's sampled vocals and good time chantalong couldn't have been more askew from Reznor's troubled tunes.

Reznor's album, 'Pretty Hate Machine', released under the name Nine Inch Nails, opened with the momentous 'Head Like A Hole', but by the time track three rolled around, with the help of On-U Sound's Adrian Sherwood and Keith LeBlanc, he was moulding the template for a brand of futuristic heavy electronic music, which was inspired, according to the sleeve, by the author Clive Barker, hip hop legends Public Enemy, This Mortal Coil and the Perry Farrell fronted Jane's Addiction. This was jarring, unnerving stuff.

By 1991, Reznor would have recruited a band and set out on a tour of the US on the inaugural Lollapalooza with Jane's Addiction, Living Colour, Siouxsie And The Banshees, Bodycount, The Butthole Surfers and Henry Rollins among others. A year later he would tour the world with Guns n' Roses, so impressing Axl Rose that the proto LA hair metal rockers would never recover and Rose would spend fifteen years working on a record which proved, on release, to be largely a pale imitation of Reznor's work.

Reznor, unlike Jo Beogaert had tapped into a kind of pulsing robotic future that was based in Kraftwerk and Depeche Mode, but carried the dark, indie stamp of The Cure, channelling the angst of thousands upon thousands of adolescent teenagers. I interviewed Reznor on the Lollapalooza tour for 'RAW' magazine, and the two incendiary performances that I saw on that long haul singled them out as being exactly in the right place at the right time, not only to transform electronic music but also the whole alternative scene.

The response at each show was amazing, as if people had witnessed something larger and more personal than a travelling concert. Jane's also had that spirit and shock effect, but while they dabbled in bawdy Hollywood and rock excess, Nine Inch Nails seemed new, dysfunctional and fucked up. They also sounded like a battalion of drugged up choppers descending.

Bearing that in mind, Reznor was still nervous and unsure about what NIN could achieve. He discussed suicide and the alienation he felt, even with thousands of people fascinated to peak into his world and desperate to find out what the tiny dot in 'Down In It' was. Undoubtedly, his uncertainty coloured his creativity, his nervousness giving NIN the edge,

In the intervening years, Nine Inch Nails have produced even darker visions with enough self-assessment to fuel a million debates. But between 1989 and '91, the future of electronic music was deftly forged by Nine Inch Nails, and their effect on rock music would be enormous.

As for 'Technotronic', the beat may well have been, but nobody with an ounce of credibility would ever have uttered the word. Nevertheless, the charts of Europe proved happy hunting grounds.

THE ORB
A Huge Ever Growing Pulsating Brain That Rules From The Centre Of The Ultraworld
Original release: 1989
BIG LIFE

As Trent Reznor was wrestling with alienation and Technotronic were filling the dancefloor, Dr Alex Paterson and Youth, formerly of Killing Joke and by then a revered producer, were experimenting with sound effects, ambient noise and samples of Minnie Riperton's 'Loving You'.

Having bubbled under the surface throughout the late 80s, the birth of Ambient House took shape when the duo were asked to do a Peel Session, and with the subsequent release of 'A Huge Ever Growing Pulsating Brain That Rules From The Centre Of The Ultraworld', a title lifted from a Blake's Seven sound effect record. The disc was released on the WAU! Mr Modo label, operated by the pair. It defied all reason, being a one track 12" of slow, multi- layered sounds that dipped into Pink Floyd's back pages, nodded to Tangerine Dream, exchanged chit chat with Eno and acknowledged a host of releases on Sky and Brain. All the while sounding new and completely different.

In an environment where the beat was being polished, sequenced and turned up to eleven, The Orb switched the drum machine off and opted to float away.

POP WILL EAT ITSELF
This Is The Day, This Is The Hour, This Is This!
Original release: 1989
RCA

Tracklisting:
PWEI Is a Four Letter Word. Preaching to the Perverted. Wise Up! Sucker. Sixteen Different Flavours of Hell. Inject Me. Can U Dig It? The Fuses Have Been Lit. Poison To The Mind. Def. Con.One. Radio P.W.E.I. Shortwave Transmission on 'Up to the Minuteman Nine. Satellite Ecstatica. Not Now James, We're Busy... Wake Up! Time to Die...

As the Orb quietly wafted away, next door there was an overwhelming racket. Stourbridge, in the UK's Midlands, isn't an exciting place, but Pop Will Eat Itself were determined to have a good time. With their heads in rock, and a few synthesizers and sequencers bubbling away, they'd discovered the possibilities of the sampler and had a thing for white boy rap. Dishevelled at best, the Poppies were considered 'Grebo', yet another genre summoned up by the NME. Their mix of industrial rhythms, an alternative rock groove and jerky sloganeering from everywhere and anywhere, including a glorious lift from Blade Runner for 'Wake Up, Time To Die' and dialogue from The Warriors for 'Can U Dig It!', soon won them a loyal army of likeminded fans.

In awe of The Beastie Boys, PWEI had some hokey raps, the line 'Give me Big Mac and Fries to go' and a host of mentions and clips from TV which said everything about their Black Country home and the nation's unemployable. PWEI had plenty of punk venom and their new technology add-ons gave them a unique edgy sound that would be toughened up in the '90s in the guise of The Prodigy.

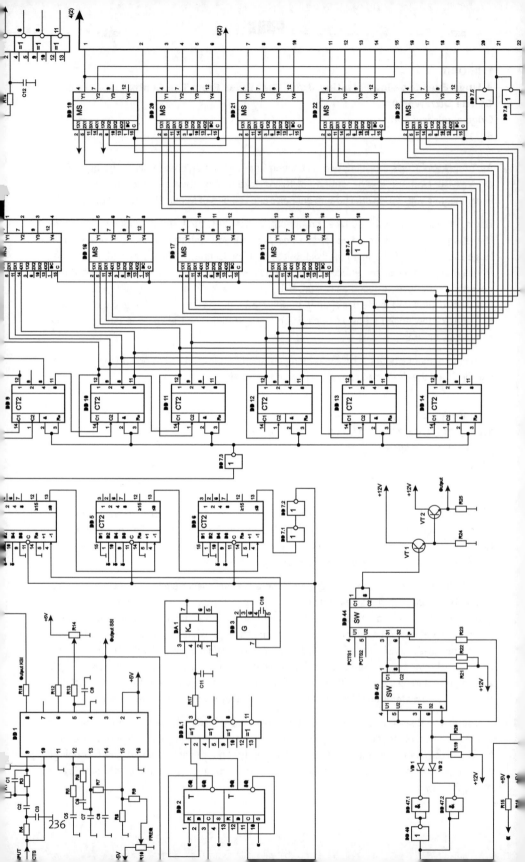

FIVE

WELCOME TO THE WORLD OF DRUG-ADDLED MULTI-SAMPLES

The '90s took shape in fields in the middle of nowhere, with police sirens wailing in the background and people looking more than a little worse for wear. Drugs were everywhere, from the core of Trainspotting to the dancefloor stimulants that elevated the DJ to the place of celebrity. When people weren't out having a good time they were a thome chilling out and listening to the latest studio bound electronic sounds.

While The Verve were convinced that the drugs don't work people were having visions. And visionaries were making sounds that couldn't have been imagined just a few years earlier. The disparate dance factions were beginning to merge, rock excess was infiltrating electronica and the key electronic acts were becoming arena pulls.

ORBITAL
Chime
Original release: 1990
FFRR

"For the average gig-going music lover, there are usually only a handful - if that - of bands in a lifetime who compel you to spend your hard-earned cash, not only on every piece of their recorded oeuvre but also, time and time again, on experiencing their live shows". So went the sleevenotes for Orbital's Glastonbury performances. Silvia Montello, head of Universal Catalogue, was a diehard fan who had selected the tracks for me to edit together, tracing their tenure down the farm from 1994. She was inspired, "There can be even fewer that have managed to grip such a loyal live audience without playing 'conventional instruments' - after all, just how exciting can it be spending an evening watching a couple of blokes on stage twiddling some knobs? No wonder the well-worn '90s phrase 'faceless techno bollocks' came about!". Quite.

Paul and Phil Hartnoll were inspired electronica fans, as Paul told Richard Buskin in 'Sound On Sound' magazine in 2006. "From the moment I heard Kraftwerk's 'Computer World' I loved the beauty and the rigidness, as well as the analogue warmth of that bubbling funk, which you only seemed to get with electronic music. I've always enjoyed that - music in 16ths, totally relentless but beautifully done. I suppose it's the whole Donna Summer 'I Feel Love' kind of thing, which always got to me".

The brothers had begun playing live on the rave scene as the decade began, and their first release was the magical 'Chime'. It became their anthem, the constant in a set that mixed heady and heavy electronica with techno, ambient spirals and air-punching motifs worthy of Vangelis or Jean Michel Jarre. If you were lucky, you'd get a dose of the theme to 'Dr who?' too. So the story goes, 'Chime' was recorded on a cassette deck in 1989 and cost less than £1 to complete. No hi-tech specs there. A year later, London Records' imprint FFRR took it to number 17 in the national chart, the discordant melody line and acid-styled bass providing an insistent, pumping groove. Where did it come from? "I just did it because I was in a happy mood, thinking about going down the pub," claimed Paul Hartnoll in 'Sound On Sound'.

"I remember the first time: somewhat sceptical," Silvia Montello wrote, "'Yeah, I've heard 'Chime', it's alright, not sure what the fuss is all about' – I had found myself, by the time 'Chime' concluded their set, propelled to the front of the stage not only by the enthusiasm of the massed Tribal Gathering festival-goers but by the sheer force of the music. Exhausted and immensely happy, it felt like a conversion, and it was the start of a special relationship with Orbital". Truthfully, that was how it happened; as soon as you saw their geeky none-chic and the cheering crowd who knew every nuance of their songs, an affection for the brothers Hartnoll was hard to evade, and 'Chime' seemed to encapsulate it all.

"The first version of 'Chime' literally came about through me replacing the stolen four-track. I'd always recorded onto four tracks and then mastered onto my dad's 1970's Pioneer cassette player - the gulf between a professional tape recorder and the sort of stuff I had was not only way too vast, but I was also ignorant," Paul told 'Sound On Sound', explaining the straight to cassette theory. "It occurred to me: 'hang on a minute, why don't I bypass the recording phase and just mix live from these instruments into six channels?'".

And he did. "I decided to knock something up. I was in a happy mood, I wasn't consciously thinking about what I was going to do, and so I just knocked up this little refrain by sampling three things from an easy listening record of my dad's, containing instrumental cover versions of popular hits".

And so a legend of the dancefloor, warehouse and deserted fields in the middle of nowhere, was born. No mean feat, and a pound well spent. A series of untitled albums followed, and the sight of the Hartnolls stooped over their keyboards with what appeared to be torches strapped to each side of their glasses became a cause for much applause and mimicking by their followers. They were a staple at Glastonbury from 1994 to 2004, and reformed for Glastonbury's 40th birthday in 2010. 'Chime', with all its overlaid samples and rising melodies, textured sound and popping rhythms, was not the stuff of teen magazines and glossy reveal-all stories. The boys in the band were too serious about what they were doing, and it would still be a few years before a techno artist graced such publications. But the time was right for acid house, and Adamski was more than photogenic; he had a dog.....

ADAMSKI
Killer
Original release: 1990
MCA

Victims of the rave were commonplace in town centres on Sunday mornings. Wandering around aimlessly, still throbbing from an evening of loved up gyration, generally confused but harmless. Adam Tinley could have been in any such crowd, blinded by the morning sun, bedraggled and looking like they were still in search of something. Anything.

Adam, with his shock of bleached hair and a designer dog with a Mohican, aided by Seal up front, giving it some proper soul, had become Adamski, eventually unleashing 'Killer', a scary synthpop moment that vibrated behind Seal's emotive vocal. He'd been Adamski before, but now he'd reached number one in the pop charts with his latest vinyl adventure and an upside down world was re-inverting itself.

"Every time I put a single out I wanted to do something different. 'Killer' was slow and heavy in mood," he told Simon Reynolds, who interviewed him for 'Melody Maker in 1990'. "It was a nothing like 'NRG' which came out before".

Adamski became acid house and rave's first real pop star, and Reynolds had a vision of his juxtaposition of music and the change he'd gone through: "It's like Picasso chucking it in to be a cartoonist for the Daily Mail, or Dirk Bogarde being envious of Norman Wisdom," Reynolds mused as Adamski sipped his Lucozade.

Adam had emerged from the faceless throng to feature in 'Smash Hits' and to start a change in acid house, which had been the territory of simple bass riffs and endless rhythm tracks before. "I wanted the music to be like 'Rebel Rebel' or 'Identity' by X Ray Spex," he told Reynolds, "I wanted to stop being at the back just pushing buttons, I wanted it to be up front".

Adamski had arrived, and his pop career was taken very seriously by the marketing heads at MCA. Nevertheless, continued success was short-lived and subsequent singles, without the groggy harmonies of Seal, the Alison Moyet to Adam's Vince Clarke, floundered. The future for Adamski, and indeed the fast changing rave scene, was always going to be precarious.

"I've got all kinds of fans now," he told Reynolds, "Teenyboppers, everything. I don't think the ravers take me seriously now though". Indeed, the spruced up image and trophy dog seemed to alienate him from the dance heads, which was a shame as subsequent singles were well worth attention. Unlike his vocalist, Adamski was to slowly slip from view.

THE KLF
What Time Is Love?
3am Eternal
Original release: 1990
KLF COMMUNICATIONS

In 1987, I was editing 'OffBeat' magazine and received a copy of 'All You Need Is Love' by The JAMMS. I couldn't believe the audacious nature of the thing when I played it, and with no information other than a phone number, I called the band and said we wanted to do an interview. How could anybody graft The Beatles' 'All You Need Is Love', MC5's 'Kick Out the Jams' and a hokey rap together and sound so angry and Scottish?

Obviously the story has become dog-eared and embellished over the years. The JAMMS became The KLF (via The Timelords), burned a million pounds, did a thrash metal cover of one of their hit songs and left a dead sheep in the foyer at the BRITS and quit the music business and deleted their extremely valuable back catalogue the next day. Genius, no less. Consisting of Bill Drummond and Jimmy Cauty, they were renaissance men, one step ahead of the PRS and MCPS, swaddled in leather hoodies and looking decidedly guilty.

'All You Need Is Love' was followed by 'Whitney Joins The JAMS', and both singles were withdrawn due to legal issues with samples, but their Timelords incarnation and 'Doctorin' The TARDIS' single topped the UK charts in 1988, mixing Gary Glitter and the 'Dr Who?' theme in a mash of wedding reception friendly pop. It was easy to have a chart hit, the pair claimed in their "The Manual: How To Have A Number One The Easy Way" opus, and the samples kept on coming with 'Kylie Said To Jason', again by the KLF, and a slew of rave-friendly singles that included the Stadium House Trilogy, a trippy trance amalgam consisting of '3am Eternal', 'Last Train To Trancentral' and 'What Time Is Love?'. The latter, perhaps their best known track, had originally appeared in 1988, a slow burning trance number bursting with sluggish energy which quickly became a pumping, war horse driven classic of the genre. The lead motif, an MK-80 derived three note riff of stupid simplicity, was recycled and reused on no less than four separate incarnations of the same single over a ten year period, including 1992' "America: What Time Is Love?" release and 2K's 1997 hit 'Fuck The Millennium'. It was a credit to that very riff that each incarnation managed to retain a fresh element.

Their singles were upbeat, their appearances on 'Top Of The Pops' became more and more overblown and obtuse as their success ballooned and, back at their Trancentral, base even more confusing things were afoot.....

KLF
Chill Out
Original release: 1990
KLF COMMUNICATIONS

SPACE
Space
Original release: 1990
KLF COMMUNICATIONS

As KLF's pop career beckoned an unsuspecting public into their world of high jinx, Jimmy Cauty, who was also a former member of the short-lived Brilliant and The Orb (both of which had also featured Youth), recorded the album 'Space', an ambient slice of melancholy downbeat chill out music that he'd perfected in his squat in South London. During the recordings, which originally began as an Orb project, he'd also entered into marathon mixing and jamming sessions with The Orb's Alex Paterson and his JAMMS cohort Drummond, adventures which eventually resulted in an ambient piece 'Chill Out'.

A cornerstone, and perhaps the key record, of the ambient house scene, 'Chill Out' was a forty four minute mix that sampled everything from Acker Bilk and Elvis through to Tuvan throat singers, all the while charting and soundtracking an imagined road trip across America. Mixed and recorded live onto DAT, and layered with synthesisers, pedal steel guitar and occasional samples from the duo's own back catalogue, it, like the 'Space' album, created a new sub genre of ambient, a flowing early morning antidote to the late night reverie of their very own chart successes.

"While electronic dinosaurs like Jean Michel Jarre and Klaus Schulze were walling themselves in with banks and banks of synthesisers, computers and electronic gadgetry, "enthused 'Record Collector' magazine, "the KLF were doing the opposite — making a crafted work with the bare necessities of musical survival".

The KLF were sound terrorists, punk composers with a wild flair for picking the right sounds at the right time. Championship chancers, their legacy remains truly impressive, their ambient pieces still standing up as influential and inspirational whilst their rave and pop sides still sound every bit as anthemic as they did in their heyday. The mix of samples, spoken parts and clever editing opened the floodgates for anyone to do it, and one can only imagine what paths the purchase of 'Chill Out' might have led "WTIL" loving teenyboppers down.

REVOLTING COCKS
Beers, Steers And Queers
Original release: 1990
WAX TRAX!

Tracklisting:
Beers, Steers And Queers, (Let's Get) Physical, In the Neck, Get Down, Stainless Steel Providers, Can't Sit Still, Something Wonderful, Razor's Edge

The Revolting Cocks had begun life with 'No Devotion' on Wax Trax! in 1985, quickly developing their electronic body music on 'Big Sexy Land' a year later. Originally consisting of Richard 23, of Front 242 fame, and Ministry's Al Jourgensen, augmented by Loc Van Acker, who Richard 23 had met in Belgium, they were a good time electronic punk idea that fused industrial concepts with pummelling beats. The band's sound soon developed into a heavy, post Nine Inch Nails thumpalong with Ministry styled percussion. Richard 23 wasn't impressed, and left due to the vintage "musical differences" clause just as their recordings became littered with samples of sound and dialogue, adding new further intrigue to their dark sound.

The title track from their 'Beers, Steers And Queers' record opened the set in brain-bouncing style, with the huge and heavy beat dominating proceedings as samples were piled on top of each other, lifted from all over the place. The song crackled with witty one-liners and subtle effects intended to further enhance its adrenalin rush. As the band's name suggests, there was more than a little ironic, tongue-in-cheek humour to Revolting Cocks, and the second track on the album, a re-imagined version of Olivia Newton John's '(Let's Talk) Physical', just sounded completely wrong, from concept to drawing board to first listen.

The band were by now morphing with various fellow industrial acts, and Finitribe's Chris Connelly was deployed on 'Physical', creating a repetitive loop of one snare beat, which made the driving, claustrophobic rhythm of the song sound like an incendiary explosion every four bars. It was the simplicity of such things, along with the polished and super clean production, that gave Revolting Cocks their merciless, menacing edge. It was a migraine-inducing thud that never let up, trading old school rock bravado with new found, sample-frenzied electronic hardcore.

PRIMAL SCREAM
Come Together
from Screamadelica
Original release: 1991
CREATION

While mainland Europe and the edgier clubs on the dark underbelly of America were protesting and venting their collected spleen about the myriad bad things in this world, in the UK My Bloody Valentine were increasing the effects on their modal guitar stew, developing a warmer, full frontal and trippy brand of sound with woozy immediacy. Synthpop, meanwhile, seemed to be ticking along just fine. But everything was about to change. The honeymoon period over, electronic music was about to become secondary.

A musical revolution was happening in Seattle, and the release of Nirvana's 'Smells Like Teen Spirit', and its plethora of hit singles and teenage friendly anthems, made everybody rethink what they were doing. Hair metal disappeared virtually overnight (although we hadn't seen the last of it as many then predicted) and anything over and above a guitar, bass and drums set up, ideally cranked up on a wall of distortion and mind twisting effects, suddenly seemed surplus to requirements to many. Of course, there were some folks heading completely in the opposite direction, waving as the grunge juggernaut passed them on the other side of the road.

Primal Scream had been engrossed in swaggering indie rock for a few years by this point, dominated by fringe aware, acid tinged indie rock and heads-down tracks such as 'Gimme Gimme Teenage Head', from their self-titled second album. But, even as they were rocking out, they were also becoming engrossed in the acid house scene, which they'd been introduced to by Creation boss Alan McGee in the late '80s. Eventually they met DJs Terry Farley and Andrew Weatherall, the latter being suitably impressed by their more mellow side, as best evidenced on 'I'm Losing More Than I'll Ever Have', a standout cut from their latest album. It was a meeting of minds that led to one of the most-acclaimed albums of the '90s, a record created whilst everybody else was buying checked shirts and embracing Nirvana's 'Nevermind' and one which proved that electronic music still had new dimensions to offer.

Seeking to explore both gospel and dub, Primal Scream discarded their indie rock roots overnight, and Andrew Weatherall was installed as producer for the single 'Loaded', which was effectively a remix of "I'm Losing More Than I'll Ever Have. It was a huge crossover hit, re-booting a whole generation of confused post-ravers. It also launched a magazine which traced the scene's hedonistic roots and set the band up to record 'Screamadelica', a pivotal album that mixed Stones-styled brass stabs, Orb-like ambience and Weatherall's house mix ideas to create a symphonic, and indeed spiritual, experience. Stones' producer Jimmy Miller and The Orb's Alex Paterson (now aided by latest cohort Thrash) lent a hand, along with many others, but key tracks like 'Come Together' were created with the deft touch of Weatherall. Featuring a choir, brass and samples of a gospel preacher, there appears to be very little band input (although one mix of the track did prominently feature vocals and guitars). Elsewhere, there was magical interplay between the band and producers, the stripped-back groove and variety of source samples giving the album a truly filmic feel.

Re-evaluated recently on its re-issue, the BBC extolled its virtues, "Weatherall had loosened up the Scream, and they would never be the same again. A whole new menu of opportunities and sonic exploration was theirs. It allowed them out of the constraints of the 'rock outfit' set-up."

But not everybody was impressed at the time; "'Screamadelica' finds Primal Scream abandoning any pretence of being a band in the accepted sense," opined Dave Roberts in his two star review in 'Q' magazine, "with a succession of pre-programmed trance dance grooves boasting give-away names like 'Don't Fight It Feel It', 'Inner Flight' and 'Higher Than The Sun' showing Gillespie's whole hearted conversion to all things psychedelic".

"Both of its time yet quintessentially timeless," the BBC claimed with some fair degree of hindsight, "'Screamadelica' still sounds like nothing else, yet all things at once. Digestible whether off your nut in a club, soundtracking a barbeque or even in indie seduction. Eighteen years down the line, it's not too much to suggest that it's a solid gold classic".

Such a glowing reverie is how we remember it now, but Roberts, back in 1991, concluded, "Through the fog of this sometimes self-indulgent soundtrack to '90s drug culture, only the excellent 'Loaded' and 'Higher Than The Sun' truly stand out". Everybody was, of course, too out of it to notice that the band rarely appeared to feature on the record, and that the album effectively constituted a compilation of visions of the modern musical landscape as seen by some of the most important people working in it at that time. With those credentials, it could hardly fail to be anything but classic.

MASSIVE ATTACK
Safe From Harm
From Blue Lines
Original release: 1991
WILD BUNCH

If, Primal Scream were met with mixed opinions, Massive Attack, emerging from the Bristol scene's Wild Bunch conglomerate, were welcomed with open arms. Their debut album, 'Blue Lines', was universally praised, their fresh, edgy trip hop sound celebrated the world over. Five star reviews, Album of the Year awards and decent sales abounded.

Writer Simon Reynolds famously said of 'Blue Lines' that it was "a shift toward a more interior, meditational sound". It was spiritual, inward looking and, indeed, the band openly admitted that they were lazily sitting around listening to everything from reggae, dub, electronic and funk, from Pink Floyd and PiL to Herbie Hancock and Isaac Hayes, soaking up local influences from their multi-cultural Bristol surroundings, thinking about what they could do but, if truth be told, not actually doing anything at all.

Produced by Johnny Dollar and Neneh Cherry's partner Cameron McVey, who would go on to manage the band, 'Blue Lines' only happened because Cherry all but forced them to make something of the sounds they were immersed in, to look at where they were and to use it.

From the rotating bass loop and Shara Nelson's sultry vocal on the opening track 'Safe From Harm', the Massive Attack sound, with its funky keyboards, stoned groove and the cut up edits imposed on 3D's vocals, cast the tune as a mini soap opera that clocked in at just over five minutes. The accompanying black and white video added further tension, a theme that they would repeat on the groundbreaking and award winning 'Unfinished Sympathy' clip and on several memorable videos throughout their career. Unlike many of their wigged out and pilled up contemporaries, Massive Attack were providing a harsh piece of reality, albeit delivered at a slo-mo, super stoner pace.

This new sub genre, somewhat lazily christened 'trip hop', relied on one solid, bubbling groove throughout most tracks. There were rarely middle eights, indeed there weren't even choruses on most of the songs, but they were heads down and utterly welcoming. 'Blue Lines' provided a comic book insight into another world, but one which grown up music fans could listen to as it lay beneath the aggression beginning to dominate hip hop and had as much to do with The Cocteau Twins and old school soul as it did with the dancefloor.

THE SHAMEN
Move Any Mountain (Progen 91)
Original release: 1991
ONE LITTLE INDIAN

Two Years before their chart topping poke at the BBC, 'Ebenezer Goode', with its immortal chorus 'E's are good', which stymied the corporation's plan to ban any drug references on air, the Shamen were coming off the back of 'Hyperreal' an ecstasy-tinged dance tune that had taken their original psychedelic ideas as Alone Again Or in a new, headier direction.

The Shamen were moving into a scene where S'Xpress, M/A/R/R/S, Jesus Jones, EMF, The Beatmasters, Baby Ford and various others were fusing all kinds of styles into grooves that work on any dancefloor and their next single, 'Move Any Mountain (Progen 91)' underlined their hippy ideas. Tragedy, however, struck when the then duo of Colin Angus and Will Sinnott were shooting the colour-drenched video for the song in Tenerife as Sinnott drowned during a break in filming.

The song's anthemic quality looked to be their last fusion of incessant dance paced synth melody lines and overwhelming positivity, but part time rapper, Mr C managed to re-direct the band and push them towards an even more E-friendly future.

SHAFT
Roobarb And Custard
Original release: 1991
FFRREEDOM

The Shamen's success had allowed them to escape the daytime TV and cereal for dinner doledrums, then the creators of 'Roobarb And Custard' were simply playing on it, mercilessly. They were either superglued to the dancefloor or polaxed on their sofa. It was a much talked about fact in the early '90s that the faces of the perpetrators of many of the rave anthems or novelty 45s were never going to be fully exposed, that they could have come from anywhere and been made by Black Lace or Rick Wakeman, but the public persona was always going to be one of a gang of blessed-out party goers "havin' it large".

The Shafts of this world were destined to be mystery guests on 'Never Mind The Buzzcocks' in years to come, and they, and their mates, could pick up on BBC hospitality for a night as they gurned to the nation's bemused TV viewers on 'Top Of The Pops', and no-one would be any the wiser. And so it was that a procession of moronically happy people would grace the TV screens every Thursday night in the early '90s, a bit like 'X Factor' now.

That said, there still had to be some form of creative process, something that would reduce drugged-up revellers to new levels of wild irreverence and cross-face smirking. It needed to have a reference point which would make it all make perfect sense. 'Roobarb And Custard' did just that.

A form of KLF-lite, Shaft had a pumping house rhythm and a touch of Italo-house piano, which they interrupted with the repetitive squelchy synth motif from the kids' UK TV series 'Roobarb And Custard', and a bit of dialogue for effect. Shaft had their moment in make up at the 'Top Of The Pops' filming and the incessant riff of the TV series was lodged in clubbers' brains, a perfect haunting refrain for the comedown nausea that would follow. It was three minutes and thirty one seconds of pure, self referential and retro hip madness, showing that, by the early '90s, all kinds of everything was possible and permissible in electronic dance music.

THE FUTURE SOUND OF LONDON
Papua New Guinea
Original release: 1992
JUMPIN' & PUMPIN'

Brian Dougans had been responsible for the visionary 'Stakker Humanoid' in the '80s, a piece of acid rave culture that had been inspirational in the scene's early days. Having teamed up with Garry Cobain, the duo, as Future Sound Of London, had released a whole string of influential bleeping techno singles and a debut album, 'Accelerator', before they created the ambient-dub classic 'Papua New Guinea' in 1992. Like any travelogue album that might have preceded it, it sounded like it was steeped in the culture of the place, and was brought bang up to date by an incessant rhythm track sampled from Meat Beat Manifesto.

On top of this pulsing rhythm were carefully placed, evocative synths and a sample of a swooping vocal by Dead Can Dance's Lisa Gerrard. A lengthy Andrew Weatherall mix and a host of other takes on the original secured the track club popularity and gave FSOL license to delve much further into what was possible with samplers, synths and time on their hands.

A string of truly influential albums would follow, along with more singles from the ever-experimenting duo who, in 2010, became the toast of Noel Gallagher and Paul Weller and looked set to further change popular music with their re-branding of their music as Amorphous Androgynous. Their DJ sets were legendary, adding a sitar player for further ambience, and, in 2010, their ten minute version of 'Let It Be', prepared for a 'MOJO' magazine reworking of the album, sounded like an out-take from 'Screamadelica', a glorious piece of recasting that a transcendental George Harrison would have freaked out over.

APHEX TWIN
Heliosphan
Original release: 1992
R&S

In many ways, Aphex Twin's 'Heliosphan' sounds like a close relative of the Andrew Weatherall remix of 'Papau New Guinea', the spacious overlapping synths sounding like a natural ambient bed partner. Hailed as 'the most inventive and influential figure in contemporary electronic music' by The Guardian, Richard D James was a DJ who began releasing records under a variety of names in the early '90s. Truly prolific, it's said that he'd preview much of his new music while driving around Cornwall with mates. In fact, the quality of his debut album, 'Selected Ambient Works 85-92', suggested that some of the tracks were actually taken from the original cassette source, but the music was something else. Aphex Twin was breaking taboos of structure and composition and shedding light on a new path the genre could take.

The album's release caused a stir on both sides of the Atlantic, with 'Rolling Stone' magazine claiming that Aphex Twin had taken ambient sound further than Eno and Q's Stuart Maconie heading down to Truro to interview him and being truly impressed that, like all musicians who'd begun to gain royalties from their craft, he'd invested his money wisely in a tank. "It's not actually a tank," he told Maconie, "it's actually classed as an amphibious armoured car".

But that was all to come. When 'Heliosphan' was being created, Aphex Twin was hosting parties on the beach in Cornwall, DJing and learning about what music he could from the poor supply of sounds that reached his far off locale. A move to London would eventually change all that. "When I was DJing," he told 'Q', "I'd only listen to techno". But, relocated to London, "Now I was hearing avant-garde stuff, German experimental rock, dub." Inevitably, he bought thousands of records and the future of electronic music would change as a result.

In 1992, the approach of Aphex Twin was to listen to music and completely break it down into its component parts, then rebuild it. Like an engineer with a handy edit button. But the key to Aphex Twin's creativity was never really that simple. Having studied electronics extensively, he built much of his own equipment, and his song structures bore no relation to the traditional, build up/break down arrangements so favoured by clubbers. His approach was that of somebody who'd heard about techno, but never actually heard any.

"This is going to sound really weird, but I'm a lucid dreamer, you see," he told Q, "I make tracks in my dreams. Sometimes I'm in my own studio, sometimes I'm in an imaginary studio or sometimes in my real studio with imaginary equipment in it. It used to be a real struggle to remember the tunes when I woke up but I'm training myself to do it".

OK, we can go with that. A thousand analysts might not but, as the Aphex Twin catalogue swelled, such revelations seemed to have some semblance of truth to them.

"I've thought about analysing where my tunes come from," James concluded, "plotting charts and graphs and so on, but I'm afraid I'll find out something I don't want to know".

FRONT LINE ASSEMBLY
The Blade
Original release: 1992
THIRD MIND

The early '90s, away from the mainstream which was now perfectly grunged up, had become dark and gothic, self-examining and hard edged in many cases. As Aphex Twin was creating post-techno ambience, , former Skinny Puppy man Bill Leeb was sculpting gothic monstrosities inspired by DAF and Portion Control. People liked it too! The singles 'Iceolate' and 'Provision' had both been singles of the week in 'Melody Maker' in 1990 but, for Front Line Assmebly's third album, Leeb and Rhys Fulber wanted to make even more startling music, stuff that would really go against the grain.

But, the recording of 'Tactical Neural Implant' didn't go as planned, and the recordings were eventually scrapped. Starting again, they decided they needed a complete change of heart and that they ultimately just wanted to make music that "sounded good". As a result they steered themselves away from the extremes of their initial influences towards a more disco-led set of rhythms, which placed them far closer to Nine Inch Nails.

Pulled from the album, 'The Blade' was a powerhouse of infectious rhythms and strident keyboards, a more engaging take on their vision which, in turn, introduced them to a much wider audience intent on embracing the 'anything goes' dance culture that was beginning to evolve all over Europe as the walls between hard dance, electronic body music, new beat, techno and acid house began to crumble.

THE PRODIGY
Out Of Space
Original release: 1992
XL

Named after the Moog Prodigy synthesiser, and the brainchild and bedroom project of Liam Howlett, The Prodigy's rise to fame beagn when his demo tape was picked up by XL and the quirky 'Charly', based around samples from the UK's "Charley Says....." public information films of the 1970s, featuring a scarily-drawn cat, became their second single release. Reaching number three in the UK chart, the sample and wonky keyboard breaks, which had them briefly labelled as Kiddie rave or Toytown techno, struck a chord with rave-goers, much in the same way that 'Roobarb And Custard' had brought incoherent memories flooding back to the emerging retro market.

By 1991, Howlett had recruited dancers Keith Flint and Leroy Thornhill to the line up, and his fascination for sampling had turned him towards the same reggae and dub sounds that were already inspiring Massive Attack, Aphex Twin and Future Sound Of London. Howlett sampled the Lee Perry-produced 'I Chase The Devil' by Max Romeo, concentrating on the immortal line "I'm gonna send him to outta space, to find another race". An anthem was born. Riddled with sci-fi synths, scratchy turntablism and Helium-fired vocals, 'Out Of Space' was propelled by a monster backbeat that slipped dutifully into the Romeo sample before thumping back and cascading with all the flailing arms that Flint, Leroy and further recruit, MC Maxim, could muster.

METALHEADZ
Terminator
Original release: 1992
SYNTHETIC HARDCORE PHONOGRAPHY

The Prodigy's dancers were larger than life and filled with an aggressive swagger that allowed them their own space on the dancefloor, heading an underground pecking order in much the same way as the seemingly flamboyant Metalheadz. Inspired by the Arnie movie, 'Terminator' by Metalheadz was one of the earliest releases by Goldie. Fascinated by breakbeats, he'd become immersed in the Bristol graffiti scene where he'd met Massive Attack's 3D and been introduced to leading lights on the emerging drum and bass scene Dego and Marcy Mac by his girlfriend Kemistry. Under the name Rufige Cru, which he'd return to many years later, he'd begun to make waves in the jungle and drum and bass clubs, before 'Terminator' was unleashed to huge adulation.

The Metalheadz moniker would become his own label a couple of years later by which time Goldie's ideas had expanded and London Records' division FFRR picked him up but back in 1992, the rampant drum machine and arpeggio synth lines cut to dialogue that sounds like it's bubbling up from beneath the dancefloor made 'Terminator' an intense five minutes with some fast edit time changes adding to the mood of good time menace.

BJORK
Big Time Sensuality
Original release: 1993
ONE LITTLE INDIAN

Both the Prodigy and Metalheadz were championing arm-flailing dance moves, a concept that couldn't have been further from the idea of Bjork slowly spinning and pirouetting on the back of a flat bed lorry as it drove through the streets of New York, as seen in the Stéphane Sednaoui-directed video for 'Big Time Sensuality', was another proposition altogether.

The fourth single from her 'Debut' album, 'Big Time Sensuality' featured the minimix of the song as prepared by Fluke, a Home Counties outfit who performed the song live with Bjork on the first MTV Awards at the site of the now destroyed Berlin Wall. Cocooned in a shell, the members of Fluke were a subdued foil for the former Sugarcubes' vocalist, whose Nellee Hooper-produced album retained more than a few of the tricks the producer had adopted on Massive Attack's debut.

"'Big Time Sensuality' is about my friends, not my lovers. It's not erotic or sensual, even if it may sound like that," admitted Bjork. Indeed the union of Fluke's clinical electronics and Bjork's wide-eyed soulful innocence made the song a teasing piece of sultry pop, a synthpop classic that didn't begin to hint at her future direction, but absolutely drew a line under her Sugarcubes career.

PORTISHEAD
Wandering Star
From Dummy
Original release: 1994
GO! DISCS

Geoff Barrow of Portishead had been the engineer on the Massive Attack 'Blue Lines' sessions and, along with guitarist Adrian Utley and vocalist Beth Gibbons, had set about creating his own brand of 'trip hop' with a more traditional sound mixed with Gibbons' raw folky voice, creating a smoother, more spacious sound than their Bristol contemporaries.

Their debut album, 'Dummy', produced three monumental singles in 'Numb', 'Sour Times' and 'Glory Box' – a great version of which was done much later by John Martyn. Throughout the cleverly arranged set, the taut mood was magnified by the minimal approach, and on the pussyfooting 'Wandering Star' the mix of samples and simple electronics paint a remarkable picture.

With a distant harmonica picked up from Eric Burdon And War's 'Magic Mountain', and Gary Baldwin adding Hammond organ to Barrow's programmed effects and Clive Deamer's drums, the track became an unclassifiable piece of music, a song that had managed to transcend all categorisation and musical genres. It just existed.

STEREOLAB
Moogy Wonderland
From Ping Pong
Original release: 1994
DUOPHONIC

Like Portishead, Stereolab defy simple categories. They were, and remain, out of kilter with everything else. What they are is impossible to clarify. Sometimes indie pop, maybe sunshine pop, a dose of French pop, Krautrock-lite, tweecore, everything else........ who knows?

I have fourteen Stereolab albums, a box set, lots of ten-inch singles and around twenty singles. I can't remember the titles of any of the tracks, but they have a strange combined effect as they lull the listener off to pastures new or imagined universes where only they make any sense. Their music is like so much cotton wool, wrapped around the listener like a comfort blanket.

Playing support to bands like Pulp in the '90s, they weren't so roundly accepted. In fact they'd be roundly cheered as they announced their last song of the set. "It's a really long one," they'd add to stifled groans. People weren't ready to relive the former days of Faust with a bit of John Cage thrown in for good measure, they couldn't handle the lengthy minimalism, even if there was the occasional chorus.

Their 'Ping Pong' was a four track EP that came out in 1994, and the second track on side one was the gorgeous, ironically-titled 'Moogy Wonderland'. Tim Ganes' Moog meanders throughout as Laetitia Sadler croons in proper "bad-a bad-a da" Bacharach style. It's a gorgeous swirling groove that revolves around their Farfisa organ and eventually descends into a revving synth noise that repeats endlessly in the run-out groove. It lasts forever and seems to have a life of its own, underlining the true out-thereness of Stereolab. And thank the Lord for them.

UNDERWORLD
dubnobasswithmyheadman
Original release: 1994
JUNIOR BOY'S OWN

Tracklisting:
Dark And Long, Mmm...Skyscraper I Love You, Surfboy, Spoonman, Tongue, Dirty Epic, Cowgirl, River of Bass, M.E.

The eerie start to 'Mm... Skyscraper I Love You' and its lengthy rotating sound said much about the collision of inner city culture, rock music and the club scene that brought about the evolution of Underworld. Their story features a complex set of circumstances that led Karl Hyde and Rick Smith from the proggy synth pop of Freur to clubland then way beyond. Freur had, in fact, run its course, and in the hiatus that followed Smith became enthralled with the music created by DJs like Andrew Weatherall and Paul Oakenfold, leading him to hook up with teenage DJ Darren Emerson before re-uniting with Hyde.

By 1994, they'd set up an experimental soundfield at Glastonbury, experimented with all kinds of techniques and released two albums before their union of sounds matured fully with the much praised 'dubnobasswithmyheadman' set. Spiked with a rock ethic, their club-ready tunes had begun to crossover. They'd hit on a rock techno fusion of sorts and, as Rupert Howe reported in 'Q', "Much of their success is down to their ability to play several audiences at once, mad-for-it clubbers, festival crowds and would-be ravers who never left their armchairs".

The duo's rock heritage allowed them to try a touch of prog fantasising, while Emerson's handle on club culture ensured that they would also reach the tripped out punters too. There was also a deep, soundtrack-like feel to tracks like 'Dirty Epic', and the endless mixes and dubs of that track, along with many of the other cuts from the album, allowed DJs to re-interpret Underworld in any way they wished, the vocals of Hyde adding another mix option as much of the trance-like music of the day was purely instrumental.

"Their debut album fair bristles with invention, tunes and satisfying noise," said Q's Andrew Collins, reviewing it on its release. "It's Underworld's all-consuming studio confidence and a healthy disregard of their genre's codebook that scores here".

THE PRODIGY
Music For The Jilted Generation
Original release: 1994
XL

Tracklisting:
Intro, Break & Enter, Their Law (Featuring Pop Will Eat Itself), Full Throttle, Voodoo People, Speedway (Theme from Fastlane), The Heat (The Energy), Poison, No Good (Start the Dance), One Love, The Narcotic Suite: 3 Kilos, Skylined, Claustrophobic Sting

With Underworld introducing rock music ideals into their armoury of heady dance beats, Liam Howlett was in the process of using cool jazz riffs, Blade Runner synths and smashing bottles to make a point. And that was just on 'Break And Enter'. By track three, 'Their Law', forged with the help of Pop Will Eat Itself, the spirit of punk rock aggro and information overload was their central pivot. If 'Out Of Space' owed its heritage to a reggae 45, then there was death metal in 'Generation', along with swinging strings, a dab of Tangerine Dream, some acid house bass and plenty more.

"A soundtrack for those British rave hordes who dodge Tory truncheons, 'Music for the Jilted Generation' thrills initiates with a political buzz Americans might miss. But the Prodigy's hard-core techno generates universal dance fever..." claimed 'Rolling Stone' magazine, "Truly trippy."

And the analysis went on: "'Voodoo People" mixes up a Nirvana-riff ('Very Ape'), with 70's 'Shaft'-style flute, and hardcore techno and comes out as a great bit of dance with a twist," claimed Martin Bates on the band's website. More Herbie Mann than Shaft in retrospect, I'd say, but who's checking. Bates continued: "Things finish off on a high note (in more ways than one) with 'The Narcotic Suite', a collection of three drug related moods. '3 Kilos' with its dreamy keyboards topped with super-fly flute and piano, 'Skylined' with its alternating wide open expanses and hard dance and the 'Claustrophobic Sting', with its dance roller coaster beats cut with screams, scary laughter, and a voice repeating "My mind is glowing!" like a mantra".

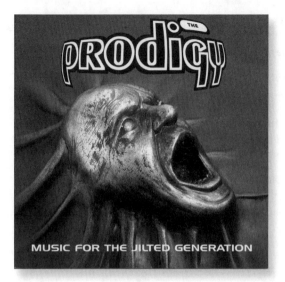

The suite was a suitable soundtrack to nights before and mornings after that were being experienced up and down the country. It was a very English experience in the mid-'90s, something that America perhaps found hard to really understand. "The Prodigy jolts an industrial sensibility with techno drive and then rides the seemingly endless grooves until we're numb... for intensely pumping dance music, this album has more life than most," concluded 'Option' magazine.

The album was of its time. Like the Clash's debut in 1977, if you didn't understand what it was about then you weren't part of what was going on. So in tune was it with what was happening that it scooped the Mercury prize, voted by a bunch of journalists who were probably as askew with what The Prodigy were going on about as anyone at the time. That said, the band were already moving into different territory and appealing to the masses. They fell into Kerrang!'s world because of their use of guitar, and their less than orthodox approach saw them outwit many of their contemporaries.

Two years after the Mercury Prize-winning escapades, Select magazine noted that, since the "breakbeat punk of 'Music For the Jilted Generation', The Prodigy have become something no-one ever expected them to be: a rock 'n' roll band. While dance outfits like Orbital and Underworld have succeeded in taking techno to the rock masses, The Prodigy have effectively gone about it more directly, and become a dance band that makes rock music. They absorb breakbeat, techno, hip hop and guitars in equal measure and spit it out in a black wall of noise. Their records are dominated by machines, but infused with a raw power that makes Rage Against The Machine look like leading lights of the Easy Listening revival. And the thing is, everybody thinks they're fantastic".

Indeed, The Prodigy had fans everywhere, as diverse as Bono and Des O'Connor. Now how did that happen?

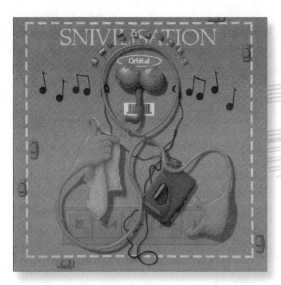

ORBITAL
Snivilisation
Original release: 1994
INTERNAL

While The Prodigy were in the process of reformatting rock music, Orbital were heading down a completely different road. 'Snivilisation' was sombre by comparison, highly textured, with a deep seam of warm and enveloping melody lines, heavily effected samples, background dialogue and the voice of Alison Goldfrapp on 'Are We Here?', the single version of which featured four minutes of silence dedicated to the Criminal Justice Bill, which had recently been passed to allow the police further anti raving powers. It had been a time of spectacular raves and the new legislation made it more difficult for such things to happen. Orbital, as did many others, saw the new legislation as a direct attack on people's enjoyment of music - something that would have repercussions on the rave scene as the '90s rolled on.

In reviewing the album for 'Q' back on its release, Andrew Collins praised the square pegness of the brothers Hartnoll, almost incredulous that they'd scored "chart hits" since 1990. "They are techno's first stars, Steve Reich in the afternoon," he punned cleverly, "True to form, their third album is no easier than its predecessors". Undoubtedly it wasn't meant to be, but in re-hearing the set sixteen years later, it certainly has retained a majestic quality, and a clever use of melody and construction which allowed them to create a much bigger sound than they had any right to. 'Q' actually made it one of the Top 25 Dance Albums of all time much later.

The now defunct 'Select' magazine, on the other hand was far more enthusiastic. "Can techno really ever be about anything? Or, should we say, anything more meaningful than fluffy clouds and getting substantially out of it. Than sheer sonic loveliness and the ruthless hedonism of the dancefloor. Well, you'd like to think so, wouldn't you?" the magazine's reviewer mused manfully. "If anyone is going to convince skeptics, it'll be the Hartnoll brothers, aka Orbital. Over two untitled albums and several compelling EPs, they've staked a claim to be the best, perhaps in the world, at this type of thing. And what is this thing? Techno does it no justice, certainly. It's modern electronic music using the studio as a compositional tool - how's that for a sexy movement title, New Wave Of New Wave! - and 'Snivilisation' is as wonderful an example of it as you're going to hear".

'Snivilisation' was a pulling together of everything that seemed so untogether, so seemingly random for the passing consumer. Kept at barge pole length by many for its explosive rhythmic patterns, it is in fact a truly tuneful experience. Alison Goldfrapp's vocal is gorgeous on a fifteen minute epic that further ripped the very fabric of tradition. And 'Attached', the closing track, sounds like a piece of modern chamber music, a fresh piece of pastoral Englishness that's Michael Nyman-esque and gloriously hopeful.

GLOBAL COMMUNICATION
76:14
Original release: 1994
DEDICATED

The complex nature of dance music and its faceless persona during the '90s was further confused by Tom Middleton and Mark Pritchard who, as Global Communication, produced this staggering album. It sounded like the music you could only hear when laying beneath the stars searching for Orion's belt. It has swathes of synthesiser and ambient echo, sounding like it was produced for some ill advised underwater movie, with added alien activity for good measure. It is Tangerine Dream and Klaus Schulze, it is Vangelis on a budget from two guys who also released dance singles under names such as Jedi Knights, Cosmos, The Modwheel, Brinkworth, Series 7, Harmonic 313, Troubleman, Schizophrenia and Spiritcatcher among many other suitably strange nom de plumes.

'76:14' was an album for returning clubbers to put on while they watched TV with the sound down. If the old story that you can play Pink Floyd's 'Dark Side Of Moon' while watching The Wizard Of Oz and the two synched up perfectly is anywhere near the truth, then Global Communication's ambient deep house in space opus would work for anything from the testcard to David Lynch's 'Eraserhead'.

AUTECHRE
Amber
Original release: 1994
Warp Records

If '76:14' was the soundtrack to late night comatosing, then Autechre's 'Amber' carried on the feeling, a year before they began to fully deconstruct their sound and experiment with glitch - the sounds of electronic equipment and computers malfunctioning made into rhythmic templates. Conversely, 'Amber' was an ambient treat that hinted at the future paths that would hugely inspire Radiohead's Thom Yorke, among others.

While Autechre were intent on a Darwinian reduction in possibilities and a return to basics, elsewhere, Varese aficionado Frank Zappa was completing his last great work, a synthetic monster that would attempt to encapsulate everything.

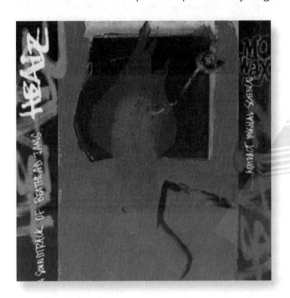

VARIOUS ARTISTS
Headz
Original release: 1994
MO'WAX

Tracklisting:
DISC ONE
Patterson – Freedom Now (Meditation). Attica Blues – Contemplating Jazz. Awunsound – Symmetrical Jazz. Nightmares On Wax – Stars. La Funk Mob – Ravers Suck Our Sound. M.F. Outta 'National – Miles Out Of Time (Astrocentric Mix 'n' Beats). RPM – The Inside. Autechre – Lowride. Olde Scottish – Wild Style

DISC TWO
DJ Shadow – Lost And Found. Skull – Destroy All Monsters. Deflon Sallahr – ...Don't Fake It. RPM – 2000. Palmskin Production – Slipper Suite. U.N.K.L.E – The Time As Come. Howie B – Head West / Gun Fight At The O.K. Corrall. Tranquility Bass – They Came In Peace. DJ Shadow – In-Flux

While Warp and Metalheadz were amassing a host of experimental electronic dancefloor acts, James Lavelle's Mo' Wax label was mixing the likes of Autechre with his own UNKLE and US crate diggers like DJ Shadow, whose sampling of all kinds of raw audio material made for some unique dance music. The 'Headz' album, sub-titled, "A soundtrack of experimental beathad jams", showcased some of the best new perpetrators of quite varied genres, painstakingly collated by Lavelle.

Two further double sets, 'Headz 2', arrived in 1996 with an even more startling line up that included Air, The Stereo Mcs and a host of lesser known acts. This time the mix was deeper and even more evocative as Nightmares On Wax, The Beastie Boys, Skull, Peshay, Roni Size and a plethora of wide ranging mixmasters were pulled together. Indeed, if anything, the new found calm that encompassed these albums was even more far reaching, as post rock from Tortoise nestled comfortably next to Money Mark, Luke Vibert and The Jungle Brothers. Both 'Headz' and these second volumes remain pivotal examples of just how splintered but amazingly cohesive dance music had become by the mid 90s.

ALEX REECE
Pulp Fiction
Original release: 1995
METALHEADZ

Following the establishment of the Metalheadz label, a host of like-minded drum and bass and jungle innovators began to release records through the imprint. Alex Reece had been DJing since the 1980s, and had begun working in studios and releasing sides for various independent labels, but it was the singles 'Basic Principles' and the mighty throb of 'Pulp Fiction' that introduced him to a wider audience. The urgent, 'intelligent' Metalheadz groove dominated the record, but the addition of jazz trumpet – which inspired the jazzstep sub genre later – really set the song apart from his labelmates.

GOLDIE
Timeless
Original release: 1995
FFRR

Tracklisting:
Timeless (i Inner City Life, ii Pressure, iii Jah). Saint Angel. State Of Mind. Sea Of Tears. Angel. Sensual. Kemistry. You & Me

Meanwhile, Metalheadz head honcho Goldie had been signed to London and retired to the studio with programmer Timecode. The author John Niven was, at the time, working as an A&R man at London Records and his fictional novel, 'Kill Your Friends', in which a jungle star disappears to the east end with a pot of cash from the label and eventually returns with a concept piece about life was, allegedly, in no way based on the true experience of the recording of 'Timeless', the centre piece of which was a 20 minute suite about, er, inner city life.

Niven's hilarious plotline and its insight into the machinations of the record industry aside, 'Timeless' was an incredible piece. It took the basic premise of drum and bass and added a soulful Vocalist in Diane Charlemagne, retained the use of Goldie's original drum and bass sparring partners Dego and Marcy Mac and bolstered the sound with an orchestra, among other things. It was spectacular, a concept piece that summed up what was in Goldie's head but also dragged drum and bass into completely new territory and forced it on a completely new audience.

FRANK ZAPPA
Civilization III
Original release: 1995
BARKING PUMPKIN

Tracklisting:
This Is Phaze III, Put A Motor In Yourself, Oh-Umm, They Made Me Eat It, Reagan At Bitburg,
Very Nice Body, Navanax, How The Pigs' Music Works, Xmas Values, Dark Water!, Amnerika,
Have You Heard Their Band?, Religious Superstition, Saliva Can Only Take So Much, Buffalo
Voice, Someplace Else Right Now, Get A Life, Kayak (On Snow), N-Lite, I Wish Motorhead
Would Come Back, Secular Humanism, Attack! Attack! Attack!, I Was In A Drum, Different
Octave, This Ain't CNN, Pigs' Music, Pig With Wings, This Is All Wrong, Hot And Putrid,
Flowing Inside-Out, I Had A Dream About That, Gross Man, Tunnel Into Muck, Why Not?,
Put A Little Motor In Em, You're Just Insultin' Me, Aren't You!, Cold Light Generation,
Dio Fa.,That Would Be The End Of That, Beat The Reaper, Waffenspiel

Delivered entirely on the Synclavier synthesiser, 'Civilization III' straddles every Zappa musical nuance, from Varese through trad jazz, kabuki percussion to classical to rock, moving on into wayward symphonic minimal systems, light opera and so on. In fact, all of the areas that had fascinated him, made him one of the key American composers and taken his reputation way beyond the guitar God or hippie icon of old.

From the off, 'Civilization III' sounds like an attempt to put the record straight on everything. The conversational explanation of why he's starting 'Phaze III' and how the whole thing will take place inside a huge piano – not to mention how he "exploited" the Haight Ashbury scene - are all laid bare, tongue-in-cheek. This extensive double set was the last thing he completed before his death in 1993, and had taken him ten years to perfect.

Categorised by Zappa as an "opera-pantomime", the project began as a vocal recording experiment in 1967, which Zappa described in the liner notes (written in 1993): "I decided to stuff a pair of U-87s in the piano, cover it with a heavy drape, put a sand bag on the sustain pedal, and invite anybody in the vicinity to stick their head inside and ramble incoherently about the various topics I would suggest to them".

Some of these tapes had turned up previously on 'Lumpy Gravy', but they provided a strange dysfunctional dialogue, like a sit com carried out inside a piano – almost reminiscent of the movie 'Being John Malkovich' in some ways – with realities blurred way further. Collected together on this set, they arguably made slightly more sense.

As David Fricke commented in 'Rolling Stone' magazine on its release in 1995, "Zappa's score is rich with the lively outlaw dynamics (knotty melodic agitation, hairpin tempo manoeuvres, mutant instrumental voicing) that have long distinguished his orchestral work". Fricke went on to point out that there was certainly a serious veneer, but that it ran alongside a homage to the timing of The Three Stooges and the creative re-invention of Spike Jones.

"In Civilization, as he did throughout his life," Fricke, who first heard the album in Zappa's studio weeks before his death, concluded, "Zappa finds power, refuge, pleasure and hope in music – the giant piano of his imagination. Like every other record he ever made, 'Civilization Phaze III' is Frank Zappa's way of saying, "Yeah, everything is fucked, but all is not lost"".

Beyond 'Civilization III's overheard dialogue and pointed irony, the music is something else altogether. At the time of its construction Zappa owned mountains of samples that could be used with the Synclavier. The result takes the listener from the kind of sax sound sought out by Coleman Hawkins to the blip of Stockhausen, the speeded up futuristic swirl of an electronic melody straight from Todd Rundgren's wilder moments through to the spacious orchestral tension of Boulez.

The mismatch of styles led to indifferent reviews, but as the internet grew in popularity numerous heads appeared positive among the disparaging few who wanted a return to 'Chunga's Revenge'.

"It is one of the most brilliant compositional works I have ever heard, within the realms of electronic music," enthused one such fan, Paul S Remington of New Jersey, who claimed to have heard the work over 100 times, while Kurt Woods, a Zappa-phile with a mere thirty platters in his collection dismissed it as "unlistenable".

For sure, it wasn't easy listening, and the jokes Zappa was so keen on reside in the spoken dialogue, which you can take or leave. There are great moments though, the Teutonic electronica of 'Xmas Values', the haunted ambience of 'Amnerika' and the lengthy 'N-Lite', with all of its taut drama and fairy tale abandon. In fact, when the mood gets more normal, like the almost traditionally rhythmic jazz vibe of 'I Was In A Drum' it's almost too accessible.

There's hokey drama too, old school Zappa, frat year stoner realism that harks back to his earliest days, but it's the creativity and dalliance into unknown territory, like the mammoth penultimate track 'Beat The Reaper', which sounds like a mass sample of old Folkways albums from around the world stitched together with wild abandon and a jazz percussionist checking his bass drum, that really stretch the boundaries.

Listening to the whole affair continuously is an effort in itself at nearly two hours, but there's something about the car exiting the garage in a rain storm on 'Waffenspiel', with its electronic storm clearing into an almost unintelligible chorus of dog barks and birdsong, that made this a stranger trip than you'd think even Zappa was capable of. Of course, after the initial dialogue at the start, the car sounds of 'Put A Motor In Yourself' take this into a perfect full circle. What have we learned?

The Synclavier, in the early '90s, was undoubtedly the sample-friendly beast of choice. Zappa had been exposed to enough outward influences to create his own unique sound, which touched on everything that his work had in the past. 'Civilization III's message of "everything's fucked" was also laced with the sentiment of 'Be positive, carry on'. You can either hop in the car and go around again – you'll undoubtedly hear things you never noticed first time around - or you could motor off someplace else.

Zappa's extensive preparation for this set was part and parcel of what was around at the time, like Cage and the early tape manipulators who made synth sounds before synths were invented, this was a visionary work that could undoubtedly be produced on an Apple Mac today for a fraction of the time and money that this great American provocateur invested. But then it wouldn't have been Zappa.

THE MOOG COOKBOOK
The Moog Cookbook
Original release: 1995
RESTLESS

Tracklisting
Black Hole Sun (original by Soundgarden), Buddy Holly (original by Weezer), Basket Case (original by Green Day), Come Out and Play (original by The Offspring), Free Fallin (original by Tom Petty), Are You Gonna Go My Way? (original by Lenny Kravitz), Smells Like Teen Spirit (original by Nirvana), Even Flow (original by Pearl Jam), The One I Love (original by R.E.M.), Rockin' in the Free World (original by Neil Young)

While Zappa had been retracing his every move and trying to make sense of electronic music and his perpetual muse, Brian Kehew and Roger J Manning Jr were adding further twists to their multi-band careers, and apparently having a laugh doing it. Seasoned power pop experts and producers and fans of all things poppy, Manning, a former member of Jellyfish and Imperial Drag, and Kehew, who'd played keyboards for The Who, Air and Hole among others, decided to relive the days of 1960's analogue synth-powered exploitation records by doing covers of contemporary material by the likes of Soundgarden and Neil Young, in quirky non-digital style.

The Moog Cookbook was the first of four albums – more recent ones have included takes on The Eels and Foo Fighters among others – which harked back to the days of the earliest bargain bin albums that would bring the authentic sound of a Moog into your back parlour. It's easy to be dismissive of such concepts, but when you hear their interpretation of Eddie Vedder's plaintive vocal on 'Even Flow' what's not to love? OK, so it's not a playlist regular, but hey.... For its retro chic and bringing of electronica full circle it warrants consideration.

LEFTFIELD
Leftism
Original release: 1995
HARD HANDS/COLUMBIA

I met Neil Barnes from Leftfield once. It was a rambunctious 'Q' Awards which saw John Lydon arrive on a horse and cart with his wife, dad and seven mates, including Neil, forming what Lydon called his "arsenal". As the day went on they proceeded to get more and more bedraggled, the high point coming when they were all sat grinning at the aftershow. Lydon beckoned me over and said, "Oakenfold is fucking rubbish". Confused, I pointed out that he hadn't been DJing for the last two hours, this was somebody else. To which the arsenal chimed in, "Well, they're fucking rubbish".

I dare say, their state of ill-repair was similar to the condition a lot of people found themselves in when they first heard Leftfield's early sides spun at clubs. Like many of their contemporaries they dabbled with dub, house and electronica, as Barnes and partner in tune Paul Daley created driving, acid-tinged grooves like 'Not Forgotten' and the Lydon-sung 'Open Up', from 1993.

Their debut album, 'Leftism', included the latter, along with 'Original', sung by Curve's Toni Halliday, the merciless opener, 'Release The Pressure', featuring reggae singer Earl Sixteen, and some great dub drum samples, plus 'Afro Left' featuring the intense mantra like vocal of Djum Djum.

Martin Aston, in his four star review in 'Q', praised the band's attention to detail - evidently the set was three years in the making and - also pointed out its "sweltering cosmopolitan flavour," largely due to its guest vocalists. He also celebrated the non-vocal moments: "Where percussive drive takes over, as on 'Song Of Life' and 'Black Flute', Leftfield unleash some of the most thumping techno to be housed under a major label".

The album also featured deep atmospheric pieces in the spacious 'Melt' and the heavy echoey backbeat of 'Storm 3000'. The set closed with '21st Century Poem', a downbeat piece of retro dialogue from Manchester poet Lemn Sissay, the whole album concluding like any rollercoaster experience that might take place on any lysergically-spiked dancefloor, with a flurry and an over the shoulder glance. With 'Leftism', Leftfield had proved that they were capable of embracing numerous other genres and, in so doing, attract a much wider audience.

AUTECHRE
Tri Repetae
Original release: 1995
WARP

Tracklisting:
Dael, Clipper, Leterel, Rotar, Stud, Eutow, C/Pach, Gnit, Overand, Rsdio

While Leftfield, Underworld and The Prodigy were welcoming the masses to their party, Rochdale's Autechre were moving out. The dance triumvirate had added melody to their stylised, often repetitive rhythms, but Sean Booth and Rob Brown opted to change the balance completely. For 'Tri Repetae', they concentrated on multi layering the rhythm elements and dropping melody to a secondary role. They sounded like they were stuck inside a machine, much like the image of Stockhausen from many years earlier wherein he listened to his creations from inside the box it was reverberating from to allow the sounds to rotate around him.

Autechre were inventing glitch, utilising found sounds, some which were simply accidental machine clicks and whirrs, which they made into multi-layered rhythms. The ambient melody lines, which would have previously sat on top and been used as textured building blocks, now sat underneath the rhythms, in the distance. When they did come to the foreground they were allowed to weave in and out of the machine-like rhythmic rotation.

"If not as immediately experimental as the fractured work by the likes of Merzbow," 'All Music' noted, comparing the duo to the prolific Japanese noise manipulator whose experiments and multi-releases had made him a cult hero of the underground, post-industrial scene, "'Tri Repetae' expertly harnesses the need for a beat to perfectly balance out the resolutely fierce, crunching samples and busy arrangements, turning from being inspired by Aphex Twin to being equally inspiring in itself".

All Music gave the album five out of five, but no review could explain the audio experience that Autechre had created. It seemed to hail from the future, it was exquisitely precise, like an even more robotic machine music, taking Karftwerk to a higher level, doing Philip Glass with toy Mecanno and being the ultimate endless piece that New Order could just switch on and retire from. Even now, it sounds like a completely offworld experience. Haunting and totally dominating.

TRICKY
Maxinquaye
Original release: 1995
ISLAND

Tracklisting:
Overcome, Moonchild, Ponderosa, Hell Is Round The Corner, Pumpkin, Aftermath, Abbaon Fat Tracks, Brand New You're Retro, Suffocated Love, You Don't, Strugglin', Feed Me

After leaving Massive Attack to explore the convergence of hip hop, soul, rock, dub and electronica, Tricky brought in Cure producer Mark Saunders to help with his debut solo album. Recorded on an ad hoc basis, with rotating players and a torrent of ideas that were assembled in the studio, Saunders ended up in a number of roles as samples were initiated and the impromptu nature of compiling the elements for each song became less and less straightforward. Song structures were adapted, Saunders legendarily used varispeed to get the right pitch on the various parts, played guitar, programmed synths and ended up as a DJ in places, while Tricky's then girlfriend Martina Topley-Bird supplied gloriously off-beat vocals which allegedly came out as heard, as everything was done in one take then adapted accordingly to fit.

It was an avant-garde way to work, almost a performance art style of recording, the end result changing as the various elements were added, thought up or created. The result was truly breathtaking - this was music that didn't sound like any of the component parts. The samples were eclectic and included Isaac Hayes, Marvin Gaye, Michael Jackson and a host of inanimate objects. The trip hop pace was slow, and the addition of some chunky guitars against Topley-Bird's breathy jazz vocal or disjointed rap added a heavy, soulful feel, with Tricky's whispered lines adding even more spooky charm to the affair. It was dark, like The Cure. The various singles did little damage to the charts but the universal praise, from 'Rolling Stone' to 'Q' to 'MOJO', was amazing.

THE CHEMICAL BROTHERS
Leave Home
From Exit Planet Dust
Original release: 1995
VIRGIN

While Tricky deconstructed sounds and seemed to be rebuilding them in a hap-hazard but audibly very successful way, the remix and DJ team The Dust Brothers, who had already released a couple of EPs under the name on Junior Boys Own, quickly found that the already well established American team with the same name really weren't very happy about their compliment gone too far. Tom Rowlands and Ed Simons duly changed their name to The Chemical Brothers in an effort to keep their card carrying drug references in tact.

Consequently, their debut album couldn't be called anything other than 'Exit Planet Dust', and the frenetic big beat rhythms and sampled dialogue, acid house basslines and relentless energy of the club staple 'Chemical Beats', along with the hip hop meets Kratfwerk collision of their first high profile single, 'Leave Home', thrust them into the charts and to the forefront of the nations dancefloors. With most of the accompanying album being presented pre-mixed, like one of their late night sessions, 'Exit Planet Dust' was perhaps a bit less than accessible to the general public, even if The Charlatans' Tim Burgess and the lovely Beth Orton lent a hand on vocals. Nevertheless, the pair soon became a household name, and their dominance of chart-friendly-yet-credentials-in-tact dance music had begun.

A genre soon followed in their wake, as the likes of Fatboy Slim (aka Norman Cook, previously of The Housemartins) and Propellerheads, hailing from Bath, went on to score huge hits and number one singles, such as the latter's re-invention of Shirley Bassey on 'History Repeating', but 'Leave Home' with it's hip hop styled one liner and immense rhythm was the nation's introduction to this huge new sound. For many, what appeared to be a booze friendly form of dance music was certainly welcomed with open arms.

The Chemical Brothers' insistent rhythms under-pinned their sound, but when they added the likes of Beth Orton's vocals, sampled Dead Can Dance hooks and contributions from a number of high profile covailist over the following years, they began to realise more soulful things might be possible. 'Exit Planet Dust' was a suitable nod towards two groundbreaking singles that would follow, turning DJs into superstars, no less....

DJ SHADOW
Stem/Long Stem/Transmission 2
From Entroducing
Original release: 1996
MO-WAX

A perennial record collector willing to sample anything to get the right groove, DJ Shadow, aka Josh Davis. even made it to the 'Guinness Book Of Records' for recording a whole album where there are no original instruments – absolutely everything on 'Entroducing' was sampled from somewhere else. In rock circles, the adulation for the album turned him into the DJ it was OK to love. His mix of hip hop, jazz, psychedelia and funk made 'Entroducing' truly unique. Amazingly, response to the album was universally positive, people becoming fascinated by its construction and the star ratings were widespread – 'All Music Guide', 'Alternative Press', 'MOJO', 'Q', 'Rolling Stone' and 'Spin' all awarded the album full marks. OK, so Spin actually gave it 4.5/5, but it's still not bad form for an album with no recognisable verses and choruses, and most of which was in fact instrumental.

It was a hugely influential crossover album constructed from loops and samples as diverse as The Beastie Boys, Metallica, Kurtis Blow, Stanley Clarke, Loudon Wainwright III, David Axelrod, Nirvana and many, many more. 'Entroducing' brought new fans to hip hop grooves and the art of crate digging as perfected by Shadow and his Solesides cohorts. And, of course, the sampler that turned those finds into songs was thrust into the limelight..

"This remains a stone classic, channelling Afrika Bambaataa's genre-splicing, DJ-booth mysticism into a fully realised studio epic..." said 'Spin' magazine, while 'Q' added, "Shadow's brief is to develop a totally sample-based idiom, weaving a cinematically broad spectrum so deftly layered that the sampling-is-stealing argument falls flat".

For most, the key piece of the album is the nine minutes plus of 'Stem/Long Stem/Transmission 2', a 'Tubular Bells'-like piece of Philip Glass book ended by atmospheric ambience filled with effects including harp and orchestra. With upfront rhythms and all kinds of sounds added for colour it defied any kind of normal construction, taking the record way out of the hip hop safety zone that Shadow started in.

The samples on that piece alone included Nirvana, Giorgio Moroder, Dennis Linde, Murray Roman, Osanna, The Mystic Number National Bank, Mother Mallard's Portable Masterpiece Company, Just-Ice and KRS-One, Meredith Monk and the soundtrack of Blade Runner. The result was phenomenal, and the possibilities of sampling seemed endless in its wake.

Meanwhile, as Davis rewrote what was accepted in hip hop, soon-to-be stadium behemoths The Prodigy were perfecting the art of bridging the gap between punk and dance.

THE PRODIGY
Firestarter
Original release: 1996
XL

As potent as The Sex Pistols' 'Anarchy In the UK', The Prodigy's teaser for their impending new album 'The Fat Of The Land' fused a wah wah sample from The Breeders' 'SOS' with a snatch of The Art Of Noise's 'Close To The Edit', but it was the addition of Keith Flint's manic vocal which took the band into entirely unchartered territory. Liam Howeltt's screaming synthesisers also played a significant role in producing dance music that truly was as palatable to metal fans as it was to clubbers. With such a potent cocktail at their disposal, world domination inevitably loomed.

"Firestarter' remains their signature tune," enthused 'Q' in its 100 Greatest Singles feature, "and it's terrifying tunnel video can be said to have warped teenage minds. Its raw power mashes all the best of metal, punk, techno and the art of noise".

It's relentless stuff, a song and sentiment that never tires. "Re-inventing Alice Cooper for the young 'uns still makes for a right rollicking mosh," concluded 'This Is Uncool'. Without doubt, 1996 was a time for independence, the underground and a different slant on things. Punk rock, even delivered by electronic samplers, just made perfect sense.

LTJ BUKEM
Logical Progression
Original release: 1996
GOOD LOOKING RECORDS/FFRR

Tracklisting:
LTJ Bukem - Demons Theme. Chameleon – Links. LTJ Bukem – Music. PFM - One & Only. Aquarius & Tayla - Bringing Me Down. PFM - Danny's Song. Peshay - Vocal Tune. LTJ Bukem - Coolin' Out. PFM - Western (Conrad Remix) Vocals - MC Conrad. LTJ Bukem - Horizons

I once saw LTJ Bukem live in Manchester in a blacked-out upstairs room at a pub. It was a thudding, industrial-styled noise, a multi-layered set of frantic beats with synths trailing off into the sweating ceiling. I was working with 'Mixmag' and had been taken to Leeds and Manchetser to try to fathom out how the club scene worked. Invariably, whether it was house or specialist, there was usually one visionary who was away with the fairies, while his mate handled the "business" side.

The majority of places we visited were handbag house or super clubs. but this place was obviously different. It was virtually pitch black and the volume was intimidating. That said, it sounded fantastic, like the first time I saw Throbbing Gristle or Nine Inch Nails. It was pretty relentless.

LTJ Bukem had been DJ'ing for years, all the while picking up like minded performers who had a penchant for throwing things into the mix that you might not, at first, expect. Bukem didn't actually release an album in his own right until the early 2000s, but this compilation, which bore his name, included several of his jazz-infused tracks as well as material from some of his contemporaries. Throughout its cascading rhythms there are lighter touches, ethereal synthesiser, spaced out sound effects and melodic synth lines that smacked of Klaus Schulze, or even Jean Michel Jarre. There was also a strange filmic feel in places, a haunting rotation of sounds that made 'Logical Progression' all the more engaging.

TRAINSPOTTING
Original release: 1996

The release of 'Trainspotting', a movie based on Irvine Welsh's superb novel, was a key event during 1996, whichever way you looked at it. A story of smack-addled Scots at the point of collapse, it's visual presentation was carried along by a suitably in your face soundtrack including two key anthems. Iggy Pop's 'Lust For Life', from the Bowie/Eno Berlin period, was central to the film's ethos and ran over the opening credits, while Underworld's 'Born Slippy.NUXX' with its memorable, Oasis fan friendly 'Lager, lager, lager, shouting' refrain, played behind the triumphant climax to the film and Begsbie's come-uppance. The movie was a social statement on the times, the music its defining soundtrack.

'Born Slippy.NUXX' had originally been released a year prior to the movie as the B-side to an instrumental track called 'Born Slippy', and has subsequently been programmed on literally hundreds of compilation albums in a string of different mixes. It's laddish chorus made the track perfect fodder for anything from "The Very Best of Trance" to ZOO magazine's hoary sets. It also became a huge turning point for electronic music, coinciding perfectly with the arrival of booze friendly Big Beat, and ushered in a string of beat-ridden single successes for 1997. The electronic 'anthem' (as these tracks were becoming increasingly known) was now not only in the clubs but also on the radio.

THE CHEMICAL BROTHERS
Block Rockin' Beats
From Dig Your Own Hole
Original release: 1997
VIRGIN

"What turned the Chemical Brothers from two trendy students with an acid house fixation into one of the biggest, most exciting acts in Britain?" asked Dom Phillips of 'Mixmag' in his introduction to the duo in the Glastonbury programme of 1997. His analysis followed them from rave hangovers at Manchester University in 1989 to starting a club a year later and releasing 'Song To The Siren' in 1993 as The Dust Brothers. In 1994 they were the kings of the remix and had developed their own awesome live sound twelve months later. By 1996, they had recorded a chart topping single in 'Setting Sun', with Noel Gallagher on vocals, and international success followed. Relentless touring underpinned their popularity, and in March of '97, they released the monstrous lead single from their imminent second album, 'Dig Your Own Hole'. With its driving bass that's often attributed to 23 Skidoo's 'Coup' and Pink Floyd, and a drum track from Bernard Purdie's 'Them Changes', 'Block Rockin' Beats' was an anthem who's title (sampled from Schoolly D's 'Gucci Again') defined the genre.

Three months later they were on the Other Stage at Glastonbury at 9.50pm, following Neneh Cherry and warming up for Radiohead's legendary, rain-sodden, no monitors performance on the main stage. They had arrived.

THE PRODIGY
The Fat Of The Land
Original release: 1997
XL

Tracklisting:
Smack My Bitch Up, Breathe, Diesel Power, Funky Shit, Serial Thrilla, Mindfields, Narayan, Firestarter, Climbatize, Fuel My Fire

The night before the Chemicals' 'Block Rocked' Glastonbury in 1997, the rain had fallen in scenes akin to the end of the world. I was in a backstage compound that was slowly turning into a lake, trying to produce the festival's Daily Paper between intermittent power cuts, when the sound of a juggernaut literally shook our pelted Portakabin. It was the first rumble of bass from The Prodigy, who had taken to the Pyramid stage. Our temporary housing shuddered like a building in 'Jurassic Park' might with the footsteps of an approaching dinosaur. Of course, as with all good Prodigy shows the power outed shortly after our portakabin moved a good two feet to the left.

The sense of expectation for this Prodigy show was phenomenal. Here was an electronic band who were headlining the Friday night at Glastonbury. They'd forsaken the smaller dance stages and, on the back of 'Firestarter', were spearheading a rock/dance crossover that would culminate in the release of their new album, 'The Fat Of The Land' on the following Monday. The rain still poured down, but the growing euphoria in the crowd was palpable as electricians did whatever they do in such times of crisis.

"The Friday night set at the last Glasto, headlining the second stage, was the pinnacle of the festival," reasoned Gareth Grundy in the programme notes as a precursor to the performance. And with a parody of Keith being featured in a Lucozade at the time, it was obviously The Prodigy's moment.

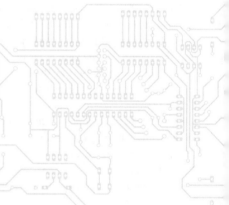

And the album? It didn't disappoint. The brash and heady 'Breathe', which had followed the release of 'Firestarter', and of course the controversial 'Smack My Bitch Up', were a three-pointed eruption of intent. It was relentless.

"It's a screaming pile up of breaks and acid noise and hollered vocals and God knows what else and it's fab," claimed 'Mixmag' breathlessly, "It's the distilled and chaotic mess of everything mad that has been happening to music in the last six years - rave and hardcore, hip hop, thrash-metal, crammed into ten tracks. Mad, bad, and dangerously up for it, it's a hell of a ride".

Alongside the singles, the rapping of Ultramagnetic MC Kool Keith - aka Dr Octagon – added further depth to The Prodigy sound, as did another Glastonbury 1997 headliner, Crispian Mills of the long forgotten Kula Shaker, who added a far eastern, if a little 'Trustifarian', feel to 'Narayan'.

'The Toronto Sun' compared the album to Public Enemy at their best, while 'Rolling Stone' reckoned, "To suggest that they are the Sex Pistols of techno would not even be such an exaggeration. What the Prodigy have done, quite simply, is to drag techno out of the communal nirvana of the rave and turn it into outlandish punk theatre -- and they've done it brilliantly".

America, primed by the video to 'Firestarter', had long been agog at The Prodigy and, without doubt, the excitement generated by 'Fat Of The Land' was awe-inspiring. Absolutely of its time, the record was a headrush of ideas and samples, the kind of barging youthfulness that had made original punk and hip hop so awkward and in your face. It was a white knuckle rollercoaster where anything could come out of Liam Howlett's bag of samples and you weren't going to argue with whatever Keith said. It just seemed right.

In 2009, The Prodigy played an astonishing set at Radio One's Big Weekend in the salubrious setting of Swindon. They tore the place apart in the style that they'd perfected over ten years earlier, as if its been one continuous expulsion of sound, a self exorcism that had started that night in Glastonbury. The power went out mid-set, of course. That was a Prodigy show.

DREXCIYA
The Quest
Original release: 1997
SUBMERGE

Tracklisting:
Intro, You Don't Know, Dehydration, Bang Bang, Antivapor Waves, Intensified Magnetism, Hydro Cubes, Aquatic Beta Particles, Hi Tide, Depressurization, Sea Snake, Aqua Judidsu, Beyond The Abyss, Lardossen Funk, Red Hills Of Lardossa, The Mutant Gillmen

While The Prodigy were going global, Drexciya, a mysterious duo from Detroit, were not so much going underground as going under water. Possibly not even on this planet. The duo dipped into techno and electro, but were essentially aloof, occasionally ambient and partially funky too. The sleeves of their records contained misleading, Sun Ra-styled prose that suggested their otherworldly nature. Nothing about Drexciya was easy, least of all finding a copy of 'The Quest', which currently sells on eBay for £50 and on the Discogs website for anything up to £75 for the double vinyl issue. Comprehending what you have when you finally get a copy is another story.

"Could it be possible for humans to breath underwater? A foetus in its mother's womb is certainly alive in an aquatic environment. During the greatest holocaust the world has ever known, pregnant America-bound African slaves were thrown overboard by the thousands during labour for being sick and disruptive cargo. Is it possible that they could have given birth at sea to babies that never needed air?" is typical of their sleeve rhetoric, this example being taken from the sleeve of 'The Quest'. It continues, "Recent experiments have shown mice to be able to breathe liquid oxygen. Even more shocking and conclusive was a recent instance of a premature infant saved from certain death by breathing liquid oxygen through its undeveloped lungs. These facts, combined with reported sightings of Gillmen and swamp monsters in the coastal swamps of the South- Eastern United States, make the slave trade theory startlingly feasible. Are Drexciyans water breathing, aquatically mutated descendants of those unfortunate victims of human greed? Have they been spared by God to teach us or terrorise us? Did they migrate from the Gulf of Mexico to the Mississippi river basin and on to the great lakes of Michigan? Do they walk among us? Are they more advanced than us and why do they make their strange music? What is their Quest? These are many of the questions that you don't know and never will. The end of one thing... and the beginning of another. Out - The Unknown Writer".

These guys were not giving much away, least of all their identities. Energy Flash #3, a Detroit 'zine, tracked them down in 1996, via email, and asked a string of burning questions that fans of the band had mustered, most of which were met with one word answers, apart from the odd statement:

Q: "Is your environment in Detroit your greatest inspiration for your music?

A: "No, it's a mental state of mind. We live like monks. No movement except air and sound".

Not helpful, and the magazine eventually gave up and tried to go along with their deep sea theme.

Q: "Would they be interested in playing an aquatic setting?

A: "Yes."

Nice one. Drexciya never gave much away. They'd certainly whipped up interest though, and 'The Quest' was their key beat-laden release, their other albums and singles being less electro orientated and heading for a more ambient sound. 'The Quest' had plenty of the Kraftwerkian notations to it, simple drum machines, the sound of oceans, and even the occasional piece of dialogue, such as on 'Bang Bang' and 'The Mutant Gillmen', but mostly it was slowly simmering and rhythmic. 'Hi Tide' had a chunkier feel, but this was multi layered sequenced synthetics, which Drexciya utilised expertly to bring their concept piece to life.

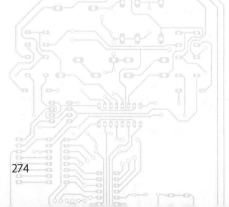

BJORK
Homogenic
Original release: 1997
ONE LITTLE INDIAN

Tracklisting:
Hunter, Jóga, Unravel, Bachelorette, All Neon Like, 5 Years, Immature, Alarm Call, Pluto, All Is Full of Love

'Homogenic' was a brave and compelling album from Bjork, even by her own intriguing standards. By 1997 she'd carved a niche with her upbeat personality and unique yet suitably accessible songs, but the suicide of Ricardo Lopez, who had been stalking her, and her desire to write an album that reflected her native Iceland cast a far more serious sheen on the creation of this much praised album. While some critics noted its "fusion of chilly strings (courtesy of the Icelandic String Octet), stuttering, abstract beats, and unique touches like accordion and glass harmonica" and 'Rolling Stone' warned that it was "certain to be rough going for fans looking for the sweet melodies and peppy dance collages of her earlier releases," 'Homogenic' was a key musical statement that informed Bjork's sound thereafter.

In the press scrum following the suicide, Bjork had retreated to Spain to record the album, and the cast of protagonists and programmers was enormous as work continued. Having written string parts on a Casio keyboard, Bjork brought in Eumar Deodato to conduct a full orchestra, which added enormous depth to a sound which revolved around the often grating rhythmic elements and took the luscious arrangements to new places. It was Mark Bell whose brilliant programming defined the sound that surrounded Bjork's distinctive vocal, a partnership that she recognised in 'Pytlik', "If I were to say who has influenced me most it would be Stockhausen, Kraftwerk, Brian Eno and Mark Bell".

The looped backbone of 'Immature', the overtly dramatic 'Bachelorette', the jerky rhythm of 'Pluto' and the Howie B produced ambient netherworld of 'All Is Full Of Love' are all astonishing, the wavering reverb on the latter track which closes the album adding to the huge sound of the set. 'Homogenic' was a bold and dramatic electronic creation that utilised more traditional instruments and song construction to give it room to breathe more deeply.

AIR
Sexy Boy
From Moon Safari
Original release: 1998
SOURCE

By contrast to Bjork's engaging and challenging new direction, the debut album from French duo Air couldn't have been more easy going. The opening cut, 'La Femme D'Argent' floated past with consummate ease, Q's review noting the whole set's "heightened state of tranquillity" in its four star review, which acclaimed it as "a fine study of the art of musical cool". By contrast, even in its subdued position after 'La Femme', the single 'Sexy Boy' remained a featherlite tune that only came into its own when remixed and the volume was cranked up. When it was taken out of the super relaxed confines of 'Moon Safari'.

"Like all great pop, it is based on a snap you to attention rhythm," exclaimed 'This Is Uncool' of the 45, and by the autumn of 1998 'Q' had written a whole piece about how 'Sexy Boy' sounded like, er, sex. I guess you had to be there. Air's position as modern day bachelor pad jazz-lite explorers was confirmed, and the super sweet 'Sexy Boy', with its deep-filled plumped up cushions of synthesisers, would always remain a classic.

The Beastie Boys had a different slant on 'sex' and electronic, as their 'Intergalactic' proved. Like schoolboys on a prank outing with new technology at their fingertips, they were childishly hilarious.

THE BEASTIE BOYS
Intergalactic
Original release: 1998
CAPITOL RECORDS

Allegedly using a vocoder to cloak the immortal line "I've got an erection" was a touch of genius, as was sampling Rachmaninoff, Les Baxter and The Jazz Crusaders. The Beastie Boys are perhaps a footnote, a sidenote even, in the progression of electronic music, although their Grand Royal magazine once devoted a whole issue to analogue synths, but 'Intergalactic' and its vocoder-vocal chorus was a classic 45, and their ongoing devotion to sampling, drum machines, synthesisers, Reason and so forth certainly renders any omission of their contributions a huge oversight.

COLDCUT (AND HEXSTATIC)
Timber
Original release: 1998
NINJA TUNE

Coldcut had been around since the late '80s, in fact they made the cover of 'OffBeat' which I edited as early as 1988, when Jonathan More and Matt Black told ace reporter Chris Coco about the construction of their excellent 'Out To Lunch' album, which was recorded at home. "We're too busy making sounds to worry about the new technology, our drum machine cost £200, the samples are crap, but it doesn't matter, we can still use them".

Coldcut were working on the hoof, much like The KLF, bringing in all kinds of sounds sources and reworking them. Their mastery of what little equipment they had provided them with a stream of releases, demonstrating their ability to find and manipulate the right sound even if, in some cases, they had to dismantle it, loop it and rework it to make it fit with the direction they wanted to go. They made hugely successful tracks, commercial slices of pop and club music that seemed to effortlessly appear. Given their other production roles, DJ outings and eventual ownership of Ninja Tune, it's fair to say the duo's fingers were in many pies.

"The sampler is like the ultimate musical instrument, you can use it to play any noise at all. In fact it's our fault that there were five records in the chart recently with the phrase 'This is a journey into sound' on them. We used it on Eric B's 'Paid In Full' and the M/A/R/R/S single and everyone sampled it, We created our own monster".

The Coldcut legacy included 'Doctorin' The House', 'People Hold On' featuring Lisa Stansfield, the groovy 'Atomic Moog 2000', 'More Beats And Pieces' and, in 1998 a collaboration with Hexstatic, who worked primarily in audio/visual media. The collaboration produced 'Timber', the video for which explained and visually represented the sawing samples, morse code, edited, stuttering vocal lines and car starting sound effects that were moulded into the five minute piece, demonstrating more than a hint of the found sound ethic. On 'Timber' everything has a part to play, everything is going on and, seemingly, no sound can't find a home in its rich stew of beats 'n pieces. The concept of listening to wood be sawn never sounded so good.

PLASTIKMAN
Consumed
Original release: 1998
NOVAMUTE

By complete contrast, you could be forgiven for thinking that nothing is going on when you listen to Plastikman. The 'Consumed' album, for Novamute, was an intense experience - at volume it was a vibrating rhythm that shook your body before often off kilter waves of synthesisers and confrontational secondary rhythms drift into play. On 'Passage (In)', the rhythms were dispensed with and you almost have to strain to hear what's going on, whilst 'Convulse (Sic)' and 'Ekko' reduce the sound to the reverberated after effects, the latter adding a pulsing throb for effect.

What were we hearing here? This was the pulsing and vibrating of machine music seemingly playing itself. Plastikman is, of course, Richie Hawtin, a British born musician who wound up in Detroit as techno was beginning to take hold. "Every time I went to Derrick May's house," Hawtin told 'The Wire' in 2008, his machines were on the floor in the corner, and they were always running. There was always this music flowing out, tracks I have never heard again".

Hawtin was inspired, and sound was everything. He made music as FUSE before releasing the classic 'Sheet One' album in 1993 and the now legendary 'Spastik' single, which 'The Wire' referred to as "a landmark of skittering, sweaty palmed tension".

A second album, 'Musik', followed but Hawtin felt it was too acid-tinged, and so a series of 12" singles under the name Concept 1 began to strip away at the sound before the next Plastikman album, 'Consumed' appeared. The record showcased the ultimate in his bare bones approach, which would then build into a reactive sound where any real time input could influence what he was doing.

"Jeff Mills (Detroit producer) and I talked about this once," Hawtin told 'The Wire' when asked about where the music was talking him, "We decided we were futurists. It's not that we know where the future is going, it's that we're trying to pull together things that are out there".

Hawtin's music certainly has the feel of the future, albeit a prospectively unpleasant one, engulfed as it in a cold, sterile sense of alienation, where every sound can be explained. On 'Consumed' even the hum of silence has its place.

ADD N TO (X)
Avant Hard
Original release: 1999
MUTE

Tracklisting:
Barry 7's Contraption, Robot New York, Skills, Steve's Going to Teach Himself Who's Boss, Fyuz, Buckminster Fuller, Revenge of the Black Regent, Metal Fingers in My Body, Ann's Eveready Equestrian, Oh Yeah, Oh No, Machine is Bored With Love, Hidden track after 0:33 of silence

Plastikman's reduction of sound to its very minimal components was giving edge to the Mute label's more experimental Novamute stable, whilst, at the main label, Add N To (X) were returning to a more traditional form of electronic music. The late '90s eerie and ethereal analogue experiments of Add N To (X) thrived on blips and squeals, X-rated video concepts and off-kilter avant-garde ideas. The London-based trio had pushed a few envelopes by the time they tackled their third album, 'Avant Hard', and although it doesn't encroach on the territory of their electroclash contemporaries who'd taken to the pop route, or indeed labelmates Depeche or Erasure, the album had a more cohesive and accessible ambience than their previous releases.

"From its Tipsy-like opener 'Barry 7's Contraption', 'Avant Hard' displays an unexpected swing towards accessibility," enthused an almost incredulous Andrew Carden in 'MOJO' magazine on the album's release. "If 'Robot New York' and 'Ann's Everyday Equestrian' still flirt with sonic over-indulgence, elsewhere tracks like 'Oh Yeah, Oh no' marry '60s pop with wigged out FX... while 'Metal Fingers In My Body' sounds like a rock anthem played out on vintage synthesisers".

Indeed, the latter was used on a Sky Digital advert to lure new customers, no doubt an ad exec-styled veil being drawn over the track's original video which featured a woman having sex with a robot, its catchy backbeat and throbbing shards of melody proving far more important.

With Alison Goldfrapp credited as an additional musician, and samples of avant-garde prog extremist Egg's 'Fugue In D Minor' hidden away, 'Avant Hard' was never in danger of being commercial, but it was an exceptional take on pulsing new beats mixed with valve-crackling authentic instrumentation.

MOBY
Play
Original release: 1999
MUTE

Tracklisting:
Honey, Find My Baby, Porcelain, Why Does My Heart Feel So Bad?, South Side, Rushing, Bodyrock, Natural Blues, Machete, 7, Run On, Down Slow, If Things Were Perfect, Everloving, Inside, Guitar Flute & String, The Sky Is Broken, My Weakness

Mute were experiencing even bigger success at the end of the '90s with 'Play', a carefully crafted, sample-heavy set that took him away from his cult following and into the pop charts and onto coffee tables all over the globe. "'Play' wasn't the first album to make a rock star out of an insular techno nerdnik," pointed out 'Rolling Stone', "but it was the first to make one a pop sensation".

As Add N To (X) had travelled back to analogue simplicity, Moby delved further to original vocalists who'd originally appeared on 78s earlier in the century. The key to 'Play' was the samples garnered from Alan Lomax's famous field recordings and the huge 'Folkways' archive owned by the Smithsonian Institute. These wayward blues, gospel and folk songs set the tone, and were enhanced with fairly primitive drum patterns and affected vocal lines from Moby and, of course, waves of lush synthesisers.

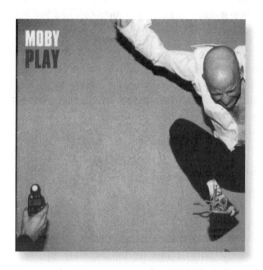

A staggering nine singles were released from the album - apparently the world just couldn't get enough of this reawakening of traditional song, from the ambient beauty of the much-sampled 'Porcelain' through to the opening 'Honey' and the evocative 'Why Does My Heart Feel So Bad?'. Moby and his sampled sound was everywhere, and in some cases the original vocalists were located and began second careers courtesy of their electronic reawakening. Some questioned the rather skewed ethics of a man who had previously earned a reputation for his outspoken, anti-corporate take on the world selling rights to so many songs from the album to be used in advertisements, but history will surely remember the music rather than the issues that surrounded it.

As the decade ended, the world seemed obsessed with electronic music and DJ culture had reached even headier heights, as The Chemical Brothers' 'Surrender' album displayed.

THE CHEMICAL BROTHERS
Hey Boy Hey Girl
Original release: 1999
VIRGIN

In May of 1999, The Chemical Brothers released what was to become probably their most instantly recognisable hit. By June they were headlining the Dance Stage at Glastonbury, and you couldn't get near the place. Twelve months on they headlined the Pyramid stage and the field became like a rolling football stadium as people vied for position. Nine Inch Nails were on the Other Stage at the same time, but the UK was gripped by the cult of superstar DJs and 'Hey Boy Hey Girl' had had a full year to bed into everyone's psyche. The Chemical Brothers could do no wrong.

On its release in 1999, 'Hey Boy Hey Girl' took a more four to the floor approach than the pair had previously been known for, but became an instantly recognisable phrase that seemed to ring from thousands of revellers whenever it was played in clubs or live. The simple sampled one liner was lodged into Britain's collected brain, cementing the superstar image for its perpetrators and elevating the art of the DJ to a whole new level.

LEFTFIELD
Afrika Shox
Original release: 1999
HARD HANDS

Leftfield also played Glastonbury, headlining the Other Stage on the Saturday, in 1999, underlining the move from specialist to mainstream for their electronic groove. Three months later they released their new album 'Rhythm And Stealth', and the single 'Afrika Shox', featuring Afrika Bambaataa. A vocoder and a rolling homage to Kraftwerk on top of a driving rhythm and an electrofunk groove, proved a perfect foil for the 'Intergalactic' robot summoning up Bambaataa's Zulu Nation. With a gloriously Teutonic melody line for good measure, it was another turning point for electronic music, and a further marriage of styles and personnel.

VNV NATION
Empires
Original release: 1999
DEPENDENT RECORDS

Tracklisting:
Lastlight, Kingdom(Restoration), Further, Legion (Janus), Saviour (Vox), Fragments (Splinter), Legion (Anachron), Standing (Still), Standing (Motion), Radius≤, Standing (Original)

Irish band VNV Nation had dabbled in electronic body music and electronica on their first two albums, and been embraced by Chicago's Wax Trax! Label. Their third set retained their palpitating rhythmic patterns but added some techno lines and verses and choruses that sounded like Editors on a New Order kick some ten years before they arrived. The mood was downbeat and austere. Utilising an Access Virus synthesiser and two cheap samplers, VNV Nation had cast themselves in a new sub-sub genre, proving again that experimentation in electronic music knew few boundaries.

"VNV Nation is one of a number of bands (such as Covenant, Wumpscut, and Neuroactive) aggressively carving a niche for themselves in the spaces between industrial and electronic music." claimed 'Pop Matters', while the band's Ronan Harris revealed their roots on the Angelindustrial website: "I was hooked on Kraftwerk from the age of seven because they were number one on the charts and every birthday my dad bought me a new Kraftwerk album. I was also into synth-pop, the whole New Romantic movement at the time, everything from Depeche Mode to Human League.

"Then, when I got older, I was getting more aggressive, and I got into things like Portion Control. I loved Joy Division, because they painted this bleak but incredibly restrained emotive and emotional landscape for me. As I got older I was listening to industrial, I liked anything electronic, the whole smorgasbord of it. The cold, enigmatic, dramatic electronic music".

The VNV influence smorgasbord had led them to the dark side and some vitriolic doomy sounds while, over in California, the pert synth pop of Joy Electric was at completely the other end of the electronic spectrum.

JOY ELECTRIC
CHRISTIANSongs
Original release: 1999
BEC RECORDINGS

It would be easy to pillory Joy Electric for their lyrics. The opening track on 'CHRISTIANsongs' is jaw droppingly odd, with its 'praise the Lord' sentiment set against the kind of classroom synth melody that The Teletubbies might come up with. Were these guys for real? Breakneck rhythms and offkey vocals on 'Children Of The Lord' follow on what is plainly a serious Christian album, which was the intent of the band's mainstay, Ronnie Martin, who "explained his frustration over Christian music groups attempting to downplay their religion in hopes for greater commercial success".

That's all fine, but the mix of Martin's heart on the sleeve lyrics and the relentless teenybop rolling synthesisers gave twee a new meaning. The Christian website 'Jesus Freak Hideout' gave it four out of five stars, as did 'All Music' and, indeed, the 'Phantom Tollbooth' website, which stated: "Of course, Joy Electric is a musical oddity in its own right. With music composed entirely of the synthesizer work of Ronnie Martin, Joy Electric makes music for the Nintendo age. Some people love it, some hate it, but everyone must admit that it is unique".

If Joy Electric were unique, then where on earth did that leave Aphex Twin?

APHEX TWIN
Windowlicker
Original release: 1999
WARP

"'Windowlicker' is the most impossible to understand noise... Conversely and wonderfully, it is also one of the most aesthetically beautiful," claimed Garry Mulholland in 'This Is Uncool'. But Karlheinz Stockhausen thought otherwise when he was sent an Aphex recording by 'Wire' magazine: "I heard the piece Aphex Twin of Richard James carefully: I think it would be very helpful if he listens to my work 'Song Of The Youth', which is electronic music, and a young boy's voice singing with himself. Because he would then immediately stop with all these post-African repetitions, and he would look for changing tempi and changing rhythms, and he would not allow to repeat any rhythm if it varied to some extent and if it did not have a direction in its sequence of variations".

Too serious? Famously, the Twin summed up his career as: "I'm just some irritating, lying, ginger kid from Cornwall who should have been locked up in some youth detention centre. I just managed to escape and blag it into music".

'Windowlicker' sounds like a song going beautifully off the rails, every time it teeters it pulls itself back and adds a new layer of intrigue. It is a provocative, edgy piece of music, eternally morphing and changing. It's offbeat and challenging yet gloriously rewarding - as you listen, you repeatedly find yourself wanting it to pull itself back into shape, and it does.... briefly. It's a triumphant, and ultimately rewarding, journey.

It's a fitting way to end the decade that brought electronic music to stadiums, from Christians and into the homes of virtually everyone. The NME, indeed, voted 'Windowlicker' Single Of The Year, to which the Twin, Richard James replied...

"Smart! Thank you very much for voting for my track/s. I've had a very good year as usual, although it was very intense, getting on a really big roll, writing new stuff constantly, really looking forward to isolating myself next year even more! Hope everyone has a totally boring New Year's party, overdoses on everything and chokes on their own vomit on the bathroom floor, make sure you lie face down just before you pass out!

Signed, Pritchad. g. Kraymes"

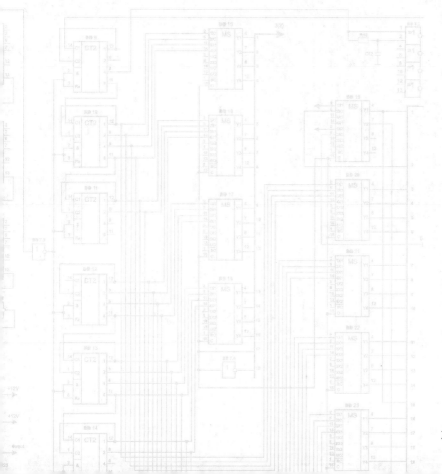

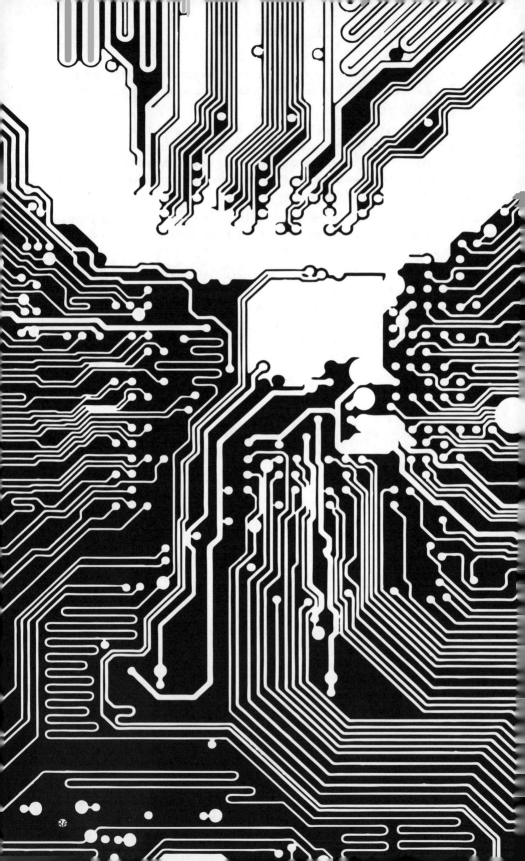

SIX

DISMANTLING SOUND AND BENDING THE CIRCUITS

As 1999 whirred to a close, the captains of industry bit their nails, terrified at the threat of Y2K, a potential computer meltdown nobody had envisaged when they invented what had become our greatest friend during the '90s. Missiles might develop minds of their own, keen to fly the coop like the bomb in John Carpenter's 'Dark Star'. Whole memory banks could be wiped and all semblance of natural order would be destroyed. As Prince's anthemic millennium closer rang around the globe, nations drew breath. Were we all doomed?

Nothing, of course, happened. Fireworks went off, 'Auld Lang Syne' was sung, people arrived at doors holding coal and bottles of whisky. Hangovers arrived sometime later.

Musically, the '90s had heralded a new wave of single-orientated dance hits and the idea that electronic music was not only listenable and saleable, but was also a key part of the musical family. Barriers had been destroyed, genres defied. Although some were still sceptical about the value of electronic music, nobody could deny it had arrived on a global scale.

The decade's fascination with electronic music had pulled it almost completely from the underground. In the new millennium, 'Mixmag', 'Ministry', 'Muzik' and 'DJ' magazine, along with a torrent of style mags, would marvel at, and be opinionated about, electronic music and its many emerging sub genres. As the new decade unravelled, even the established critics, from 'Q' and 'MOJO' through to 'The Guardian', also hipped to these new sounds. New gadgets were emerging by the day. How could anybody not marvel at this new futuristic dream world?

GOLDFRAPP
Utopia
Original release: 2000
MUTE

"Despite the lingering suspicion that they make music solely for graphic designers," 'NME' jested about 'Utopia', the second single from the album 'Felt Mountain', "Goldfrapp's art-hop is undeniably enchanting". The traditional press were also intrigued by the new dance music, and Pitchfork, of course, probed further: "Taking cues from apparent influences, ranging from Marlene Dietrich to Siouxsie Sioux to Björk, Alison Goldfrapp has constructed an album that's simultaneously smarmy and seductive, yet elegant and graceful".

NME called the album "cold, desolate and old-fashioned" and argued that 'Felt Mountain' was not a "bad concept" but that "Portishead got there first, and managed to update the spy-film vibe with a hefty dose of break-driven twilight melancholia".

"If Austin Powers had been a film noir flick," Pitchfork countered, "it's soundtrack would probably sound something like 'Felt Mountain'. The hushed vocals, the crying analogue synthesisers, and the sustained seven chords all evoke amazingly strong images of things past".

The concept retro futurism was applauded, and 'Q' magazine included the album in its list of the top 50 albums of 2000, whilst 'Utopia' bedazzled the club crowds with its many remixed identities. The 2000s were about to become the remixed decade, with everything seemingly restructured and rephased for easier listening pleasure. 'Utopia (Genetically Enriched)', for example, sparkled with Bowie-esque melancholy and lush synthesisers. It was heroic, futuristic and joyous. Perfect for the new thinking that would surely accompany the new millennium.

Everything would be different, whilst remaining comfortably familiar, and Goldfrapp's use of analogue equipment on 'Utopia' made the track feel comforting in a proto future retro kind of way. Remixes by the Bad Seeds' Mick Harvey (slow and ethereal) and Jori Hullkkonnen (housey and tub thumping), along with Tom Middleton's 'Acid Dub Edit' and a vocal version with strident back beat, plus the super phased 'Sunroof' mix, ensured that 'Utopia' had been stretched from just under four minutes to a total of just under 40 minutes of evocative, soulful minimalism. Perfect pop music, whichever way you cut it, and presented in such a non confrontational manner - there was a tailor-made interpretation for anyone who was half interested.

APOPTYGMA BERZERK
Kathy's Song
Original release: 2000
POLYDOR

Everyone seemed just simply overjoyed to have survived the turn of the century, and in Norway the previously chunky and frenetic Apoptygma Berzerk (APB to you and me) decided to lighten up for the new millennium. They had been making electronic body music since 1993's 'Soli Deo Gloria' album, laden with hard-edged, rhythmic grooves, but by album three, 'Welcome To Earth', they'd seen a new light rising, and a few crop circles too. They became players of future pop, a super-lite descendent of the industrial rhythms and dance friendly beats they'd been utilising in the '90s, and effectively crossed over to the sunny side of the street.

"On 'Welcome To Earth'," 'All Music' noted, "they keep things dense and mildly sinister (lots of chord washes in minor keys), but they give in to their poppier side on the choruses... welcome relief from the skull-numbing techno rhythms".

The band's new vision was riddled with stories of alien sightings and a fascination with "natural" phenomena, such as crop circles, and the album provided much of the material that would comprise their live sets throughout the decade. The single cut, 'Kathy's Song', became one of their biggest hits in Europe, with remixes by VNV Nation, Beborn Beton and Ferry Corsten helping out. The latter strips the track back into an anthemic house piece clocking in at close to eight minutes, and significantly added to the band's mystique and, indeed, their audience.

COVENANT
Dead Stars
Original release: 2000
WHITE LABEL 12

In neighbouring Sweden, meanwhile, Eskil Simonsson, Joakim Montelius and Clas Nachmanson were developing similar ideas. As Covenant they'd been inspired by Kraftwerk, The Human League, and by EBM pioneers Front 242 and Nitzer Ebb. They'd also loosened up and partially ditched the darker, edgier rhythms by 2000 with their album 'United States Of Mind'. The DSO website enthused about their new direction, claiming that their "typically harsh, staticky blasts of audio have been significantly smoothened out, flirting with the simple repetition of dance-pop".

Yet again, the remix was key in extending the appeal of the band, with club and dub mixes allowing the phased synth lead line and baritone rasp of 'Dead Stars' to hint at their heavier roots whilst also playing out as a far more accessible slice of dream pop, or even shoegaze as it was known in some circles.

"'Dead Stars' provides enough evidence that they can still write perfect EBM with self-referential lyrics like: "We find our songs in fashion magazines" and "We find ourselves in pictures on the net"" commented DSO as it concluded that perhaps Covenant weren't entirely forsaking their Blade Runner-infused beginnings. Any original fans shouldn't panic.

RADIOHEAD
Kid A
Original release: 2000
PARLOPHONE

Tracklisting:
Everything in Its Right Place, Kid A, The National Anthem, How to Disappear Completely, Treefingers, Optimistic, In Limbo, Idioteque, Morning Bell, Motion Picture Soundtrack

From the obscure to the stadium filling... If pop success beckoned for electronic acts, no-one had told Radiohead. They'd already become huge on the back of 'OK Computer', had headlined Glastonbury and toured the enormodomes of world and were by now being roundly imitated by hundreds of bands, as "They're the new Radiohead" became a well worn journalistic cliché and served as an unmanageable weight around the necks of many potentially interesting new bands. If fans of Covenant were re-assured and asked not to panic, Radiohead were about to cause mass hysteria in the ranks of the faithful. For 'Kid A', they decided to go someplace else. And not just musically. There were no pictures, no group interviews – all were done individually – and no discernable pop singles. The book 'No Logo' had caused something of a reaction in Thom Yorke.

"While making 'Kid A', there was a wall chart of song titles that Phil Selway was frightened to look at," claimed 'Q' in a Radiohead special issue. Back on its release, the magazine had enthused: "The urge to smack Thom Yorke briskly around the chops – Eric and Ernie style – grows more irresistible with each passing day. Here's to their bloody-minded cussedness". 'Kid A' certainly got a reaction, and took on that long forgotten role of pop music in getting people thinking. Yorke and co were heroically heading in a new direction.

"Like its most obvious forebear, David Bowie's 'Low,'" suggested 'Select' magazine, "what's not present is as important as what's actually here. The main absentees, then, are choruses, coherent lyrics, crescendos, and guitars... But, really, what do you want for sounding like Aphex Twin circa 1993? A medal?"

'Everything In Its Right Place' with its memorable repeated line about waking up sucking a lemon, which Yorke explained was about the face he'd worn for the last three years, opened the set, and the frightening title track, with its barely coherent vocodered vocal, followed. The Ondes Martenot was introduced for 'The National Anthem', and it was quite apparent that this was not to be the 'OK Computer Pt 2' that many craved.

Evidently, Jonny Greenwood and Thom Yorke were apparently the enthused pair who jumped up and down and cajoled the rest of the band into things, and all was not plain sailing in the studio. Its easy to see why – in one instance, Ed O'Brien supplied a feedback mantra that was re-warped in Cubase and sat alongside Yorke giving out a weather forecast (on 'In Limbo'), whilst funereal chants and the proverbial kitchen sink were also employed.

"The sonic scribbles of 'Kid A' are far more stimulating than their regular grind...", The Wire reckoned, "Along with Primal Scream's 'Exterminator', 'Kid A' is a vital work. Anyone remotely interested in contemporary music should listen to it at least once". Just the once?

On the album's closing cut, 'Motion Picture Soundtrack', Q reckoned that Yorke sounded "like he's got a mouthful of ulcers, ending the set on an "oddly undernourished note".

As a whole piece, 'Kid A' was brave, majestic and groundbreaking. 'Billboard' exclaimed that it "immerses listeners in an ocean of unparalleled musical depth. It is, without question, the first truly groundbreaking album of the 21st Century". 'Spin' magazine saw the new soaking of sound as nothing short of revolutionary: "Radiohead have completely immersed themselves in the studio-as-instrument, signal processing, radical stereo separation, and other anti-naturalistic techniques. Even the precious guitars - saturated with effects and gaseous with sustain - resemble natural phenomena rather than power chords or lead lines. Essentially, this is a post-rock record.... 'Kid A' is not only Radiohead's bravest album but their best one as well".

And, how could they follow that? Simple - in June the following year came 'Amnesiac', further studio-based antics and effectively a sister album to 'Kid A'. People were beginning to understand what they were doing. Sort of.

"Either Yorke's lyrics are better this time, or the comparative voluptuousness of the vocal performances make it easier to tune in, or we've finally grasped what he's been getting at since abandoning 'OK Computer's more straightforward man-vs-society musings," said 'Q'. 'MOJO' reckoned the album was "Deliriously provocative" and "as splendidly other and awkward as its sister album".

On 'Amnesiac', the studio was further dismantled, but seemed to make more sense. So much so that Radiohead fan sites assembled 'Kid Amnesiac', a more flowing amalgamation of the two albums, even producing cover art for the DIY enthusiast. For those interested, the tracklisting ran: The National Anthem, Like Spinning Plates, Dollars and Cents, Idioteque, Morning Bell, How To Disappear Completely, In Limbo, Everything In Its Right Place, Packt Like Sardines In A Crushd Tin Box, Optimistic, Knives Out, Pyramid Song, Treefingers, Motion Picture Soundtrack.

Now that's something we can all do with friends at home. Unlike watching Add N To (X)'s 'Plug Me In' video, which added new dimensions to their sullen image and experimental musings....

ADD N TO (X)
Plug Me In
Original release: 2000
MUTE

'Add Insult To Injury' was the fourth album from Add N To (X), being a hybrid of two mini albums which had followed the release of 'Avant Hard'. The video for the album's 'Plug Me In', an 18-certificate lesbian romp, certainly attracted viewers to a tune that was previously an eerie piece of disjointed indie underground synthesiser meddling. The band's otherworldliness was as experimental and haunting as something from the cutting room floor of 'Kid A', a downbeat, unnerving sound that felt a tad uninviting at times. The whole thing was sharply brought into focus by the video clip.

Perhaps it was unrelated to their offbeat collages of sound, but whatever the reasoning it caused all kinds of controversy and, as a marketing tool, attracted a host of previously uninterested people to the world of post-industrial synth pop.

BONOBO
Animal Magic
Original release: 2000
TRU THOUGHTS

While Add N To (X) were creating brooding, malevolent music, British musician, producer and DJ Simon Green was defining the downtempo groove of 'Animal Magic', an album of samples and ethereal grooves that often got lumped in with lesser releases of the Ibiza hangover generation. Without doubt, Bonobo's music was always a cut above that theme bar mix tape genre, as Green preferred to dabble in jazz, lush strings and all kinds of out-there samples. 'Animal Magic's follow up sets, 'M For Monkey' and 'Days To Come', from 2006, further enhanced his reputation. The latter was roundly applauded by 'Prefix' magazine: "This time around Bonobo sounds fuller and better defined. But that's not the only difference: For the first time he makes room for vocalists, employing the talents of the mysterious Bajika (who also collaborated heavily with Ubiquity's Radio Citizen) and labelmate Fink".

That said, it's those earlier less formulated mixes on 'Animal Magic' that still stand out, underlining his influences from Sun Ra through to Stereolab and ratcheting up his music above and beyond his contemporaries.

If Bonobo's bag was all about relaxation and cool jazz tones, utilising well chosen samples to lull the listener into a secure sense of super comfort, Squarepusher's jerky creations were using similar source material with an entirely different result. The edits were fast and frenetic, choppy and precise, developing a syncopated new jazz groove in difficult time signatures with a scratchy DJ tricks and digital trickery adding further dynamics to the jittery structure.

SQUAREPSUHER
Tommib
Original release: 2001
From Go Plastic
WARP

'Tommib', from 2001's 'Go Plastic' album, couldn't be further from the fast paced chop up of sound that dominated the rest of the record. It's a gentle, lilting piece of choral music that's been used on the soundtracks of 'Lost In Translation', 'Marie Antoinette' and a thousand TV links. It was truly evocative, though, a downtempo moment that allowed the rest of the album to be as intense as it wanted to be. And 'Go Plastic was intense. It needed the 'Tommib' moment simply to breathe.

'Go Plastic' was, according to 'MOJO', "An album which makes his previous excesses seem conservative... Dazzling though this bombardment is, it's a draining experience". That couldn't have been closer to the truth. Like Miles Davis' later period romps, the post funk attack of, say, 'Directions', 'Go Plastic' is relentless, frantic and, frankly, exhausting. "What's striking is that he's less wacky than he's ever been, instead pursuing a rougher, more complex sound,' suggested 'The Wire' magazine, while 'Q' noted that "Tom Jenkinson shares Aphex Twin's mischievous way with a beat, but lacks his respect for melody".

Amazingly, perhaps, 'Go Plastic' was an engaging experience, but not everyone could cope with the whole set. 'Tommib', the quiet between the storms, held it together, probably being a much more restrained option for some. 'Rolling Stone', in emperor's new clothing style, remarked: "For sheer virtuosity, you gotta hand it to the guy - he sure can make a lot of really weird noises. But who cares?"

AUTHECHRE
Confield
Original release: 2001
WARP

By 2001, Warp Records had grown from a stylish, on-the-money dancefloor label into a key protagonist in the progression and evolution of electronic music, much like Brain and Sky in the early '70s and Mute in the late '70s and '80s. Its roster included Aphex Twin, Squarepusher, Boards Of Canada, Stereolab and many others, and it had also been truly supportive of the painstaking experiments of Autechre and their slow deconstruction of sound and, to a growing extent, rhythm.

"They've all but abandoned 4/4 grooves, discarded bass as an inefficient distraction and fractured their beats into splintery beatlets that detonate in flurries," claimed American magazine 'Blender', while 'MOJO' saw the duo as unfathomable groundbreaking noise terrorists, "The mind-boggling intricacies and moody, broody sound-sculpting on tracks like 'Pen Expers' find Autechre zooming off, leaving their followers eating cosmic dust".

Like Squarepusher's 'Go Plastic', 'Confield' was not easy listening. The mood was slower and more considered, with pulses and vibrating sequences delicately overlaid onto each other, and the titles themselves added to the feeling that the album, as hypnotic as it was, was created in some kind of isolation, seemingly out of sync with the world. 'Eidetic Casein' rumbled like it was being overheard from another space, the occasional feedback or white noise glitch accentuating its remote feeling, and the penultimate track 'Lentic Catachresis' sounded even more obtuse, the final third reverberating like it was in complete meltdown. "'Confield' not only documents the future of IDM," 'Alternative Press' proclaimed, "it also cements Autechre's name in the pantheon of sonic visionaries".

ZERO 7
Destiny
Original release: 2001
ULTIMATE DILEMMA

The gentle, spacious sound of Zero 7, couldn't have been farther from the claustrophobia of Autechre and Squarepusher. Emotive, downtempo and soulful, thanks to the vocals of Sia Furler and Sophie Barker, Zero 7's 'Destiny' was the stand out track from their debut 'Simple Things' album. The creation of Henry Binns and Sam Hardaker, Zero 7 mixed trip hop and ambient jazz to create a new breed of ultra smooth lounge music with an electronic sheen. "They're the British Air, and they're very good," announced 'NME'.

"The distinctive, dulcet tones of Australian born Sia Furler," the BBC's website says, "embellish the lush instrumentation of 'Distractions' with more husk than a wheat field, whilst the vocal partnership with the sublime and as yet unsigned Sophie Barker on 'Destiny' soar on a summer thermal to new heights". Quite.

Zero 7's Radio 2 breakthrough proved that the art of relaxation and its accompanying soundtrack might just have mass appeal, and certainly seems to have inspired that particular BBC journalist to some flowery prose into the bargain.

ROYKSOPP
Melody AM
Original release: 2001
WALL OF SOUND

Tracklisting:
So Easy, Eple, Sparks, In Space, Poor Leno, A Higher Place, Röyksopp's Night Out, Remind Me, She's So, 40 Years Back/Come

While Zero 7 appealed to the masses through AOR Radio, and especially BBC Radio 2, Royksopp were, perhaps, unlikely chart entries who managed to garner equal appeal for their less obvious chilled sounds.

Named after a puffball mushroom, Norwegian duo Royksopp managed to crossover with their distinctive, hugely whistleable melodies. The gorgeous 'Epie', from 'Melody AM', was one of three Top 40 singles in the UK, as the band delivered luscious layered synths, multiple melody lines and infectious motifs that were the stuff of a thousand ad campaigns.

"Quite unlike any other chill out album you're likely to hear," said 'Playlouder's erstwhile reviewer, "'Melody AM' takes low rider funk and splices it with '80s synth-pop ambience and analogue dub techniques to create a truly inspiring epic pop landscape which neither strays into questionable light classical territories, nor worrying prog rock terrain".

On second listening, nearly ten years later, the album sounds wonderfully simple, like well-tuned pop music should be. Back in 2001 it split the audience in the US, 'Pitchfork' finding it "Wildly

296

experimental and unique, 'Melody AM' belongs in the collections of fans of lush keyboard instrumentation, '70s soul, new age and Boards Of Canada-style strangeness alike," while 'Rolling Stone' was less convinced, "Royksopp show a debt to art rock, but they replace Pink Floyd's paranoia with a mood of late-night sorrow".

Sure, there was plenty of melancholy in there, but It had a joyous sense of seriousness. Perhaps America's confusion had been created by the adrenalin headrush that met the arrival of Fischerspooner and the general excitement of the short-lived 'electroclash' genre. Unlike Royksopp's considered, soul-less beauty, this brash departure had taken the idea of Soft Cell's sleaziness and magnified it 100%.

FISCHERSPOONER
Emerge
Original release: 2001
MINISTRY OF SOUND

Rumours abounded that the duo of Fischerspooner were courted by many labels, eventually signing to Ministry Of Sound in the UK for a staggering one million pounds. The hype never transferred to mass sales and the band were eventually dropped without recouping, but not before the single 'Emerge' was released, heralding what seemed to be the battle cry for a whole new generation of haircuts.

'Emerge' was the first anthem of electroclash, and Fischerspooner's moment. Capitalising on the history of synth pop, it had "a synth line that bears a strong similarity to 'Blue Monday"," according to 'Pop Matters', "but takes the song in another direction, as Spooner spouts the album's own mantra of "Sounds good / Looks good / Feels good too", and the song bursts into frenetic beats and an incredibly catchy chorus".

But catchy choruses weren't enough, and the movement had few survivors from the original Electroclash festival that took place in New York the same year. The Guardian called electroclash and minimalist techno "two of the most significant upheavals in recent dance music history," but it had peaked by 2004 and its legacy was patchy at best. Apart from Fischerspooner, Peaches (with her scarily forthright androgynous image), Chicks On Speed (bottled off supporting the Chili Peppers in London) and Miss Kittin And The Hacker (repeating the same sensual European coldwave sound with their early releases) were the key instigators, while Felix Da Housecat (DJ whose second album was scuppered by big star allegiances) and the likes of The Faint also gained attention.

THE FAINT
Danse Macabre
Original release: 2001
SADDLE CREEK

The development of the internet, and with it the ability for anybody, absolutely anywhere, to voice their opinion on music helped focus attention on electroclash. While the traditional press were stuck in old school formats, hundreds of websites, and a good dose of viral marketing, created huge interest in bands long before they'd even thought about touring outside of their home territory. The Faint's reputation preceded them

"They've taken bits of dance, new wave, gothic, and pop and stirred it all up into a fat mixing pot of sound to create an album that's not only fun but actually has a message," claimed the Almostcopol.com website rather bloatedly, "There are bits of everything, from Gary Numan to Depeche Mode and New Order, as well as newer groups like Covenant, that pop up on the disc, and although there's a definite dance edge, the group also doesn't forget to rock once in awhile".

Poorly written but sincere, their sentiments were mirrored by 'Pitchfork', who announced that,

"Though The Faint's last album, 'Blank-Wave Arcade', was lyrically obsessed with sex, 'Danse Macabre' seems to keep coming back to gothic paradoxes; the living die by agenda suicide and mannequins are brought to life. Paralysis and involuntary movement or actions are common themes - although paralysis is more likely to mean being trapped in daily routines than in coffins, and involuntary movements are caused by social pressure rather than satanic possession. Still, these subjects seem well suited for synth-heavy anthems that lack subtlety in their thumping draw towards the dancefloor".

On such advice, thousands of bedroom-bound Goths immediately pricked up their ears and The Faint sounded like a band with promise. And, when the ailing Melody Maker finally decided to get behind the genre, electroclash was away and running, if a little slowly.

MISS KITTIN AND THE HACKER
Frank Sinatra
Original release: 2001
DJ HELL

Miss Kittin And The Hacker were also riding the electroclash rollercoaster. The duo had met at the start of the '90s in rave conditions and released their debut EP 'Champagne' in 1998. According to Kittin's website, 2001 was when her career really took off: "Miss Kittin and The Hacker finally release their first album on Gigolo," she recalled, "My voice appears on a song with Steve Bug, an album with Felix Da Housecat, an album with my Zurich friend Goldenboy. I am suddenly welcome in France after five years of absence. I took my first holidays in thtree years. After shooting the video of 'Je T´aime Moi Non Plus', a Serge Gainsbourg cover with Sven Vath, I decided to move to Berlin".

Like Twitter gone mad! The album featured the club favourite 'Frank Sinatra', which the duo had recorded earlier for release on the DJ Hell label in 2000. Kittin revealed the song's origin to the Phinnweb site.

 "I love Frank Sinatra and the American crooners and romantic jazz in general. I was looking for a rhyme to 'area' and here it came. What you don't know, is when I said 'He's dead', I really thought he was... A friend told me it was funny because he's still alive... I couldn't believe it and felt guilty, especially when he died three months later..."

"As career highlights go," 'Pitchfork' argued, "never mind first bows, it's a pretty enviable one - over the Hacker's brilliantly stupid rinky-dink ur-techno backdrop, Caroline Hervé speak-sings self-absorbed bon mots like "To be famous is so nice/ Suck my dick/ Kiss my ass," over and over with a dispassionate cadence". Music had come a long way.

FELIX DA HOUSECAT
Silver Screen (Shower Scene)
From Kittenz And Thee Glitz
Original release: 2001
EMPEROR NORTON

Kittin also turned up on the second album by Felix Da Housecat, a move that wasn't applauded by 'Pitchfork': "With guests drawn from outside of his usual circle, the record quickly becomes Felix's New Power Generation-equivalent. Quite why he didn't reject Miss Kittin's contributions ('Voicemail', 'Madame Hollywood' and 'Silver Screen - Shower Scene'), is uncertain, though it likely has something to do with a severe lapse of judgment".

"At least for 'Silver Screen - Shower Scene'," the outraged website continued, "Felix breaks out a devastatingly massive club groove. The Godzilla bassline pounds hard enough it's actually easy to ignore Miss Kittin's twittering about nicotine and "endless pleasures in limousines"".

It was deadpan stuff with plenty of French film noir posturing from Kittin, which actually came to life on the Jacques Le Cont Thin White Duke Mix, but if Kittin's attempts at sensual arousal fell on deaf ears at 'Pitchfork', Peaches was offering a whole different set of innuendo under the electroclash banner....

PEACHES
Set It Off
Original release: 2001
EPIC

Merrill Beth Nisker, better known as Peaches, is a Canadian-born electronic musician and performance artist based in Germany. Initially praised as a more extreme example of electroclash's dirty dancing, by the release of 'Set It Off' in 2001 she'd carved a niche as an electronic tease with some scary credentials.

"'Set It Off' is a moronic slab of two-note electro-clatter fecklessly nailed to a grimy, Hi-NRG rhythm with Peaches strutting her sexlessly smooth stuff over the top," the inkie 'NME' declared. "It'll use you, abuse you and you'll wake up in the morning to find it has stolen your cash card... Filthy, trashy and not entirely unlike Gary Numan after a sex change operation, Peaches is a winner all the way," claimed the paper's Jim Wirth.

While Kittin then proceeded to disappear back to the underground, Peaches was embraced as the more acceptable face of angsty-sex strangeness. 'Fatherfucker'. From 2003, was suitably controversial, and by 2006's impressively titled 'Impeach My Bush' album, she'd become hip enough to be able to enlist guest musicians Joan Jett, Queen Of The Stone Age's Josh Homme, The Gossip's Beth Ditto and Feist to perform on several of the tracks.

"Peaches has always trafficked in subversion. On her fourth full-length album, 'I Feel Cream', what she subverts - time and again - are preconceived notions of who Peaches is and what she does," her website applauded on the 'Bush' follow up. "Having held the attention of international audiences for a decade, now she reveals new dimensions of her artistry".

Back in 2001, 'Set It Off' had a swagger and poise, and also some traditional rock muscle - it was far bigger than the sum of its parts. Peaches also had the look, she was weird and strange and dangerous and not adverse to donning a false beard when the mood struck. By contrast, Richie Hawtin, aka Plastikman, had continued to minimise his sound and sported a fatherland haircut that was all 'Sound Of Music' Von Trapp family. Hawtin was a businessman, and his extra curricular activities began to raise a few eyebrows. The world perhaps wasn't ready for techno tea towels.

RICHIE HAWTIN
DE:9 Closer To The Edit
Original release: 2001
MUTE

The Richie Hawtin Minimalist Techno DE9 series ran to three albums, over which he reduced his techno sound yet further, utilising the decks, effects and 909 rhythm machine of the title to create new, unique mathematically-precise mixes. The liner notes on 'Closer To The Edit' explained the technique of reducing the various samples to their most basic elements, then reconstructing them into new pieces. 'DE:9 Closer To The Edit' looped these sounds in Final Scratch Pro, and resulted in a whole new album (the second in a series of three, in fact) that had been created from bits of all his other albums.

Was this electronic music gone mad? Was this acceptable eccentric behaviour from one of the established icons of techno or just part and parcel of further strangeness that seemed to have invaded the genre. Indeed, was this music created just because it could be?

'Fact' magazine, in 2010, listed the ten maddest things Richie Hawtin had done and the album was in there. Way up front. But so was his haircut and his collaboration with Sven Vath for a Novamute album in 2002 wherein the first track featured the duo and mates having dinner, the track being 'T Bone Steak'. 'Fact' also noted Hawtin's initial remarks on the project, "After recording, sampling, cutting, and splicing over 100 tracks down to their most basic components, I ended up with a collection of over 300 loops, ranging in length from 1 note to 4 bars. I then started to recreate and reinterpret each track, putting the pieces back together as if an audio jigsaw puzzle - using effects and edits in between each piece. This 53 minute piece, consisting of over 70 tracks and 31 ID points, represents what those loops became, and how their interactions created something that had not existed before".

"Like what, house?" quizzed 'Fact' before also lambasting Hawtin's clothing and jewellery range and his rather expensive beach towels, not to mention the well-publicised reason that he did The Cube tour in 2008 - "What is apparent is that the Cube is a highly advanced communications device that responds positively to the presence of humans and interacts accordingly," Hawtin's manifesto explained, "By acting as a central hub it seems to allow us to direct our thoughts, collect and share ideas, transcend language and interconnect musically in ways previously not possible. We're still in the early stages of research but it seems our destinies have somehow become interlinked".

Perhaps it's the excitement of the unknown, the one-up manship of understanding what the future holds or even what the flick of a switch could do. Whatever, Richie Hawtin's brand extensions and the "power of the cube" set him apart as being completely out there, much in the same way that the Dadaists and George Clinton in 'Mothership Connection' mode, not to mention Sun Ra, had been much earlier. From his techno beginnings he'd managed to reduce music to a mere hint of what it was supposed to be, or could be, and was selling the commemorative T-shirt and tote bag too.

VITALIC
Poney Part 1
From OK Cowboy
Original release: 2001
CITIZEN

In 2001, electronic music was allowed to be different, to do things because it could. The blips and bleeps were uncontained and unexplained, and the vibrant video world supplied further opportunities for this new generation of experimenting composers to explain the noise they made with their vision of where such music should sit in the world. In 2001, we'd already seen Add N To (X)'s explicit visuals for 'Plug Me In', whilst Peaches and Miss Kittin's salacious pouting and innuendo also transferred well, but whatever next?

For 'Poney 1', a swaggering synth-led instrumental from his throbbing 'OK Cowboy' album, French electro stylist Vitalic needed to add a further dimension. He teamed up with ace video maker Pleix and delivered a simple, yet highly chic glamour reel of well-manicured dogs being thrust into the air, their pampered coiffeurs exploding like so many idolised hair metal bands. Running in slow motion, it begged the question "What does this have to do with the ridiculous effect-heavy lyrics of the song?", but it looked funny and there was neon on it too, which seemed to keep everybody happy.

DAFT PUNK
Discovery
Original release: 2001
VIRGIN

Tracklisting:
One More Time, Aerodynamic, Digital Love, Harder, Better, Faster, Stronger, Crescendolls, Nightvision, Superheroes, High Life, Something About Us, Voyager, Veridis Quo, Short Circuit, Face To Face, Too Long

Fellow French men in suitably nondescript robot masks with metallic hands, Daft Punk were taking the possibilities of electronic imagery even further, and their 'Discovery' album provided a new benchmark for synthpop in the process.

"It set the tone for the best pop, dance and hip hop in ten years, and it was French," squealed Joe Muggs in 'Word' magazine. "They gave us an album shot through with club-music joie de vivre, but it was as much Derek And The Domninos as it was Derrick May".

"No moment of 'Discovery' is left unfilled with an idea, a sonic joke, a spark of brilliance...." echoed 'Q', giving it the full five out of five treatment. "A towering, persuasive tour de force which ultimately transcends the dance label". Indeed, 'NME' concurred, "Daft Punk have pulled off a brilliant wheeze by re-inventing the mid-'80s as the coolest pop era ever. And not even the officially approved retro-kitsch cool of Madonna's lukewarm excursions into post-Daft terrain, but all the bubble-permed, sports-jacket-and-jeans excesses they can muster.... Mostly, though, 'Discovery' is simply fantastic pop".

And, with 'Harder, Better, Faster, Stronger' they sounded like a tipsy version of Kraftwerk, a happy go lucky bunch of replicants who would be sampled continuously in the following years. Daft Punk were timeless in their retro-futurism, and they had all the accoutrements of a mass media proposition. Their songs fitted perfectly into adverts, films and computer games. They were faceless pop stars, they commanded time, it was all about the melody line and they had plenty of them.

"No matter what we've done, music, videos, robots, tours, electronica, we like it to have a timeless feel and be universal," claimed Guy Man. But 'Rolling Stone' weren't so sure, "Not enough of this album delivers on the promise of [lead single] 'One More Time'" they groaned. Ah well, you can't have everything.

"Two hundred years from now," Guy Man responded, "We hope you'll get it... like Mozart or Taxi Driver". We live in hope.

FENNESZ
Endless Summer
Original release: 2001
MEGO

Tracklisting
Made In Hong Kong, Endless Summer, A Year In A Minute, Caecilia, Got To Move On, Shisheido, Before I Leave, Happy Audio

If Daft Punk's futuristic French vision was cajoled into three-minute robotic sketches, Vienna's Christian Fennesz was painting in a far more expansive style. With a nod to the experimental side of Sonic Youth and with some surrounding glitch noise a la Autechre, his 'Endless Summer' album was Squarepusher-lite, a multi layered, effected guitar and laptop concoction that sounded scarily experimental in places before lulling you into submission with more ambient and spacious interludes.

"Imagine the electric guitar severed from cliché and all of its physical limitations, shaping a bold new musical language," offered the 'American City' newspaper. "If the Beach Boys represent the ideal of angelic clarity at the near end (of the spectrum), and white noise is the sonic chaos in the distance," laboured 'Pitchfork', "Fennesz currently owns the territory about 2/3 the way down the scale".

"The treacherous, pockmarked terrain of glitch electronica is a curious place to go for a holiday. Usually, the work of Christian Fennesz and his accomplices at the Viennese Mego label is characterised by skips and blips and tiny damaged noises, an unsentimental avant-music of laptops and dysfunction. 'Endless Summer', though, is weirdly blissful, possessing an indefinable emotional pull," reckoned 'NME'. Glitch pop, as a genre, was in the process of establishing a palatable position that wasn't too scary – well, most of the time.

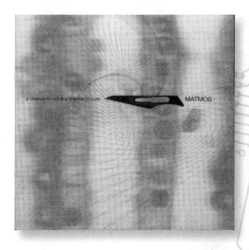

MATMOS
A Chance To Cut Is A Chance To Cure
Original release: 2001
MATADOR

Tracklist:
Lipostudio... And So On, L.A.S.I.K., Spondee, Ur Tchun Tan Tse Qi, For Felix (And All the Rats), Memento Mori, California Rhinoplasty

While Fennesz was appropriating sound to translate The Beach Boys into the avant-garde, San Francisco's Matmos were. To put it simply, employing the sampler to reflect their hometown's fascination with surgical procedures. Their 'A Chance To Cut Is A Chance To Cure' sampled bonesaws, liposuction and plastic surgery, added a few rhythmic glitch patterns and sounded remarkable, with all the unspoken scariness of Throbbing Gristle and the subversive anarchy of the characters in 'Fight Club' who steal human fat waste to make soap, they were edgy but dressed in lab coats. There was something unwholesome about the concept but, like 'Nip And Tuck', it seemed harmless enough on the surface.

"To the duo's credit, Matmos avoids making 'A Chance To Cut Is A Chance To Cure' grisly or gross," clarified 'All Music'. "Andrew Daniel and Martin Schmidt approach the album's concept with their usual playfulness and an appropriately clinical detachment, resulting in some clever and surprisingly diverse songs".

Indeed, the album was a celebration, an inquisitive journey into surgery that leaves the listener wondering just what was that noise, much like Coldcut's inspirational 'Timber', but with a far more personal end result. The sample methods and reasoning apart, 'A Chance To Cut Is A Chance To Cure' created a perfectly triggered soundscape.

"A splendid piece of work; compelling even when shorn of its conceptual and procedural backdrop, and infinitely more invigorating when considered as one with its making," concluded 'The Wire'.

LADYTRON
Seventeen (Darren Emerson Remix)
Original release: 2002
NETTWERK

Ladytron began life in the summer of 1999 in Liverpool, and almost immediately caught the attention of 'Melody Maker'. Their Roxy Music inspired name and electronic throb was different. They didn't sound like other synthpop bands of the day, and their songs seemed to appeal merely to the trendier fashion-led magazines. They seemed to be endlessly nearly doing something but getting no further than that initial fanbase. They were constantly on the verge of breaking through, but their art school schtick somehow didn't allow it.

In 2002, they released their second album, 'Light And Magic', which spawned the club hits 'Seventeen', 'Evil' and 'Blue Jeans', all of which, like the album itself, were influenced by the emerging electroclash scene which, ironically, had originally been ignited when the chief perpetrators heard their earlier singles.

'Seventeen' seemed to own more than a passing debt to Miss Kittin And The Hacker, while, in an ongoing piece of baton passing, the song was remixed by Underworld's Darren Emerson and that remix was then used as the backing for a track by Harlem-born rapper Miss Bank$, which sounded like it had direct lineage to modern day electronic rapper Uffie, then some eight years in the future.

The cross pollination of electroclash and electronic pop music with hip hop and RnB would take an even more significant turn when Ladytron worked with the already multi-selling Christina Aguilera on her album 'Bionic'. Ladytron had taken their pert electronica to new audiences, while LCD Sound System were about to add a touch of wry humour to the proceedings.

LCD SOUNDSYSTEM
Losing My Edge
Original release: 2002
DFA

The 'Zimbio' site proclaim that, "In 2002, in the wake of 9/11, pundits were declaring irony dead. Assuming they were talking about Generation X, they were right on," they mused. The reference to Generation X was to the Douglas Coupland recognised generation of hip new things who were "hip" to whatever they felt it was right to be hip to but who struggled to hold down a conversation with the majority of the rest of the world on anything else.

'Losing My Edge' was the song for them. A mega list of the coolest things they could have claimed to have done over a vibrant electronic backbone, it allowed a post terrorism American youth to see beyond the cooler than thou 'I was there' mentality of the super cool kids, to recognise that there was more to music than make up. And you could dance to it too.

"Even today 'Losing My Edge' reads like a hipper-than-thou blog post," remarked the 'Pretty Much Amazing' blog of the lengthy rhythmic electronic groove that accompanied the song's wired dissection of popular music and the urge to be key player in the crowd. 'The Guardian' described the song as "an eight-minute, laugh-out-loud funny dissection of cool over a dirty electronic beat". It was just that.

Name checking "the first Can show in Cologne", "kids in Tokyo and Berlin", "art-school Brooklynites" and attendance at "the first Suicide practices in a loft in New York City" plus claims to fame that included being "the first guy playing Daft Punk to the rock kids" amongst other one-liners, LCD's James Murphy let the hippy do the talking.....

"I was there in the Paradise Garage DJ booth with Larry Levan,

I was there in Jamaica during the great sound clashes,

I woke up naked on the beach in Ibiza in 1988"

....before name-checking The Beach Boys, Modern Lovers, Niagra, This Heat, Pere Ubu, The Human League, The Normal, Mantronix, New Order, The Sonics and a whole lot more. It was an arch piece of black humour which set LCD up as spokespeople for the a new, more time sensitive crowd who seemed set on dancing while Rome and their record collections burned.

KYLIE MINOGUE
Can't Get You Out Of My Head
Original release: 2002
PARLOPHONE

Prior to the release of the hugely successful 'Fever' album, Kylie had been a soap legend, teeny bop icon and fledgling disco diva. She'd duetted with The Pet Shop Boys in 1999 before spending quality time at the top of the UK charts the following year with 'Spinning Around' and 'On A Night Like This', not to mention further duetting duties with Robbie Williams on 'Kids'.
Her follow up album, 'Fever' was something of a departure as she moved into synthpop and disco, inspired by Madonna's 'Girlie Show'. It gave her a Top 20 hit with the coy 'Your Disco Needs You', but its monster cut, 'Can't Get You Out Of My Head', elevated her to a completely different stratosphere. Topping the charts all over the world, the song's electronic beat and Kylie's singalong chorus ensured it stuck in the cerebral tract with everybody as it sold in excess of forty million copies.

The song's strident rhythmic beat had all the elements of modern synth pop, it captured the imagination of the gay scene, dominated clubland and, through her past triumphs, appealed to a now grown up generation of teeny boppers. It had everything. But that wasn't enough. The masterstroke was recognising that people's comparisons with New Order's 'Blue Monday' were no bad thing and, when invited to play at the BRITS alongside Gorillaz, The Strokes and Basement Jaxx performing a 'mash up' mix of the two songs, fittingly retitled 'Can't Get Blue Monday Out Of My Head'. Pure genius, and a moment which allowed the Kylie juggernaut to cruise into the darker recess of the New Order fan base. Kylie was ubiquitous, the song was omnipresent.

LEMON JELLY
Lost Horizons
Original release: 2002
XL

As the decade rolled on, electronic music infiltrated not only the world's charts but, in the clamour to make adverts and soundtracks relevant, the world of TV and films. By 2008, Lemon Jelly, a duo of creative dance fans brought up on the mighty 23 Skidoo, A Certain Ratio and the burgeoning electronic scene, would be heard on Friskies cat food ads and trails for the cult show 'Heroes'. Their electronic swirl was lilting in the background as much as Sigur Ros were at the tail end of the decade.

After a string of 12-inchers on their own Impotent Fury label, the partnership of Fred Deakin and Nick Franglen took their carefully selected samples and downtempo beats to XL, first releasing the catch all album 'Lemon Jelly.ky', then their first album proper, the spacious 'Lost Horizons', an engaging romp through styles, sounds and genres that spawned endless pieces of background music but was, in itself, a cohesive package. The set was accompanied by some intense graphic images, which added to their hypnotic mantra-like sound and became as important as the music

on 2005's follow up '64-'95', which was released simultaneously with an animated DVD version of the music, an idea that harked back to Stakker Humanoid and the first hits of acid house.

'Lost Horizons' had a super real worldview, from the sleeve in. It was a highly coloured, multi-textured place where the duo's very Englishness was accentuated; the sound was saturated (as was the colour on the sleeve), whilst they always waved homewards with simple motifs and melodies that suggested the place they'd come from. Their work seemed to suggest overheard micro-melodies and re-imagined new symphonies, their pastoral elegance powering their vision.

BOARDS OF CANADA
Geogaddi
Original release: 2002
WARP

Tracklisting:
Ready Let's Go, Music Is Math, Beware the Friendly Stranger, Gyroscope, Dandelion, Sunshine Recorder, In The Annexe, Julie and Candy, The Smallest Weird Number, 1969, Energy Warning, The Beach At Redpoint, Opening the Mouth, Alpha And Omega, I Saw Drones, The Devil Is In the Details, A Is to B As B Is to C, Over the Horizon Radar, Dawn Chorus, Diving Station, You Could Feel the Sky, Corsair, Magic Window

Scottish brothers Mike and Marcus Sandison had been producing music since the late '80s, manipulating samples and comparing and contrasting analogue synths with more traditional instrumentation. Like Lemon Jelly, they were interested in re-drawing the world they saw using wide-ranging influences, from The Beatles through to the Incredible String Band, whose delicate balance between traditional folk and contemporary psychedelia can be traced through to the Boards' music. They also pulled samples of dialogue, but their inspiration was darker, more chilling and included takes influenced by their interest in numerology and cult leaders like David Koresh. Boards Of Canada were from a far more challenging place, and because of that they split opinion.

"'Geogaddi' is marvelously vague, as unconcerned with the real world as gangsta rap is obsessed with it," said 'Rolling Stone' in their review. "It's also a lovely, strangely comforting collection of electronic introspection, mood and shadow". 'NME', though, were far more enthused; "It's easily the electronic album of the year, but for all that, it doesn't break particularly new ground. The point s that what ground is broken is done so with exquisite artistry". 'Q' recognised that Boards Of Canada were succeeding in their creative mix where label mate Aphex Twin was throwing new spanners into his works, declaring the album "Satisfying in every way that Aphex Twin's 'Drukqs' wasn't".

Aphex Twin comparison aside, 'Geogaddi' wasn't particularly easy listening, more a consuming drive into unknown territory, signposted by occasional recognisable sounds and melodies. It possesses an odd narrative which blows through the twenty three sketches that make up its twisting flow. The track titles add further drama to what seems to be the soundtrack to an overnight car travelogue into a futuristic world of Philip K Dick's concoction, a claustrophobic, twisting journey that takes you into some pretty dark experiences before you reach the open air again.

Electronic music continued to add dark and meaningful depth to the world of entertainment, and Boards Of Canada were motoring to another far off desolate state of mind while the rest of the UK was glued to their Saturday night TVs, busily making heroes of people who shouldn't be, stunned into submission by the fly-on-the-wall, big brother reality of 'Pop Idol' and its imitators. A world where people from nowhere were suddenly on the front of newspapers for doing nothing newsworthy. Meanwhile, Boards Of Canada were happily emptying the exhaust from their car into the cab.

RICHARD X
Being Nobody
Original release: 2003
VIRGIN

It was perhaps with a touch of irony that seasoned bootleg mash up DJ Richard X chose specially created group Liberty X, the losers on ITV's 'Popstars' series, to sing on his fusion of Chaka Khan with his beloved Human League. One would hope so. The resultant 'Being Nobody' took everything from the originals to create a dancefloor-friendly radio-prescribed pop masterpiece.

Such fusions would spawn crossover hits for 2 Many DJs and many others who would splice together familiar tracks by Nirvana, Christina Aguilera. Brittany Spears and just about everybody else, but this track was a real group (sort of) cast against two vintage 45s.

As a result of the interest in X's Girls on Top mix 'Freak Like Me', a marriage of Adina and Gary Numan which had been copy-recorded as it was mashed by Sugababes in 2001 to create a number one single, he was was signed to Virgin, for whom he created 'Being Nobody', a mash-up of Chaka Khan's 'Ain't Nobody' and The Human League's 'Being Boiled', with Liberty X filling in the blanks. It was a huge club, then pop, hit, proving that an electronic bandage could quite easily cure anything if it had a suitable rhythm,

BENNY BENASSI
Satisfaction
Original release: 2003
DATA

'Satisfaction' was a slow grinding trance tune featuring the crowd-teasing one liner, "Push Me, Then Just Touch Me, Til I Can Get My, Satisfaction". It was accompanied by a video featuring scantily-clad women with power tools, thankfully wearing gloves and protective goggles if little else.

A piece of Italian house which Benassi had dubbed "hypnotech", 'Satisfaction' became a Ministry Of Sound anthem, whilst its video (clean and explicit versions both available on iTunes) virtually launched the idea of FHM Music TV and provided a source of interest for hundreds of faceless house artists across Europe. Now they could go to the ball, lurking in their geek editing garb behind clips of ladies who wouldn't know the right side of a phase, echo or flanger setting.

The gloves were off in the sampling stakes and the Stephen Hawking-esque synthesised vocals that Radiohead had first utilised on 'OK Computer' became the central pivot of 'Satisfaction', an international dancefloor smash with a varispeed acid house-like pulse.

GOLDFRAPP
Strict Machine
Original release: 2003
MUTE

Alison Goldfrapp was the complete antithesis of such behaviour. The light and fluffy confines of 'Felt Mountain' had positioned her as thinking man's crumpet, a cerebral muso bent on creating multi-layered symphonies of soft and charming sample and synch friendly pop. All created with her partner in crime, whose name nobody could remember. It all seemed quite Sunday school, until she delivered her second album.

On 'Black Cherry', Goldfrapp stepped out as a Kylie-styled diva amid a sea of Lemon Jelly-ish graphics. With a supporting cast of male dancers wearing husky masks, she produced a piece of glam pop and became the princess that the songs demanded.

'Strict Machine' and its evocative groove re-cast her as a gay icon as well as a pop star, and her set at the New Tent (later the John Peel stage) at Glastonbury on the Saturday night, heralded by the event's programme as "electro-glam, Krautrock and none-chilled carnality", was a defining moment.

COLDER
Crazy Love
Original release: 2003
OUTPUT

Electronic music, with all its cold and alienating instrumentation, had come into the parlour and was quickly and unceremoniously warming itself by the fire of commercial success, but there was also a troublesome darker edge manifesting itself, most notably among the likes of Nine Inch Nails and a slowly unravelling Depeche Mode. Dark was still a good colour to sport.

Marc Nguyen Tan, a graphic designer, DJ and remixer, released his debut album 'Again' in 2003 under the name Colder. Recorded in Paris, it spawned two dancefloor singles in 'Crazy Love' and

312

'Shiny Star', the former a throbbing slice of slowed down electronica that didn't warrant a sexy video at the time but has since had several uploaded to Youtube, adding a touch of vampiric bloodlust and general S&M tomfoolery to the tune.

All that stuff fitted perfectly, and 'Crazy Love' has the feel of estranged exotica, with lush melodic synths at half speed spiralling over its driving rhythms. As the title suggests, it's sex music with all the trappings of robotic urges.

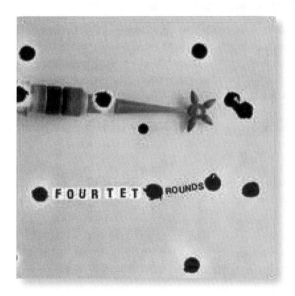

FOUR TET
Rounds
Original release: 2003
DOMINO

Kieren Hebden had originally released the bewitching 'Thirtysixtwentyfive', 'Dialogue' and 'Glasshead' on Output, Trevor Jackson's label, which was also the home of Colder. Mixing jazz time signatures and hip hop rhythms, Hebden pulled together all kinds of samples and melody lines to create symphonic sounds. Now signed to Domino, his third album, 'Rounds', capitalised on the folktronica tag he'd mustered with his previous sets and took it quite literally when he added samples of mandolin and, believe it or not, a rubber duck.

"A trove of bewitching melody and subtle invention, 'Rounds' succeeds not only as a meticulously conceived piece of art but also as a moving expression of human warmth," reckoned 'The Guardian', while 'Q' recognised it as "maverick electronica without the headaches".

'Rounds' was indeed a thing of beauty, the smorgasbord of samples utilised by Hebden to create a pillow-soft sound with melodic motifs littering the unexpected rhythmic pulses that, in places, seemed as natural as breathing out and in.

M83
Dead Cities, Red Seas, Lost Ghosts
Original release: 2003
MUTE

Tracklisting:
Birds, Unrecorded, Run into Flowers, In Church, America, On A White Lake, Near A Green Mountain, Noise, Be Wild, Cyborg, 0078h, Gone, Beauties Can Die

Much like the Four Tet of 'Rounds', M83 were headed down a deep electronic dream pop avenue, and, on this their second album, sounding like My Bloody Valentine without the volume meeting Vangelis let loose with a church organ. The brainchild of Anthony Gonzalez, from Antibes in the South Of France, their suitably spacey sounds were named after a spiral galaxy, Messier 83, and 'Dead Cities…' mixed deadpan pop melodies with huge swathes of old school synths. The heady, ethereal 'In Church', 'Gone' and 'On A White Lake, Near A Green Mountain' all sounded like travelogue epics of the kind Sigur Ros would have been proud of, while '0078h' had a choppy, introverted sense of quirky oddness with its guitars hinting at even more hybrid post rock in the future.

'Pitchfork' enthused about their "dense new layers of sound," and that the "keyboards throb, quiver, arpeggiate, and drone with such unbridled intensity that there's rarely any space (or need) for anything else".

DATAROCK
Computer Camp Love
Original release: 2003
ELLET

M83's attention to detail in terms of production and source keyboards was something that Norwegian duo Datarock didn't have time or money for. In 2003, Ketil Mosnes was 17 and Frederik Soroea was a year younger, surprising really as an early EP's lead tune, 'Computer Camp Love', name-checks the Commodore 64 and resounds with the tinny charm of a Casio keyboard and the maturity of well-heeled musos. Datarock were doing it for themselves, and the punky charge on 'The New Song' – see, no time even for song titles – sounded like Ultravox! circa 'Young Savage'.

'Computer Camp Love' was placed in the 100 best songs of the year at 'Rolling Stone' magazine, and when their 'Fa Fa Fa' was picked up for a Coca Cola advert, a series of computer game synchs followed and their quirky DIY bedroom electronica gained a global post-ironic following. Not bad for two teenagers singing about "boogers".

FRENCHBLOKE AND SON
Sexy Model
Original release: 2004
F&S

By 2004, the proliferation of mash up mixes and people's general ability to reshape virtually anything in their home studio, or just on their trusty Mac, meant that there was a string of 45s creeping into the high street shops that were suitably illegal and, in many cases, hugely listenable. The Beastie Boys/Led Zeppelin hybrid 'Immigrant Check' and White Enemy's union of The White Stripes and Public Enemy were just the tip of the iceberg.

Frenchbloke And Son was Stuart Mclean, an Optimo DJ who moved from Glasgow to Harlow in England and first gained notoriety with 'David Fischer', a "mash up" of Craig David and Fischerspooner. In 2004 he turned his attention to a whole host of hybrids including a collision of Kraftwerk's 'The Model' and Right Said Fred's 'I'm Too Sexy', which made 'Sexy Model'.

315

"All the tracks are created in Sonic Foundry's Acid Pro, which seems to have been created solely for this purpose," Mclean revealed on the 'Modsquare' site. "With some tracks it is solely an instrumental with an a capella placed on top. Other tracks can be more tricky to create, if there's no instrumental available you have to create your own taking the key parts out of the track you want to cut-up".

The result, as with the b side, 'Neon Love Cha Cha Cha', which used a chugging Casio rhythm and Justin Timberlake among many other bits and pieces, was a brand new tune which whimsically sent up both original parties. Frenchbloke's schtick was very much tongue in cheek, as was The Diff'rent Darkness, which came out around the same time with a re-telling of the other Darkness's heavy metal moment from 2004.

THE DIFF'RENT DARKNESS
I Believe In A Thing Called Love
Original release: 2004
GUIDED MISSILE

Sounding like a throwback to The Flying Lizards and their covers of 'Money', etc, The Diff'rent Darkness completely revamped the hair metal revivalists' biggest tune, employing Katrin Geilhausen on deadpan vocals over a perfectly harmonious analogue synth interpretation of the original track. The single also featured their take on 'Get Your Hands Off My Woman' and 'Love On the Rocks On Ice', and, apparently, The Darkness themselves were involved in the project. Alas, their career never recovered after its release.

THE KILLERS
Somebody Told Me
Original release: 2004
LIZARD KING

While the singles market was overflowing with clever mash up ideas and electronic music seemed to be the staple sound of clubland, the arrival of Las Vegas band The Killers' debut album, 'Hot Fuss', added a new dimension to synth pop. Here was an established band set up, with a vocalist doubling on synth, producing singles with an unmistakable flavour that could be traced way back to Duran Duran's synthier moments. While album tracks like 'On Top' leaned closer to synth-led melody, it was 'Mr Brightside', voted song of the decade by Absolute Radio, and the gorgeous 'Somebody Told Me', with its sweeping synth line which leads into the chorus, that showed off their mix of traditional rock instrumentation and old school analogue keyboards.

"Our most Vegas-influenced song on the album," chirped singer Brandon Flowers of 'Somebody Told Me' and its gossip heavy lyrics, "Sin city, the Strip. It's where I grew up and of course it affects the songs I write. This song has a lot of sexual energy".

HIEM
Chelsea
Original release: 2004
ATLANTIS RECORDS

Sexual energy doesn't come into it when you live in the north of England, as Hiem's debut single perfectly explained. Sexual tension featured strongly though. The single was one of those lurking in the singles rack at Rough Trade in 2004 that stood out for all its northern charm and working class storyline – and of course because the shop's Nigel House insisted, "you've got to hear this".

Over a hypnotic electronic rhythm that smacks of repetitive analogue droning, before it spiralled into a proper verse/chorus structure with reverbing accentuation, the song followed the journey home of a would-be footballer who's ball is "nicked" by Donna and Chelsea, two taunting teens decked out in football shirts. It was oh, so English.

Delivered in a brusque Sheffield accent, the single draws a line between the repetitive nowheres of the two girls eventual lives, perfectly monotoned over the endless looped rhythm, as the vision of their giro-fuelled "two kids and the occasional male stripper" lifestyle disappears in a hail of feedback and the vocalist concludes "Thank fuck I didn't marry that Chelsea".

A gem as regional as mushy peas, Hiem, Nick Eastwood and David Boswell, used the mundane electronic melody to accentuate the hopelessness of their subjects' lives, conjuring up a wonderfully understated take on the just how grim it can be up north. The duo continued to release singles throughout the noughties, garnered support from Steve Lamacq and worked around the Sheffield scene with The Human league's Philip Oakey and Pulp's Jarvis Cocker among others, but it was this primal reworking of The Normal's 'TVOD' that made such a staggering impact when first heard. It renewed faith in electronica and added a touch of humour, much like Bill Bailey's 'Das Hokey Kokey', a Kraftwerkian take on the much loved working men's club dancefloor filler that he performed in full Teutonic style on his 'Part Troll' tour in the same year. This was electronic music explained to the masses, with liberal amounts of tongue in cheek humour. God knows what Ralf und Florian would have made of it.

In 2004, electronic music ingratiated itself with many new audiences. The likes of America's The Crystal Method continued to mine the Nine Inch Nails template on 'Legion Of Boom' ("an album that breaks little new ground, but further entrenches the Method as America's finest producers of dance music made for rock 'n' roll people" - 'Rolling Stone') and the Domino signed Junior Boys kicked back into synthpop on 'Neon Rider' ("Pop music isn't abstract enough and abstract music isn't pop enough," they explained to the 'Careless Talk Costs Lives' fanzine, as if to sum up their slant of music).

Electronic music was changing and things were about to take a dramatic shift as LCD Sound System switched gear and, in the UK, dubstep stripped things back even further.

LCD SOUNDSYSTEM
Daft Punk Is Playing At My House
Original release: 2005
DFA

After the success of 'Losing My Edge', LCD Sound System released 'Give It Up' and 'Yeah' before their debut eponymous album, which opened with the monumental 'Daft Punk Is Playing At My House'. Like 'Losing My Edge', it captured an ironic celebration of one-up manship in music. 'Daft Punk...' appealed to the hipper than thou fraternity, and also to the wider audience who wanted to be invited to the party.

As with 'Losing My Edge', here was a simple melody line, performed over relatively dark beats, which gave a kind of shrouded mystery to a celebration of everything that was good in electronic music. It was mindless, but it was intelligently subtle. James Murphy had his finger on the pulse and, inevitably, a witty line set it all off.

LCD Sound System captured the mood of a time and place, a wild and irreverent party animal set to dance 'til dawn, with an American vibe of laissez faire. By contrast, dubstep was reflecting a bass-heavy London scene that had started at the end of the '90s with music that was "tightly coiled" and, to all intents and purposes, as avant-garde at its inception as it was as it began to attract wider audiences.

SKREAM
Midnight Request Line
Original release: 2005
K MAG

Pirate radio, post jungle ideas and the discovery of reggae dubplates had influenced the early days of dubstep. But, with Radio 1 support through John Peel, Annie Nightingale and Mary Anne Hobbs, the scene's secrecy, while adding more than a hint of danger to the proceedings, began to make iconic figures of its producers and Djs, whose names sounded like tags found on any high street wall. D1, Skream, Digital Mystikz, Benga, Joe Nice, Kode 9, Pinch, Hijak and a host of others emerged armed with basic drum machine lines and hovering synth stabs.

It was a scene that had been bubbling under in clubs for a while, spreading west from the far east end of London, and the release of Skream's 'Midnight Request Line', with its wayward typewriter, distant gunshot and wavering synth line which cemented everything that had gone before, representing a watershed moment that brought a whole new crowd into dubstep with the view that, perhaps, this music wasn't as scary as originally thought and, maybe, the stripped back electronic patterns were leading somewhere new and different, albeit with a body-shaking, vibrating bass element to the mix.

"Skream says he made 'Midnight Request Line' while experimenting with new musical elements. Until then his tracks had been simpler and moodier, in keeping with the 'dark garage' style championed in the early 2000s by DJs such as Hatcha," reckoned one of the genre's more understandable websites. "Unlike the stripped-back, garage-style sound of much early dubstep, 'Midnight Request Line' has a sophisticated melodic structure. It has a slightly eerie feel due to the minor chords Skream uses and, importantly, it changes key halfway through, giving the track a sense of progression that is often missing from bass-heavy genres like dub".

Dubstep was moving out of the garage and from the pirate radio stations into more accessible locations. Within time it would even be nominated for a Mercury Prize.

KODE 9 AND SPACEAPE
9 Samurai
Original release: 2006
HYPERDUB

QUARTA 330
Sunset Dub/9 Samurai
Original release: 2006
HYPERDUB

I remember going to XL in around 2006 with Andy Roberts, the head of Kiss Radio programming. The discussion with Richard Russell from the label was very much about MIA and Dizzee Rascal, Wiley and co. The conversation was about how unpalatable music made on a Gameboy or console was and how grime's success was suffering from the abrasive nature of the sounds.

Of course, since then both MIA and Dizzee Rascal have gone on to forge their own niches and both gained international reputations, something that wasn't envisaged at that stage. Around the time of the discussion at XL, Kode 9's dubstep reshaping of Quarta 330s' console bending sound on '9 Samurai' slowed things to a haunting two step bass throb with a melody line that sounded like it came straight from a Russian state funeral. Snatched dubplate dialogue further added to the tension of the insistent blunted electronic pulse.

"People need to remember what is interesting about these musics - jungle through to dubstep," Kode 9 told the 'Spannered' website. "They can weave together every single music ever, potentially, at that speed, with those basslines. There's no reason why there shouldn't be aspects of techno, hip hop, reggae, soul, electro, house... I mean it's just a speed. The danger right now is that it has become dominated by half-step. But I'm sure that won't last".

People were intrigued by these new sounds, and even more so by the detached dialogue that ran through them, and the debut album from Burial proved to be a turning point for the music. The album received a Mercury nomination and opened the door for dubstep and two-step.

BURIAL
Burial
Original release: 2006
HYPERDUB

Tracklisting:
Untitled Start, Distant Lights, Spaceape, Wounder, Night Bus, Southern Comfort, U Hurt Me, Gutted, Forgive, Broken Home, Prayer, Pirates, Untitled

According to Derek Walmsley in 'Wire' magazine's Dubstep primer, a line can be drawn back to the Metalheadz label for the inspiration to Burial's self-titled debut, the record presenting a mix of dubstep, two-step and house music with hints of soulful vocals, a huge echoey soundtrack styled with swathes of ambience and a deep earthy message both spoken and suggested.

"Where was dance music in 2006, as the clubs surrendered to happy house?" asked the short-lived 'Observer Music Monthly'. "The mysterious Burial offered one way forward, with this first, mournful, dubstep masterpiece". These words weren't delivered lightly - Burial's William Bevan had produced a haunting soundscape that sounded like a distant, disturbed descendent of Massive Attack at their most leftfield.

Their previous 'South London Boroughs' EP had been intriguing, but on this debut set they switched from taut, almost directionless rhythms to the ethereal synths of 'Night Bus' and the precise backbeat of 'U Hurt Me', which sounded like a 23 Skidoo outtake with its mystical wind sounds, and the dysfunctional bachelor pad soul of 'Broken Home'. Like a Channel 4 documentary soundtrack of darkening old London, it just needed the images added.

HOT CHIP
The Warning
Original release: 2006
EMI

Tracklisting:
Careful, And I Was A Boy from School, Colours, Over And Over, (Just Like We) Breakdown, Tchaparian, Look After Me, The Warning, Arrest Yourself, So Glad To See You, No Fit State, Won't Want

Wikipedia sums up the second album from Hot Chip as an exploration into "the theme of contradiction" as well as "slower and darker aspects of electronic music" with the use of "strange violence" in songs.

As Burial were treading similar boards but only exposing the more frightening aspects of a slowly evolving violent world, Hot Chip had forsaken the synth pop of their debut and undertaken a painstaking examination of themselves, their mood swings and the circumstances around them. Gone were simple pop songs, to be replaced by Freudian analysis.

'Stylus' magazine noted that "The fact that Hot Chip can take all these conflicting moods, string them together and make of them a satisfying whole is testament to their understanding of the classic rubric of the pop album - an identifiable, unique sound that has enough room to allow for variety and enough consistency to keep the listener's attention".

Sure, there were still palatable singles on show, but this was a much more serious and darker beast than before, and subsequent albums would go even further, using their sense for irony to allow them to hit out against the injustices of the world and, on the video for 'I Feel Better' from 2010, boy bands too.

KLAXONS
Atlantis To Interzone
From Myths Of The Near Future
Original release: 2006
POLYDOR

While the big hits from 'Myths Of The Near Future' were 'Golden Skans' and 'It's Not Over Yet', the wailing synth line on the soulful stomper 'Atlantis To Interzone', with its death metal meets Electric Six middle eight, made it a real standout. The album itself was lauded by the 'NME' - after all, here was a band who were opinionated, could quite plainly also be pop stars and you could dance to their songs too.

"'Myths Of The Near Future' is charged with the same spirit which fuelled legendary rave pranksters The KLF's period of pop subversion," the 'NME' trilled, and the songs reference points, the lost city of Atlantis and a suburb of William Burroughs' mind gave it a trippy, drug-related edge and plenty of venom.

NME's KLF comparison was more than evident on the track, but while KLF were more atuned to late night rave rhythms, Klaxons seemed intent on switching between Sex Pistols' thrash and the kind of Pop Will Eat Itself originated madness that had inspired The Prodigy. Klaxons seemed set on starting the party as soon as was physically possible.

THE KNIFE
Silent Shout
Original release: 2006
BRILLE

If Klaxons' favoured position was in your face, The Knife, a Swedish electronic duo, preferred to be at home wearing Venetian masks. Karin Dreijer Andersson and Olof Dreijer sampled fame when Jose Gonzalez had a hit with their song 'Heartbeats' in 2006, but it wasn't until they somewhat surprisingly announced a live tour and an impending DVD release of the shows that reknown for their own work arrived.

'Silent Shout' was the result, and opinions were nothing if not mixed. "A hideous mess of electro noodling and maddeningly obtuse, tuneless vocals," suggested 'Q' magazine, while 'Drowned In Sound' reckoned that "This is one of the most rich and accomplished albums of recent times. Essential".

Undoubtedly, 'The Captain', with its chipmunk vocals, is a strange one, but for the most part the Kraftwerk keyboards and synthetic percussion is usefully gothic and gloomy. Sure, they were taking themselves mighty seriously, as the sleevenotes revealed: "It starts in complete darkness. A darkness with gothic dimensions, a darkness to get lost in. It could be the mysterious forests playing such a crucial role in the tale of the Grimm brothers. Or the threatening and labyrinthine cityscapes used by Fritz Lang," but why not. Somebody has to be the Rick Wakeman, and nobody else was donning a cloak in 2006.

"A freaky, moving masterpiece," mused 'Spin' magazine, while 'The Guardian' also enthused wildly. "It's anybody's guess what a fan of the Gonzalez and Royksopp tracks will make of this beautiful, haunted record, but its dark ingenuity is the kind that keeps electronic music alive".

COLDCUT
Man In A Garage
From Sound Mirrors
Original release: 2006
NINJA TUNE

Coldcut had been charged with keeping electronic music alive for quite some time. They were originally the kings of house but, as they told 'The Word' in 2010, "There's nothing wrong with people coming together under one rhythm, but when the rhythm takes over so there isn't anything else allowed, that's a problem, so we decided to be the resistance".

And the resistance was highly productive. The Ninja Tune label, run by Black and fellow Coldcut man Jon More, has been responsible for releases by The Bug, Bonobo, The Cinematic Orchestra, Daedelus, The Herbaliser, Kid Koala, Mr Scruff, Roots Manuva, Toddla T and a host of others, and their offshoot imprint Big Dada scooped the Mercury Prize in 2009 with Speech Debelle's 'Speech Therapy'.

Back in 2006, Coldcut's 'Sound Mirrors' featured a wealth of guest vocalists, including Annette Peacock, Roots Manuva and, on 'Man In A Garage', John Matthias. It wouldn't have sounded out of place on Hot Chip's new album, with its skittering rhythm and selection of synth sounds and samples whizzing by. Like every Coldcut recording, it managed to transcend any simple genre-specific limitation and set its own agenda, a perfect example of the possibilities of a modern electronic studio if you had the basis of a good song to start with.

AUDION
Mouth To Mouth
Original release: 2006
SPECTRAL SOUND

Audion's main man, Matthew Dear, is renowned for his own version of pop-orientated electronics but, under the name Audion, he was able to produce the kind of evocative electronic mantras that Manuel Gottsching, or even Richie Hawtin, might have been proud of. At close to thirteen minutes, 'Mouth To Mouth' is a pulsating groove with claptrap drum machine and hi-hat aplenty, which rotates as electronic notes oscillate, building into a tumultuous piece of multi-layered electronic noise with that incessant rhythm still revolving around your brain as audio ray guns are fired into your temples.

There's something amazingly old school about 'Mouth To Mouth', from the tinny drum machine's synthetic bongo sound through to the whirring shards of noise that infiltrate the song, like the soundtrack to a robotic face off. It's original release was also accompanied by the shorter (eight minutes) slow pulse of 'Hot Air', a glitch-riddled smoulderer that sounded like the noise of the last shuttle to Mars, interrupted by a drunken varispeed melody that threw the focus with consummate ease.

MATTHEW DEAR
Asa Breed
Original release: 2007
GHOSTLY INTERNATIONAL

'Asa Breed' couldn't have been further from Audion. Applauded by 'Stylus' magazine as being Dear's more accessible album, and with favourable comparisons to a "happier TV On The Radio" and Eno and Byrne's 'My Life In The Bush Of Ghosts', plus Talking Heads from the same period, it was certainly his greatest pop vision.

"This year's most unexpected pop masterpiece," quipped Philip Shelbourne from 'Pitchfork', and 'The Wire' chirped in with, "'Asa Breed' might make you rethink everything you thought you knew about guitars, drum machines and pop itself".

"A work of electronic focused songcraft that leaves everything else in it's dust," concluded 'URB', and, from the opening hum of 'Fleece On Brain', it sounded like a more accessible take on 'Low', with it's overlapping synth lines embracing a more fluent dance feel. Even when the pace slowed, on 'Deserter', the layers of sound felt warm and enveloping, and Dear's vocal comes across as an old friend you're just glad to hear from again.

'Asa Breed' was a one man pop dream, a futuristic and wonderfully compulsive set, a carefully created multi-track gem that allowed Dear to create new structures for pop music.

SHY CHILD
Noise Won't Stop
Original release: 2007
WALL OF SOUND

If Matthew Dear's vision was purely a reflection of his pop upbringing, brought to life through the use of the studio, then Shy Child's was the result of being exposed to a wealth of dance clubs where all hell was breaking loose. I once booked them onto a stage at Glastonbury in 2007 after hearing this track on a demo sent by their agent - the synth-powered riff and Pete Cafarella's voice, backed by Nate Smith's machine like drumming, sounded like the perfect score for any TV documentary about people passing out in clubs. This was the music from the greatest binge ever.

Live, they didn't disappoint, with Cafarella sporting a guitar styled synth far too big for him and Smith pounding away at his kit. It was akin to some of the coolest synth pop sounds, and the audience were hooked, which was remarkable in itself as it was pretty early in the day. Cafarella's driving synth pulses and choppy lead melody lines proved irresistible, and this was clearly something far greater than the sum of its parts.

HOLY FUCK
LP
Original release: 2007
YOUNG TURKS

Holy Fuck were just as intense. I first saw them do their own set at the Bowery Ballroom as part of the CMJ Festival in 2004, where they also backed the rapper Beans on a bill headlined by Devendra Banhart. They were amazingly haphazard, with what seemed to be a thousand instruments and bits and pieces that they'd plug in and unplug. It was chaos. The duo of Brian Borcherdt and Graham Walsh were producing music that didn't ought to work but somehow managed to.

The key to their sound was that they'd mix and match all kinds of effects with things like a 35mm film synchronizer, wherein they would pull and rewind the loops of film to accentuate the soundtrack. By 2007, their first album saw the addition of a bass player and drummer, and the result was a more focussed but no less extravagant and variable sound.

It seemed the possibilities live were endless, but catching them on tape was another thing. "It's formula is pretty much stretched to breaking point by the end of the album's 37 minutes, and it's hard to see quite what else Holy Fuck can do," reckoned 'The Wire', but the cuts 'Super Inuit' and 'Lovely Allen' proved truly influential and inspirational to electronic bands that followed.

In 2010, I booked them onto the Queen's Head stage at Glastonbury, where they played with bass and drums. As ever it was a mad scene of wires everywhere, with random elements added and discarded as the set progressed. It was an awesome performance, a riot of sound made by what seemed to be spontaneous invention. Like the futurists who we started this long haul with some pages ago, Holy Fuck had not only destroyed the rules of naming a band, but also redefined the way that music was created.

THOU SHALT ALWAYS KILL
Original release: 2007
SUNDAY BEST

Seeing the video for 'Thou Shalt Always Kill' for the first time was a truly memorable experience. Here was a severely bearded man rapping over multi-layered keyboards and edits with a thumping relentless rhythm. And the lyrics were just taboo. The duo topped it by spoofing 'X Factor' and attempting to cover 'It Ain't No Fun' by Snoop Dogg with the desired reaction from Sharon Osbourne and Simon Cowell. Fun enough, but 'Thou Shalt Always Kill', with Dan's driving, rhythmically pushy melodies and Pip's clever lyrics, was just superb, a new crunching sound that seemed to revel being set against the poetic prose of Scoobius.

The duo played at Glastonbury in 2009 and 2010, the latter performance being seen by over 2,000 people who'd opted to miss Stevie Wonder to hear their abrasive, beat-ridden riffs. They had taken synth pop and turned it on its head. This was not Erasure revisited, this was a hip hop-soaked, banging house-paced sound, with the bass synths ripping at the eardrum and the occasional melody working like a soundworm eating away at the anvil.

LADYHAWKE
My Delirium
Original release: 2008
ISLAND

A year before Dan Le Sac And Scroobius Pip's first performance at the Queen's Head, the stage had welcomed Florence And The Machine and Elbow, among others, but one of the highlights of the weekend was the diminutive Pip Brown, aka Ladyhawke. Clutching a guitar and looking set to riff like an AC/DC fan, Brown's Ladyhawke instead revealed a twin synth core that drove the songs, allowing her vocal to lift the mood on her tales of deadpan excitement, most notably on the standout single cut 'My Delirium'. There was something oh, so familiar about the song, and it had a killer hook in the best tradition of synthpop.

"Ladyhawke is unlikely to win any awards for originality, but you'd be hard pressed to find a more consistent and hook-laden debut all year," was the 'All Music Guide' view, while 'NME' cast their memory back to the fey glam pop of the '80s, "Ladyhawke's louche synthetic pop is brazenly Bananarama, ridiculously 'Rio', and wonderfully Waterman, but the lack of posing – her sheer scruffiness – makes it the first credible '80s pop record since ABC's 'The Lexicon Of Love'".

But was almost like Pip Brown didn't want to be Ladyhawke, and when she played the following year at Radio 1's Big Weekender she was almost apologetic for not being enthused. Very cool.

METRONOMY
Nights Out
Original release: 2008
BECAUSE

Tracklisting:
Nights Intro, The End Of You Too, Radio Ladio, My Heart Rate Rapid, Heartbreaker, On The
Motorway, Holiday, A Thing For Me, Back On The Motorway, On Dancefloors, Nights Outro,
What Do I Do Now?

Unlike Ladyhawke, Metronomy couldn't have been any happier to be doing what they were doing. In 2009 they played on the Queen's Head, and in the smallest tent imaginable at Bestival, on the same bill as Kraftwerk. Metronomy reflected some of the futuristic austerity of their German forefathers, but their outfits, complete with light up breast plates, and their synth constructions, which stray from funereal marches to cod reggae, Vangelis-lite and Todd Rundgren-esque synthpop melodies, made for a truly joyful experience on their second album, 'Nights Out'.

"It's a sleeping giant of a dancefloor creeper that will be everyone's favourite new electro album in approximately six months' time," reckoned 'NME' on its release, while 'Drowned In Sound' accentuated their upbeat vibe, "The joy and longevity emanating throughout is at once jubilant and effortless: a luminescent pop-not-quite-masterpiece…'Nights Out' is eminently worthy of your time and investment".

'MOJO' was more restrained in its enthusiasm, but added the Eno-influenced David Byrne to their obvious touchstones. "At its best, as on 'Heartbreaker,' the singing has the deadpan charm of Talking Heads or Kraftwerk, adding to the likeability of men who know its better to be a robot than a hippy".

M83
Saturdays = Youth
Original release: 2008
EMI

By complete contrast, M83 were done with robots. They had spent more recent times quietly sanding down the rougher edges of their sound, and the addition of rolling synths and chunkier guitars behind Anthony Gonzalez's vocal seemed to waft them back to the electronic pop of Frazier Chorus, A Flock Of Seagulls, China Crisis and a host of other '80s bands whose music had seemingly been snuffed out by contemporaries with better conceived images and more driving storylines. In 'Saturdays = Youth', M83 had delivered a beautiful album.

"As super-stylised as its sounds and emotions are, 'Saturdays=Youth' always seems genuine, even when it feels like its songs are made from the memories of other songs," 'All Music Guide' commented, while US magazine 'Paste' recognised that, "The clear standout is 'Kim and Jessie,' which convincingly recaptures the magic gloss of Tears For Fears with a propulsive undercurrent and an elegant use of space. One of the best songs of 2008 so far, it's the key destination in a stunning journey". Indeed, there's much of Tears For Fears' production style and bits of OMD in there too. Even a touch of Simple Minds on 'We Own The Sky', a more spacious sound that impressed 'Billboard' magazine, "Though nothing quite reaches the heights of past work, there's ambience to spare on 'We Own The Sky' and the lush 'Highway of Endless Dreams'".

Everyone could catch something of their former '80s self in the album and 'The Guardian' summed it up by saying, "To call 'Saturdays=Youth' derivative is to pay it a compliment, because every retro synth sounds calibrated to provide the maximum nostalgic rush".

CRYSTAL CASTLES
Crystal Castles
Original release: 2008
DIFFERENT

Tracklisting:
Untrust Us, Alice Practice, Crimewave, Magic Spells, Xxzxcuzx Me, Air War, Courtship Dating, Good Time, 1991, Vanished, Knights, Love And Caring, Through The Hosiery, Reckless, Black Panther, Tell Me What To Swallow

While M83 were harking back to days of innocence and poor haircuts, Crystal Castles were the hoody-wearing robots of the dancefloor. These shoegazing extremists, who'd adopted the blips and squeaks of Quarto 330's Gameboy electronica and added some embittered vocals, were angsty and in your face. The sleeve of their self-titled debut featured them heads down and sullenm and their performance on 'Skins', in a nightclub where heaving drug-addled bodies blurred into each other, seemed the perfect setting for their heated, aggressive sounds. The album positively palpitated with sound from Ethan Kath, the explosive 'Xxzxcuzx Me' and the seemingly unhinged 'Alice Practice' both being particularly full-on assaults, but there were also more spacious textured sounds, such as the heady 'Crimewave'. All topped with the offbeat vocal style of Alice Glass. Crystal Castles didn't look like or indeed sound like much else.

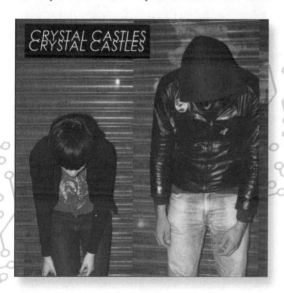

"The benchmark for 2008's best electronic record has been set," trumpeted 'MOJO' magazine. "It is also, perhaps more importantly, an album absolutely overloaded with spine-tingling, pulse-quickening electro noises," added 'NME'. A year on they played the 'NME' stage at Reading, and the keyboard bound Kath shook his head like a Ramone while Alice Glass seemed possessed. The music was intense, and when Glass's vocal disappeared at the end of the set, even though she was giving it everything, the density of Crystal Castles' sound was amazing.

"At its best, it makes for exhilarating listening, as on 'Crimewave', the bleep-funk soundclash that drives 'Air War' and the unexpectedly tender 'Courtship Dating'," ,Q, concluded. At a time when the electronic revival was skulking in underground clubs in London, Crystal Castles were always an oddball confection, like Royal Trux meeting Suicide with a Commodore 64 for company.

MSTRKRFT
Fist Of God
From Fist Of God
Original release: 2009
DIM MAK

Even with guest appearances from John Legend, E-40, N.O.R.E., and Lil' Mo on their second album, 'Fist Of God', there was general consternation and not a lot of love in the room from the critics for MSTRKRFT. The Canadian duo of Jesse F Keeler and Al-P had been widely praised for 2006's 'The Looks', but their expanded sound and a host of guests confused some people.

The 'NME', though, were still onboard - "Peppered with hip-hop connections (E-40, Ghostface Killah, Freeway), equally informed by raw Chicago house and the riff-worshipping of Jesse's previous (DFA 1979), and finally free of the omnipresent vocoder, it's near-essential stuff," but the seemingly hip cokemachineglow website were less committed, "It's all so cold and empty and irritating". As the proliferation of a million very young megacritics enlarged through easy access to the internet, there were some who saw little time for history.

To my mind, though, 'Fist Of God' was a rousing and punchy set, as 'The Guardian' rightly spotted, stating that "Their second album is a guest-packed party record built from monster beats, churning synths and power chords, and if there's nothing here that Daft Punk haven't done before, it wins points for sheer muscular euphoria". The title track alone was worth the entrance fee, seemingly a super-smooth realisation of what fellow countrymen Crystal Castles had created in a shed somewhere with intermittent power supply. MSTRKRFT operated from the big house.

LA ROUX
In For The Kill
Original release: 2009
POLYDOR

"Remarkably, with this astounding debut, an unassuming 21-year-old from SW2 has revitalised a forgotten form to make one of the finest forward-thinking British pop albums of recent memory," the 'NME' were quick to offer. For here was a true return to blue-eyed synth pop with discernable tunes. During 2009, La Roux went from bit part players on an emerging scene to a position where stories ran in the press that vocalist Elly Jackson was insuring her quiff to maximise her image.

By August bank holiday weekend, they played a small tent at Reading and you couldn't get near the place. Two weeks later, at Bestival, they played a tent six times as big and it was a heaving mass of bodies. "That voice. That quiff," the programme for Bestival mused, "There's no denying Elly Jackson's star quality and La Roux's all-conquering pop nous".

La Roux could do now wrong - the wholesome synth pop image, the hair, the great songs, including the singles 'In For The Kill', 'Bulletproof' and 'Quicksand', had catapulted the unlikely duo to new heights. They looked nervous at Bestival, but they were almost willed to succeed.

Their debut album, 'La Roux', received mixed reviews, and there was question about the vocal prowess that lurked beneath the quiff. "Things dip slightly in the middle, when Jackson's reedy vocals are exposed against a mid-tempo backing, but it's a minor quibble," suggested 'MOJO', but the 'Under The Radar' site was far less supportive, "Between the shrill, semi-anonymous voice of Elly Jackson and Ben Langmaid's clunky, paint-by-numbers beats, La Roux's eponymous debut already feels dated".

Without doubt, the La Roux sound was designed to be just that. A year on they shared a session with Heaven 17 for Mark Jones' 6Music show 'Back To The Phuture'. By then, Elly Jackson seemed more comfortable with herself and, even though Glenn Gregory was in fine voice, she stole the show. Synth pop was returning to its inspiration as Jones' show also featured Little Boots with Gary Numan. The '80s had been reborn, and all of its synthetic charm remained perfectly intact.

In the January issue of the 'Observer Music Monthly', La Roux were hailed as making "a felicitous mix of '80s synths and dazzling hooks... with emotional substance". In their Top 20 picks for the coming year, the group lay behind Karima Francis and Magistrates and ahead of Dan Black (deftly produced elctro-tinged songs), Empire Of The Sun (dance rock and psychedelic whimsy) and Florence And The Machine (languishing at number 20). No room for Fuck Buttons, then.

FUCK BUTTONS
Tarot Sport
Original release: 2009
ATP

In 2008, Bristol's Fuck Buttons had released a throwback to the bedroom psychosis of cassette-only post-industrial releases. 'Street Horrsing' contained grinding sound sculptures in 'Okay, Let's Talk About Magic', 'Colours Move' and 'Race You To Your Bedroom/Spirit Rise', while 'Sweet Love For Planet Earth' and 'Bright Tomorrow' were more inviting, tempered and textured soundtracks.

"When we first started to make music together, we got hold of whatever signal processors we could lay our hands on. Because we were students, they were often cheap things, kids' toys and so on", the Buttons told the 'Residential Adviser' website, "We'd find 'em at car boot sales. We were making quite harsh abrasive music at the time, so I guess it's a juxtaposition of the harsh sound — the "fuck" bit — then the "buttons" representing the signal processors that we use all the time".

By the recording of 'Tarot Sport', they'd embraced techno rhythms and timings and brought in Andrew Weatherall to help with the production. The result was an awakening of a new electronic possibility. It was a monster sound.

"'Street Horrsing' was a great record, but 'Tarot Sport' is a cut above. Perhaps surprisingly, it's also a welcoming album, and one of the best of this already fruitful year," reckoned 'Pitchfork', while 'MOJO' concluded that "If 'Street Horrsing' was a bit of a lark, then 'Tarot Sport' plays an altogether more serious game," and 'Q' continued the positive feedback, "With 'Tarot Sport', Fuck Buttons have made a career-defining album that will resonate with anyone who has ever spent a night with their head in the speaker stacks and gone home marvelling at the ringing in their ears".

Second time around, Fuck Buttons had managed to make huge strides, and their live performance at Green Man in 2010 was phenomenal. Suitably, they headlined the Far Out stage on Friday night, the programme suggesting that "Losing yourself in a Fuck Buttons live set is to achieve transcendence between yourself, the listener, the band and the universe". Nice.

WILD BEASTS
Two Dancers
Original release: 2009
DOMINO

Wild Beasts were the headline act for Saturday at that same Green Man in 2010, also on the Far Out Stage. Like Fuck Buttons they had completely changed after their debut album, 'Limbo, Panto'. Suddenly, here was a band who'd embraced electronic music and the possibility of a dance beat but retained some of the darker edginess of rock. And they had songs too. Clash magazine noted that 'Two Dancers' was "affecting, audacious, captivating of fantastical flourishes," while NME announced that, "Wild Beasts have undergone a sea change, and this beautiful album is a treasure that deserves plundering".

'Two Dancers' was a clever departure. While their debut concentrated on the musichall and vaudeville pouting of Hayden Thorpe, using all kinds of musical input to create a suitably theatric sheen, the new album mixed Thorpe's flamboyance with the deeper vocal of bassist Tom Fleming, giving greater context and contrast. Live, the juxtaposition allowed them far greater width and appeal, and the success and positive reaction to 'Two Dancers', was staggering. Many people made it album of the year for 2009.

ANIMAL COLLECTIVE
Merriweather Post Pavilion
Original release: 2009
DOMINO

Tracklisting:
In the Flowers, My Girls, Also Frightened, Summertime Clothes, Daily Routine, Bluish, Guys Eyes. Taste, Lion In a Coma, No More Runnin, Brother Sport

Labelmates Animal Collective picked up even more album of the year accolades for 'Merriweather Post Pavilion' in 2009, something that the band themselves were quite amazed by. They told 'MOJO' magazine, when given top honours there, that they'd been doing the same thing for years, quizzing why it should be this album that suddenly captured everyone's attention.

Indeed, 'Merriweather Post Pavilion' was no more easy on the ear than their previous albums, so how had this release made the commune-like band, with their ever changing line-up, suddenly be in the right place at the right time? A cursory listen across their many albums might suggest that they were doing similar things in places, but without doubt they'd wandered into as many genres as you could imagine before the release of 'Merriweather' in January 2009.

By the spring they'd been nominated for a 'MOJO' award, and by Glastonbury at the end of June they were headlining the Park stage. Come September they headlined the Green Man festival, and their rise to such stardom seemed to completely bemuse them.

I first saw Animal Collective in one of their psychedelic neo-experimental folk phases at SXSW. The place was rammed and we had to watch through a wire fence from outside, it was a spiritual and uplifting experience, strangely Pink Floyd in places. I followed their progress afterwards and studiously bough the albums, but they were erratic. It wasn't until 'Strawberry Jam' in 2007, that they seemed to be heading towards a strange hybrid of The Beach Boys and electronic music, a vision that 'Merriweather Post Pavilion' delivered.

The album's use of electronics, samples, sequencers, drum pads, keyboards and a lyrical content that appeared to be both mystical but everyday and ordinary by turns, even backwards in places, created further mystery around the album, and the video for 'My Girls' was yet another strand to their bow, an animated slice of futurism where the band simply melt.

The show at the Park was truly phenomenal, the minimal stage antics were embellished with a music-triggered light show and, as I'd lost my glasses earlier in the day, it seemed to me that there was a walrus with a light on its nose in charge of drums stage left, with an abominable snowman on the other side. It added to the psychedelic nature of the proceedings, without a doubt.

By Green Man the album had become an obsession, on repeat on my iPod, but that show ran late and the lights didn't work. Some of the magic was absent, and my new bi-focals had tempered the spectacle. That said, it was at times majestic, and the album remains one of the true great electronic albums of modern times, embracing new technology and throwing up even more possibilities through its song construction. It was a left of centre generation's soundtrack to 2009, and a fitting place to leave the decade. The future seemed certain to be even more exciting.

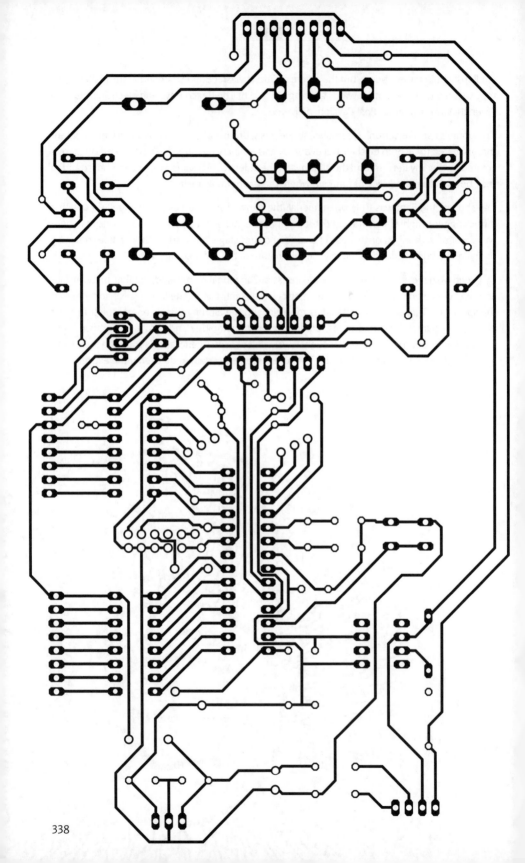

SEVEN

WARPED WORLD, BUDDHA AND THE POST-DUBSTEP EXPERIENCE

As the broadsheets and fashion magazines struggled to find a conclusion for the "noughties", 'MOJO' selected its Top 50 albums of 2009. Fuck Buttons made it in at number eight, while Animal Collective's 'Merriweather Post Pavilion' was number one. "We're stumped on why this was so popular," admitted Panda Bear, before commenting on their Glastonbury performance, "Sometimes you can just feel that it's more than just stage and audience, that there's something deeper going on," and explaining why Green Man wasn't such a success, "I take full responsibility. I was really drunk, too drunk to play. I'm still licking my wounds. Everyone makes mistakes, you have to live and learn".

Elsewhere in the magazine, artists from Paul Weller to Corinne Bailey Rae were asked to reveal their favourite album of the year. There was no mention of Animal Collective throughout, but Holly Johnson, vocalist with Frankie Goes To Holywood, beamed about buying a book on the recording techniques of Joe Meek, "It included a CD of 'I Hear A New World', which I'd never heard and it blew me away – it was like Ziggy's space odyssey before David Bowie recorded it".

How that revelation might affect Holly's future recordings is another thing, but it suggested that these influences and ideas in electronic music are things that are passed down, only to rebound off other artists and return to make sounds that are new. Or differently sequenced at the very least.

THOM YORKE
The Eraser
Original release: 2006
XL

In 2006, Thom Yorke's 'Eraser' album started life as an idea for the closing credits of Richard Linklater's trippy 'A Scanner Darkly' film interpretation of Philip K Dick's book. The piece, 'Black Swan', slowly evolved into the album 'Eraser', wherein Yorke and Jonny Greenwood moved on from 'Kid A' and 'Amnesiac', utilising the various influences that had sparked those albums.

"A keen fan of Warp Records acts like Plaid and Autechre, it was Yorke who seemed keenest to shed instruments and fling himself across the stage to the synthetic rush of 'Idioteque'," recalled 'NME' in its review, pointing out that the album wasn't "simply Thom being difficult. Nine tracks arranged by Thom with long-term Radiohead producer Nigel Godrich, plus occasional instrumentation – albeit warped, filtered, digitally twisted out of shape – culled from Radiohead sessions, 'The Eraser' is less a splinter project than a chance for Thom to play dictator with the master tapes; to rewire Radiohead into his own vision".

The simplistic drum sounds, off-kilter melodies and redux nature of the sound allowed Yorke room to let his voice become a further instrument to be tampered with, to let the lemon-sucking howl be the perfect foil for the machinations of the studio.

"Musically, the 'Kid A' acolytes will be on familiar ground," 'NME' continued, "There's nothing here as immediately gripping as 'Idioteque', but that song's hallmarks – tractor-beam synths, hissy percussion, mechanical propulsion – form this record's backbone".

The album was followed by various live performances that mixed in Radiohead songs and gave them a new context and, in 2008, Thom was invited to do a station takeover on NPR. His playlist included 'Falling Into Place' and 'Nude' from Radiohead's 'In Rainbows', the Eurocrunk techno of

German duo Modeselektor with 'Kill Bill Vol 4,' from their BPitch Control album 'Hello Mom!', Madvillain's 'Meat Grinder' from 'Madvillainy' and 'Vose In' by Autechre from 'LP5'.

Yorke's interest in Plaid and Autechre had been well-documented, and in 2009, when Warp celebrated its 20th birthday with a lavish ten-inch box set, it was an opportunity to revisit the label's catalogue and realise how Steve Beckett's label had gone from releasing cool dance 12-inchers by Coco, Steel And Lovebomb to underpinning and supporting the development of modern electronic music. Here was a label with a vision that had stuck to its guns.

In 2010, Mute's Daniel Miller received the MOJO Medal at the MOJO Honours List, an accolade that meant I had to edit down from 30 selected videos a two-minute clip of the best of Mute Records. It was, of course, impossible. The wealth of material, from Fad Gadget covered in chicken feathers doing 'Back To Nature' to Throbbing Gristle, Depeche Mode, Erasure, Add N To (X)'s 'Plug Me In', Plastikman, Moby, Goldfrapp, Panasonic and many more gave far too much variety before even considering Mute's more mainstream acts like Nick Cave and Richard Hawley. I got it down to five minutes and still it was rich with glorious moments from the Mute archive. Like Warp, the sheer breadth of the Mute catalogue was quite staggering, and with the addition of the recently remastered Kraftwerk catalogue – which was nominated for best compilation at the ceremony – the position of both Mute and Warp as central to the history of electronic music was cemented.

The awards also honoured Jean Michel Jarre and, again, editing a presentation package from the enormous visual spectacles he had put on in Beijing, at the Place De La Concorde in Paris, at Lyon, Docklands in London and in front of one a half million people in Houston, Texas, was a real eye-opener. Jarre's ability to experiment with sound, as well as provide some gorgeous melody to such vast audiences was quite staggering, and his influence on dance music couldn't be overstated enough.

Undoubtedly, in 2010 there was a growing interest in electronic music, from its roots to its halcyon days in the '80s and beyond. Tears For Fears had reformed and played in Australia in the summer and Heaven 17 revisited their 'Penthouse And Pavement' album, playing it live at the Vintage festival. Meanwhile, Gary Numan's Pleasure Principal tour was sold out in the UK and, as 2010 came to a close, there was huge press interest on his arrival in Mexico and the States.

The year also saw La Roux play on the Other Stage at Glastonbury to around 30,000 people. They were joined by Heaven 17's Glenn Gregory for a driving version of 'Temptation', before closing their set with 'Bulletproof' and 'In For The Kill' to rapturous applause. Amazing in itself as the band's underground late night club vibe somehow transferred to a huge audience in the middle of the day. Glastonbury also welcomed a host of returning electronic heroes as it celebrated its 40th year, with both Orbital and The Orb triumphant and more than a little nostalgic.

THE ORB
Baghdad Batteries (Orbsessions Volume III)
Original release: 2009
MALICIOUS DAMAGE

Tracklisting:
Styrofoam Meltdown, Chocolate Fingers, Baghdad Batteries, Raven's Reprise, Dolly Unit,
Super Soakers, Suburban Smog, Orban Tumbleweed.,Pebbles, Woodlarking, Oopa

The Orb's 'Orbsessions' series had previously focussed on material from their catalogue that was rare or unreleased, but volume three, which was also released in a cardboard box with a host of artefacts, featured new recordings by Alex Paterson and Thomas Fehlmann. In keeping with their material that was set aside from more commercially successful releases, 'Baghdad Batteries' was a serious work, bolstered by the surrounding paraphernalia – documents, pictures, random explanations and so on.

The duo's fascination with the Baghdad batteries, which could supply electricity when powered with grape juice, said something about the austere nature of the recordings. Billed as Dr Alex Paterson and Professor Thomas Fehlmann, it smacked of early electronic technicians donning white coats in front of banks of overwhelming equipment. The set also included an additional CD of alternative interpretations that stretched the envelope yet further.

Away from the mainstream, The Orb's 'Orbsessions' were deconstructed further on this bonus disc, which featured over 40 minutes of almost accidentally overheard ambience, like the slow 'Mutant Ambience' and 'Suburban Ambience', but it was the lengthy looping effects on 'Styrofoam Capital', and its thudding beat, that seemed to best sum up the lavish nature of the boxed version of 'Baghdad Batteries' with all its collectibles and diversional texts.

THE SHOOTING STAR EXPERIMENT OF LIGHTS
The Sound Of The World Collapsing
Original release: 2008
REVERB WORSHIP

Tracklisting:
The Sound Of The World Collapsing, Faces From The Past

Outside of the mainstream, the DIY ethic was completely intact , and the search for the future of electronic music had led to some hugely entertaining finds. The Norman's Records mail order service turned me on to Fieldhand and Northerner, but there were smaller indie websites offering limited edition, short run items by a wealth of bands that remain unheralded. I say bands, undoubtedly, as in the great days of DIY cassette-only releases, many of these acts must be one person, locked in their back room with way too much time on their hands.

The Reverb Worship label specialises in noisey agit-folk, booming overlaid synths and generally scary concept items. In limited runs of 50, they have a wealth of releases including items like 'The Sound Of The World Collapsing', which does sound just like it says on the tin. The echoey, doomy feedbacked sound on the title track burrows deep into the psyche, while 'Faces From The Past' could be sourced from any lo-budget ghost film. And, like all Reverb Worship CDs, it came in a homemade sleeve that just added to its unique quality.

MOUNT VERNON ARTS LAB
The Séance At Hobs Lane
Original release: 2001
GHOST BOX

Tracklisting:
The Fog Detonator, Hobgoblins, The Mandrake Clu, Dashwood's Reverie, The Black Drop,
Sir Keith At Lambeth, The Submariner's Song, The Vauxhall Labyrinth, While London Sleeps,
Warminster 4, Percy Toplis

The Ghost Box label is again a DIY concern, but their releases don't come in handmade sleeves, rather beautifully-designed and stylish packages that reflect the label's studied identity. This is serious stuff, and although there are some similarities in the seismic noise at the beginning of 'The Séance At Hobs Lane' and 'The Sound Of The World Collapsing', 'Hobs Lane' has a narrative that's far more obvious, according to the sleevenotes by Lawrence Norfolk, which talk of the teams digging underground tunnels in London. "Their world is a soundscape in which synthesisers burble and thrum. Strange crashes sound from the bottom of shafts". This period piece of synthesisers and effects are summoned up at a séance where Isobel Campbell plays cello, Portishead's Adrian Utley is on ARP2600 and minimoog, Teenage Fanclub's Norman Blake strums a guitar and Drew Mulholland does magical things on EMS VCS3 and Theremin among other wayward instruments.

The sleeve warns that, "The forthcoming end of the world will be hastened by the construction of underground railways burrowing into the infernal regions and thereby disturbing the Devil". The words of the Rev Dr John Cumming, from 1860, seemingly caught in the analogue synthesis and repetitive rhythm of the whole affair.

RICHARD PINHAS METAL/CRYSTAL

RICHARD PINHAS/MERZBOW/WOLF EYES
Metal/Crystal
Original release: 2010
CUNIEFORM

Tracklisting:
Bi-Polarity (Gold), Hysteria (Palladium), Paranoia (Iridium), Schizophrenia (Silver),
Depression (Loukoum)

If Mount Vernon Arts Lab were in danger of disturbing the Devil, then Japanese noisenik Merzbow had already raised him and made his ears bleed since releasing his first cassettes in 1979. Literally hundreds of albums and CDs later, Merzbow is in the midst of a lengthy re-issue program while still collaborating with different musicians and producing hugely challenging work. In 2010 he worked closely with French avant-garde guitarist Richard Pinhas for a second time, along with American noise terrorist Wolf Eyes, recording 'Metal/Crystal' a double CD that also featured Antoine Paganotti (drums), Didier Batard (bass), Patrick Gauthier (mini-Moog) (all ex members of Heldon and/or Magma) and Jerome Schmidt (electronics).

Merzbow's music over the decades has always been challenging and, in many cases, extreme. But his following around the world has become huge, and the clamour for earlier limited edition releases is nothing short of phenomenal. In fact, in 2000 Extreme Records released a 50 CD box set called Merzbox. It was lapped up.

In the middle of the noise, Masami Akita's Merzbow persona also delved into what has best been described as dark ambience. In 2010, as well as the Pinhas and Wolf Eyes collaboration, Akita released part 13 of his '13 Japanese Birds' series, as well as 'Graft', 'Ouroboros', 'Marmo', 'Untitled Nov 1989', 'Spiral Right/Spiral Left', '9888A', an EP, two live albums and another collaboration with Chrome Peeler. His output remains prodigious.

The Pinhas and Wolf Eyes double is suitably abrasive, with all three main protagonists pushing the sound barrier while the rhythms are held together, a feature that hadn't always been part of the Merzbow plan. The 20 minutes plus of 'Schizophrenia (Silver)' and 'Depression (Loukoum)' are strikingly powerful,l and the project's translation of crystals and metals into sound has all the selected wisdom of its method of creation oozing from the speakers.

WINTER NORTH ATLANTIC
A Memento For Dr Mori
Original release: 2009
BOLTFISH

The influence of natural materials on music wasn't something that had happened in isolation. Ed Carter, the man behind Winter North Atlantic, is a young and enthusiastic Newcastle-based musician who I met at Green Man this year. He was there performing a piece created by mapping the surrounding hills, feeding the results into a computer and translating it into a musical form. It was an intoxicating experience, lying on the grass listening to his layered synths set off against acoustic instruments, surrounded by the very hills that had created the work.

His 'A Memento For Dr Mori' was a similar mix of real and synthesised sounds, a similarly evocative piece that Norman's catalogue enthused over as Carter managed to "drift effortlessly between folk and electronic, creating an emotive and uplifting sound. They embrace acoustic guitars, analogue keyboards, violins, accordions to great effect, crafting a sound that sits somewhere between the Bracken/Hood/Declining winter school of thought and Four Tet, as well as having a little in common with groups like Town And Country and Pullman".

And, as is the way with discovery, a need to get hold of those Norman's comparison acts would further aid the journey into new electronic sound which seemed, in 2010 to be coming from many unlikely sources, wrapped in many different styles. Without doubt, the slow ambient feel of Winter North Atlantic couldn't have been further removed from the sound of Tobacco.

TOBACCO
Maniac Meat
Original release: 2010
ANTICON

Tracklisting:
Constellation Dirtbike Head, Fresh Hex (Feat. Beck), Mexican Icecream, Lick The Witch,
Sweatmother, Motorlicker, Unholy Demon Rhythms, Heavy Makeup, Grape Aerosmith (Feat.
Beck), New Juices From The Hot Tub Freaks, Six Royal Vipers, Overheater, Creepy Phone Calls,
TV All Greasy, Stretch Your Face, Nuclear Waste Aerobics

Helmed by Tom Fec, who is a member of Pittsburgh's neo-psychedelic troupe Black Moth Super
Rainbow, Tobacco is an abrasive concept. While Black Moth have an edgy indie feel, Tobacco
couldn't be more pushy and in your face. They're positively loud and snotty.

"Tobacco is his harder tack – the place he goes for aggressive, edgy, hip-electro that is consistently
flying off at odd angles," 'NME' explained. "Fec tempers the heaviness by adding his own sweetly
vocodered vocals to the likes of throbbing Neu! Vs Fat Truckers opener 'Constellation Dirtbike
Head', and the downbeat plurality-party anthem 'Mexican Icecream'".

It's a huge sound that had already impressed Beck, who guested on Tobacco's second album
'Mainiac Meat', a heads down adrenalin-rush that seems to be wallowing in deep mud piles of
sound. "You could ask, what's happening here?" quizzed 'Feminist Review' online, "A better
question is, what isn't?".

Tobacco seems to have the needle blowing red on all the dials, a huge throbbing noise that
somehow hints at melody too.

SLEIGH BELLS
Treats
Original release: 2010
MOM + POP

Tracklisting:
Tell 'Em. Kids, Riot Rhythm, Infinity Guitars, Run The Heart, Rachel, Rill Rill, Crown On The Ground, Straight A's, A/B Machines, Treats

Falling somewhere between Sonic Youth and Crystal Castles, Sleigh Bells' debut was originally picked up on by MIA and bears some relation to Tobacco. Derek Miller's goal in life seems to be simply making an enormous noise. More rhythmic and ordered for sure, it also manages to transcend its beats and grunge setting by adding the tuneful poppy vocals of Alexis Krause to add power to the play off of styles.

The Brooklyn-based duo formed when Miller quit Florida hardcore band Poison The Well and moved to New York. Writing music while waiting tables, he eventually, so the story goes, served Krause, asked if she could sing and the partnership began. Sure, there are hardcore elements in there, but the chugging beats and effects-heavy guitar are pulsing with sequenced synths, indescribable noise and Krause's sweet, sweet vocal for a perfect contrast.

UFFIE
Sex Dreams And Denim Jeans
Original release: 2010
ED BANGER

Tracklisting:
Pop The Glock, Art Of Uff, ADD SUV (ft. Pharrell Williams), Give It Away, MCs Can Kiss, Difficult,
First Love, Sex Dreams & Denim Jeans, Illusion of Love (ft. Mattie Safer), Neuneu, Brand New
Car, Hong Kong Gardens, Ricky

While Sleigh Bells seemed to have arrived from nowhere – even if Miller's labour of love took five years to come to fruition - the slow birthing process of the debut Uffie album seems to have taken an eternity. It was 2006 when 'Pop The Glock' crept out, a monstrous vocodered and effected piece of electronic pop with plenty of innocent menace from the much-hailed rapper.

Four years on, and after sessions with producers including Madonna-collaborator Mirwais, Mr Oizo and Sebastian, plus Uffie's ex-boyfriend DJ Feadz, 'Sex Dreams And Denim Jeans' sounds somehow watered down, like there's too much vocoder and effects and no real substance in there. In fact, even 'Pop The Glock', a permanently playlisted weekly spin when I was DJing on MOJO Radio in 2006 and 2007 seemed to have lost its edge.

"For an artist whose talents seem designed around her rhymes," reasoned 'The Guardian', "it's hard to be too enthused when they include nuggets like: "These are the best crackers I've tasted for a long time – can you put some cheese on it for me?"

That said, from the sleeve's half asleep pictures of Uffie through to the songs themselves, there's a strange futuristic sheen on the proceedings. Like a Stepford Wife, Uffie seems oblivious to what's going on, her voice and the songs seem to have been completely robotised. Perhaps, underneath the huge weight of expectation, it's like she's letting the machines do the talking, albeit in an affected and emotionless voice.

MAGNETIC MAN
Magnetic Man
Original release: 2010
COLUMBIA

With dubstep still confounding the major labels, existing in its own single-friendly space on pirate radio and in clubs, and with the departure of Annie Nightingale and Mary Anne Hobbs from Radio One suggesting that those confines might be best, what better time to bring together three producers and form what's been heralded as a dubstep supergroup. The arrival of the debut album my Magnetic Man – featuring Skream, Artwork and Benga – had already caused much written analysis even before it came out, and the response was mixed.

"Their debut fails to translate dubstep's speaker-blowing underground sound into comparably interesting pop," claimed 'The Guardian', while Skream, aka Oliver Jones, told 'Q' that, "We want to fuse dubstep with proper songs. I'd love to get a number one. You've got to think big and we are ambitious people, we want to change things".

'Q's review of the set concluded, "The elephant in the room is that, like jungle, drum and bass and garage before it, dubstep is not really an album genre," reasoned Dan Hancox. "Magnetic Man is at its best when it's at it's prettiest, either thanks to vocal contributions or, on the standout track 'Ping Pong', a shuffling instrumental garage number with an irresistible keyboard riff".

There are some great electronic moments on Magnetic Man's debut album, such as the vocodered vocal on 'The Bug' and Ms Dynamite's vocal on 'Fire', but the trio had moved way beyond dubstep already. The pop simplicity of 'Boiling Water' has the jungle rhythm, 'Mad' sounds like an outtake from some Krautrock interlude, while 'K Dance' has a bit of Pink Floyd to it and 'Crossover' could be from any synth pop period.

"Some of my mates didn't like dubstep," Skream told 'NME', "but now they're hearing me on the radio and realising that all that time I spent at home in the bedroom wasn't wasted".

SKREAM
Outside The Box
Original release: 2010
TEMPA

Tracklisting:
Perferated, 8 Bit Baby (featuring MURS), CPU, Where You Should Be (featuring Sam Frank), How Real (featuring Freckles), Fields Of Emotion, I Love the Way, Listenin' To The Records On My Wall, Wibbler, Metamorphosis, Finally (featuring La Roux), Reflections (featuring dBridge & instra:mental), A Song for Lenny, The Epic Last Song

Skream's bedroom antics were all coming to fruition in 2010. He'd already begun to move away from dubstep and into a host of dance-framed styles. His second album under his own name, 'Outside The Box', realised an affinity with old school rave, much as on Magnetic Man's debut single 'I Need Air', along with rumbling breakbeat, hip hop, drum and bass and a host of in between docking stations of recent dance history.

The guest vocalists add soul and further eclectic dimensions to the mix and, if anything, Skream's solo set avoids the poppier elements of Magnetic Man's controlled elements that are undoubtedly set to appeal to chart and radio programmers alike.

As 2010 draws to a close, electronic music as a pure form is being swallowed by everything surrounding it. The complete version of dubstep that appealed across the board on Burial's 'Untrue' album, or the wonky pop created by Sleigh Bells and Tobacco, seem a long way from Magnetic Man. La Roux's next move, likewise Little Boots, has all the foreboding of second album blues, and the purity of electronic sound seems harnessed in the most part to other things that could make it easier on the ear. There are, of course, people out there who know no better and who are lost in their electronic vision, and from them, perhaps, a new direction will be found.

VARIOUS ARTISTS
Astro:Dynamics
Original release: 2010
ASTRO:DYNAMICS

Tracklisting:
Lukid – Pleurisy, Jay Prada - Nina's Strut, Tapes – Oberheimer, Slow Hand Motëm - Love Is The
New Evil, Clause Four – Daze, Mike Slott - Music's Fun, Coco Bryce - The Cliché, Slugabed
- Clunk Clunk, Crackazat - Party In The Clouds, Bnjmn - It's Not a Joint, Rekordah - Candy
Flossin', Professor Ojo – Focus, Metske – Isotopic, Subeena – Rakeeh, Lower – Heartbroken,
The Blessings – Lungebob

The Astro:Dynamics CD was put together by the fresh-faced Rekordah, who was, at the time, still in his second year at college writing a thesis on astro dynamics. He looks frighteningly young. But he's damn enthusiastic about what he's doing.

The music on the collection is roundly listed as abstract, bass music, dancehall, dubstep, dust-riddled (I like that one), electronic, garage, hip hop, instrumental, progressive hip hop, wonky and Camberwell. It is a collection of rhythmic electronica that bore a sticker in the Sounds Of The Universe record store to the effect that it was the 'Future' of electronic music. It is quite an astonishing collection. It's underplayed and incomplete in parts. Iit stutters, as on Oberheimer's 'Tapes', there's plenty of console noise on Jay Parada's 'Nina' Strut' and a drum pattern that sounds straight out of the Animal (from The Muppets' portfolio on Mike Slott's 'Music's Fun'.

The 'Sonic Router' website reckoned that it featured "a veritable who's who in modern UK 'beats'. Names like Lukid – whose first two albums on Werk Discs pre-empted a whole heap of great music in their own right - Lucky Me's Mike Slott and The Blessings sit in perfect harmony with Stoke Newington's Subeena and SR's new favourite obsession, Coco Bryce". Indeed, Bryce's klaxon and rap over a swirly console rhythm and intruding synth drum effects has a strange, itchy kind of viral feel that seems to continue even after the tune has long ended.

But, is this future of electronic music? Is there enough here?

In October 2010, Paul Morley, ZTT founder, Art Of Noise member and author of 'Words And Music', which described how we should listen to everything as, in that way, we could discover the future of music, revealed that he was listening to La Monte Young's 'Death Chant', Miles Davis' 'Dark Magus', 'King Tubby Meets the Rockers Uptown', Can's 'Tago Mago', Public Image Ltd's 'Metal Box', Cabaret Voltaire's 'Voice Of America', and various other things, which all had led him to "abstract spatial electronic music released on labels such as Hot Flush, Tectonic and Kode 9's Hyperdub".

The latter amalgam he compared to having "ideas about form and formation, decay and growth, mystery and consciousness as single-minded as Stockhausen". The piece was accompanied by a photograph of Ikonika, one of Hyperdub's signings. Obviously, I had to find out more.

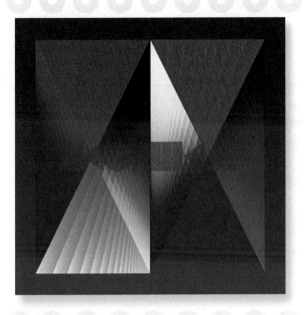

IKONIKA
Contact, Love, Want, Have
Original release: 2010
HYPERDUB

Tracklisting:
Ikonklast (Insert Coin), Idiot, Yoshimitshu, Fish, R.e.s.o.l., They Are Losing The War, Millie,
Sahara Michael, Continue?, Heston, Psoriasis, Video Delays, Look (Final Boss Stage), Red
Marker Pens (Good Ending)

From the opening track 'Ikonklast', it's clear that this is video gaming music gone mad. It's minimal
journey, from inserting a coin in the arcade through to the 'final boss stage' of 'Look', singles it out
as probably the first concept album of dubstep, or post dubstep, or whatever the console-friendly
new sound is. Inside the set there are melodies that seem askew with the rhythms and, in some
cases, with the sub-melodies, but it is a striking album and one which the buzz on the internet
seems to think was even more brave as it followed the successful Burial albums. As a whole
piece this is a complete statement, over and above the insistent groove of the first single lifted
from the set, the shuddering 'Idiot'. 'Contact, Love, Want, Have' is a soundtrack to an imaginary
video game, a futuristic 'Dungeons And Dragons' experience, the idea of which seems so much
a part of the recurring idea of what electronic music could be about. Descended from dubstep,
it is stripped down to what you could perceive as the minimum. Like Richie Hawtin's reductive
theories, like 'Astro:Dynamics', this work is constructed from basics that you feel probably just
waiting to blossom into something bigger.

FM3
Buddha Machine
Original release: 2006

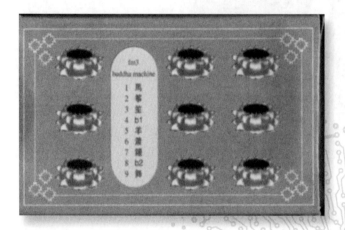

FM3
Buddha Machine 2
Original release: 2006

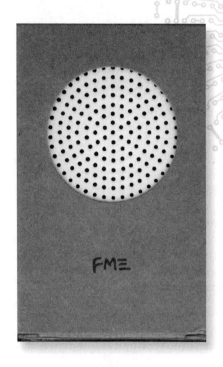

BUDDHA MACHINE
Throbbing Gristle
Gristleism
Original release: 2010

The Buddha Machine was created as a simple aid for art installations by the Chinese group FM3. Christiaan Virant and Zhang Jian were the first electronic group in China, and the inspiration for the Buddha machine came when they found a "small Buddhist chant device in a temple in South West China".

The duo designed and perfected their own box, a nine loop collection of sounds taken from their previous recordings which they intended to be released in a limited run of 500. Now, 20,000 units later, the box has a reputation of its own – "People use the machines to put their babies to sleep, agitate their cat, or pacify their dog," the duo told Eric Nakamura in 'Giant Robot' magazine. Brian Eno bought five of these ambient sound creators in Rough Trade, with plans to record with them, and German band Monolake have already created the album 'Layering Buddha'. An exhibition of 1,000 machines all set off at once in a gallery in Rome provided further depth to the legend, and the minimalist nature of the machine gave it a reputation as the "anti iPod".

A whole album of machine recordings were released as 'Jukebox Buddha' in 2006, featuring tracks from Blixa Bargeld from Einsturzende Neubauten and Nick Cave's Bad Seeds, The Orb's Thomas Fehlmann, On U Sound's Adrian Sherwood and The Sun City Girls among others. Two years later, a second machine was released with pitch control, and, in 2010, Throbbing Gristle, pioneers of electronic sound since the explosion of punk, released 'Gristleism', a set of three boxes in red, white and black featuring 13 loops with loop selector and pitch control, including 'Persuasion', 'Hamburger Lady' and the lengthy 'Heathen Earth' reduced to a minimal drone.

Could it be the drone of the Buddha machine harks back to the Telharmonium or Dynamophones, or even the abstract sounds that came out of the Futurists' first meetings, or perhaps the general hum that emanated from the CSIRAC computer? Have we somehow come full circle in terms of our expectations of electronic music?

CREDITS

A VERY LONG LIST OF ALBUMS, SONGS AND PERFORMANCES FEATURED IN THIS BOOK

CHAPTER ONE:
THE EARLY YEARS - ARTISTS, INVENTORS AND ECCENTRICS GO ELECTRONIC

LUIGI RUSSOLO - The Art Of Noises

TRISTAN TZARA, MARCEL JANCO AND RICHARD HUELSENBECK - L'Amiral Cherche Une Maison A Louer

GEORGE ANTHEIL - Ballet Mécanique

CLARA ROCKMORE - The Art Of The Theremin

OLIVIER MESSIAEN - Trois petites Liturgies de la Présence Divine

DR SAMUEL J HOFFMAN - Music Out Of The Moon

PIERRE SCHAEFFER - Etude aux Chemins de Fer

THE CSIRAC COMPUTER - First computed music

BERNARD HERMANN - The Day The Earth Stood Still

HERBERT EIMERT - Klangstudie I

MICHEL PHILIPOTT - Etude Number One

JOHN CAGE - The Williams Mix

VLADIMIR USSACHEVSKY - Sonic Contours

BRUNO MADERNA - Musica Su Due Dimensioni

KARLHEINZ STOCKHAUSEN - Electronic Musiche (1952-60)

KAREL GOEYVAERTS - Komposition Nr. 5

PIERRE HENRY - Le Voile d'Orphée

HUGH LE CAINE - Dripsody

MICHAEL KOENIG - Klangfiguren I

ERNST KRENEK - Pfigstoratorium (Spiritus Intelligentiae Sanctus)

JOHN PRESTON (NARRATION) - The Sounds And Music Of The RCA Electronic Music Synthesizer

OSKAR SALA - Concertando Rubato

LOUIS AND BEBE BARRON - Forbidden Planet

TOM DISSEVELT AND KID BALTAN (The Elektrosoniks) - Song Of The Second Moon: The Sonic Vibrations Of...

VARIOUS ARTISTS - The Sounds Of New Music

IANNIS XENAKIS - Diamorphoses

LUCIANO BERIO - Perspectives

EDGARD VARESE - Poeme Electronique

BBC RADIOPHONIC WORKSHOP - Quatermass And The Pit

GYORGY LIGETI - Artikulation

THE IBM 7090 COMPUTER AND DIGITAL TO SOUND TRANSDUCER - Music From Mathematics

RAYMOND SCOTT - BC 1675

RICHARD MAXFIELD - Sine Music (A Swarm Of Butterflies Encountered Over The Ocean)

CHAPTER TWO:
THE SIXTIES - FROM INVENTION TO EXPLOITATION

KID A - Original Release 2000

LUCIANO BERGIO - Visage

FORREST J ACKERMAN - Music FOR ROBOTS

THE TORNADOS - Telstar

JEAN JACQUES PERREY - Musique Electronique Du Cosmos

LEJAREN HILLER AND ROBERT BARKER - Computer Cantata

ILHAN MIMAROGLU - Le Tombeau d'Edgar Poe

TZVI AVNI - Vocalise

COLUMBIA-PRINCETON - Electronic Music Center

THE GRAHAM BOND ORGANISATION - Baby Can It Be True?

BEAVER AND KRAUSE - The Nonesuch Guide To Electronic Music

PERREY AND KINGSLEY - The In Sound From Way Out

THE BEATLES - Tomorrow Never Knows

EMIL RICHARDS - Stones

MORT GARSON - The Zodiac Cosmic Sounds

PINK FLOYD - See Emily Play

PIERRE HENRY - Messe Pour Le Temps MoDerne

TERRY RILEY - A Rainbow In Curved Air

MORTON SUBOTNICK - Silver Apples Of The Moon

SILVER APPLES - Silver Apples

TRANS-ELECTRONIC MUSIC PRODUCTIONS, INC. PRESENTS - Switched-On Bach

PINK FLOYD - Set The Controls For The Heart Of The Sun

LA MONTE YOUNG - Drift Studies

STEVE REICH - Pendulum Music

THE LOVE MACHINE - Electronic Music To Blow Your Mind By!

RUTH WHITE - 7 Trumps From The Tarot Cards/ Pinions

THE WHITE NOISE - An Electronic Storm

WILLIAM SEAR - The Copper Plated Integrated Circuit

MARTY GOLD - Moog Plays The Beatles

MIKE MELVOIN - The Plastic Cow Goes Moooooog

RICK POWELL AT THE MOOG - Switched-On-Country

CLAUDE DENJEAN - Moog!

CHAPTER THREE:
MOOGS, HEADS, THE INVENTION OF AMBIENCE AND A MOVE TO BERLIN

TANGERINE DREAM - Electronic Meditation

THE FIRST MOOG QUARTET - The First Moog Quartet

ORIGINAL SOUNDTRACK - A Clockwork Orange

WENDY CARLOS - A Clockwork Orange Original Score

BEAVER AND KRAUSE - Gandharva

THE WHO - Baba O'Riley

YES - Roundabout

TONTO'S EXPANDING HEAD BAND - Zero Time

HOT BUTTER - Popcorn

BILLY PRESTON - Outa-Space

STEVIE WONDER - Talking Book

ROXY MUSIC - Virginia Plain

THE EDGAR WINTER GROUP - Frankenstein

KRAFTWERK - Tongebirge and Tanzmusik

VANGELIS - Creation Du Monde

KEN FREEMAN - Infinity + One

MIKE OLDFIELD - Tubular Bells

THE PEPPERS - Pepper Box

ENO AND FRIPP - (No Pussyfooting)

TOMITA - Snowflakes Are Dancing

PHILIP GLASS - Music in Twelve Parts

THE COMMODORES - Machine Gun

SPARKS - This Town Ain't Big Enough For The Both Of Us

EDGAR FROESE - Aqua

NEU! - Isi

PARLIAMENT - Mothership Connection

TANGERINE DREAM - Ricochet

KLAUS SCHULZE - Totem

BRIAN ENO - Discreet Music

DIONEE-BREGENT - Et Le Troisieme Jour

JEAN MICHEL JARRE - Oxygene

AUGUSTOS PABLO - King Tubby Meets The Rockers Uptown

DONNA SUMMER - I Feel Love

GIORGIO MORODER - From Here TO Eternity

DAVID BOWIE - Low

CLUSTER AND ENO - Cluster And Eno

KRAFTWERK - Trans Europe Express

SUICIDE - Ghost Rider

THE NORMAL - Warm Leatherette

ULTRAVOX - Systems Of Romance

ORCHESTRAL MANOEUVRES IN THE DARK - Electricity

THE HUMAN LEAGUE - Reproduction

CABARET VOLTAIRE - Nag Nag Nag

THROBBING GRISTLE - Hot On The Heels Of Love

FAD GADGET - Back To Nature

GERRY AND THE HOLOGRAMS - Gerry And The Holograms

THE FLYING LIZARDS - Money

STEVIE WONDER - Journey Through The Secret Life Of Plants

YELLOW MAGIC ORCHESTRA - Solid State Survivor

THOMAS LEER AND ROBERT RENTAL - The Bridge

ROBERT RENTAL AND THE NORMAL - Live At West Runton Pavilion

DR MIX AND THE REMIX - I Can't Control Myself

TUBEWAY ARMY - Replicas

M - Pop Muzik

CHAPTER FOUR:
SOUNDTRACKS, SAMPLES AND THE FRACTURED DANCEFLOOR

ORCHESTRAL MANOEUVRES IN THE DARK - Enola Gay

HUMAN LEAGUE - Only After Dark

CABARET VOLTAIRE - Three Mantras

CHROME - New Age

THROBBING GRISTLE - Distant Dreams (Part Two)

ROBERT SCHROEDER - Floating Music

JOHN FOXX - Underpass

ULTRAVOX - Vienna

DEPECHE MODE - Just Can't Get Enough

ORCHESTRAL MANOEUVRES IN THE DARK - Maid Of Orleans

THE HUMAN LEAGUE - Dare

HEAVEN 17 - (We Don't Need This) Fascist Groove Thang

JAPAN - Tin Drum

LAURIE ANDERSON - O Superman

KRAFTWERK - Das Model

DAF - Der Räuber Und Der Prinz

DIE KRUPPS - Wahre Arbeit, Wahrer Lohn

COLIN POTTER - Here

Escape From New York OST

Blade Runner OST

THOMAS DOLBY - She Blinded Me With Science

TEARS FOR FEARS - Mad World

SOFT CELL - Torch

BLANCMANGE - God's Kitchen

YAZOO - Don't Go

A FLOCK OF SEAGULLS - Wishing (I Had A Photograph Of You)

TRIO - Da Da Da

AFRIKA BAMBAATAA AND THE SOUL SONIC FORCE - Planet Rock

THE TWINS FACE TO FACE - Heart to Heart

TUXEDOMOON - Divine

NEIL YOUNG - Trans

DEPECHE MODE - Everything Counts

HERBIE HANCOCK - Rockit

EVELYN THOMAS - High Energy

NEW ORDER - Blue Monday

CYBOTRON - Clear

CABARET VOLTAIRE - Fascination/The Crackdown

SOZIALISTISCHES PATIENTEN KOLLEKTIV - Leichensrei

FRIEDER BUTZMANN - Incendio

NOCTURNAL EMISSIONS - Drowning In A Sea Of Bliss

SEVERED HEADS - Since The Accident

OMD - Dazzle Ships

THE ART OF NOISE - Close To The Edit

HOLGER HILLER - Jonny

MANUEL GOTTSCHING - E2-E4

HAROLD FALTERMEYER - Axel F

SILVER POZZOLI - Around My Dream

SKINNY PUPPY - Assimilate

PORTION CONTROL - Psycho Bod Saves The World

ERASURE - Sometimes

MARSHALL JEFFERSON - Move Your Body

RHYTHIM IS RHYTHIM - Nude Photo and Strings of Life

PHUTURE - Acid Tracks

FRONT 242 - Master Hit

NITZER EBB - Join In the Chant

THE PET SHOP BOYS - Actually

JEAN MICHEL JARRE - Revolution Industrielle

YELLO - The Race

A GUY CALLED GERALD - Voodoo Ray

HUMANOID - Stakker Humanoid

S'EXPRESS - Theme From S Express

LIL LOUIS - French Kiss

808 STATE - Pacific State

NINE INCH NAILS - Down In It

TECHNOTRONIC - Pump Up The Jam

THE ORB - A Huge Ever Growing Pulsating Brain That Rules From The Centre Of The Ultraworld

POP WILL EAT ITSELF - This Is The Day, This Is The Hour, This Is This!

CHAPTER FIVE:
WELCOME TO THE WORLD OF DRUG-ADDLED MULTI-SAMPLES

ORBITAL - Chime

ADAMSKI - Killer

THE KLF - What Time Is Love? and 3am Eternal

THE KLF - Chill Out

SPACE - Space

REVOLTING COCKS - Beers, Steers And Queers

PRIMAL SCREAM - Come Together

MASSIVE ATTACK - Safe From Harm

THE SHAMEN - Move Any Mountain (Progen 91)

SHAFT - Roobarb And Custard

THE FUTURE SOUND OF LONDON - Papua New Guinea

APHEX TWIN - Heliosphan

FRONT LINE ASSEMBLY - The Blade

THE PRODIGY - Out Of Space

RUFIGE KRU - Terminator

BJORK - Big Time Sensuality

PORTISHEAD - Wandering Star

STEREOLAB - Moogy Wonderland

UNDERWORLD - dubnobasswithmyheadman

THE PRODIGY - Music For The Jilted Generation

ORBITAL - Snivilisation

GLOBAL COMMUNICATION - 76:14

AUTECHRE - Amber

VARIOUS ARTISTS - Headz

ALEX REECE - Pulp Fiction

GOLDIE - Timeless

FRANK ZAPPA - Civilization III

THE MOOG COOKBOOK - The Moog Cookbook

LEFTFIELD - Leftism

AUTECHRE - Tri Repetae

TRICKY - Maxinquaye

THE CHEMICAL BROTHERS - Leave Home

DJ SHADOW - Stem/Long Stem/Transmission 2

THE PRODIGY - Firestarter

LTJ BUKEM - Logical Progression

Trainspotting OST

THE CHEMICAL BROTHERS - Block Rockin' Beats

THE PRODIGY - The Fat Of The Land

DREXCIYA - The Quest

BJORK - Homogenic

AIR - Sexy Boy

THE BEASTIE BOYS - Intergalactic

COLDCUT (AND HEXSTATIC) - Timber

PLASTIKMAN - Consumed

ADD N TO (X) - Avant Hard

MOBY - Play

THE CHEMICAL BROTHERS - Hey Boy Hey Girl

LEFTFIELD - Afrika Shox

VNV - Nation Empires

JOY ELECTRIC - CHRISTIANSongs

APHEX TWIN - Windowlicker

CHAPTER SIX:
DISMANTLING SOUND AND BENDING THE CIRCUITS

GOLDFRAPP - Utopia

APOPTYGMA BERZERK - Kathy's Song

COVENANT - Dead Stars

RADIOHEAD - Kid A

ADD N TO (X) - Plug Me In

BONOBO - Animal Magic

SQUAREPSUHER - Tommib

AUTHECHRE - Confield

ZERO 7 - Destiny

ROYKSOPP - Melody AM

FISCHERSPOONER - Emerge

THE FAINT - Danse Macabre

MISS KITTIN AND THE HACKER - Frank Sinatra

FELIX DA HOUSECAT - Silver Screen (Shower Scene)

PEACHES - Set It Off

RICHIE HAWTIN - DE:9 Closer To The Edit

VITALIC - Poney Part 1

DAFT PUNK - Discovery

FENNESZ - Endless Summer

MATMOS - A Chance To Cut Is A Chance To Cure

LADYTRON - Seventeen (Darren Emerson Remix)

LCD SOUNDSYSTEM - Losing My Edge

KYLIE MINOGUE - Can't Get You Out Of My Head

LEMON JELLY - Lost Horizons

BOARDS OF CANADA - Geogaddi

RICHARD X - Being Nobody

BENNY BENASSI - Satisfaction

GOLDFRAPP - Strict Machine

COLDER - Crazy Love

FOUR TET - Rounds

M83 - Dead Cities, Red Seas, Lost Ghosts

DATAROCK - Computer Camp Love

FRENCHBLOKE AND SON - Sexy Model

THE DIFF'RENT DARKNESS - I Believe In A Thing Called Love

THE KILLERS - Somebody Told Me

HIEM - Chelsea

LCD SOUNDSYSTEM - Daft Punk Is Playing At My House

SKREAM - Midnight Request Line

KODE 9 AND SPACEAPE 9 - Samurai

QUARTA 330 - Sunset Dub/9 Samurai

BURIAL - Burial

HOT CHIP - The Warning

KLAXONS - Atlantis To Interzone

THE KNIFE - Silent Shout

COLDCUT - Man In A Garage

AUDION - Mouth To Mouth

MATTHEW DEAR - Asa Breed

SHY CHILD - Noise Won't Stop

HOLY FUCK - LP

DAN LE SAC Vs SCROOBIUS PIP - Thou Shalt Always Kill

LADYHAWKE - My Delirium

METRONOMY - Nights Out

M83 - Saturdays = Youth

CRYSTAL CASTLES - Crystal Castles

MSTRKRFT - Fist Of God

LA ROUX - In For The Kill

FUCK BUTTONS - Tarot Sport

WILD BEASTS - Two Dancers

ANIMAL COLLECTIVE - Merriweather Post Pavilion

**CHAPTER SEVEN:
WARPED WORLD, BUDDHA AND THE POST POST-DUBSTEP EXPERIENCE**

THE ORB - Baghdad Batteries (Orbsessions Volume III)

THE SHOOTING STAR EXPERIMENT OF LIGHTS - The Sound Of The World Collapsing

MOUNT VERNON ARTS LAB - The Séance At Hobs Lane

RICHARD PINHAS/MERZBOW/WOLF EYES - Metal/Crystal

WINTER NORTH ATLANTIC - A Memento For Dr Mori

TOBACCO - Maniac Meat

SLEIGH BELLS - Treats

UFFIE - Sex Dreams And Denim Jeans

MAGNETIC MAN - Magnetic Man

SKREAM - Outside The Box

VARIOUS ARTISTS - Astro:Dynamics

IKONIKA - Contact, Love, Want, Have

FM3 - Buddha Machine

FM3 - Buddha Machine 2

THROBBING GRISTLE - Gristleism

ABOUT THE AUTHOR

Dave Henderson wrote for 'Sounds' in the early '80s, where he championed bands such as 23 Skidoo, Severed Heads and Cabaret Voltaire. He launched both 'Underground' and 'OffBEAT' magazines and edited 'DJ' magazine. He has also worked for 'Q', 'MOJO', 'Select', 'Mixmag' and 'Kerrang!'. He has worked with the Glastonbury Festival since 1997, editing the programme, launching the daily paper and 'Glastonbury Review', producing the Queen's Head stage and exec producing 'Glastonbury: The Film'. More recently, he produced Vintage At Goodwood and the ICA Beck's Futures Chemical Brothers in Trafalgar Square event and curated R.E.M.'s ICA film and photo exhibition. He lives in Wiltshire with a lot of records and runs the Righteous and Other Sounds record labels.

THANKS

Special thanks to Richard at Cherry Red for editing and encouragement, Adam at Cherry Red for saying, yes, let's do it. Emma, Lewis and Maia for putting up with me listening to strange music early in the morning. Sir David of Black for making it all look coherent.

Apologies to everyone I've missed out, and there are many. Great bands from Kas Product to Kap Bambino, Attrition to Konstruktivits, Chris And Cosy and UNKLE to Tik And Tok, the endless Sky and Brain people I've been listening to and Plaid, Clark and Flying Lotus who were all on the cutting room floor.

I wish I'd still got a copy of Soylent Green's cassette that I put out in the late '70s. Two guys with stylophones and a vocalist - genius! And, of course Fujiya & Miyagi. Not really an electronic band as such but a great inspiration when doing this project

Sources include the archives of 'Q' and 'MOJO', both of which I'm very grateful for, various credited websites, 'The Guardian', 'Giant Robot', 'Observer Music Monthly', 'Careless Talk Costs Lives', 'Plan B', 'Sound Projector', 'The Wire', Garry Mulholland's excellent books, my old issues of 'Sounds', 'OffBeat' and 'Underground', 'Zigzag', 'Dark Star' and the 'NME'.

Other things that were important:

My favourite record shops: Rough Trade and Sounds Of The Universe

OTHER TITLES AVAILABLE FROM CHERRY RED BOOKS:

You're Wondering Now - The Specials from Conception to Reunion
Paul Williams

Celebration Day – A Led Zeppelin Encyclopedia
Malcolm Dome and Jerry Ewing

All The Young Dudes: Mott The Hoople & Ian Hunter
Campbell Devine

Good Times Bad Times - The Rolling Stones 1960-69
Terry Rawlings and Keith Badman

The Rolling Stones: Complete Recording Sessions 1962-2002
Martin Elliott

Embryo - A Pink Floyd Chronology 1966-1971
Nick Hodges and Ian Priston

Those Were The Days - The Beatles' Apple Organization
Stefan Grenados

The Legendary Joe Meek - The Telstar Man
John Repsch

Truth... Rod Steward, Ron Wood And The Jeff Beck Group
Dave Thompson

Our Music Is Red - With Purple Flashes: The Story Of The Creation
Sean Egan

Quite Naturally - The Small Faces
Keith Badman and Terry Rawlings

Irish Folk, Trad And Blues: A Secret History
Colin Harper and Trevor Hodgett

Number One Songs In Heaven - The Sparks Story
Dave Thompson

Kiss Me Neck – The Lee 'Scratch' Perry Story in Words, Pictures and Records
Jeremy Collingwood

Prophets and Sages – 101 Prog Rock Essentials
Mark Powell

Random Precision - Recording The Music Of Syd Barrett 1965-1974
David Parker

Bittersweet: The Clifford T Ward Story
David Cartwright

Children of the Revolution – Glam Rock 1970-75
Dave Thompson

PWL: From The Factory Floor
Phil Harding
Goodnight Jim Bob - On The Road With Carter Usm
Jim Bob

Tamla Motown - The Stories Behind The Singles
Terry Wilson

Block Buster! – The True Story of The Sweet
Dave Thompson

Independence Days - The Story Of UK Independent Record Labels
Alex Ogg

Indie Hits 1980 – 1989
Barry Lazell

No More Heroes: A Complete History Of UK Punk From 1976 To 1980
Alex Ogg

Rockdetector: A To Zs of '80s Rock / Black Metal / Death Metal /Doom, Gothic & Stoner Metal
/ Power Metal
Garry Sharpe-Young

Rockdetector: Black Sabbath - Never Say Die
Garry Sharpe-Young
Rockdetector: Ozzy Osbourne
Garry Sharpe-Young

The Motorhead Collector's Guide
Mick Stevenson

Fucked By Rock (Revised and Expanded)
Mark Manning

The Day The Country Died: A History Of Anarcho Punk 1980 To 1984
Ian Glasper

Burning Britain - A History Of UK Punk 1980 To 1984
Ian Glasper

Trapped In A Scene - UK Hardcore 1985-89
Ian Glasper

The Secret Life Of A Teenage Punk Rocker: The Andy Blade Chronicles
Andy Blade

Best Seat In The House – A Cock Sparrer Story
Steve Bruce

Death To Trad Rock – The Post-Punk fanzine scene 1982-87
John Robb

Johnny Thunders - In Cold Blood
Nina Antonia

Deathrow: The Chronicles Of Psychobilly
Alan Wilson

Hells Bent On Rockin: A History Of Psychobilly
Craig Brackenbridge

Music To Die For – The International Guide To Goth, Goth Metal, Horror Punk, Psychobilly Etc
Mick Mercer

CHERRY RED BOOKS

Here at Cherry Red Books we're always interested to hear of interesting titles looking for a publisher. Whether it's a new manuscript or an out of print or deleted title, please feel free to get in touch if you have something you think we should know about.

Please visit www.cherryredbooks.co.uk for further info and mail order

books@cherryred.co.uk
www.cherryredbooks.co.uk
www.cherryred.co.uk

CHERRY RED BOOKS
A division of Cherry Red Records Ltd,
Power Road Studios
114 Power Road
London
W4 5PY

OTHER SOUNDS

RELEASED IN JANUARY 2011

Two examples of vintage electronic music from the very pages of Journey To A Plugged In State Of Mind. Available through Cherry Red Records distribution, launching a new imprint which focuses on sounds from a new dimension.

OTHER ONE
MUSIC FOR A RETRO-FUTURE

Featuring the early work of Jean Jacques Perrey, Dissevelt and Baltan, Raymond Scott, the Barrons, The RCS Electronic Synthesizer, IBM 7090 and Edgard Varese with dogs, electronic melodies, fairground noises, whistling, spaceships, early rhythm generators, echo, men in white coats, computers the size of houses and orchestras being tortured.

OTHER TWO
KLANGSTUDIE AND KOMPOSITION

Featuring Herbert Eimert, Bruno Maderna, Karel Goeyvaert and Pierre Boulez
with booming rhythms, interstellar interference, drones, chimes, bells, alien transmissions, the sound of the wind, wonderful reverb, cut up and backwards tapes and a riot of varispeed.

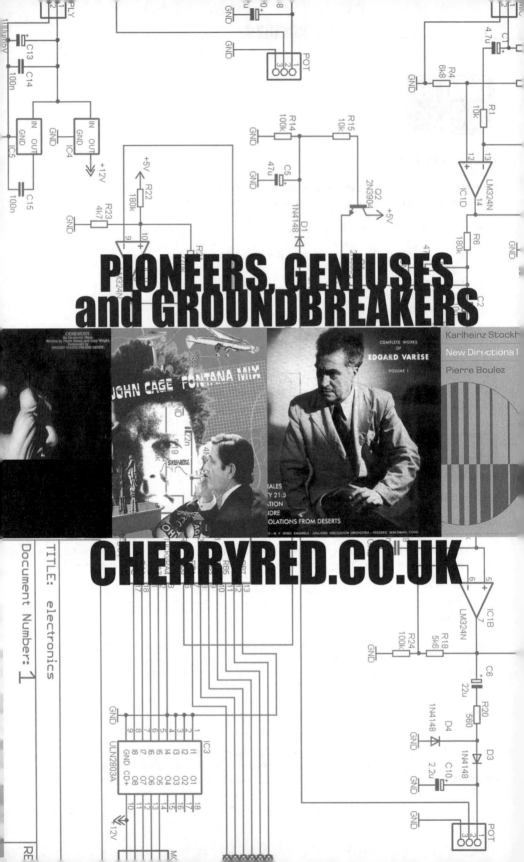

PIONEERS, GENIUSES
and GROUNDBREAKERS

CHERRYRED.CO.UK